I0592182

Henry Scott Holland, William Smyth Rockstro

Memoir of Madame Jenny Lind-Goldschmidt

Her early art-life and dramatic career, 1820-1851. Vol. 1

Henry Scott Holland, William Smyth Rockstro

Memoir of Madame Jenny Lind-Goldschmidt
Her early art-life and dramatic career, 1820-1851. Vol. 1

ISBN/EAN: 9783337394493

Printed in Europe, USA, Canada, Australia, Japan

Cover: Foto ©Raphael Reischuk / pixelio.de

More available books at **www.hansebooks.com**

MEMOIR

OF

MADAME JENNY LIND-GOLDSCHMIDT:

HER EARLY ART-LIFE AND DRAMATIC CAREER.

1820-1851.

FROM ORIGINAL DOCUMENTS, LETTERS, MS. DIARIES. &c.,
COLLECTED BY MR. OTTO GOLDSCHMIDT.

HENRY SCOTT HOLLAND, M.A.,
CANON AND PRECENTOR OF ST. PAUL'S.

AND

W. S. ROCKSTRO,
AUTHOR OF "A GENERAL HISTORY OF MUSIC," "LIFE OF HANDEL," "LIFE OF MENDELSSOHN," ETC.

IN TWO VOLUMES.—VOL. I.

WITH PORTRAITS AND ILLUSTRATIONS.

LONDON:
JOHN MURRAY,
ALBEMARLE STREET.

NEW YORK:
CHARLES SCRIBNER'S SONS,
745, BROADWAY.

1891.

Dedicated

BY GRACIOUS PERMISSION

TO

HER MAJESTY

THE QUEEN.

LIST OF ILLUSTRATIONS (VOL. I.)

PREFACE.

THE following memoir tells its own tale, and requires no further explanation. The justification that we offer for the date at which it closes is given in the body of the book. Nothing therefore remains for the Preface to deal with beyond a few matters, chiefly personal, upon which it may be well to say a word.

It will be seen from the title-page that the whole of the materials used in these two volumes have been procured, and sifted, and sanctioned by the one who alone could act with complete, intimate, and legitimate authority. Everything possible has been done under this competent and exact scrutiny to secure that the memoir should be trustworthy and authentic; and, for further warrant, the sources whence the materials have been drawn have been continually recorded in the Notes.

For the use made of the materials thus industriously collected, the two authors are solely responsible; and this general responsibility they have shared in common, so far as was practicable. But, within that common responsibility, each has undertaken separate sections of the work, so that to the one has fallen the story of Madame Goldschmidt's life so far as it belonged to Sweden, together with that part of it which followed her farewell to the stage; while the other has taken in hand the whole of her dramatic and musical career in its European development.

A divided authorship must, perforce, lessen the effect which follows on perfect unity in ideal and in expression; but, on the other hand, a personality such as hers, which was as unique in moral character as it was rare in artistic quality, lends itself to double treatment. Even if such a treatment involve some repetitions, the completeness of the impression may nevertheless gain thereby.

It only remains to thank those who have more especially contributed to the material placed at our disposal. Such thanks we do, indeed, express in the pages of the book itself to all who have so helped us; but some there are without whose aid it would have been simply impossible to make the book what it is; and to these we desire to pledge our peculiar gratitude.

First of all we would do so for the privilege of the Dedication so graciously accorded to us, which is, moreover, beyond its own direct favour, a witness to the personal and immediate interest taken in the work by Her Majesty the Queen.

Then we would offer our heartiest thanks to Her Majesty Queen Marie of Hanover for the vivid reminiscences which she so freely and willingly contributed out of her private records.

We beg leave to thank His Majesty the King of Sweden and Norway for the use of his father's—King Oscar I.— autograph letter. And we thank, for the use of autograph letters and papers that were invaluable—

In Germany.

Herr Rudolph Wichmann (member of the German Reichstag).

The family of the late Felix Mendelssohn-Bartholdy.

Frau von Hillern,

Herr Kammersaenger Joseph Hauser,
Herr Dr. Edouard Brockhaus,
Frau W. von Kaulbach, and
Fräulein Auguste von Jaeger, at Vienna.

In Sweden.

Judge Carl H. Munthe,
Count A. L. Hamilton,
Herr Krigsråd C. L. Forsberg,
Madame Anna Hierta-Retzius, and
Count G. Lewenhaupt (of the Swedish Embassy at Paris).

In England.

Mrs. Vaughan,
The Lady Rose Weigall,
Mr. Augustus Hare,
Mrs. Salis Schwabe, and
The Baroness French, of Florence.

Nor can we fail to name in the list of our special benefactors—

Miss Jessie Lewin, the late Mrs. Grote's literary executrix;
Madame Schumann, who wrote out for us with ready affection her remembrances of old days;
Mrs. C. T. Simpson, for the MS. record by her father, Mr. Nassau Senior, by the aid of which it was possible to track our way through an anxious episode in the spring of 1849;
Madame Wetterberg (*née* von Platen), who with permission of Baron Ugglas, the owner of Fröken von Stedingk's MS. Diary, furnished us with the valuable extracts from her aunt's journal;

Miss Olivia Frigelius, of Stockholm, for her excellent
aid in reviewing and correcting the details of our
Swedish narrative;

Fru Celsing (Louise Johansson), for autograph letters and
valuable information.

And, in thanking Mr. and Mrs. Grandinson for the use of
the precious Lindblad letters, we cannot but express our
gratitude to him also for the pains, zeal, and accuracy with
which he worked on our behalf to make the account of the
life in Stockholm true and full.

H. S. HOLLAND.

W. S. ROCKSTRO.

March, 1891.

CONTENTS OF VOL. I.

CHAPTER V.

DISCOVERY.

CHAPTER VI.

CHARACTER.

CHAPTER VII.

PILGRIMAGE.

BOOK II.—ASPIRATION.

CHAPTER I.

IN PARIS, 1841.

CHAPTER II.

THE MAESTRO DI CANTO.

CHAPTER III.

THE STUDENT.

CHAPTER IV.

WITHIN SIGHT OF THE GOAL.

CHAPTER V.

UNDER WHICH KING?

CHAPTER VI.

THE RETURN.

BOOK III.—ACHIEVEMENT.

CHAPTER I.

HOME: AND AFTER?

BOOK IV.—MASTERY.

CHAPTER I.

IN DRESDEN.

CHAPTER II.

AT THE COURT OF BERLIN.

CHAPTER III.

THE NEW OPERA HOUSE.

CHAPTER IV.

THE DÉBUT.

CHAPTER V.

DAS FELDLAGER IN SCHLESIEN.

CHAPTER VI.

THE BUNN CONTRACT.

BOOK I.

———

ANTICIPATION.

JENNY LIND,—THE ARTIST.

CHAPTER I.

INTRODUCTION.

JENNY LIND—the name carries music with it to English ears.
The memory is very tender and fragrant of her who, to our
joy, found, for so long, a home among us. And yet it may
well be questioned whether we English have even yet formed
an adequate estimate of her gifts and character.

For what is it which we have in our minds as we recall
her name? It is, first, some tale of the wonderful days when
all London went mad over her singing. We have heard
people tell, as their eyes kindle with the old passionate
delight, how she came tripping over the stage in the *Figlia*,
and how the liquid notes came rippling off her lips. We
hear of the hours they waited in the historic crush at the
Opera in the Haymarket; of the feverish energy with which
they toiled to catch one glimpse of her passing. We
remember, with a smile, some picture in an old copy of
Punch, or the *Illustrated London News*, of scenes in the Opera
passages on a Jenny Lind night.

And then we add to this memory of that surpassing
triumph, the thought of one whose purity and simplicity
won all hearts to love the girl who, in the hour of her overwhelming success, remembered others rather than herself,
and poured out her money in charities, and devoted her

B 2

marvellous gifts to the relief of poverty and the healing of pain.

That is our English picture, and it is good and pleasant enough; and it is quite true, so far as it goes. But it is strangely imperfect and fragmentary. It assumes that her operatic career is to be identified with the brief passage of those London seasons, and that her fame is a private possession of our own here in England, where she lived and died. There prevails no general conception that the English visits were but the latter episodes of a long dramatic experience—an experience which had begun, with extraordinary promise, before she had passed out of her childhood, and which had already won to her the same enthusiasm which greeted her in England, not only in her own Swedish home and in the kindred capital, Copenhagen, but in the great musical centres of Germany—Berlin, the Rhine, Leipzig, Munich, and Vienna.

Nor was it only the enthusiasm of the general public for a most beautiful voice, which had been already given her; but it was the authoritative chiefs of the musical art who had signalised in her the arrival not only of an exquisite singer, but of a supreme and unique artist. The admiration for Jenny Lind was not a mere popular fever, such as has now and again followed the steps of some favourite of the Opera. Its peculiar force lay in this—that it held enthralled the highest and best minds in Europe. It was the men of genius who recognised in her something akin to themselves. In her native land it had been those who dominated in the musical and literary world who were drawn to sing, and write, and talk of her—Geijer, historian and poet; Lindblad, the "Schubert of Sweden"; Bishop Thomander, Fredrika Bremer, Topelius. At Copenhagen it is the chief artists and poets, and writers and sculptors of the day who are profoundly sensitive to her influence—Jensen, Hans Andersen, Thorwaldsen, Melbye,

Œhlenschläger. In Berlin it is Meyerbeer, who can talk of nothing else but this marvellous Swedish girl. In London it is Moscheles, who writes, "What shall I say of Jenny Lind? It is impossible to find words adequate to describe the impression she has produced. This is no short-lived fit of public enthusiasm. So much modesty and so much greatness united are seldom, if ever, to be met with." It is Thalberg, Taubert, Schumann, who welcome her into the elect company of the masters, "who know." It is Tieck and Kaulbach at Berlin, it is Grillparzer at Vienna, who are her friends and her hosts. And, finally, it is Mendelssohn himself, who, as will be seen in the letters that follow, is fascinated by her personality, and feels all his gifts roused in him to compose something worthy of her, and is eager and on fire to put out all his power in an opera which she may sing, and bends before her judgment as to his own place and career, and delights to share with her the deepest motives and convictions with which he sets to work at the *Elijah.* Does not our picture of the Haymarket crush rather fade into insignificance as a standard of Jenny Lind's position as an artist when we recall the high notes of the soprano in the *Elijah,* giving out the cry of Seraphim to Seraphim, "Holy, holy, holy, Lord God of Sabaoth," and remember that it was with her image before him that Mendelssohn wrote that music—that it was to catch the peculiar beauty which he loved in her voice that the high F sharps ring out so appealingly in the "Hear ye, Israel"? And have we at all realised that she was one of whom he could say, "She is as great an artist as ever lived; and the greatest I have known"? *

The question that we have put was one which her visible

* Recorded by Mrs. Grote, in her Note-book, as said to her by Mendelssohn in 1846. *Cf.* Mendelssohn's words to Hans Andersen, at p. 288 of this volume.

presence would at once suggest. Surely those who first saw her in much later life must have instinctively felt a jar between the popular ideal and the realisation; not that she was less than their expectation, but that ·she was so much more than the general report tended to convey. They had come to be introduced to her, murmuring perhaps to themselves some air from the *Sonnambula*, or the *Figlia*, with which her early fame was associated; but the air was forgotten when they found themselves in her presence; that strong and solemn face, with its deep lines and grey pathetic eyes, with its grave dignity, with its serious exaltation—what had this face in common with an Opera of Donizetti? Charm, animation, lightness, grace—these, no doubt, she had at command, and she could brim over with gaiety and humour; but not in these lay the impression she produced—not here was the dominant note struck. Rather one felt oneself to be facing a character of emphatic force and vigorous outlines—a character that it was difficult to imagine curbed within the conventional artificialities of the Italian drama. It had far more of the impressive pose of a powerful tragedienne. Even the name of "Jenny Lind" seemed to be inadequate to the occasion. It is a name which English lips caress with affection, having in it the sense and sound of some homely and endearing diminutive. But here, one felt, was something more than affectionate diminutives could express; something more than a delicious singer; something more, even, than the pure and simple and beneficent woman. All this there certainly was, but with it and above it was that which startles and quells and even alarms—something of a rare and majestic type, which broke through the ordinary layers which encrust and imprison our average human life; a character solitary and distinct, dowered with strange intensity, retaining its free original spontaneity, drawing ever on its own resources, independent and somewhat contemptuous

of those external tests and standards by which the mass of
men guide their hesitating judgments. Susceptible, indeed,
she was, as an artist must be, to outside influence and
atmosphere, but her individuality had not succumbed, or lost
its sharp and unique distinction under this liability to
sensitive impression; it had never yielded to the grinding
years. It retained, obviously and undeniably, the rarity and
the grandeur of genius; and all who had eyes to see knew, at
a glance, that here before them was a pilgrim-soul, aloof and
uplifted,

" One of the small transfigured band,
Whom the world cannot tame."

It is to justify this high estimate of her powers and gifts
that this book is written. It starts from the level of
Mendelssohn's judgment of her. If, indeed, she was the
greatest musical artist that he had ever known, it is well
worth while to ask whence her capacities took their rise, what
was their artistic development, what are the special notes
and features which were most characteristic of her genius.
The very existence of an artist who responded to Mendelssohn's Ideal, is bound to set us thinking. What was the
secret of her sway? In what was she emphatically herself,
individual and unique? What elements of power and skill
did she owe to external influences? The book proposes to
respond to such questions as these; and, with this end in
view, after lightly tracing the records of her birth and early
infancy, it offers a sketch of her dramatic career from the
year 1829–30, when she first passed within the doors of
the theatre, to the year 1850–51, when, after having bade
farewell to the stage for ever, she signalised her new position
by her triumphant passage to the New World beyond the
Atlantic. Within those full twenty years she was a Child of
the Drama in an intimate and peculiar sense. Within that
time she won the experience, under the pressure of which the

gifts with which she was endowed received their impress, and moved forward to their perfection. By the close of those years she had gained everything that gave its unique character to her artistic genius; for, not only had she proved her complete mastery over all the manifold opportunities and material of the operatic stage, but she had already, in earlier days, by her singing of selections from the *Creation*, and the *Seasons*, and more especially by her marvellous rendering of the soprano part in the *Elijah*, in London, on behalf of the Mendelssohn Scholarships, on December 15th, 1848, attested her supremacy in that domain of art which was so singularly congenial both to her special capacities and to her spirited temper, and through which she was, in after years, to carry such a high message to her hearers—the domain of sacred Oratorio.

Those twenty years, then, contain the secret of her growth as an artist. The years that followed, besides the splendid opportunities which they brought her of exercising the powers which were already matured, added, also, to this, much which matured and deepened the woman's inward history—added the good gifts which she herself had, by hard necessity, most pitifully lacked in her early days—the gifts of tender domestic love, of watchful devotion—the background of warmth and confidence which belongs to home, and husband, and children. All this would, for herself, measured by her own balances, be of priceless worth in the estimation of her life, and for those who knew and loved her, it would be of inexhaustible interest. But it is the *artistic* life, alone, of an artist, over which the world has a positive and undeniable claim. The rest is a matter for private judgment, for personal consideration; it may be made public or not, according to the decision of those who have full right over it. But an artist is, in a sense, public property; his or her art makes direct appeal to public

judgment ; it offers itself as a public endowment to the world
at large.   Its development, its movements, its story, are
public facts.   And it is due to mankind, when it gives to an
artist a generous and unstinted welcome, that it should know
the peculiar growth and training, the advantages and the
perplexities, the hindrances and the helps, through which
that gift, which was at last so triumphant, won its slow way
forward out of darkness into light.   Such a story may not be
without profit, if it aids men to understand how better to
cherish and foster those germs of genius which are to be found
scattered in such strange freedom, amid conditions which
seem least calculated to rear them in hardihood and grace.
And, certainly, the tale of Jenny Lind may well be told for
the sake of bearing splendid witness, to all those who feel
themselves stirred by some inherent native power, of the
unconquerable force with which a pure and strong individuality, if it be true to the inner light and loyal to the outward
call, can dominate circumstances, however harsh and rude,
and can, with a single eye on the far goal of artistic perfection,
and upheld by faith in God, move straight to its aim with an
unswerving and irresistible security, shaping its passage, amid
pitfalls and snares, over this perilous earth with a motion as
free and sure and faithful as a star that passes, in unhindered
obedience, over the steady face of heaven.

Nor will it be without significant interest that those twenty
years begin with her earliest attachment to the Royal
Theatre in her own home-city of Stockholm, and end with
her tribute-gifts, made out of her wonderful winnings, as
thank-offerings to that theatre and home to which her heart
had so often and so tenderly turned.   The years of her main
artistic growth are those in which, whatever her successes
elsewhere, Swedish influences dominated her life.   It was
from the Swedish stage that she derived all her dramatic
training.   It was Swedish literature, Swedish literary men,

who first made her sensitive to the high motives that were at work within her. It was in their company, under their encouragement, that she learned the truth and power of her own spiritual promptings. It was to carry back to her beloved Stockholm the rich fruits of her Parisian discipline that she toiled in exile. And even though, as an artist could not but do, she felt her spirit expand when she found herself taken into the full sweep of the musical forces at a great centre like Berlin, still her Swedish heart beat true to the old home-country, and it was out of her innermost self that she bent herself, as soon as the currents of her public triumph carried her far abroad, to the sweet task of securing for Sweden, out of the gains that Europe and America poured into her lap, records and pledges of her faithful remembrance of the needs and necessities of her own people, and her fatherland.

CHAPTER II.

CHILDHOOD.

" A CHILD of the Drama "—so we have named her—and not
without reason; for it was within the shelter of the Royal
Theatre at Stockholm that she first found the comfortable
warmth of a steady and a tender home, in which her child-
heart, with its intense affections, could freely and candidly
expand. She was hardly ten years old when she came under
the guardianship of the Royal Theatre; and throughout
those nine early years, she was a forlorn little pilgrim, often
passed about through the hands of strangers, and pitifully
deprived of that deep security which a fixed and stable
home-life inbreeds in us through its traditional sanctities and
immemorial kindnesses.

Her birth, which took place in the parish of St. Clara, in
Stockholm, on October 6, 1820, found both her parents somewhat under difficulties. Her father, Niclas Jonas Lind, son of
a lace-manufacturer, seems to have been able to do little or
nothing towards providing a home for mother and child. He
was very young, only twenty-two years old; he had, through
lack of energy, failed to continue his father's business, and
at this time, kept the ledgers at a private merchant's house;
in virtue of which office he is entered as " Accountant " in
the church register at the baptism of his little daughter,
who was christened, on the day after her birth, with the
name " Johanna Maria."

Such a post would, no doubt, bring him in but little; and

perhaps he was not very likely to make the most of what he got. For he was good-naturedly weak; much given to music of a free and convivial kind, such as was widely popular in Sweden at that day, when the influence of Bellman was at its height. This brilliant Anacreontic genius, whose songs are to the Swedes what those of Robert Burns are to Scotchmen, though he had himself died as long ago as 1795, had, under the *régime* of Gustavus III., gained a sway which enthralled the people during the first thirty years of the century. His songs were sung with unbounded enthusiasm; great popular feasts were held in his honour. Even now, we understand, on Bellman's Day in July, his admirers gather to pour libations before his bust; and still a Society meets every month to sing his songs. In 1820 this poetic thraldom was in full possession; and Mr. Lind had a good voice, and took an eager part in the musical festivities. Such a life, it will be easily understood, does not tend to foster steadiness or thrift; and he was perfectly unable to provide mother and child with either lodging or board, though he probably contributed to it in some slender way. All the practical management had to be left to the energy and determination of the mother, who was, at the time, making her own way through the world under conditions which were not favourable to a baby's entry on the scene.

She was, herself, of very respectable burgher-stock. Her maiden name had been Anna Maria Fellborg; but she had been first married, in 1810, at the age of eighteen, to a Captain Rådberg. Her marriage had proved very unhappy, owing to the bad character of the husband; and after about eighteen months she obtained a divorce from him in the High Ecclesiastical Court, the Court assigning to her, in decisive recognition of her husband's misconduct, the custody of a little daughter who had been born to them, called Amelia Maria Constantia, together with aliment to the amount of half Rådberg's income, whatever that might be. She was thus thrown upon her own unaided exertions; but she was a woman of great force of character, well-educated for her circumstances, resolute not to be beaten.   She got along, in one way or another, chiefly by means of education; and in 1820, at Jenny's birth, was keeping a day-school for girls, one or two of whom she also boarded; it was one of these little boarders, nine years older than Jenny, who became afterwards so helpful to her as companion and friend—Louise Johansson, whose name will frequently recur in the course of our story.

A baby would be, no doubt, a most tiresome inconvenience in the management of such a household; and so her mother seems to have placed the child, at once, under the care of Carl Ferndal, who was organist and parish clerk of the church at Ed-Sollentuna, some fifteen English miles out of Stockholm. She was tended by this man and his wife for about three years, her mother visiting her, it seems, at intervals, and spending with her the summer of 1821. Owing to some dispute with the clerk, she took Jenny back in 1824, probably in the early part of the year, to Stockholm; but it is possible to believe that those early years in Sollentuna were not without some influence on the child's character, for they seem to have woke up in her, from the very start, that innate and instinctive sense of the country which was so noticeable in her.   The instinct itself is, indeed, native to the Swedes, for whom "the country" is a passion; and this national characteristic held, in her, a deep-rooted dominion. Somehow, one felt, in her company, as if she had come out of the country. She was in close touch with all that belongs to a simple peasantry. She knew the tones of its songs; and the rhythm of its dances; its simplicity, its charm, its pathos—all were hers. Something of its native depth and dignity seemed to have passed into her. She ever felt herself at home in the country; she breathed there freely; she revelled in its wild flowers, in contrast with cultivated garden-flowers for which she had little love. She had an intense delight in the songs of wild-birds, with whose ways and habits she had intimate acquaintance. She enjoyed, especially, the expanse of wide waters. She delighted to be at large; she hated crowds, and the pressure of a city, and the unresting stir of society. She did not desire the constant company of many fellow-creatures; the town-instincts did not draw her. Her need of music might bring her to live there where she could best satisfy it; but her heart was, naturally, away in country-scenes, where men were not too thick and near; and where God seems closer; and where the soul can feed its own high thoughts, somewhat aloof and alone, unfretted by man's insistent noise. Yet, after these first four years, she was brought up altogether in a city, winning the sight of the country only in her holidays. Something, surely, sank down very deep into the tiny baby, as she toddled in and out of the clerk's house, in the village of Sollentuna—something, which made her at home, ever, amid trees and fields—and something which was still strong in her to the end, linking the first days in the Swedish village to those last hours when she waited for her death, hid in the English home, where she had made for herself a refuge of peace, amid the sweet solitude of the Malvern hills.

Back, however, to Stockholm, she was then quickly brought; and there, in her home, she, most likely, found a new arrival in the person of Fru Tengmark, her grandmother on her mother's side, now in her second widowhood, who had, hitherto, lived with one of her daughters, Fru Perman, at Östersund, in the north of Sweden, but who had now come to press her claim for admittance into a certain Home for the Widows of Stockholm burghers, an established and endowed institution of some importance in Stockholm.

Already, in 1822, the old lady had put in her plea that she was unable, at an age which made employment impossible, to save herself, by her own efforts, from need; but it was not until 19th August, 1824, that rooms were finally allotted to her. Jenny, therefore, it would appear, found her at her mother's house; and she seems to have received from Fru Tengmark a more kindly and appreciative treatment than it was in her mother's nature to bestow upon her. She always spoke of her grandmother with strong admiration and affection. Above all, she took in from her a profound impression of religion; and it was to her that, in after-years, she was accustomed to trace back those spiritual influences which became the very soul of her life.

It was the grandmother who was the first to detect the musical gifts of the child; and this detection left a profound impression on the child herself, as if she, too, then first made a discovery of what was in her through the surprise which she found herself producing in others. The story formed her earliest distinct memory. Coming up from the country to the town, she was struck by the music of the military bugles that daily passed through the street; and one day when she fancied herself alone in the house she crept to the piano on which her half-sister used to practise her music, and, with one finger, strummed out for herself the fanfare which she had caught from the soldiers. But the grandmother was at hand, and, hearing the music, called out the name of the half-sister, whom she supposed it to be; and little Jenny, in terror at being found out, hid under the square piano; she was so small that she fitted in perfectly; and the grandmother, getting no answer to her calls, came in to look, and presently discovered her, and dragged her out, and was astonished, and said, "Child, was that you?" and Jenny, in tears at her crime, confessed; but the grandmother looked at her deeply, and in silence; and when the mother came back she told her,

and said : " Mark my words, that child will bring you help."
And, after that, the neighbours used to be called in to hear
her play. As she told the story in later years, she would reproduce most vividly the frightened look of the child creeping
away to hide ; and the significant look of the wonder-struck
grandmother as she took in that it was indeed the tiny creature of three years old who had played the tune. She never
forgot the historic " fanfare " ; and, as the earliest signal of
her after-career, it is given in the form in which she herself
committed it to the memory of her daughter.

At this day-school Jenny continued with her mother, for
three or four years ; but, at last, the only boarder, Louise
Johansson, was taken away, and her mother found herself
hard pressed for funds. She determined to go out as governess ; and, perhaps with this intention, answered an advertisement stating that a certain childless couple were anxious
to have a child to take care of. It turned out that this
couple lived in the very same Widows' Home, in which Fru
Tengmark had rooms, the man being the Guardian or Steward
of the Home—a thoroughly comfortable and respectable position, by right of which he occupied the Lodge at the gate.
This all seemed to fall in admirably, as Jenny would have the
companionship of her favourite relation. So thither she was

sent, probably in the year 1828 ; and her mother retired from Stockholm and took a place as governess, in Linköping, carrying with her her daughter Amalia Rådberg to help her in her educational work.

For a year and more she lived in the Widows' Home, but there is nothing recorded of her life there until we come to the famous incident which brought about her removal, and which fixed, for ever, the lines of her future career. It came about in this fashion. "As a child I sang with every step I took, and with every jump my feet made." So she herself records in her letter to the Editor of the 'Swedish Biographical Lexicon,' written in 1865 ;* and, apparently one of the forms which the perpetual song took was addressed to a cat, "with a blue ribbon round its neck," of which she was very fond The rest of the story shall be given in her own words as they were taken down by her eldest son, to whom she told it at Cannes in the spring of 1887. "Her favourite seat with her cat was in the window of the Steward's rooms, which look out on the lively street leading up to the Church of St. Jacob's, and there she sat and sang to it ; and the people passing in the street used to hear, and wonder ; and amongst others the maid of a Mademoiselle Lundberg, a dancer at the Royal Opera House ; and the maid told her mistress that she had never heard such beautiful singing as this little girl sang to her cat. Mademoiselle Lundberg thereupon found out who she was, and sent to ask her mother, who seems to have been in Stockholm at the time, to bring her to sing to her. And, when she heard her sing, she said, "The child is a genius ; you must have her educated for the stage." But Jenny's mother, as

* The **Editor** of this Biographical Dictionary had written to her to ask if she could give him any account of her artistic training. She wrote back a most characteristic letter, of which fragments only were inserted in the Dictionary, among the "Addenda" to Vol. viii., New Series, p. 363 (1868). The letter is given in full in the Appendix to the present memoir.

well as her grandmother, had an old-fashioned prejudice
against the stage; and she would not hear of this. "Then
you must, at any rate, have her taught singing," said Mademoiselle Lundberg; and the mother was persuaded, in this
way, to accept a letter of introduction to Herr Croelius, the
Court-secretary and Singing-master, at the Royal Theatre.
Off with the letter they started; but, as they went up the
broad steps of the Opera House, the mother was again
troubled by her doubts and repugnance. She, no doubt, had
all the inherited dislike of the burgher families to the
dramatic life. But little Jenny eagerly urged her to go on;
and they entered the room where Croelius sat. And the
child sang him something out of an Opera composed by
Winter. Croelius was moved to tears and said that he must
take her in to Count Puke, the head of the Royal Theatre, and
tell him what a treasure he had found. And they went at
once; and Comte Puke's first question was, "How old is
she?" and Croelius answered "Nine years old." "Nine!"
exclaimed the Count; "but this is not a Crèche! It is
the King's Theatre!" And he would not look at her, she
being, moreover, at that time what she herself (in her
letter to the 'Biographical Lexicon') calls "a small, ugly,
broad-nosed, shy, gauche, under-grown girl!" "Well," said
Croelius, "if the Count will not hear her, then I will
teach her gratuitously myself, and she will one day as-
tonish you!" Then Count Puke consented to hear her
sing; and, when she sang, he too was moved to tears; and,
from that moment, she was accepted; and was taken, and
taught to sing, and educated, and brought up at the
Government expense.

So she told it in her own graphic manner; and what these
last words imply we must now see, for they mark the most
crucial event in her life. We have seen how her mother re-
pelled the thought of the stage. It was a deep-rooted tradi-

tional repugnance; and her child, in after-years, when she
herself had come strongly under the influence of the same
repugnance, used to regard it as inherited from her mother.
"She, like myself, had the greatest horror of all that was
connected with the stage." So she wrote in 1865. How
far these words about herself need qualification, we shall see
as our story advances; but as, in its later years, this repugnance played so vital a part in fashioning her life, it may be
well to note it here at its first appearance, where it makes
the mother hang back, at the very door of the theatre, and
is only overcome by the entreaties of the eager little child,
longing to give proof of her gift. Those stairs, so haunting
to the two who then crept up them, were to become familiar
enough to the little feet which then first felt them. Up
that broad flight she stepped on to the platform on which,
for twenty years to come, she was to live out her life, and
win her unexampled victories. As she pulled at her mother's
unwilling hand that day, she took the step which determined
her whole destiny.

For, radical as her mother's dislike might be to the stage,
yet fate, on the one hand, was too strong for her, and, on
the other, she was pressed sorely by her straitened means.
Croelius and Count Puke were not going to let their new-
found treasure slip through their hands. They made an
immediate offer to relieve the mother of all direct responsibility for her child's maintenance and education; they
proposed to adopt her into the School of Pupils, which was
attached to the Royal Theatre, looking to repay the expenses,
which they risked, through the after-success which they
anticipated. It was a generous proposal; it came at a
moment of pressure when it was almost impossible to refuse
the opportunity of relief; and the mother yielded. To her it
still seemed an act by which, in her own words, used afterwards to the directors of the theatre, she was " sacrificing her

own child to the stage." But circumstances were unfortunate,
and she could not but agree. So Jenny passed over from the
Widows' Home to become a little nursling of the Drama; and
the world owes a debt of genuine gratitude to the directors
of the Theatre Royal for so quick and bold a recognition of
the wonderful gift which lay hid in that tiny body. Rare,
indeed, in the annals of art is it that the official authorities
are so swift in their appreciation of strange and exceptional
genius or so ready to make a venture on its behalf. And the
chief honour, in a deed most honourable to all concerned,
must lie with Herr Croelius. It was his insight that saw
what there was in the "shy, gauche, and ugly, under-grown
girl;" it was his courage that laid compulsion on the natural
unwillingness of Count Puke. "The person," she herself
wrote in the letter we have already quoted to the editor
of the 'Biographical Lexicon,' "whom alone I have to
thank for the first discernment of my gift of song was the
Court Secretary Croelius, Singing-master at the Theatre
Royal. He told me all that which in later years came to
pass." It is pleasant at this point to read a letter from
the old man himself to Jenny Lind, written from Stockholm, 4th March, 1842, in answer to a letter of hers from
Paris, in which "her kind heart," as he says, has expressed
its gratitude to him. He fears to put himself forward
too much lest he should seem to be claiming that which
her later masters had done for her; "but," as he writes,
"when your talent and your other excellent qualities
called forth general homage, I considered I had a right to
present myself as your admirer and friend. My interest in
you is, and will always remain, the most genuine. Your
honour, your success will be the comfort of my old age and
a balm for my sufferings." He died that year. His kindly
features, quaint and dignified, are recorded in the accompanying sketch, on which she herself, long afterwards, wrote her

witness to the goodness of him who was "the first to discern her gifts," and whose insight and courage determined her career.

So closes her early childhood. Hitherto she has sung as Nature bade her, singing to herself, singing to her cat, singing "at every step and jump which she made with her baby feet." Something, indeed, she may have caught from her mother, who was qualified to teach music, and from her half-sister and the day-pupils who used to practise on

Croelius
my first
dear old
singing-
master

who caused me to
be engaged
at the R. Theatre
at Stockholm
1829

the piano on which Jenny made her first famous experiment; and she would have heard her father, who used to come in the evening and sing, while her mother played the guitar, when the little one lay probably in bed. And, even at Sollentuna, she would have listened, in baby-wonder, to Ferndal as he played his organ in the church. But her young life had been, as we have seen, strangely wandering, chequered, and untutored, and nearly everything she had must have come from her own instinctive spontaneity. She

was now to pass at this tiny age into a school devoted
to the drama, under the definite training and discipline
of skilled masters in music. In Croelius' room she made
her début; there she found her vocation. The little
foundling of Nature was henceforward to become the child
of Art.*

* Her half-sister, Amalia, who, during the break-up of the home,
wrote affectionately to her "dear little Jenny," urging her to pray to
God to keep alive "our dear good mother," and to bring back the
pleasant days, seems to have appreciated the gifts of the child; for in
the P.S. to a letter written on March 21th, 1830, which was found preserved among Madame Goldschmidt's papers, she wrote: "Whatever
you do, pray cultivate your music, for then you will make your mark."

CHAPTER III.

The Royal Theatre, at Stockholm, into which Jenny Lind passed in the September of 1830, was to be, for the next ten years, the scene and centre of her life. In it she found a nursery for her child-talent; a school to direct her entire development; a playground in which she tasted the delights of companionship; a home, which watched over her with fatherly interest and authority; a stage on which she was greeted with unstinted appreciation. It became, for this spell of years, the pivot of all her efforts, the focus of all her associations and hopes, the environment within which all her gifts opened and discovered themselves.

The theatre was subsidised from the Royal Civil List, and was directed and controlled by the office of the Lord Chamberlain. Its chief officer was a Royal Director (Intendant), under whom, among other officials, was the Chief of the Singing Department. The first office was occupied, at the time of Jenny's entry, by Count Puke; while the second was filled by Herr Croelius, who was dignified with the title of Court Secretary. The official finances came under the supervision of Herr Forsberg, an official in the War Office, who was charged with the honorary superintendence of the Theatre-School. He took an almost fatherly interest in Jenny Lind; and she retained an intimate and affectionate friendship with his family, until her death.

The theatre stands in the heart of Stockholm, close to the

Norrbro (North Bridge) overlooking the wide basin of the
Norrström: it is a large, handsome building, facing the street
known as the Gustaf Adolf's Torg, with its basement and
double stories, on the second of which, in fine and airy
rooms, was housed the School of Girls attached to the theatre,
into which Jenny was now introduced, herself the very
youngest of all, as we may gather from Count Puke's complaint that Croelius was treating the theatre, as if "it were a
Crèche."

The "Directors of the Royal Theatre," * as its authorities
were called, were in the habit of boarding out the pupils at
some certified home, or homes, in the town, under the charge
of some lady with whom the theatre made terms for food,
lodging, and educational supervision. And, here, we come
to a rather curious arrangement, which might, if it had been
happily carried out, have combined, most fortunately, Jenny's
new conditions with her natural home-relations. Her mother
had moved back to Stockholm just before Jenny's entry at
the theatre: she had taken, in the spring of 1830, a
flat in No. 4 Quarteret Hammaren, in the Jakobsbergs-
gata. Had she taken it for the very purpose of boarding
the pupils of the theatre? It is impossible to say: but,
certainly, this parish of St. Jacob is close at hand; and, very
soon after her return, she appears to have been intrusted by
the Directors with some of their boarders; and, among them,
probably, her own little daughter. It is true, that the first
formal records of this arrangement that we possess do not
begin until the years 1832–1833, but we have no notice of
where Jenny boarded during the two intervening years, and
the fact that her mother already had taken, in 1830, the
house in which she is found boarding the children in 1832–
1833, seems, certainly, to suggest, that Jenny may have been
placed with her from the beginning. And, indeed, this is

* K. Teater Direktionen.

made almost certain by the fact that her very earliest recollections of the Theatre-School, as she often told her daughter, was her running to the school, to keep herself warm, in the cold winter mornings, dressed in the vivid smart colours, which her mother and half-sister loved, and which she so hated that she used to pull the bright feathers out of her bonnet as soon as she was out of sight of home. Anyhow, in 1833, the thing took shape in a legal contract, drawn up between the " Directors " and Jenny's mother, which implies, by its language, that it was formularising an arrangement, which had been going on already in some tentative fashion, at least since April, 1832. The conditions of the bond are most precise, and remarkable; and their definite precision is, itself, a witness how clearly the authorities had perceived, and proved, the value of the gifted child, for whose sake they were prepared to make so remarkable a venture. They begin by stating that they have, already, since April, 1832, been paying for * "Jenny Lind's board and education," and that, through the progress she has made since then, they have " formed the best hopes of her usefulness for the theatrical profession," and that they " desire to attach this young talent, by more definite conditions, to the Royal Theatre." They wish, therefore, to close a contract with her mother, with the terms of which, as they carefully insert, " Jenny Lind has declared herself satisfied." The child is to be received in the capacity of " actress-pupil at the Royal Theatre "; and cannot, without the consent of the directors, be released from her engagement until she have, through her after-efforts, " made restitution for the care and expense bestowed on her education."

---

* " Jenny Lind " appears as the formal name, even in the official document. Only once, *i.e.* in the Confirmation certificate, 1836, does the full name of her christening reappear, " Johanna Maria Lind." In the letter to the Biog. Lexicon, she herself says that she was " never called Johanna."

"During her growing years, and until she is competent to be allotted a fixed salary, she is to receive, at the expense of the Theatre, food, clothes, and lodging, together with free tuition in singing, elocution, dancing, and such other branches of instruction as belong to the education of a cultivated woman, and are requisite for the theatrical profession." The carrying out of this instruction is then committed to her mother, who engages to teach her "the Piano, Religion, French, History, Geography, Writing, Arithmetic, and Drawing." She is also to see to all matters of "food, fire, furniture, and clothing, bedding and washing"; and to have for her a tender mother's care.

For these purposes she will receive from the Directors 250 Riksdaler Banco (*i.e.* 20 guineas), while Jenny herself will be given two Riksdaler Banco every month for pocket money, out of which she is to pay (poor child!) for her own needles and tape as well as for silk and cotton towards the mending of her clothes; this will leave not very much over for Jenny's private purposes; but on the other hand she is to be allowed the use of a pianoforte belonging to the Royal Theatre, of which her mother pledges herself to take proper care; and moreover, after the 1st July, 1835, she will actually be supplied with a chest of drawers, as well as bedstead and bedclothes, at the special cost of the Royal Theatre. Her mother is to see to it that the *aktris-elev* carefully observes the hours for lessons, rehearsals, and representations. The Royal Directors are to judge when the little creature will become competent to enter as actress with a salary from the Civil List, after which a new contract will be made, by which she will be pledged to remain for ten years in the service of the Royal Theatre for such a salary as the Directors, having proper regard to her talent and usefulness at the time, shall decide to grant her; but, in case "the aktris-elev Lind, contrary to the good hopes entertained on her behalf, were for one reason or another to prove of no use to the Royal Theatre, or, again, if she were to fail in that obedience she owes to the Royal Directors, it shall have full right to discharge her from the theatre after three months' notice, in which case the contract is to lapse."

So runs the deed, signed, on behalf of the Directors, by P. Westerstrand, who had succeeded Count Puke as Intendant, and by Carl D. Forsberg, of the War Office; and, below their signatures, Jenny's mother declares herself to be satisfied with the proposed conditions.

Such was the bond. It resembles in general outlines other agreements of the kind; but it is exceptional in its details, and in its special care for the "high talent" which it desires to attach to the theatre. The assumption of an almost paternal authority by the Directors is quite in accord with its habitual tone. In the case of Matilda Ficker, for instance (afterwards the well-known Mme. Gelhaar), who had only a grandfather alive, the bond declares that the "Direction undertakes a father's duties towards her, and acquires, also, a father's rights": wherewith it will decide about her residence, education, occupation, and conduct. Both this bond, and that with Jenny Lind's close friend "Mina Fundin," * are made when the child is about fourteen years old, which was, perhaps, the usual age.

The present bond has been given almost in full, not only for its intrinsic and historic interest as marking a momentous epoch in Jenny Lind's career, but also in order to bring out the conception which is there embodied, of the educational qualifications requisite for a pupil of the theatre. The completeness of the instruction proposed is most striking. We

---

* Wilhelmina Christina Fundin, daughter of the Precentor of St. Klara Church, Stockholm; she was born in 1819, entered the Elev School 1833, and remained there until 1841. She remained connected with the Royal Opera until 1870, when she retired on a pension.

may smile at the long list of subjects in which the little
girl is to be schooled, or at the abrupt appearance of
" religion " sandwiched between the piano and the French
language.   Doubtless, these numerous branches of study
were but touched in an elementary manner: but, still,
they are recognised as essential: and the remarkable phrase
stands which declares that the training for the dramatic profession includes all that belongs to the " full
education of a cultivated woman."   There, in that phrase, is
a distinct ideal.   It implies that the drama is no narrow,
specialised function of a mere expert; but is an affair in
which the entire mind and character of the artist are concerned, so that the theatre itself may well spend its money
in securing, not only the technical and professional training,
but also that the pupil shall have the intelligence developed
and fertilised, so that it be level with the average culture of
the time.

And then, again, the completeness of the more professional
instruction is well worth notice.   Elocution, dancing, the
piano—all are necessary to perfect the dramatic singing.
The memory of this completeness in her early theatrical
education left an indelible impression on Jenny Lind.   She
felt that she owed to it so much that contributed to, and
enriched, the full effect of her musical gift; and especially
she valued her trained skill in expressive and beautiful
motion, gained in the dancing school at the Theatre Royal.
She moved exquisitely.   Her perfect walk, her dignity of
pose, her striking uprightness of attitude, were characteristic
of her to the very last; and no one can fail to recall how
she stood, before, and while, she sang.   Her grace, her
lightness of movement were all the more noticeable from
the rather angular thinness of her natural figure; and there
can be no doubt that they threw into her acting a charm
which was positively entrancing.   She knew the value and

necessity of all this completeness of training; she felt its
lack in those who had entered on the operatic stage by
accident as it were, taking it up only when fully grown
simply on account of possessing a beautiful voice. She missed
in them the full finish of the perfected art; no beauty in the
singing could quite atone for the ignorance of dramatic
methods, and of all that constitutes the peculiar environment
of the stage.

We shall see how deeply this early ideal of all that was
involved in the technical training coloured her intentions,
when she was planning the endowment which she, at first,
desired to devote to the theatre-school where she had served
her own apprenticeship. And this ideal still lived in her, to
play a large part in those interests, and anxieties, with which,
even at the very close of her life, she worked to found a
School of Song, at the Royal College of Music, in South
Kensington, and which she embodied in a memorandum
drawn up by her, at the request of H.R.H. the President,
before entering on her official post.

To what degree the full education of a cultivated woman
was actually attained in her case, it would be hard to
exactly define. A great musical gift like hers carries culture
with it; and, then, she had, all her after-life, revelled in the
society of the most cultivated men in Europe. So that it is
difficult, from knowledge of her in later days, to say how
much she had gained out of the formal instructions given her
in childhood. But, naturally, these can only have been of an
elementary and superficial type. She never possessed the
sure mental instincts which are the fruit of a literary
education. Her judgments on books, for instance, depended,
for their brilliancy, on her unaided and unconventional
spontaneity, and on her rapid perceptions. But they had not
the proportion, and balance, that comes from accurate knowledge, or trained intellectual discipline. One felt that she

had never had this, in the strict sense. She was, so to
speak, at the mercy of any book that interested her ; she had
no secure sense of its limitations ; she did not know how to
place it. Evidently, the education had been quite simple
and unscientific.

Nevertheless, the list of general studies named by the
Directors was not merely nominal; pains were taken ; the
instruction was given. Religion, in spite of the hostile
proximity of French on the one side, and of the piano on the
other, was carefully attended to; and her Confirmation certificate, given her on May 10th, 1836, witnesses, by the hand
of the rector of St. Jacob's parish, Herr Abraham Pettersson,
that she passed the public examination in the Christian
doctrine of salvation " *with distinction."*

For French, she went, probably, to the classes of M.
Terrade, teacher to the Royal Theatre; the instruction was
slight, but a certain degree of conversational French was in
free use in Stockholm at the time, and would be habitual
round about the theatre. Still, before her visit to Paris in
1841, she thought it necessary to take special lessons; and
she had, when there, as we shall see, to grind at the grammar ;
so that her early knowledge must have been quite unscientific.

As to the piano, she, certainly, gained, at some time in her
early life, a complete mastery over it, which stood her in
good stead, and afforded her great enjoyment in later years.
It was true that she had injured her left hand, when young,
while striking fire with a flint on tinder, which to a certain
extent crippled its full use; and, besides, she feared to
fatigue and contract the vocal organs by serious practice on
the piano. But, in spite of this, she handled it freely, and
finely; she delighted to improvise on it, which she did with
a touch of genuine genius ; and part of the peculiar charm of
her northern songs, as she sang them, came to them from her
delicious playing of the accompaniment. There seems to be

no doubt that, from quite early days, and more especially at about the age of sixteen, she could use it with easy familiarity; for, while still at this school, she used to "coach" the other girls through the musical parts of the plays, beating them out, herself, on the piano.

She had an eager and intense appreciation of her native literature; but, no doubt, this would be largely due to the influence of the Stockholm literary world, into which she was heartily welcomed at the time of her first triumphs; and, above all, to her intimacy with Geijer and Lindblad and Beskow.

A specimen of her drawing still remains—some painted flowers, done in the exact and formal manner of the day, but bearing sufficient witness to her having had the regular lessons; and those, probably, from her mother, who has left designs of the same type.

One accomplishment must be mentioned with special honour, her sewing. She worked magnificently. "Madame's stitches never come out," is the later testimony from her maid to her powers. And she loved to do a piece of work, designing it herself, and achieving it, with the thoroughness of an expert.

Her knowledge of history was very vague, and general; nothing very definite, probably, was made of that, at the theatre-school.

German, which, afterwards, she loved, and pronounced beautifully, she did not begin until after her twenty-fourth year; her limited knowledge of it was a difficulty, as we shall see, at the first *début* in Berlin under Meyerbeer in 1844; she went to Dresden to work at it in July, 1844; but, even as late as the year 1848, wrote it incorrectly.

English was only slowly won, after her English visits. Her usual speech in this country at that time was French.

So much for her general education and accomplishments;

but we have been anticipating the course of our story, to which we now return.

The little girl, then, started in the spring of 1833, with what might well seem good hopes. Her career had taken a definite shape; she was provided for, if nothing went wrong, for years to come; she was to receive a regular education; and a future position was assured to her. In the meantime she was to be housed, and cared for, by her own mother, in the happy companionship of other girls. Among these companions, and boarding with Jenny, at her mother's house, were several who subsequently filled considerable positions on the royal stage; *e.g.*, Charlotte, and Matilda Ficker (afterwards Mesdames Almlöf and Gelhaar), and Fanny Westerdahl, prominent in Tragedy and severe Comedy.

Mdlle. Bayard, the lady superintendent of the school, was a person much respected; and the pupils were sure of enjoying care and attention from her. Jenny seems to have been exceedingly happy both with her, and with the other girls; but, alas! her trouble came from where we might least expect it—from her mother. Was it that her strong, and resolute nature had been warped by early disappointment?—that the early marriage with Captain Rådberg at eighteen, with its rapid disillusion, had left serious damage behind it on temper, and character? Certainly, the world had gone hard with her. She had had to fight her way along for herself, under the burden of straitened circumstances. These things are apt to tell; if they do not sweeten, they sour. And she was somewhat proud, and stubborn, and self-willed. She, probably, fretted at the sense of being below the conditions which her burgher blood might expect and justify. From passages in her letters, we shall see, that she was quick to resent a slight, and hard to pacify. She had a strong idea of her rights. She would not yield them, even to her own convenience. Altogether, from her recorded words and expressions, we can feel that she was one for whom things would not run smoothly,—one to whose exasperated sensitiveness life would never prove an easy, sleek, comfortable affair. There is a tone of defiance in her, as if she were at war with her fellows. She had a touch of haughty pride in her, which would find itself engaged in many battles. It is perfectly natural to suppose that she had got a bit worsened by the vigour of the strife. She had not much softness of sympathy to spare; she did not make people love her. She was apt to show herself cross-grained, violent, harsh; and this, not only to others, but also to her child.

Before going on to tell the pitiful story of this early harshness, it may be well to remember that the daughter's memory of her mother was not all dismal and unkind. Their characters had, probably, many elements in common; her mother's force, her mother's haughty persistence reappeared, to some extent, in Jenny Lind. She, too, was not apt to take life too easily. And, again, she warmly recognised all that she owed, at this early time, to her mother's talents, and resolution, and effort. There was, below all the divergence, a strong tie of underlying attachment. The actual intercourse was, indeed, unhappy; it was marred by cruelty, and narrowness, and suspicion, which left a life-long shadow on the child. But it was not without something in it, which could, under brighter circumstances, open out into the tenderness and gentleness which belong to the name of mother. It is comforting to find with what emotion Jenny Lind could look back on the past, in spite of its bitterness, when death had closed the record. It was, indeed, far on in life when this death occurred; but it may soften us, as we approach the story of Fru Lind's faults, to read, by anticipation, the words, in which her daughter sums up the tale. It was in America, in 1851, that the sad news reached Jenny Lind; and, reviewing the event, she wrote to an old friend in Sweden:—

" My mother's death I have felt most bitterly ; everything
was now smooth and nice between us ; I was in hopes that
she would have been spared for many a long year . . . and
that, now that she was quieter and more reasonable, I might
have surrounded her old age with joy, and peace, and tender
care. But the ways of the Lord are often not our ways.
Peace be with her soul ! " *

The affection is there, and the deep bond of blood ; but,
alas ! there had been bad days when all had *not* been so
" smooth, and nice," and when the mother had *not* been
" quiet and reasonable."

It is these bad days of which we have now to speak. It
appears that the pupils found the treatment they received
from her too stern and hard ; and they were soon removed to
rooms at the top of the theatre itself ; and placed under the
charge of Mdlle. Bayard. Here they fared excellently ; and
were extremely happy. Jenny, who remained at her mother's,
used to visit them there ; and it was now that she struck up
her intimate friendship with one of the pupils, Mina Fundin,
who became her favourite playmate, and with whom she kept
up, for life, an affectionate relationship. This lady is still
alive, residing in Stockholm. It would seem that the contrast
between the lonely severity of the home and the lively
society of the theatre-rooms was too much for Jenny ; and,
at last, after some bout of harsh treatment, on the 30th of
October, 1834, she took matters into her own hands, and ran
off to Mdlle. Bayard. The Directors saw the merit of the
proceeding, and allowed her to remain there. But her
mother was not a person to acquiesce in such an arrangement, and the result was a long dispute with the theatre for
the recovery of the child. It can serve no good purpose,
now, to follow the track of this unhappy wrangle. It is
enough to say that the mother was not content, until she had
applied the pressure of the law against the Directors ; that,

* Written to Herr Carl Forsberg, of the War Office, in August, 1852.

at first, she only rested her appeal on the bond with the theatre, and that, when this failed, in January, 1835, she set to work with a more determined effort. Mr. Lind, who had, hitherto, kept in the background, was called to the front to take part in the struggle; and, together, they combined to make good their full parental claims over their child. Such a claim, once formally established, and put in force, was, necessarily, irresistible; and the theatre was obliged to surrender Jenny, by a final judgment of the Royal Upper Town-Court, on the 23rd of June, 1836; and was, also, directed to recognise the existing contract of 1833 as still standing, and to pay, therefore, to the parents the stipulated sum for Jenny's keep, which was owing from January 1st, 1835, to April 1st, 1836, together with lawyer's fee, etc. There the quarrel ended; on June 6th the theatre notified to the parents that Jenny would return to their house on July 1st, to be boarded at the old terms; and both Mr. Lind, and his wife, countersign the notice.

It is pleasant to think that, in spite of these most uncomfortable proceedings, the little creature over whose person home and theatre were fighting so strenuously was spending a most happy time at Mdlle. Bayard's; and it is delightful to read the brimming letter which she wrote, in the very thick of the wrangle, in August 1835—the very first word that we actually possess from her pen. It is written from Skytteholm, a place lying on one of the inland lakes which, in Sweden, are called by the pleasant name of "Sweet-Waters," where the pupils were taken for their summer holidays. It is addressed to the mother of her little playfellow, Mina Fundin—the Mina mentioned in the letter, who has made such desperate resolutions from which she is only saved by the state of her nerves and the motherliness of the "sensible old woman." With Mina's mother, Jenny is evidently on the brightest and most affectionate terms. Here is the letter:—

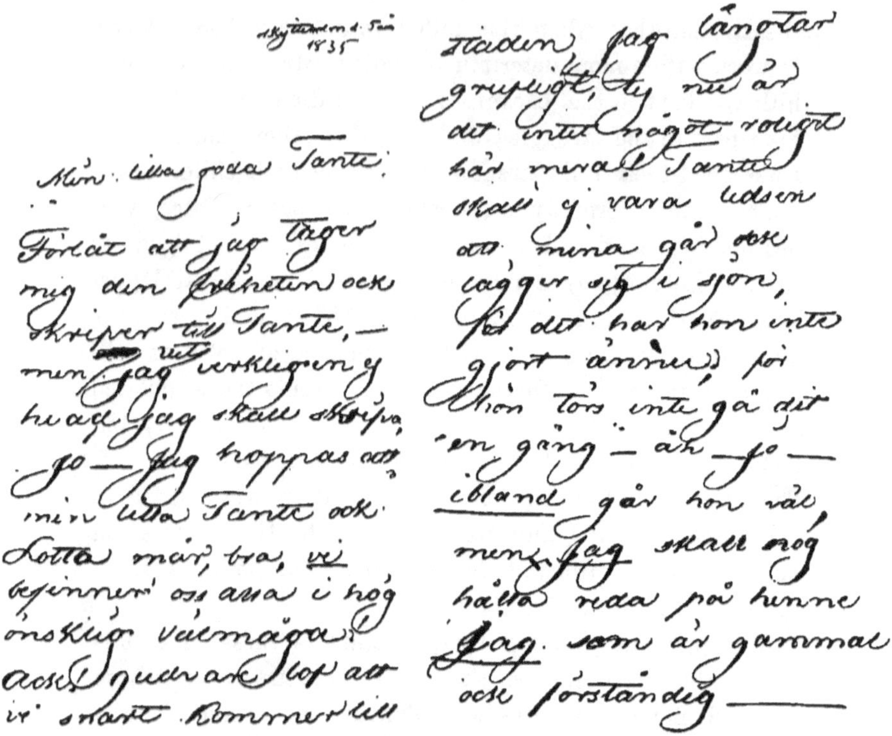

[handwritten Swedish letter — two columns]

[Translation.]

Skytteholm, 5 Aug., 1835.

MY DEAR LITTLE AUNTY,

Pardon me for taking the liberty to write to you—but —I really don't know what to write about! Yes, I know! I hope that my little Aunty and Lotta are quite well;—*we are flourishing, all of us!*

Ah! thank God! soon we return to town; I long dreadfully, for now there is no more fun down here. You must not feel uneasy, Aunty, about Mina going to drown herself, for she has not yet done so, because she is too nervous even to go near the water—Oh, yes!—*occasionally* she does run the risk

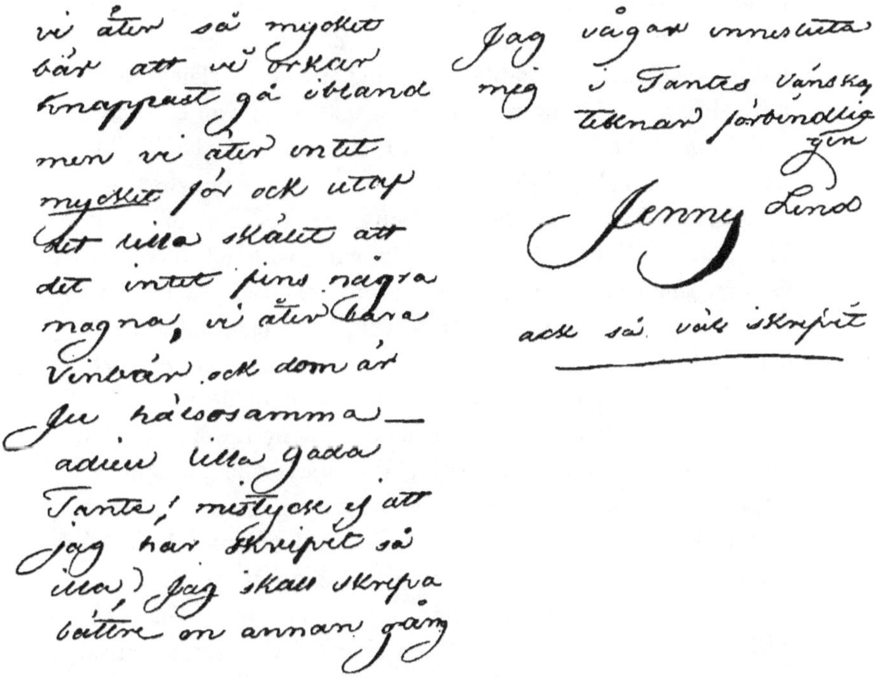
vi äter så mycket
bär att vi orkar
knappast gå ibland
men vi äter intet
mycket för ock utaf
det lilla skälet att
det intet fins några
magna, vi äter bara
Vinbär ock dom är
ju hälsosamma —
adieu lilla goda
Tante; misstycke ej att
jag har skrifvit så
illa) Jag skall skrifva
bättre en annan gång

Jag vågar innesluta
mig i Tantes vänska
teknar förbindlig
gen
Jenny Lind

ock så väl skrifvit

of it, but *I* will look after her—*I*, who am a sensible, old woman.

We eat fruit in such quantities that sometimes we are not able to walk, but we can't get so very much, for the simple reason that there are so few ripe ones; we only eat currants, and those are most wholesome, aren't they?

Adieu, kind little Aunty! Do not mind my having written so badly, I shall write better another time. I venture to enclose myself in Aunty's friendship.

Yours truly obliged,

JENNY LIND.

Oh! how beautifully written!

The applause of the last phrase refers to the signature, a facsimile of which is here given, that we may all enter into her burst of enthusiasm over it. The tone of the letter is delicious,—simple, gay, and tender. They must have been bright days out of which such words came; and it must be confessed, we fear, that some of the brightness was probably left behind her, on the day when she returned to her own mother's house on the 1st of July. The nature of the return, to begin with, was not likely to be very auspicious; and, then, there was the partial loss of her merry companions. However, there is a letter from her mother to Mr. Lind, written on the 2nd of August, 1836, which tells of Jenny's intense happiness: "You may imagine how Jenny enjoys herself among the hay-stacks every day. Do you know, the child enjoys the pleasure of country-life with all the lively brightness of innocence." "And she has with her, to share her enjoyment, Mina, of whom she is so fond." "It is a treat to listen to their charming little duets together, which, no doubt, one day will enchant papa, too." At the close of the letter comes a postscript: "Welcome home, sweet papa, and do take care of your health; this is the wish of your faithful daughter, Jenny." This is all happy, enough: and there must have been many times like this, in which all went smoothly, and the relations of the household were free and affectionate.

And, in the mean time, too, success is coming, and continually growing, to enliven, and enhearten the days. Whatever the struggle, and trouble, that her life brought in it, certainly of one grief, which is apt to darken the days of young artists, she was absolutely free. She was never troubled by a lack of recognition. From her earliest childhood, her gifts were felt to be surpassing; and this feeling never flagged. From the beginning of her dramatic career to its close, it is one unbroken triumph; and she had this

singular good fortune of finding her way to the exercise of
her gifts, before a sympathetic public, as soon as she had
them to exercise. We shall see, in the next chapter, the
way in which this happened, and the direction which her
success took. We shall see that this risk on her behalf,
which the Theatre Royal ran, and to which we have ventured
to give cordial praise, was one which justified itself, by
practical results, almost as soon as it had been run. The
theatre had hardly sown before it found itself reaping. The
child, whom Count Puke thought more of an age for a
Crèche than a Royal Theatre, was already, before she
was in her teens, bringing grist to the Royal mill.

CHAPTER IV.

CAREER.

WE have seen that it was the child's *musical* talent that,
first, evoked the wonder of her neighbours. The stupor of
the grandmother at the baby's fanfare on the piano; the
amazement of the passers-by at the song which was being
confided to the ears of the patient and appreciative cat;
the tears that started to the eyes of Croelius—these are the
earliest signals of her marvellous gifts. But we, now, have to
recognise a new characteristic, which was almost more phenomenal than her singing. Indeed, it may well be doubted
whether, during her first ten years at the Royal Theatre,
it did not surpass her voice in witnessing to the presence in
her of a unique genius. This was her *dramatic* power. It
was through the marvellous acting which she combined with
her singing, that, as a tiny child, she won her first triumph,
and fascinated the spectators: and, as we shall learn from
the deeply interesting account of the development of her
voice given to this volume by a contemporary critic,* it
was not her vocal power alone which, at her earliest operatic
period, would account for her overwhelming attractiveness.
Precocious and extraordinary as her child-voice had been,
both in versatility and in tenderness, yet her early woman's
voice did not exhibit or develop its after-gifts of high sonority
until after her return from the Paris training. It was still
thin, and veiled. Rather, at that time, the secret of her

* See page 156.

success lay in that intense and irresistible identification of herself, voice and all with her part, which is the highest proof of dramatic genius.

In later years, those, who heard her sing in Opera, would often say, that if she had not been the greatest singer in the world, she would have been the greatest actress. And we shall see the evidence for the truth of this anticipation, if we glance over the early records of her performance at the theatre; and we shall, also, understand through what years of actual experience it was that she had obtained that thorough mastery over all the detail and method of the stage, which made her acting so consummate.

The long list of her performances, kept in the records of the Royal Theatre, reveal to us that already, in the very first year of her admittance to the school, as a little creature of ten years old, she made her appearance on the boards, on November 29th, 1830, in a play called *The Polish Mine*, described as a "Drama, with Dance"; and in which she played the part of "Angela." "Angela" is a little girl of seven, who has been carried off to a wild castle in the hills by a tyrant lord, to amuse and cheer her mother, whom he has seized and shut up as his prisoner. The child is to amuse the company at a grand fête in the castle, and contrives, in an improvised dance, to convey to her mother comfort and affection. But, on recognising her father disguised among the guests, in pursuit of his wife, a cry of surprise escapes her; the father is detected, and all three, father, mother, and child, are thrown into prison in the Mine. There little Angela succeeds in getting hold of the warder's key while he is speaking with her mother, and in opening the barrier without being discovered. The father and mother are thus enabled to meet, and to fly, with their child, from the Polish Mine; after a series of exciting adventures, they make good their escape; all is made right. It is a part full of occasions

for the brilliant little dancer, whose ingenuity and skill are
the key to the plot. The play was repeated five times in the
December, and twice more in the January, following. On
March 18th, 1831, she made her first appearance in the play
that is noticed in the newspaper quoted below; it was called
'*Testamentet*, a Drama,' in which her part was that of
"Johanna." She appeared, in this character, for the third
time on April 14th, 1832, and on the 24th April, 1832, we
have the following notice of her appearance in a periodical
for literature and art, called *Heimdall*, which signalises the
extraordinary significance of her child-efforts. The paper
begins by an apology for not having, long ago, put on record
the wonder that had already for some time been aroused.
"We take this opportunity," it writes, " of performing a
long-neglected duty—that of calling attention to a young
pupil of the theatre, Jenny Lind, only ten or eleven years of
age, who has, several times appeared in the play *Testamentet*
which preceded *Fidelio*. She shows, in her acting, a quick
perception, a fire and feeling, far beyond her years, which
seem to denote an uncommon disposition for the theatre."

This play *The Will* is a charming piece by Kotzebue;
and the part taken by Jenny is one which would give
delicious opportunities to her arch and winning grace. It
is impossible, as one reads the part, not to picture her every
look and gesture, so admirably is it suited to qualities in
her which were vividly present to the very last. We
venture to extract a scene from it. The plot turns on an
old Colonel wounded in the wars, who has been carried,
unknown to himself, to the house of a daughter whom he
had utterly cast off for a marriage of which he disapproved.
He is full of gratitude for the care with which he has been
nursed. His heart is stirred with a longing for home : he is
longing to leave his fortune to his kind nurses ; but the
daughter, who has recognised him, keeps ever out of sight ;

and he only sees her two children, Henriette and Johanna.
Henriette, the eldest, having been told by her mother who
this old man is, has been singing him a song which he had
loved in long-past days, "O sweet, and holy Nature!" He
has broken down under the strain of bitter memories: and
he has to beg her to cease singing, and to send him her little
sister, for "the gracious child knows so well how to charm
away all bitterness." After a sad monologue, bewailing the
loneliness in which he is drawing near to that last hour,
when there will be no one ever to say over him, "Here lies
a brave man in peace!" Johanna (Jenny) comes springing
into the room, saying:—

"Good morning, dear old Colonel!—'Mister Colonel,' I
ought to have said! My mother scolds me, if I don't!"

"Col. Good morning, little Jacky! Come, and be merry
with me! Do some of those funny tricks, that you are so
fond of! And call me 'Colonel,' plain and simple, please!—
Or, what do you think of calling me 'Papa'?

"Joh. Papa? Oh! that I could never do! My papa is
in the picture upstairs, and he is so beautiful, and young,
and kindly——

"Col. Well, I own I am not young and beautiful: but
kindly!—*that* I am, indeed! Don't you believe it?

"Joh. Oh yes! very often you are!

"Col. You must remember how ill I was: sick people
cannot be very kind to others: but now, you shall always
find me bright and good, right until I go away.

"Joh. What? Must you go away from us?

"Col. Certainly: in a few days.

"Joh. Are you in earnest?

"Col. I am, indeed.

"Joh. Oh! don't go away from us! We all love you so
dearly!

"Col. Do you love me?

"Joh. Oh! yes! At first, you know, I was very frightened
of you; but now—not a bit!

"Col. And how did you get over your fright?

"Joh. Why, because when you are as kind as you were,
no one could help being fond of you. And when you are
dull, and cross, then I just take myself off.

"COL. Ah! then, to-day, my Jacky will not take herself off, will she?

"JOH. Yes, I will, if you ever again call me 'Jacky'! that is a *dreadful* name!

"COL. Why dreadful?

"JOH. I don't know. But there are such *lovely* names in the books which my sister reads; and specially nice English names, like Liddy, and Betty, and Arabella! Oh! if only they had asked *me* before I was baptized, I would have chosen the very loveliest of them all!

"COL. It was, really, a great shame that they did not ask you.

"JOH. My mother says, that she only had two names to give to her daughters, because my grandfather had but two names, John, and Henry!

"COL. John Henry! Why, those are *my* names, too!

"JOH. Once I cried over the stupid name, Jacky. But, then, my mother began to cry, too, and she said: 'Dearest child, you bear a name which reminds me of a noble man!' Now, I don't know at all why I should remind her of him. But then mother began to cry; so, you see, since then, I don't take any notice of it!

"COL. Well, let me try and teach you why you have the name. I am too old, you say, to be your father, so will you try to think that I am your dear old grandfather, John Henry?

"JOH. Yes! All right! But then, you know, you must never go away!

"COL. Or will you come with me, when I go?

"JOH. Away from mother? Oh! what a horrid thing to do!

"COL. Well, but, some day, you will have to leave her, when you go to be married.

"JOH. Ah! yes! when I am married! I say! have you got a son?

"COL. Why?

"JOH. Why, because, if he is nice, I would marry him and, then, we might all stop together.

"COL. No, Jacky! I have no son—no child at all!

"JOH. Poor old man!

"COL. (*sighing*). Yes, indeed!

"JOH. It's a shame! A horrible shame! I should have been so glad to have married your son!

"Col. Why so glad?

"Joh. Why, because you are rich; and, then, I should be rich; and I could help my sister!

"Col. What is there that she needs?

"Joh. I'll tell you.   Only, you must promise never to betray me!

"Col. I promise faithfully.

"Joh. Well, you know, she loves the head-ranger, and the head-ranger loves her; and my mother says that it is all right: she often says, 'It would be the joy of my old age!' But he has nothing, and we have nothing: so nothing can be done.

"Col. Dear me!   Is that how it stands?

"Joh. Ah! if only I could manage that mother should be able to say to me 'You are the joy of my old age!'   That would be lovely!   I declare that if only I could do that, I would not mind calling all my own children, 'Jacky!'

.   .   .   .   .   .

.   .   .   .   .   .

"Col. Listen to me, dear child!   I have an idea.   If it was in your power to make your sister rich enough to marry the head-ranger, would you not do it?

"Joh. Of course I should!

"Col. Well, then, you *can* do it.

"Joh. You are only laughing at me?

"Col. No!   I promise you!   Come away with me; be my little daughter; and I will give your mother enough money to buy this joy for her old age!

"Joh. Oh! that's very hard!   Where shall we have to go?

"Col. Far, far away from here.

"Joh. Oh dear! and shall I never see my mother again?

"Col. Oh yes!   I shall let you have a beautiful carriage with four beautiful horses, and you will jump into it, and cry 'Coachman, drive me quick to mamma!'

"Joh. Will you really give me that?

"Col. I promise it.

"Joh. And I shall, then, bring joy to my mother's old age!

"Col. Yes, you alone! of your own self!

"Joh. Come along, you dear old Colonel; I will be your daughter.

"Col. Away we'll go, my Jacky!   Only wait a minute! I must go and arrange things.   (*Goes out*).

"Joh. (*alone*). Oh! How happy mother will be! and my
dear sister! and the head-ranger! And it shall be a splendid
wedding! and we will have the musicians to play! Oh yes!
we must have musicians! My old man must not refuse me
that, or else I won't go with him! Oh dear! I wish I was
not going! I shall cry so; and the others will cry too; for
they all love me!—Ah! but then just think what it will
be when I come back in the beautiful carriage with four
horses; and say 'Coachman, drive me home!' and away
we go, over stock and stone, until we draw up here at
our own house, prr! prr; and mother will put out her
head at the window; and cry 'Jacky is come! Jacky is
come!'"

Such was the delightful part played by the tiny little girl
of ten years old. Every word in it would suit her—the
merry quickness of the child, the sudden turns from gaiety
to tears, and back again to gaiety, the mysterious con-
fidences, the prattling innocence, the brimming affection.
In all this she would instinctively revel. It will be seen
that the part gave great scope for versatile acting; and no
wonder that the *Heimdall* was fascinated.

In the year preceding this notice, 1831, she had played, for
three nights, in what is called by the serious name of "an
historic drama"—*Johanna de Montfaucon*, in which she took
the part of "Otto"; and, besides this, had appeared five
times as "Jeannette," in a "Comedy, with Dance," called
the *Pasha of Suresne*. During the following year, 1833, she
appeared in twenty-two performances—her new characters
being "Louise" in a bagatelle in one act, called *The Students
of Småland*, and "Georgette," in a drama of five acts, called
Thirty Years of a Gambler's Life, which ran for ten nights
during November and December; and was constantly repeated
in 1834. This early brilliancy was apparently at its very
height in 1834—when, on June 24th of that year, a paper,
The Daily Allehanda seems quite bewildered by the child's
extraordinary power. "In the play known in its French

form as *La fausse Agnès*" (so it writes) "there is a child's part which is rendered with an almost incomprehensible, a really unnatural cleverness, by Jenny Lind." This cleverness must indeed have been almost incomprehensible : for it leads the critic to indulge in an anxious complaint that the little girl's "temperament seems readily to lean to everything that is not of a serious character." So absolutely had she disguised herself by the freedom with which she had thrown herself into her part! All that deep impressive seriousness, which was the innermost note of her being, had absolutely vanished out of sight; and the paper feared for her lightheaded frivolity! Yet, in calling, as it does, upon Jenny's instructors and guardians to see to it that the danger be averted, and that "her happy natural gifts, high-spirited as they are, should be carefully and judiciously dealt with," the *Daily Allehanda* was giving proof of a tender and noble solicitude for the good guidance of the child. And it does more. For it goes on to complain of the immoral character of this play, in which she was allowed to appear; it speaks strongly of the deep ethical corruption of the society which it portrayed, and of the responsibility incurred by those who permitted a child to put out her powers in a part so full of "coquetry, boldness, and heartlessness." It does honour to the press of Stockholm that it should have made this protest. As we read it, we shudder at the terrible perils which were swarming round the child. Here was a case in which her very innocence of evil, at that tender age, allowed her to revel in the fun and the audacity of such a character, without any of the checks which a knowledge of the villainy in it would have suggested to a pure mind. Her very innocence is used to encourage her to abandon herself to the fling and swing of the scandalous play. So perilous was her path! Yet along it she moves, untainted and unhurt, in the security of the pure in heart, with such sure feet as those with which, on Raphael's canvas, St. Margaret passes, without an effort, or a fear, in maiden gentleness, over the writhing Dragon and through the gate of Hell.

It is not to the credit of the Directors, that they let her appear in two more performances of this abominable play, in the year after the protest had been made. The play, itself, was a sign of the French influence, which began to make itself felt in Sweden during the reign of Adolf Fredrik (1751–1771), mainly owing to the sway exercised by the France of the Grand Monarque over civilised Europe; and which culminated, under Court pressure, during the reign of his son, Gustaf III., who was, for political reasons, murdered at a Fancy Ball in 1792. Since then, the national literature has gradually thrown off this malign shadow; and has recovered its own native inspiration. But, in 1830, the older atmosphere, with its corruption, still widely pervaded the Swedish theatre.

She appeared, altogether, twenty-two times in 1834, and twenty-six times in 1835—the principal new character being " Pierrette," in a drama from the French in three acts, called *The Foster-Son*, which ran for thirteen nights in the course of the year; and "Leonora" in a vaudeville, with music by Berwald, called *The New Garrison.*

In several of these plays, there seems to have been music and dancing; possibly, too, some singing from Jenny. At any rate, she sang publicly at some concerts in the theatre, during these years; taking part in a duet from *La Straniera*, with her master Herr Berg, on November 24th, 1832; and in a trio, on November 28th, 1835. And long before this there appear to have been performances given, in private rooms, by Herr Berg, in which to exhibit her phenomenal talent, the news of which spread abroad: for, in the *Heimdall*, the periodical from which we have already quoted a description of her acting, there is the following record given, in its number for April 24th, 1832 :—

"Her (*i.e.* Jenny's) remarkable musical gift, and its precocious development, have made quite a sensation in the circle in which she has appeared, guided by her master, Herr Berg. Her memory is as perfect as it is sure; her receptive powers as quick as they are profound. Every one is, thus, both astonished, and moved, by her singing. She can stand a trial, in the most difficult *solfeggi*, and the most intricate phrases, without being bewildered; and whatever turn the 'improvisation' of her master may take, she follows his indications with the liveliest attention, as if they were her own. Nothing can be more interesting than to listen to Herr Berg with this little pupil by his side; and one is tempted to believe in a magnetic 'rapport' between them, so entirely do both seem to be one soul and one heart.

"If this young genius does not ripen too prematurely, there is every reason for expecting to find in her—although alas! not until the distant future—an operatic artist of high rank."

This is a fascinating little glimpse of the child of twelve, absorbed in her teacher, miraculously interpreting and reproducing his mind. It is an omen of the receptive speed, with which she, afterwards, absorbed, in a short ten months, everything which Garcia had to teach her. Her innate originality of character did not at all stand in the way of her rapid assimilation as a pupil. Her musical genius carried her into the very heart of what was set before it, with extraordinary rapidity of insight. We shall find many instances of this. And, here, it leads us to dwell, for a few moments, on the name of this, her early master.

Berg had succeeded Croelius, as Head of the School of Singing, within a year, or so, after her entry at the theatre. Already, in April, '32, he had made the child entirely his own, in the manner described in the periodical. Croelius had the merit of first believing in her; but it is Berg, who is to be credited with her entire training for the Swedish stage. It was out of delicacy for Berg, that good old Croelius forebore from pressing his claims upon her grateful remembrance, in the beautiful letter to her which was given at the close of Chapter II. He, evidently, took the most intense and devoted interest in her from the very first; and she became the intimate friend of his home. He was a clever and cultivated musician, confident, sanguine, and eager; well considered in Stockholm society. How far he succeeded, and how far he failed, in developing her full powers of song, we shall be better able to judge when we have seen her pass from out of his hands into those of the great Parisian master, whose help she afterwards sought. At least, we can say this—that Berg, to his infinite credit, never appears to have shown himself wounded at the prompt reversal of method, which took place as soon as she had passed under the new training. He neither seems to have been irritated at her resolution to seek further instruction elsewhere; nor do we hear of his being slow to recognise the immense improvement which was the result. He remains always her devoted admirer; and she is ever drawn towards him by strong affection. Their relations keep warm and intimate to the very end. It is he who, by her desire, accompanies her long afterwards to England, in 1848. It is his deep personal influence on which the King of Sweden relied, when he sent him to Lübeck, in 1849, to try to persuade her, if possible, to sing yet again in opera, at Stockholm. Her own feelings towards her first teacher cannot be better expressed than in the words which she wrote at that time to her guardian, Judge Munthe, in November, 1849.* "Herr Berg arrived so unexpectedly! I was delighted to see him! Oh! God! those memories

---

* This letter, together with all the others addressed to Judge Munthe which are made use of in this book, have been kindly supplied by Judge Carl Munthe, his son.

of childhood! At this unexpected meeting with him, remembrances of all kinds from my early years arose in my soul! We all, indeed, have our shortcomings, that is certain—therefore, let us cover them over! Herr Berg is one of my nearest friends; and gratitude is a feeling that I love, and desire to cultivate. . . . And old friend Berg is interwoven with the history of my whole life."

Such, then, was her master; alert, talkative, confident, with a quick-eyed face, not unlike Schubert in type; too pressing, perhaps, in his zeal for his pupil, to estimate the overstrain on her powers—an overstrain, forced on, no doubt, by theatrical necessities behind him, but constantly noticed and feared by the Press of the day.

In 1836, there is no record of Jenny Lind appearing at any concert; but her dramatic engagements continue, and some of them, with music, and singing. And, especially is to be noted her first attempt in an Opera, during the month of February, when she played "Georgette," for four nights, in a "grand opera," by Lindblad, called *Frondörerne.* Long afterwards, in 1860, he sent her the piano-score of this, his only Opera, then newly published, and wrote on the fly-leaf, "not even *your* singing could save it!" But, on its revival in the same year, it met with warm appreciation, and Geijer refers to it in glowing terms.*

Apart from this, the year was not specially signalised; she made rather fewer appearances, only eighteen during the year, her new parts being "Emilie" in a comedy with song from the German called *The New Blue-Beard*—and "Carolina," in a big drama in five acts, of Kotzebue's—called *The Un-known Son.* She sang again in the popular vaudeville, *The New Garrison,* which had for its second title *Seven Girls in Uniform;* and just at the close of December, she took the part of a girl in Sacchini's opera *Œdipus in Athens*—the

* Collected Works, vol. viii., Ed. 1873-75.

masterpiece of that composer, which retained its popularity
at the Paris Academy right down even to 1844. It depends
for its effect mainly on its use of the chorus. It was given
only once, in this December at Stockholm, perhaps for some
special occasion.

The 1st of January, 1837, marks a new departure. According to the contract of 1833, with the mother, the Directors
were to decide at what date Jenny Lind should be given a
fixed salary, as actress at the Royal Theatre. Hitherto the
money paid her by the Directors, has been simply an
arrangement for her keep; she has performed, on their
behalf, under this arrangement one hundred and eleven
times, besides her appearances at concerts. It is now considered time to give her a fixed and salaried position, after
which she is still bound, by the original contract, to be in
the service of the Directors for ten years, if they require it
of her. Her salary is fixed at 700 R. D. Banco; about £60 a
year.* And, certainly, she was to do a lot of work, in the
course of the year, in discharge of her obligations under the
bond. She appeared ninety-two times on the boards; in
twelve new characters. Four of the pieces were produced for
the first time in Stockholm. The parts varied greatly in
character: "Betty," in a drama, with music, chorus and
dancing, called *Jenny Mortimer;* "Zoe," in a comedy of
that name, by Scribe; and "Marie," in another of his
comedies called *Adèle de Sénanges;* "Justine," in a verse-
comedy of five acts, from the French, called *The Jealous Wife;*
"Lovisa," in a burlesque comedy, with song, by Nicolo
Isouard, called *The Ludicrous Encounter;* "Rosa," in a two-
act comedy by the Princess Amelia of Saxony, called *The
Bride of the Capital;* "Erik," a boy's part in a drama, with

---

* In estimating these figures concerning her fixed salary, it must be
remembered that there was, besides, "Play-money," *i.e.* a bonus given
on each appearance.

music and dancing, called *The Fisherman;* " Laura," in *The Sentinel*, a comic Opera by Rifaut; " Fanny," in *Marie de Sivry*, a drama in three acts. Here was a great deal of bright and light business; and besides this, there was work of a more serious kind: " Emma," in a three-act tragedy in verse, by Delavigne, called *The Sons of King Edward;* " Clara," in *The Bride of the Tomb*, an historical drama in five acts, which ran for eight nights on end; " Dafne," in Victor Hugo's *Angelo Malipieri;* and " Fräulein Neubrunn," in *The Death of Wallenstein*. Two performances were given of Mozart's *Zauberflöte*, in which she sang as " Second Genius."

Evidently, she had a wide range of characters; and she must have accumulated a mass of dramatic experience. It will be noticed that this is all in her sixteenth and seventeenth years; and this disposes of a familiar rumour that, at that period, her voice entirely failed, and that she had to lie by. There was no positive pause in her work. The year 1836 was, no doubt, one in which she did least; but, then, it was the very year in which she first used her voice in a grand opera. The year 1837 was, as we see, a time of growing, and incessant work, and is the first year of her *official* engagement. The rumour arose from her own pronounced opinion that it is a time at which a girl's voice absolutely requires rest; to which opinion she had been brought by her bitter experience of the damage done to her own vocal organs by the absence of this needful relaxation. Her voice was terribly tried by the exertions of that particular time, which made demands upon it just when it was not in a fit condition to respond. It was no peculiarity of her own voice which was in question; it was the normal conditions under which all voices develop into their final state. She ought to have had the repose for quiet and orderly growth, which all need, and which she was not allowed.

Before 1837 quite closed, a noticeable event took place,

full of prophetic meaning, to our heroine. A new name is becoming important in the operatic world,—the name of Meyerbeer; his fame stands high in Berlin and Paris; and the Royal Theatre is anxious to test the prospects of his popularity in Stockholm. So a concert is arranged, in which a part of the fourth act of *Robert de Normandie* should be tentatively given. Oddly enough the part of the Opera selected for the experiment was one that is not generally given when the work is performed as a whole. It is the scene in which, after a chorus of women, the Princess Isabella recognises the face of the girl, Alice, as she enters; and learns from her what she bears to Roberto from his mother. Four performances of this excerpt were given in the course of that December; and Jenny Lind was chosen to sing the short passage in which " Alice " appears. There is a melodious phrase, twice repeated, in the recitative, and a pathetic cadence at its close. The tradition still lives of the instantaneous effect produced by her on those who heard it. It was a short flight; she just felt her wings; she was to hear much more of Meyerbeer, and of " Alice." For the moment all is still again. It is but a passing trial. We must wait a little longer.

CHAPTER V.

YET it is to be but a very little longer; for we now come to the year which was, to her, the epoch, the turning-point of her career. It had opened with an immense run, for twenty-two nights, all through January and February, of a French melodrama in two acts, *The American Monkey*, in which she played "Hyacinthe." Then followed three performances of the serious tragedy, in verse, *The Sons of King Edward*. And, then, on the night of March 7th, came the moment of moments. "I got up, that morning, one creature:" she herself often said; "I went to bed another creature. I had found my power!" And, all through her life, she kept the 7th of March, with a religious solemnity; she would ask to have herself remembered on it with prayers; she treated it as a second birth-day. And rightly; for, on that day, she woke to herself; she became artistically alive; she felt the inspiration, and won the sway, which she now knew it was given her, to have and to hold.

She achieved this in the character of "Agatha" in Weber's *Freischütz*.

She used often to tell how, in studying this part in preparation for her *début*, with Madame Erikson, one of the chief leaders and teachers in the school, of whom she was very fond, and who did much for her, she, one day when they two were alone, was seized with a desire to satisfy her teacher, and put her whole soul and power into her

portrayal of the character—only to be met with dead silence.
"Am I, then, so incapable and so stupid?" she thought, till
she saw the tears trickling down her teacher's face; and all
Madame Erikson could say was, "My child, I have nothing
to teach you; do as nature tells you!"

The day of her *début* was an agony; but, with her first
note, she felt all fear and nervousness disappear. She had
discovered herself; and, certainly, the discovery was absolute.
The experience of that night was final. "She had found her
power." That is her own record of what happened on that
evening. We know not all the details; but, evidently, the
expression signifies, not merely that she had the witness in
herself to her own capacity, but that she received proof, from
without, of the mastery she could exercise over others. She
who was perfectly accustomed to a public audience, and to
the applause of a public audience; she who had, already, for
years, won her steady successes; she, who had already charmed,
and astonished, and excited; still, felt that all this success
had never shown her the real potency which it was in her to
wield. Still, for her, that 7th of March, was a disclosure, a
revelation, a new thing. It was not so much a better edition
of that which had preceded it. It was a step out into a new
world of dominion. Something happened that night which
had never happened before. She knew, at last, where it
was that she stood; and what she was to do on the earth.
She caught sight of the goal. She learned something of her
mission. For, to her religious mind, the discovery of a gift
was the discovery of a mission. She saw the responsibility
with which she was charged, through the mere possession of
such a power over men. The singer, with the gift from God
—that is what she became on that night. "She went to bed
a new creature."

The memory of that eventful moment remained perma-
nently recorded in the shape of two silver candlesticks,

presented to her by the Directors of the Royal Theatre, "in remembrance of March the 7th," so the inscription ran. It was the first of the many tributes that were made her in her life; and it had, as such, a peculiar value which no after-gift could exceed. We can fancy the joy of such a tribute, paid by the spontaneous admiration of those who could best appreciate her task, to the young girl of seventeen. She held those silver candlesticks, in special affection; and left them, at her death, to her daughter.

The *Freischütz* was given nine times in the course of 1838; but, for most of the year, she returned to her old parts which she had already played, appearing in melodrama, comedy, and burlesque. Her most popular character seems to have been "Lovisa," in *The Ludicrous Encounter*, which she played as late as February 1st, 1839. She undertook one new dramatic character, "Marie," in a drama of that name by Herold, with music and dance. This was the last play that she appeared in before she passed over to opera, playing it for three nights in April, 1839. After that, the opera possessed her wholly. And this was heralded, before the year 1838 was out, by three signal operatic appearances: *i.e.*, "Emmelina," in Weigl's *The Swiss Family*; "Euryanthe," in Weber's opera, which ran for four nights in the first half of December; and "Pamina," in the *Zauberflöte*, for four more nights, before the year was over. In all, she had made, for her salary of £60, seventy-three appearances.

In 1839, her success bore its fruit in a rise of the salary to 900 R. D. Banco. She appeared, in the course of the year, only fifty-three times; but, perhaps, this is to be explained, by the growing importance of her operatic parts, and the gradual dropping of the light comedy characters in which she had figured hitherto. She sang the part of "Laura" in an opera called *Le Château de Monténéro*, by Dalayrac—a famous composer of the French school, whom not even the Reign of Terror

could deter from producing new operas. She repeated
" Agatha" four times. She appeared in a character which
she greatly enjoyed, and in after years frequently repeated
—that of " Julia" in Spontini's *Vestale*. In spite of her
enthusiasm for Weber, she was very fond of this work of
Weber's historic opponent. It was one of her famous *rôles*,
in the great days at Berlin, and on the Rhine.

But the event of the year was her appearance in her
traditional part of "Alice" in *Roberto*, by which she was
destined to win her most memorable triumphs. It was a
character in which her splendid dramatic power fused itself
with her gifts of voice, so as to leave an indelible impression
of force and of beauty on the imagination of those who saw
and heard. It was a part which drew on her own vivid personality, with its intensity of faith, with its horror of sin,
with its passionate and chivalrous purity. Voice, action,
gesture, and living character were all combined into a single
jet of dramatic individuality.

She opened, in this part, on May 10th and, evidently, with
overwhelming effect; for she has to play it for twenty-three
times before the year is out, and to repeat it for twenty-three
more, in the following year. It is on "Alice," that the interest
is concentrated, in Stockholm drawing-rooms, when Jenny
Lind's name is announced as a guest. She will have to sing
the part 60 times, on those same boards before she has
done, between the 10th of May on which she first sang it,
and the 30th of December, 1843, when she will give her last
performance of it in the Royal Theatre.

Bournonville, a distinguished composer of operatic ballets,
in Copenhagen, of whom we shall hear more later on, writes
in his 'Theatrical Life' of this performance:

" She was only eighteen when I first heard her, but had
already so eminent a talent, that her performance of 'Alice'
could be compared to the best I had seen and heard in Paris.

Although her voice had not yet reached the high development it afterwards attained, it already possessed, even then, the same sympathy, the same electric power, which now makes it so irresistible. She was worshipped."

The year 1839 was marked by several appearances at concerts in the Royal Theatre: on February 11th, and February 14th, she sang some verses of Berwald's, the Royal Capellmeister, in connection with the tableau vivant of Saint Cecilia; on March 10th, when she sang an aria from *Oberon*, as well as in a quartette; on April 13th, when she sang a recitative and aria from *Fidelio*, and on April 20th, a recitative and aria from *Tancred*. On November 5th, it is noticeable that she sang in a duet from *Norma*, the first signal of her interest in that drama: and on November 16th, she sang, for Kellerman's benefit, a romance of his, accompanied by a violoncello solo. But, above all, on May 12th, she gave her first great concert on her own behalf. At this, she sang a recitative with aria, from *Anna Bolena*, and in a duet by Mercadante: besides giving a scena from the second act of the *Freischütz*.

Not only at Stockholm did she sing. We find her at Upsala on the 19th June, giving a concert in her own name, in connection with the great Whitsuntide festivities, of which that university town is, annually, the scene. Here, for the first time, she had the fascinating triumph of an escort home, accompanied by the Students' Song. And here, too, is the first note of danger given, as to the strain that is being put on her voice. Evidently, her inner genius is already beating against the bars of her technical skill. In her "strivings after perfection" she is attempting more than her present knowledge and training enable her to express. She "surpasses the limits" which, according to the paper, "Nature has set"; though, indeed, it was not "Nature," but the lack of knowledge, which had set the limits. "Nature" was yet

imprisoned, waiting for the sure insight of the Parisian
master to set it free to overleap the limits against which it
was now, ineffectually, struggling. It is just about this time,
in May, 1840, that the famous Swedish historian Geijer, who
was a most sympathetic admirer, notices " a certain inequality
in her acting" in the part of "Lucia." Something there was,
which was, as yet, missing to her full development. Here is
the interesting extract from the *Correspondenten*, a journal of
politics and literature, in which the tone of warning or alarm
is so gracefully struck.

"We could hardly name any musical treat, given in Upsala,
which has met with a more general appreciation than Fröken
Jenny Lind's concert, last Sunday. The spacious hall was
required in order to prevent a crush amongst the public,
which in number, no doubt, was nearer two thousand than
one thousand persons. The well-merited applause, which
the charming singer earned, burst forth in the most spontaneous manner, in repeated plaudits and cries of ' Bravo,'
during the concert, whence she was escorted home with the
Students' Song, which was offered again, later in the evening
before her lodgings. The modest bearing which is so noticeable in this gifted singer contributes, in no mean measure, to
enhance the enthusiastic reception, with which she will
always be greeted by an impartial public. But she herself,
and those who, in one way or another, are disposing of her
talents, ought to bear in mind that an artist's strivings after
perfection can, in the case of a delicate physique, easily
become a devouring fire. May we err in our conjecture, but
there seems to be some foundation for the fear that this
enchanting voice not rarely surpasses the limits which Nature
itself has suggested. From here Fröken Lind, according to
report, went to Gothenburg, having, however, promised to
visit us again, later on."

At Gothenburg, Jenny Lind had a most delightful rest for
the summer. She stayed there all July, singing indeed at a
concert now and again, but without any serious work, and
in hearty enjoyment of the delicious open-air country-life
which was so near her heart. Her mother is with her, and

writes to Mr. Lind on July 12th, 1839, a vivid account of
the pleasant days, in which we can feel how the public excitement is working round Jenny, who " receives many visits
every day from all possible artists and amateurs."

" In my last letter I gave you an account of our pleasant
journey, etc. We have now settled down temporarily at the
sweetest little spot, called ' Gubbero,' belonging to the Russian
Consul Lang, whose chief property is separated only by a
garden from our lodgings which consist of three furnished
rooms with ante-room. I think this year we should not
travel any further, for, truly, we could not wish for a better
place to spend the summer than this one. Besides, for grea
part of the day, we have the company of the Consul's charming family. His wife was my school-fellow and there is a
daughter of Jenny's age. All this makes time pass in a most
agreeable way ; and, moreover, we have a great many visits
every day from all possible artists and amateurs. Our Jenny
recruits herself daily, now in the hay-stacks, now on the sea
or in the swing, in perfect tranquillity, while the town people
are said to be longing for her concert and greatly wondering
when it will come off. Once or twice she has been singing
in rather good circles, the divine air of ' Isabelle ' from
Robert le Diable. Nearly everybody was crying—one lady
actually went into hysterics from sheer rapture ; this has got
abroad already. Yes, *mon petit vieux,* she captivates all,
all ! It is a great happiness to be a mother under such
conditions. She sends fondest love to her papa, wishing from
all her heart to meet you in quite good health. About the
20th, Jenny will give her first concert—everyone says she
ought to raise the usual price."

The last touch is as eminently characteristic of Fru Lind,
as it is unlike her daughter. We find the same note again
in an amusing bit of disappointed complaint with which she
closes a most pretty account of a surprise which they had
had, earlier in the year—an account which we insert here,
not only as a graphic story of the way in which Jenny was
responding to the buzz of popular enthusiasm which already
began to besiege her, but, also, as illustrating what Fru

Lind here notices, of Jenny's power to draw tears of joy, by her singing. Ever in her voice rang the sympathetic vibration, at which tears flow. As it had been at her earliest interview with old Croelius at nine years old, so it is now with this old Baron, when she is all but nineteen.

"Do you know," writes the mother from Stockholm, on the evening of Feb. 22, 1839, "the other day we had a curious visit, a certain Baron de G—, an old *gentilhomme*, who had travelled all the way from his country-seat, with the hope of seeing and hearing Jenny in the *Freischütz*, but he was disappointed, through a change of performance, owing to Almlöf's indisposition. Randel* (whose patron this man is) undertook to forward, in the most delicate way, his request to me and to our Jenny, that he might call upon us and be allowed to hear, ever so little, the voice of the adored one, so highly spoken of in his own part of the country. Jenny agreed, and so they came—Randel, Baron de G—, and his son. Little Jenny was liberal, the noble aspect of the old man prepossessed her in his favour, she sang both her grand airs. The old man was delighted, and this was clearly visible, because he could not keep back his tears. Our little home looked particularly neat, and chocolate was served, and they parted with us, quite charmed. But probably, it ends there! For who rewards talent in our country; even when people are ever so rich?" And "what," she asks in this same letter, "has this good, this incomparable Jenny for her increased labour? Not even the advantage of providing for her indispensable wants, without incurring debt! But I say, like you, 'Come day, comes counsel'; we shall see."

These characteristic passages, which we have quoted to illustrate the stir of fame that is moving about the daughter, will well serve to explain a domestic crisis which we are now approaching—a crisis which had, for its issue, an event that told deeply upon Jenny Lind's artistic development. For, indeed, as we read them, we cannot but be conscious that this mother, proud as she is of her wonderful child, and delighting

---

* Randel was, then, 2nd Leader of the R. Orchestra. He became 1st Leader in 1861.

in the glow of her success, yet lets drop expressions which
reveal the gulfs that gape between the two temperaments.
Every one who reads can understand why it was that, in
spite of the pleasant, and affectionate intercourse of these
summer holidays at Gothenburg, there was something which
would make mother and child impossible companions for one
another. This practical and determined mind which was bent
on acquiring the just profits that were due from a public
that talked so enthusiastically about "our incomparable
Jenny"—how it must have offended the primary instincts of
the artist herself? How was it conceivable that she should
tolerate this insistent voice in her ear, suggesting always how
easy it would be to raise the price of the tickets; while she
was, on the other hand, shaping steadily, into clearer vision,
her recognition of her gift as a charge from God, to be used
in His service, for the help of mankind? There might
be much affection, at heart, between the pair, but companionship, there could not be. They had antagonistic consciences :
and neither of them had the temper that easily yields. This
very letter from which we have been quoting contains a most
characteristic instance of the temper of which we are speaking—a temper which was bound to fill a house with the
noise of clash and quarrel, such as would be misery to
one who needed in her home, shelter, softness, refuge, ease,
and peace. Here is the story :—

"I must tell you" (she writes) "that I have just returned
from the theatre with rather a long face, to find that no seat
is accorded to Jenny's mother, although there still were
empty seats, and, besides, the performance had already
begun. M——, with his insinuating smile, asked me to
wait on the chance of there being room after the second piece
had begun. But I answered, as no place is accorded me, I
shall go without altogether,' and so I left. Z—— is always
overbearing and rude. This is the gratitude we get for our
leniency with these people. Jenny, on hearing of this mis-

adventure, went straight up to Z——, and gave him to understand her annoyance at my not having a seat. His answer, that there could not be room for everybody's mother, was just like him; but Jenny's remark on this took him a little down; a messenger was despatched to offer me a seat on the first tier; but, to Jenny's surprise, mother was gone —and best so!"

This episode is amusing enough; and, moreover, no one who knew the daughter can resist the recognition of qualities in her which vividly recall the mother in this most characteristic scene. Certainly they bore likeness to one another. But, then, this would only make matters worse where, as in this case, the mother's sensitive haughtiness had all been brought to the surface by the unfortunate hardships of her life. Her jealous pride in Jenny seems to have rather aggravated than soothed her sense of wrong, her irritability, her suspicion. We cannot be surprised if such an atmosphere became intolerable, and if explosions occurred.

So it was that, towards the end of 1839, Jenny took the decisive step which, finally, separated her from actual home-life. It came about with a certain touch of humour. She had, some time before this, pressed her old friend, Louise Johansson, now engaged in a *Magasin de Modes*, to take a spare room, which was to be let in the Linds' house. This secured her a companionship which she greatly valued, and, through which, things were tolerable. After a year Fru Lind proposed to raise her terms: and, when Mdlle. Louise could not agree to this, she lost her temper, and declared that both Jenny and she were welcome to leave her roof.

This was told to a well-to-do relation, Mdlle. Apollonia Lindskog, known to Jenny as "Tante Lona," living with a sister of Mr. Lind's father, Fru Strömberg, who, having adopted Mr. Lind at his father's death, was known to Jenny as "Grandmother." These two ladies agreed to receive the exiles: but how were they to manage the transfer? In this

R. Theatre.

Bank Palace.

STOCKHOLM.

[To face p. 65.

way. Jenny packed all her clothes into a large wash-basket
on the plea that they were to go to the dressmaker. She,
then, invited her parents to a performance of *Roberto*, in
which she played "Alice:" during which time Louise put
up her things, and sent them off to Mdlle. Lindskog. Next
morning, at breakfast, Louise announced that she wished to
leave her present lodgings. Fru Lind, with much heat,
broke out into her old phrase, and declared that if so, she
might take Jenny with her. Jenny, then, took her at her
word; and left the house, going, first, to Herr Berg, and,
then, joining Louise at Mdlle. Lindskog's. Her parents appeared there, to claim her: but found themselves unable to
force a girl of nineteen from the house of so near a relation.
Yet Jenny, in fear that they might yet succeed, on a Sunday
shortly after, left the house, escorted by her maid, Annette,
and turned her steps toward the Bonde Palace, close to the
theatre, overlooking the Norrström, in which lived the
famous musician, Adolf Fredrik Lindblad, the chief of
Swedish song-writers, her warm admirer, and friend. Into
his family she was received: she found, in Madame Lindblad
a second mother: and from Herr Lindblad himself, and from
the society into which he brought her, she inhaled an influence, which affected her entire development, artistic, intellectual, and moral. Of this, we shall have more to say in
the following chapter. In his house she remained until her
final departure for Paris in July, 1841. Back to rooms in
that house, she came, on her return to Stockholm in 1842.
There was her home. There she could rest at peace. There
she found the sympathy, the understanding, the inspiration,
which her nature ardently needed. Though in some points
endowed with a "Finnish" stubbornness, she was, in others
singularly self-distrustful, uncertain, easily unnerved. She
greatly needed an atmosphere of affection to give her confidence, and security. She was passionately domestic; she

must have the assurance of love about her, to save her from the miseries of suspicion and of distrust, into which her lofty idealism was very apt to lapse, unless buoyed against the shock of rough and hard facts by the encompassing force of sympathetic intimacy. It was not that she did not have affection for her parents: on the contrary, she held them very deep in her heart. But it was impossible for them to enter into her motives and aims: and, moreover, Fru Lind had a certain twist of temper which made actual life with her exceedingly difficult.

So it happened: and Jenny, now, could at last bring together her life into a single whole. Her daily surroundings were no longer in collision with her artistic inspiration. Rather, they aided, fed, succoured it. Her spirit breathed an air that was congenial, and bracing: her heart found warmth, and nourishment in the cherishing kindliness of a family. The year must have been a happy one. It was full of success. It opened with a brilliant continuation of her "Alice," in January, to be repeated in April, and all through November. She sang, again, in her former parts of "Agatha;" "Euryanthe;" "Pamina;" "Julia" (the *Vestale*); and "Marie," in Herold's operatic drama of that name. All is, now, Opera: not a single one of her old comedy parts does she play. Her career in pure acting is alas! over altogether. She adds, to her score, two important characters; "Donna Anna," in *Don Juan*: and "Lucia" in *Lucia di Lammermoor*. This last part, one of her famous rôles, had a furore. She introduced it into Stockholm on May 16th and played it for twenty-eight nights in the year. It was after her thirteenth performance of "Lucia," that, on June 19th, 1840, a number of the actors, together with members of the orchestra, and chorus, gathered before her dressing-room, and serenaded her: and, on her return home, she was presented with a silver tea and coffee service, which was ever highly valued by her, and was left, by specific direction in her will, to her eldest son. The donors appeared in gala costume, among them being his Excellency Count J. G. de la Gardie, Count Carl de Geer, Count Carl Axel Löwenhjelm, Count Gustaf Trolle Bonde, etc., etc. Lindblad's eldest daughter, now Mme. Lotten von Feilitzen, remembers well how Jenny Lind had to go to the window, after receiving the present, to wave her handkerchief to the crowd that had collected below in the street. Altogether, she made sixty-nine appearances. In the half-year that remained, before her departure for Paris, she played forty-nine times more, chiefly in *Lucia* and *Roberto* and the *Freischütz:* her new parts were " Alaida " in Bellini's *Straniera;* and in a selection from Gluck's opera " Armida," for a single performance. She sang in eight concerts at the theatre, in 1840, and in two more in 1841. In two of them she sang a duet from *Jessonda*, with Herr Günther: and in three, she sang a duet from *Norma*, with her playmate at the school, Fru Gelhaar.

Two special events may be, finally, noticed. First, she goes again, at Whitsuntide, to Upsala: and we have a letter of Geijer, written at the time, which speaks of the intense interest of Lindblad in his charge.

" Lindblad, who in the general enchantment is particularly enchanted with Mdlle. Lind, was also here and staying with us. He left this morning, upon which Upsala may be likened to a barrel from which the bottom has been taken out, so that the contents run away."

And our old paper, the *Correspondenten,* has some graceful words which we cannot but insert, for, besides the warm and intelligent enthusiasm of its praise, it uses the symbol of the nightingale which became, afterwards, her familiar patronymic.

" But, in addition to Nature's beautiful singing-birds, there came, flying thither on Whitsun eve a nobler nightin-

gale, the famous Jenny Lind, whose arrival many a one has
heartily looked forward to. For, indeed, she has been the
object of a homage, such as, in its truest form, can be given
only in a city of culture and of youth. True, it is in the
first place, a great, an extraordinary talent one admires in
her; but how infinitely is the value of this artistic power
increased by the unpretending, modest, charming manner,
in which it presents itself to an enraptured listener. With
her all seems Nature, simple and glorious, so as to make
one forget what great influence Art has also exercised on
her development. It is by this harmonious combination
of a noble nature and art, that Fröken Jenny Lind in
every respect stands out as of exceptional and unalloyed
worth."

So goes the judgment of Sweden. It could not be better
expressed. It embodies, exactly, the constant impression,
which, year after year, in far lands abroad, she is to create.
Somehow or other, wherever she is to go, and whatever her
triumphs in Denmark, Germany, England, and America, no
one can succeed in recording his experience without arriving
at this very identical conclusion of the Upsala periodical.
Always he finds himself saying, that "great and extraordinary
as is the talent which one admires in her, how infinitely is
the value of this artistic power increased by the modest
and charming manner in which it offers itself to the enraptured listener!" That is it. That is what everyone feels:
and what everyone tries to say. We shall find that type of
comment quite invariable. It is this especial interest of her
singing to which we propose to devote the following chapter.
Here, we pause, for a moment, in our narrative of her early
dramatic career, and take note of where we stand. We
have followed her from the lowest rung of the ladder,—a
tiny mite in the theatre-school, performing its first miraculous feats—to the high platform on to which she has
passed, in secure possession of unqualified supremacy on
her native stage. Nothing has interrupted, or broken this

sure progress. Nothing has come to traverse, or criticise it.
It has been a steady upward movement towards its final
bewildering triumph. As a child, she had fascinated by her
acting: as a singer, her very first *début* had been to her an
immediate and unmistakable revelation of her supreme
powers. Her nation have greeted her with acclamation.
Their enthusiasm for her voice can only be outdone by their
enthusiasm for herself. So it is, as we look back along the
road she has travelled. Her troubles have all been domestic.
As an artist, her career has been unchecked, and unclouded.
She might well think that she had, at twenty, already touched
the summit. All the world about her was ready to assure
her that it was so. How little she herself thought so, we
shall soon see.

But, before doing so, we are bound to stop, and review the
personal character, which had developed under these conditions. What type of person was the Jenny Lind, of whom
all Sweden was now talking? In answering this general
question, we shall not refuse the help which records and
memorials of her in her later life supply, in emphasising
those distinct and enduring lines, which formed the unchang-
ing ground of her character. And we do this with confidence, because nothing comes out more obviously from the
records of her story, than the absolute and continuous
identity, from end to end, of the main elements of her personality. Always, at all periods of her life, the terms used
to describe her are the same. Always the same person
walks, and speaks, and stands, and sings, whether it be the
simple girl in her sweet modesty, or the grown woman in
full possession of her assured powers. Whatever men tell
us of her, whatever she does, or says, we recognise her at
once. A single phrase, or pose, or gesture is enough. "That
is Jenny Lind," we say; no one can mistake it. Whether it
come early, or whether it come late in the day, it is all of a

piece; it tells the same tale; it leaves the like impression; it belongs to the same picture.

We need not, then, be at all afraid to mingle the evidence yielded by differing years, and varying places: for, indeed, it is only by so doing that we can receive the full impression of this strong and unbroken continuity of type, which was so marked a feature in her character.

CHAPTER VI.

CHARACTER.

THERE are artists, in whom their art is so predominant, that, like a despotism, it concentrates all efforts and capacities upon itself. The man is absorbed within his main interest. Through it alone does he find energetic vent. In it he verifies the attributes of genius : he gives evidence of something in him which is surpassingly excellent : but, outside its ring-fence, in all the other departments of life and character, he shows himself as ordinary, and unremarkable as the rest of us. His artistic genius does not flow over, and animate, his other sensibilities, and gifts : it abides in itself : and seems, even, to drain originality out of all rival channels ; so that we might think the man commonplace, and dull, until we saw him transfigured and illuminated in the exercise of his own peculiar talent. This is a perfectly possible type of genius : and, because it exists, men are loud in asserting the proverbial disappointment often felt at meeting, in society, some one who has been, through his gift, the inspiration of their lives. In the ordinary affairs with which all are concerned, this glorious hero, this poet, this musician, with whose fame the world is ringing, shows no particular power, has no especial facility, may, indeed, prove himself inferior in judgment and in insight, to many a man who prides himself on making no claim to be a genius. More especially, in the field of executive art, involving curious, and special facilities of organization, we may expect to come across such surprises as this.

All the more noticeable then is it, that, in the case of
Jenny Lind, the surprise is all the other way. There is a
universal consent, in all who record her influence, that what
they experienced was the effect of a character whose genius
penetrated every corner of her being, so that her unique gift
of song appeared but as an incidental illustration of the
originality which was everywhere in her. Even those who
felt her singing most profoundly, felt ever as she sang, that
she was more than her singing: while those whose lack of
musical perception made them impervious to her special
talent, experienced as much as any the full fascination of her
personality. This impression of her belongs to her early, as
well as to her after years ; and it cannot be better given than
in an expressive phrase, used long after our present date,
indeed, but which vividly and exactly embodies what was
already so characteristic of her. "After all, I would rather
hear Jenny talk, than sing, wonderful as that is," writes
Mrs. Stanley, the wife of the Bishop of Norwich, to her sister,
Mrs. Augustus Hare, in September 1847, after a rapturous
account of what her singing had been. Surely, a most
striking remark to make: and one which cannot be too
emphatically reiterated, as giving a cue to the indescribable
impression left by this great artist on the memory and the
hearts of those who came nearest to her. "I would
rather hear her talk than sing!" And at the very moment
when the words were written there was another person,
in that palace at Norwich, who gave a cordial adhesion
to this sentiment. There could be no better instance of
Jenny Lind's social impressiveness than her intercourse with
Arthur Penrhyn Stanley, son of the Bishop of Norwich,
afterwards the famous Dean of Westminster. He was a man
of the highest type of culture, of sensitive imagination, of
most delicate intellect—a man, too, who was habitually in
contact with all the finest minds and the richest experiences

of his day—and yet he was absolutely excluded from even
the slightest sympathy with all that made her " the greatest
artist whom Mendelssohn had ever known," for he was
unable to enjoy one note of her music; and still, though her
voice is no more to him than an inexplicable interruption to
their conversation, he was absorbed under the sway of her
personal fascination, and became her life-long and intimate
friend.

And, again, far down her career, the same instinctive
impression greets us, showing how from first to last, this was
her typical character. We quote from notes made by Mr.
Parker Willis, at the time of the American tour, in
November 1850, published in 1856 in a work called ' Famous
Persons and Famous Places.' These notes express, with
wonderful felicity and vividness, the particular point on which
we now are dwelling. For they tell how the author, after
being enthralled by the magic of her singing, obtains the
privilege of intercourse with her; and the effect on him is
just that recorded in Mrs. Stanley's happy phrase. He
cannot resist the impression that she could have written at
least as brilliantly as she sang; and that, somehow, it is only
circumstances that have chained her to what he ventures to
call " her lesser excellence." He feels as if she were a
" Poetess whom song has hindered and misled." He notices,
especially, as the key to her character, her " singularly
prompt and absolute power of concentration." " No matter
what the subject, the ' burning glass' of her mind was
instantly brought to bear upon it," " her occasional anticipa-
tions of the speaker's meaning, though they had a momentary
look of abruptness, were invariably the mile-stones at which
he was bound to attain, ... and the graphic suddenness
with which she would sum up, could receive its impulse from
nothing but genius." And, after much more, he winds up
with this remarkable conclusion :—

" In reading over what I have hastily written, I find it expresses what has grown upon me with seeing, and hearing the great songstress—a conviction that her present wonderful influence is but the forecast and shadow of a different and more inspired exercise of power hereafter. Her magnetism is not all from a voice, and a benevolent heart. The soul while it feels her pass, recognises the step of a spirit of tall stature, complete and unhalting in its proportions. We shall yet be called upon to admire rarer gifts in her than her voice."

It would be hard to give better, or fuller expression than this, to the sense that we desire to convey—the sense, the feeling that Jenny Lind was, not less, but more, than her Art. What men saw, and found in her was, not that a common piece of the stuff of human nature had been caught up, by the artistic inspiration, into some unspeakable heaven, and been transfigured by some sudden and strange glory which carried the human spirit beyond itself. No! rather they felt that here was a character of supreme value, of unique excellence, which had contrived to find its way down into the world's scenery, through the particular channel provided for it by song. Music gave it its chief opportunity for discovering itself to men; but it itself stood above the Art which it used as its finest medium of communication. Hence the intensity of spiritual interest, which greeted her singing. Men seemed to themselves not so much to be listening to a voice, as to be catching sight, through the door which music opened, of a high and pure soul, moving down to them, through the pathway of song, out of some far untainted home of purity and joy. It was this soul which they greeted with such amazement, such warmth; it was its felt presence which made the tears start, always, to their eyes as they listened. It was Jenny Lind herself, who, by means of her wonderful gift, was the revelation to them of the heights which it was still open to men to attain.

And, because this was so, we desire, both in the present chapter, and in chapters to come, to dwell, especially, on the *social* impression produced by her, wherever she went. This book, it is true, is a memoir of Jenny Lind as the artist. But the distinction, which we have attempted to draw between the two types of artists, will make it clear why, in her case, it is impossible to dissociate her artistic success from her effect as a woman, as a personal character, upon the people among whom she came. She was one of those whose art reveals a character behind it, out of which its own excellence is drawn ; and, in estimating that Art, therefore, we inevitably find ourselves drawn into the presence of this inspiring force of character which it disclosed. It would be impossible to represent the effect of Jenny Lind, as an artist, without making it continually clear what it was which Mrs. Stanley meant when she said in 1847, " After all, I would rather hear Jenny talk than sing," or, as she wrote again in the same year : " Her singing is the least part of her charm ; she has the simplicity of genius."

We shall have frequent occasion, as our story proceeds, to call attention to this significant characteristic ; as, for instance, to note that wherever she goes, over the cities of Europe, she is, somehow, always found to be staying in the house of someone who is of special, and even European, reputation. Men of this high stamp seem, always, to foregather with her ; she has the entry ; she finds her home with them. And, again, in her own city of Stockholm, where the circumstances of her life, with which we are familiar, might be expected to stand somewhat in her way, and where there was, necessarily, so much, in her bringing-up, which would make it difficult for her to break down social barriers, nothing is more remarkable than her complete acceptance, before she has passed her girlhood not only into those circles where details of birth and position are supposed to be of vital importance, but what is far more, into those high literary intimacies where nothing but character counts.

Let us give illustrations of this. Here is a most graceful and brilliant picture of a soirée in Stockholm in 1839, which we cannot but give as a whole. It is perfectly trustworthy, being the record of a lady, still living, in whose old home the scene took place. Evidently, as all who read it must feel, the impression of that marked evening stamped itself upon the girl's brain, so that every detail stood out sharp and clear, when, in 1887, nearly fifty years later, she wrote out the sketch for a periodical called the *Dagny*—published by the "Fredrika Bremer Association," the object of which is to further the cause of those women who are anxious to make their own living. The lady, who wrote it, herself 'the daughter of the house' mentioned in the narrative, intended to send it in a letter to Madame Lind-Goldschmidt herself, in order, by reminding her of the evening it records, to interest her in the Fredrika Bremer Association; but, before the letter could be sent, the news of her illness and death reached Stockholm; and it was, then, published in the *Dagny*, as a memorial of her who had gone. Here is the account:—

"It is a cold winter's evening in the year 1839. In the house of 11 Regeringsgatan chandeliers and lustres are gradually being lit. Along the street is stopping a row of closed carriages, which, each in its turn, drive up to the entrance. Footmen in livery open the carriage-doors and smart women, followed by men in uniform, get out cautiously and disappear through the porch of the faintly illuminated passage. A few minutes later the fresh arrivals find themselves in the cloakroom, the wraps are taken off, silk dresses are rustling, shawls are draped, a look in the glass is directed to the fantastic head-dresses, while the men are touching up their plumed cocked hats or straightening their gold-fringed epaulettes—and now they enter the glowing suite of rooms, either in groups or one by one.

"In the first *salon*, where various musical instruments are seen, they are received by the host, Baron L———, an elderly man, with noble features, shaded by silver-grey hair, of dignified deportment, and an air of kindliness and refinement about him generally. Passing through a smaller antechamber, the guests now proceed to the great, half-round *salon*, where the hostess is awaiting them. She is a tiny little lady, about thirty, youthful in her movements, with expressive eyes and a smile of great fun, as well as of courtesy, round her lips. With an unconventional and graceful movement, she gives her hand, introducing the people to one another, showing that she understands the art of forming acquaintances, right and left, by means only of a few words.

"There comes Baron B——, with his wife and daughters, one of whom, later on, married a Minister for Foreign Affairs, whilst the other became the mother of Sweden's greatest poet in our times. In their wake are seen Baron F——, the great Chamberlain to the King Carl Johan, and General C——. There some fashionable young ladies are advancing, surrounded by their court of a few officers and civilians. Behind these are seen the popular violinist in the Court-Chapel, Herr Elvers, a young cellist, Herr F——, etc., etc. And now there appears a striking couple; it is Count and Countess B——, both bearers of great historical names, and she a queen in the realm of beauty. A murmur of homage follows her as she moves on and she is scarcely seated before a crowd of admirers throw a ring round her. However, all of a sudden, the whispering becomes louder, changing tone altogether, while every head is directed towards the ante-chamber.

"On the threshold stands the host and by his side, shaking hands with him, a young girl, with an abundance of curls round the pale cheeks; a gown in simple style softly clings round the maiden figure and there is a dreamy, half absent, and fascinating look in the deep-set eyes.

"The hum is increasing still more when the old nobleman leads the visitor into the midst of his guests; but he has not time to pronounce her name, it is already on everybody's lips, and is now flying round the room with a subdued sound: *Jenny Lind! Jenny Lind!*

"The beauties of the season are forgotten and, what is more, they forget all about themselves; flirtation is suppressed; etiquette is sinned against unpunished; and as soon as the new guest has been cordially welcomed by the hostess, and by her, personally, introduced to the principal ladies, a

crowd of the high assembly gathers round the plain-looking
young girl, thus for once justly conceding the preference of
genius to birth—of beauty of soul to beauty of features.

" A singular liveliness is breathing through the hitherto
rather formal company. The hostess attracts both young and
old to her animated conversation with the honoured guest;
and every one is gratified who catches a word or a look from
this Jenny Lind who, for the last few weeks has, as 'Alice,'
in *Robert le Diable* and ' Agatha ' in the *Freischütz* captivated
and enchanted both themselves and the whole Stockholm
public.

" Somewhat monosyllabic, at the start, amongst all these
strangers, the guest begins, by-and-by, to shake off her
reserve. She smiles an incredulous smile when one of *la
jeunesse dorée* compares her to ' la divine Malibran,' and laughs
openly at some old general's grotesque flattery. To a sentimental inquiry as to what heavenly thoughts had filled her
mind when, the preceding evening, she had, as ' Alice '
embraced the cross, she answered, a little hesitatingly : ' I
believe I was thinking of my old bonnet.' But, wherever
she encounters genuine and deeper understanding in the
compliments uttered, her answers are sympathetic, almost
humble.

" By her side stands the clever pianiste Mina Josephson, a
sister of one as yet unknown to fame—Axel Josephson. A
girl of fourteen, the eldest daughter of the house, timidly
approaches her in order that by her she may be introduced
to Jenny Lind, who bestows upon her a warm pressure of
the hand.

" How the gay party went on, how the musical programme
was opened by the daughter of the house and her teacher,
after which followed one of Beethoven's most beautiful trios;
and how Jenny Lind sang the ' Lieder ' of Geijer and
Lindblad as they never were, nor ever more will be sung—
we must here only glance at. And further how the host and
hostess were obliged to check the too eager wishes of their
friends to hear more and ever more—in order to show that
the object of the invitation had been the personal acquaintance of the charming artist, not only the enjoyment of her
song lovely though it be. That Jenny Lind was satisfied
with her evening, and, in this *milieu,* found several of her
most enthusiastic, and faithful admirers, is quite certain.
And, as she was the first operatic singer received in the best

society of the capital, in which she became a dear and
honoured guest, it has seemed of some interest to preserve a
few details of her appearance in this domain.

"In the memory of the writer of this paper, Jenny Lind
stands out a unique apparition, like no one else, simple,
unpretending, but dignified—penetrated by a sort of sacred
responsibility for her mission—the mission of Art in its
lofty purity—which she felt that God had confided to her."

The last touches of this graphic record will serve to
justify our insistence on this social aspect of Jenny Lind's
life; and to redeem our motives from the suspicion of any
unworthy interest in these formalities of society. For it is
just through this lofty sense of artistic mission that she took
her place amid her fellows. As at Stockholm, so everywhere,
it is this, her spiritual sense of responsibility, which gave her
social distinction, and carried her, in dignified ease, through
these surroundings. It is deeply interesting to notice how it
is exactly this characteristic, here noted by the Swedish
lady as the secret of Jenny Lind's effect upon those about
her, which afterwards won to her the intense devotion of
the Stanleys at Norwich. "Every morning when she got
up, she told me," writes Mrs. Stanley, "she felt that her
voice was a gift from God, and that, perhaps, that very day
might be the last of its use." And Arthur Stanley repeats
this, as if this was what gave her such fascinating interest.
It was this, which secured her that aspect of independence, of
detachment, which is so vital, if an artist is to preserve moral
dignity, in face of a "society" which is too apt to flatter
itself that it is doing a favour to those to whom it kindly
permits an entry, and which is encouraged in this self-
flattery, if the artist is obviously grateful for the attention.
Nobody could see Mademoiselle Lind for two seconds, and
suspect her of any such flattery. She moved about "like an
apparition": like one "with a mission": charged with a
serious responsibility. That is her social character: that is

her note, her charm, as this paper beautifully records: and this made all touch of over-deference to external position absolutely impossible to her. No one could mistake that free independence: that moral "detachment." Indeed, criticism on her social qualities, would turn on the very opposite defect to that at which we have been hinting. It might be said that this spiritual aloofness gave a sense of haughtiness to her manner in public, and with those who were not intimate. There was a "hold-off" look—a drawing away, a critical survey of a new comer, which made many an introduction to her, in after years, a moment of supreme agony to those who had, perhaps, dreamed of that happiness for hours and days before, but who now that it had come, and that she was looking them over with a cold and lofty gaze, could only pray that the earth might yawn, and swallow them up, before things had gone any further. It was a severe ordeal: and, unquestionably, no worldly rank, or position, would have the slightest effect in modifying its severity.

Again, this spiritual attitude of one "charged with a mission," made "Society" most distasteful to her. She never could care, the least, for it as such; she hated its frivolous distractions, its social pettiness, its wearisome routine; it had no attraction for her. She liked "intimates." And "Society," therefore, in admitting her, never felt that it had done her a great kindness, or that she hung on its favours. Rather, it knew that something was there in her, which made all social distinctions become very small matters indeed. For the standards, which her presence forced to the front, were not "social" but moral and spiritual: and it was impossible to have intercourse with her, without becoming conscious of this: and, tried by those standards, it was she who brought the honour, not society which conferred it. "There is no one," writes Mrs. Stanley, in 1847, "who does not feel, that it was an honour for the Bishop, to have given her the protection of this house."

In this temper of moral independence, she passed up, out of the struggles and clouds of her childhood, into the full sunlight of success, with absolute ease, without a shadow of encumbering consciousness, without a breath of worldliness ever crossing her spirit. She retained, without even an effort, all her inherent and native simplicity, her freshness, her undaunted sincerity. Never did she slacken, for a moment, her demand that the worth of men should be estimated, wholly and utterly, according to their moral value Never, for one instant, did the mists of conventionalism dim her vision, or confuse her insight. She had one set of balances; and one only. She never even seems to have been tempted to exchange them. Swept up, in the sudden rush of an overwhelming success, out of obscurity into the company and the friendship of princes and kings, this girl, in her simple-hearted virginity, kept a conscience as true and fine as steel. No illusion bewildered her: no worldly splendour ever succeeded in beguiling her. Failings of another type might be laid to her charge. She could be hasty, and hard, sometimes, in her judgments. She was liable to misunderstand people. She had vehement impulses, and equally vehement reactions, which were apt to gain for her, from those who knew her little, the character of capricious fitfulness. She could magnify slight lapses into great sins. A certain spiritual haughtiness there was in her; a certain suspicion of the motives on which she, by bitter experience, learned that men too often act. All this might be said. But one thing it was for ever impossible, even for an enemy, to imagine: that Jenny Lind ever condescended to lower the steady standards by which she tested all human worth, high or low, rich or poor. Thus it was that she secured, as we shall hear, "a homage" from the best society in Stockholm, which was quite peculiar in its type. "Homage!" that is the very word to express what it was that was given her. One feels it, in the delightful refusal of the lady of the house, in the *Dagny* sketch, to ask her to sing again, lest she should seem to have been invited for her singing, and not for her personal qualities. It was this complete acceptance of her, in her own independent character, which worked a real and lasting change in the social respect given to actors and actresses in Stockholm, by which the difficulties that had stood hitherto in their way disappeared. And this absolute sincerity of character which won her this homage as a girl of nineteen, remained so entirely untouched to the last, that every gesture and every look, recorded in that graceful portrait of her behaviour on her earliest *début*, is familiar to those who only knew her in the latter years of her English life. That is the very lady whom they knew: every phrase recalls her. They can see her, as she stands there, at the entry of the *salon*, when the old nobleman is receiving her: rather monosyllabic, at first; and, then as she shakes off her reserve, responding, to any genuine speech, with a sympathy, that is "almost humble." They can feel her as she bends and smiles incredulously, at the pretty compliments paid her by the young men: they can positively hear her laugh as the old generals come up to fumble out their "grotesque flattery": they can catch the very ring of her voice, and the very look in her arch eyes, as she meets the earnest inquiries as to the nature of her secret thoughts when clasping the cross in the scene from *Roberto*, with the frank statement that "she was thinking of her old bonnet!" "A unique apparition, like no one else; simple, unpretending, dignified!" How much the words recall! How many a similar scene was embodied in them! To the very last hour of her life, they would have been the only possible description of her. Surely, a singular force of sincerity lay in her, which could make that early picture of her so speak to those who saw and loved her forty years after, as if it were alive with her very presence, and instinct with her very tones! Not a jot or tittle of that intense and spontaneous originality of hers had " the world " succeeded in moulding to its own liking, or society in refashioning according to its own convention. There she stood, from first to last, " a unique apparition, like no one else ; simple, unpretending, dignified." The notes of Mr. Parker Willis from which we have already quoted, describing her in America in 1850, convey, admirably, the identical impression, which belongs to this *Dagny* sketch and which belonged to her throughout:

" the freshness, and sincerity of thoughts taken as they rise— the truthful deference due to a stranger, and yet the natural cordiality *which self-respect could well afford*—the ease of one who had nothing to learn of courtesy, and yet the impulsive eagerness to shape word and manner to the want of the moment—these, which would seem to be the elements of a simple politeness, were all there ; but in Jenny Lind, somehow, they composed a manner which was altogether her own. A strict lady of the court might have objected to the frank eagerness with which she seated her company like a schoolgirl preparing her playfellows for a game at forfeits ;—but it was charming to those who were made at home by it. In the seating of herself in the posture of attention, and disposal of her hands and dress (small lore sometimes deeply studied, as the ladies know) she evidently left all to nature—the thought of her own personal appearance never once entering her mind. So self-omitting a manner indeed, in a case where none of the uses of politeness were forgotten, I had not before seen."

In saying all this, it is not intended that she could be ever called, in the strict sense, a " conversationalist." Her talk was not continuous enough, to give it the character. Her lack of literary and scientific education forbade it. She talked as an artist, not as a conversationalist. She dropped out a vivid sentence, a pungent epithet; she shot out a

sudden, and brilliant expression : she put one in possession
of a whole situation by a gesture, or a glance : but she did
not follow up a theme, or argument : she did not carry on
a train of thought, or help a conversation to develop a
sequent thread of consecutive reflection. That would not be
her manner. She would be dramatic, abrupt, intense : but
she could not yield herself to the stream of a common discussion, carrying all along in a persistent process, according
to the Socratic ideal of talk.

And here, as we speak of her social effect, it is necessary
to touch upon her personal appearance. Yet how useless it
seems !   No words can be used which will not convey a
wrong or exaggerated impression to those who never saw
her : and to those who have seen and known her, no words
are necessary. Her features were strong, and homely ; of a
usual Swedish type, we believe : very pliable, and expressive,
especially about the nose and the mouth ; and it was this
expressive pliability, which allowed such strange, and delicious
transformation to pass over it, as it changed from repose to
action. We shall come upon a vivid description, in the
course of this book, in which the contrast between her actual
appearance as it first caught your eye, and that which she
became when once she began to speak, or move or sing, will
be spoken of as nothing short of " transfiguration." *   At the
start, you would pronounce the face plain ; but, then, it lent
itself to express, in a peculiar degree, the winning simplicity,
and freshness of girlhood : it was full of animation, and into
it, moreover, there ever passed the singular grace of her
" pose," and her movements.   It was a face which it was
delightful to watch.   It could express everything with a
graphic intensity that made one laugh from pure joy.   It
could brim over with fun : it had an irresistible archness,
when she was amused : it was capable of an almost awful

* Cf. page 108.

Jenny Lind about 16 years of age from a picture by A.J. Fägerplan.

solemnity : and it could, when she was suspicious and on her guard, become absolutely stony. A transparent countenance, indeed, on which every emotion revealed itself with unqualified spontaneity. It was the ever-changing mirror of her soul, and therefore became charged with interest : a speaking face, which could captivate by its overflowing vitality, until it became delightful to observe, and to remember, for its own sake ; and this illumination from within, combined as it was, with the buoyant movements which filled her whole body, gave her, both off and on the stage, whenever she was animated, that positive charm, that personal fascination, which is associated, generally, with beauty.

She was, firmly, persuaded of her own plainness. Her description of herself, as a girl, has, already, been given, in all its comic exaggeration, " broad-nosed, ugly, gauche," etc. And Mr. Parker Willis notices that she was perfectly indifferent to the photographs taken of her, and allowed, " with careless willingness, painters, and Daguerreotypists to make what they will of her." Perhaps, this indifference renders touching one tiny hint of her finding a humble pleasure in a compliment to her looks. It was on an occasion when she appeared, at a Stockholm party, in a tableau-vivant, as Carlo Dolce's St. Cecilia : and it was said that she looked exceedingly like the picture : and she took special delight in this personal resemblance to the Saint Cecilia ; and after her death there was found, among her private stores of little mementoes, the rouge-card used at the tableaux, with her own writing on the back to say that it had been given her by Fredrika Bremer as a memorial of that evening.

The picture on the opposite page is taken from an original panel, which was in her own possession, which has no story, but which, devoid though it be of artistic merit, and common and crude in its workmanship, yet seems to preserve the likeness of what she was when about eighteen years old. It

is the earliest record we have of her appearance : and though
the artist has not the skill or the insight to give the animation that illuminated the face, or the movement that gave it
its grace, he has preserved the main outlines.

She was five feet three to four inches in height : but she
held her head so erect and had trained herself so carefully
in standing and walking that she appeared to be taller.

All the portraits taken of her, take notice of the fine mould
of her arms, and especially, of their characteristic position, in
repose, with her hands clasped on her lap.   In the Stockholm
days, she wore her hair in bunches of curls at each side of
the forehead, as is the case in Södermark's portrait of her,
painted in 1843, which she had in her own possession.
About the year 1844, she seems to have adopted for herself,
that wavy droop of the hair, laid down low about her ears,
which became so familiar and noticeable a mark of her
appearance, that it alone sufficed to make a likeness resemble
her.   As long as the lines of her hair were given, one knew
whom it was intended, at least, to portray.

The main elements of her character, as of her type of
countenance, were radically national.   She was a down-
right and typical Swede.   She was fond of dwelling on the
artistic capacities of her people, to whom she owed her own
quick sensibilities, her alert and receptive imagination, her
vivacity of temperament.   She believed them to have all the
artist's possibilities in them, with all the attendant perils.
And, in view of these perils, to which all such gifted natures
must be liable, it is remarkable that she should have included
within this national groundwork of her character, a profound
moral stability, a depth of seriousness, such as would be rare
in any race ; and, moreover, with this, she had a persistence, a
stubbornness, which, among Scandinavian races, is traditionally
attributed to the Finn.   And if she had the vivacity of her
people, she inherited also from it the strong, passionate feel-

ings, and affections, which make the home-relationships, in
Sweden, so rooted, and so deep; and, also, that undertone of
melancholy, into which such artistic sensitiveness is prone to
re-act,—an undertone, which seems to creep, like the sighing
of a wounded spirit, out of the black heart of Swedish pine-
woods, and to hover over the wide surfaces of her inland
waters. Such notes of pathos underlie the songs of her
people : and she was a true Swede when she wrote of herself,
" When I am alone, you have no idea how different I am—so
happy, yet so melancholy that tears are rolling down my
cheeks unceasingly."

This personal impression, which we have faintly suggested,
told, as we have said, not only upon the higher social circles
of Stockholm, but also upon the literary and cultured society,
where, again, she formed affectionate intimacies with the few,
and the best.

There was Johan Thomander, Professor of Theology at
Lund, of which place he was, afterwards, bishop, a celebrated
preacher, and an eminent member of the Swedish Academy.

There was Fredrika Bremer, the famous novelist, and indefatigable philanthropist.

There was Baron Bernhard von Beskow, a distinguished
author, member and permanent Secretary of the Academy,
whose name, as Intendant of the Royal Theatre, will appear
in connection with the Lind Scholarships.

There was Atterbom, one of Sweden's best poets, an
eminent student in the history of literature ; University Tutor
of Philosophy,—a man of peculiar gentleness and amiability.

Then, again, we might mention the Count Jacob Gustaf de
la Gardie, Grand Master of the Ceremonies, and a warm friend
of poetry and art, the owner of a superb library of 12,000
volumes ; who was one of the first to detect the great gifts of
the child-singer.

Here was the environment into which the girl of nineteen

found herself admitted, and, within which she made fast
friends.   But two names must yet be mentioned, which
embody a special interest in her life.

First, A. F. Lindblad, the famous song-writer.   We have
seen into what close contact they had been drawn.   In his
house she found a refuge, and a home, through which she
was brought into constant contact with the higher culture of
the Swedish capital.   Lindblad was born in 1801, and
studied music in Berlin, under Zelter: and also in Paris,
between 1825–27, after which he returned to Stockholm, and
lived there until 1864, when he moved to near Linköping.
His renown rests, chiefly, on his songs.

"They are eminently national, and full of grace, and
originality, tinged with the melancholy which is characteristic
of Swedish music.   In short songs, in which extreme simplicity is of the essence of their charm, his success has been
most conspicuous." *

There can be no doubt that Jenny Lind's intimacy with
Lindblad had an immense influence on her musical development.   Besides the vital effect of his personality, she heard
at his house all the best instrumental music of the great composers then flourishing: it was there that she was first introduced to the music of Mendelssohn,—especially, to the
Songs without Words, which had, just at that time, taken
Europe by storm.   Nor was she herself merely receptive: she
brought power to bear on Lindblad, which had a positive
effect upon his work.   The effect has been emphasised by
Professor Nyblom, in a memoir on Lindblad in 1880 in
which he mentions that there were few only who were able
to render his works in the right manner: and, among those
few, was "Jenny Lind: who impressed the individuality of
her genius, in flaming letters, on not a few of the composer's
works of that time when she had her home in his family :—

* Grove's ' Dictionary of Music,' Art. "Lindblad."

works easily identified, and made interesting and precious to those who are willing and able to observe the mutual attraction and meeting together of two burning artist-souls!" She wrote herself, in 1832, after having read this biography of Lindblad:

"I have to thank him (Lindblad) for that fine comprehension of Art which was implanted by his idealistic, pure, and unsensual nature into me, his ready pupil. Subsequently Christianity stepped in, to satisfy the moral needs, and to teach me to look well into my own soul. Thus it became to me, both as an artist, and as a woman, a higher chastener."

So she described her spiritual progress, looking back to the influence of Lindblad as anticipatory of that yet deeper hold of the meaning of Art which was given her under the later dominance of the full Christian ideal. Not only did she repay, in counter-influence, all the attention that Lindblad concentrated upon her, but also, she by her singing, carried his songs into fame all over Europe. And still, in long after-years, in England, in hours of lonely quiet, or at times when she was depressed and needed comfort, she would sit at the piano, and "croon" over to herself those songs of Lindblad's, which had in them, so many memories—memories, that had passed into her very being, of far days in the old country, when those sounds, so saturated with the inspiration of her home, were, first, in her ears, and she was tasting the spring sweetness of her fresh young powers.

And, lastly, we must mention the great name of Erik Gustaf Geijer, a man at the very summit of Swedish literature. Born in 1783, he became Professor of History, at the University of Upsala, in 1816: where his lectures had unexampled popularity. In spite of the offer of a bishopric, Professor he still remained, planning the great history of Sweden, of which his introduction was a masterpiece of skill and knowledge: and producing various historical works. He

was much occupied with political and economical specu-
lations; and, for thirty years, continued to be one of the
chiefs of the Swedish literary world. He died on April 23,
1847. Besides his historical and political work, he had a
real talent for music; and published a volume of songs, of
which Lindblad wrote a famous account.* Through music,
he crossed the path of Jenny Lind; and in her he took a most
warm interest.

" Jenny and I have become very good friends," he writes
in January 1840. "I call her 'Thou': and she calls me
'Uncle.' She is a simple attractive being. Lindblad, and
Madame Lindblad both stand to her in almost fatherly, and
motherly relation, which becomes both parties very well.
All the same, I am afraid she is a kind of 'comet' which
may interfere with their domestic peace, for comets have tails:
and their house is besieged by Jenny's admirers, who now
may be said to consist of the whole public."

Again, in March, he writes, "Jenny Lind sang two of my
songs, *i.e.*, '*The Drawing-Room or the Wood,*' and '*Spring,
will it come?*' It was quite excellent. I went behind the
curtain to thank her, and accompanied her home to her
door. I do not think lightly of the good graces in which
I believe myself to stand with her."

For her he wrote songs, both words and music: and it is
in one of these songs, that we discover the record both of his
estimation of her character, and, also, of the profound effect
which such an estimate, coming from such a man, had upon
her to whom it was addressed. And, indeed, we cannot
wonder at this effect: for the author of the song is not afraid
to acknowledge, in this fresh young girl, the signs and omens
of that supreme genius, which is the highest born of Heaven,
and which, yet, because it is highest, is also as a " consuming
flame," to which the devoted and sacrificial Will must yield
itself, as a victim, offered on an altar. The deep and serious
import of such momentous words, addressed to her by the

* *Cf.* Biography in Geijer's Collected Works, 1873-75.

highest intellectual authority of her native land, and ranking
her, the young opera-singer from the Theatre School, with that
rare band of spiritual heroes whose lives are as a torch lit by
divine fire, must have been as a revelation: and the traces of
this remain on a copy of these verses, in her own handwriting, found among her papers, across the bottom of which
she has written, " On these words I was launched into the
open sea." To her, they marked the date at which she felt
herself a public, an historic, character. For her, they contained the secret of her mission, of her expectations, of her
future. It was his insistence, as we believe, which urged her
to seek a wider world: and, now, from him she learned with
what spirit she was to make her venture. She was to move
out into the open day of her fame, not to win a reputation,
not to enjoy, not to taste triumph, not to satisfy her own
craving for expression, not to find a world of honour, and
wealth, and ease. Nay! She was to be clad about with
prophetic solemnity. She was to yield herself to the stern
necessities of genius: she was to consume, in giving: the
steps up which she was ever to be passing, were to be the
steps of an altar: and she was the sacrifice. Such were the
words that were behind her, when she found herself " launched
into the open sea." *

We give them in a free and rough translation—

> " Oh! if from you Eternal Fire,
> 　　Which slays the souls that it sets free—
> Consuming them, as they aspire—
> 　　One burning spark have fallen on thee!

> " Fear not! Though upward still it haste,
> 　　That living fire, that tongue of flame!
> *Thy* days it turns to bitter waste;
> 　　But ah! from heaven—from heaven it came!"

* They were printed, with music, in the ' Linnaea Borealis Poetisk
Kalender,' 1841:
　" Mod och försakelse. Till en ung Sångerska den 24 December, 1839.
　" (Upsala, 1840.)　　　　　　　　　　(Signed) E. G. G——r."

CHAPTER VII.

PILGRIMAGE.

THE sign of the sacrifice was already upon her, in the year
1840. On the surface, she had everything which could satisfy
her. She had become the idol of the National Drama. She
had been made Member of the Royal Swedish Academy of
Music in 1840, and had received the high official recognition
by being appointed Court-singer, on the 13th of January,
1840, by His Majesty, Carl Johan. This was an honour
which her mother had, already, been anticipating, from the
summer of 1839, and had rejoiced over the fact that it
included a salary. "It is a great mark of distinction," she
writes to her husband; "and a great joy for us!" She had
the best social "world" at her feet. She enjoyed the
delightful companionship of some of the most cultivated men
and women in Sweden. Her position at the Royal Theatre
was assured her. The Directors were, at the very moment,
proposing to her a fresh, and advanced contract. Indeed we
shall see that their zeal outran their discretion and their
proper consideration for her; for they were but too anxious
to use her gifts, at the risk of overstraining them. Her
popularity was at its height; she was pursued with
enthusiasm. The musical authorities of Stockholm had no
more to teach her; they were content to praise her, as the
perfect exponent of their art.

And, yet, what was it that worked within the girl's heart,
and told her that all this was as nothing—told her, that, far

from having reached the end, she was not even at the beginning—told her that her art had secrets yet to unfold to her, and that this adulation which encompassed her was but a prophecy of what she ought to become hereafter ? What was this insistent whisper of some buried conscience within her, which spoke to her alone—spoke of some perfection which could be sought and found elsewhere? As she bowed in courteous acknowledgment of the loud plaudits of an enthusiastic theatre, she heard, above all the genial tumult this "still, small voice" within, which said to her, "Yes ! you may, some day, live to deserve that kindly, that encouraging applause ; but, to-day, you know that, by rights, it is not yours ! You know not, as yet, how to merit it. It is given you, in spite of yourself. But you have that in you which may, indeed, deserve to receive that which is generously offered you, in anticipation, to-day. Far away, over the sea the secret is kept which will unlock the shut doors, and will set free your true self. Far over the sea, there is a power at whose touch the sleeping queen will wake and spring to life. There it is that you will know what now is hidden from your eyes. There it is that Art will disclose the mystery, which is now felt but not perceived—the mystery, that moves veiled behind the glory of to-day's success." It was the inspiration of genius which spoke to her. She had but her own soul to trust to. She had no ideal, no articulate standard given her, by which to test herself ; yet she knew her lack, she felt what she was missing. And, in so feeling, she knew, also, that, to discover the ideal, to win that which was lacking, all her present triumph must be surrendered, must be thrown to the winds. The voice within must be obeyed at all costs ; out over the sea, far from home and its happy honours, she must seek, alone, and undirected, the meaning of the mysterious summons. Surely, the pressure of the prophetic words was upon her :

> " Fear not, though upward still it haste,
>   That living fire, that tongue of flame!
> *Thy* days it turns to bitter waste;
>   But ah! from heaven—from heaven it came!"

So it was that she took her own resolution. We give it in her own remarkable words. They were written in answer to the new proposals made by the Directors, who, on the 15th of December, 1840, "wishing," as they said "most particularly, to attach to the Swedish stage, a talent so eminent as the Court-singer, Fröken Jenny Lind, make her the highest offer of which their regulations afford them the power." This highest offer was, it is true, not extravagant; it ensured her £150 a year; it provided her with all her costumes out of theatrical funds; it allowed her one "benefit" every year; and special "extra service money for the parts in which she appears." It offered her the months of July and August for study abroad; and promised to try to extend this interval. The engagement was to last for the full period permitted, *i.e.*, three years.

To this, Fröken Lind sent the following answer:

"*To the Directors of the Royal Theatre.*

"In reply to the letter from the Directors of the Royal Theatre, dated 15th December last year, I have the honour to state as follows: The musical and dramatic capabilities, which, from my earliest years, I have felt myself to possess, have, thanks to the cultivation received at home, though hitherto insufficient, still been able to attract some attention to my dawning talent; but it is not with half developed, if even happy, natural gifts that an artist can keep his ground; and, greatly as I prize the appreciation I have been fortunate enough already to win, I feel I ought to consider it not so much a homage to the artist I was and am, as an encouragement to what I might become.

"With this conviction and in order to attain the artistic perfection open to me, I have thought it a duty to do what

I can, and not to draw back before any sacrifice, either of youth, health, comfort or labour, not to speak of the modest sum I have managed to save, in the hope of reaching what may, perhaps, prove an unattainable aim. In consequence I have decided on a journey to, and a sojourn at, some place abroad, which, through furnishing the finest models in art, would prove to me of the greatest profit.

"It is, then, chiefly this journey which constitutes the real obstacle to my immediately accepting, in its entirety, the kind offer of the Directors of the Royal Theatre; for it defers, for another year, the possibility of my re-engagement. I am in hopes, however, that the Royal Directors will not disapprove of my resolution, all the more as it aims solely at perfecting myself in my art; while all sacrifices, inseparable from a similar undertaking, will fall on myself alone. Trusting that the Royal Directors will accord to these reasons due consideration, and, in accordance with the request made in their kind letter, I beg leave to submit my counter proposals.

"On returning to my native country, next year, I undertake to serve at the Royal Theatre for the two following years at the salary proposed by the Royal Directors in the above-mentioned letter of the 15th December last, but with the following modifications; that my engagement, for each year, may not exceed eight months, viz., from 1st October unto the following 31st May, so that a leave of the four months, June, July, August and September may be accorded to me.

"Furthermore, I must, rather as a humble petition, than as a condition for my return to the service of the Royal Theatre, express my wish to be free this year from next 31st May, since in the beginning of June an opportunity offers for me to start on my intended journey in company with a family without whose protection I should not venture to undertake it. I hope the Royal Directors will, kindly, give due weight to this invaluable advantage, and, in view of its importance to me, excuse my earnest request.

"JENNY LIND.

"Stockholm, 9 February, 1841."

A notable document, this. Had she any counsel to aid her in its production? Did Berg, did Lindblad advise the step? We have no record of such advice from them. Both,

indeed, seem to have agreed to the step, and to favour its
carrying out; for Berg is found with her at the start in Paris;
and it is only out of her own delicate affection for her former
master that she delays her beginning with the next one.
Moreover she owns to having consulted him as to what was
to be done when it became clear to him as to her, that he had
no more to teach her. But nothing is said of his suggesting
a remedy. Lindblad, also, visits her in Paris, and interests
himself in her final fortunes there. But, still, there is no
sign of their being the prime movers. No evidence exists
of her seeking other counsel than her own heart in making the
final decision.

Yet two influences there were that told strongly upon
her at the time, and urged her forward. The first was
theoretical and ideal: it was that of Geijer. He was clear
that she belonged to mankind, rather than to Sweden, and
he pressed upon her the necessity of widening her range of
knowledge and skill. She, herself, attributed the momentum
that drove her afield to Geijer's insistence. "He kicked me
out . . . into the great world," she would say, with humorous
vigour. The second influence was direct, and practical.
It was the example of Belletti, the celebrated barytone,
then singing with her at the Royal Theatre.* He showed
her, vividly, what scientific singing in the great Italian
manner really meant; and he would be able, if consulted as
to where such style could be gained, to say at once,—"At
Paris, under Garcia."

The decision, then, from which she is not to draw back,
even at "the sacrifice of youth, health, comfort, and of her

---

* Dahlgren's important History of the Swedish Stage has the following
about Belletti (born in 1813, at Sarzana): "Giovanni Battista Belletti,
came from Italy encouraged to do so by the sculptor, Professor Byström,
who had made his acquaintance at Carrara; he remained connected with
the R. Opera from 1839—1 July 1844."

modest savings" appears to be largely the issue of her own insight, and deliberation. Later on, in Paris, she speaks as if it were her own "artistic conscience" whose dictates she had obeyed. Certainly, it was left to her own courage and resolution to find the funds by which to carry it out. And it was, for this end, that she had already in the summer of 1840 set out on a provincial round of concerts, accompanied by her father; in which she, probably, wore out what remained of her voice after the hard work of the theatrical season, but, in compensation, won triumphant successes and accumulated supplies that would carry her through a year's training at Paris, whither she was determined to go and discover the true secret of song.

We have a letter from her written, in the middle of this tour, towards the early part of July, to her friend Louise Johansson, from Malmö, at the extreme south of Sweden whence she could actually see Copenhagen, in which she records how things have gone in the series of towns through which she has passed. "The journey has gone off well enough, thank God! That is to say, the roads were so bad that the wheels, now and then, sank a foot deep into the mud, and it was very horrid sitting about in the atrocious weather; but as soon as I arrive in a town, and see the exceeding great kindness and friendliness the people have for me, then I feel it wicked to grumble. You cannot think to what an extent they all vie with each other in serving me. It is quite astonishing!"

She tells how they began at Norrköping; how she slept through a thunder-storm; how they went to some country seats, with Herr Cederbaum, and Baron Ahlströmer; how they got to Ekesjö on Midsummer Eve; and how, at Qvarnarp they were received for a whole week by the kindest and most amiable people she had seen for a long time. "I shall not have so much fun any more, this

H

summer," she laments, "and besides—be this said without conceit—my departure was regretted, for they all cried, both young and old." Then on to Wexiö, Christianstad with its tiny theatre crowded, and so to Malmö. She is to visit Copenhagen from there, without singing; and, then, to pass through Helsingborg, Jönköping, Linköping and Norrköping, back to Stockholm, giving concerts at each place by the way. She asks most earnestly after her grandmother; not her dear old Mme. Teugmark who had died in 1833, but Fru Strömberg, a connection of her father's. She fears lest she be already dead; if not, she sends her, with deep respect, her fondest love, and an assurance that "Papa is quite well! God grant I may not come home too late to see her!"

After some messages to her Aunt Lona (*i.e.,* Apollonia Lindskog) the letter closes with a commission which shows how very early in life her characteristic charities had begun:

"My dear Louisa, would you be kind enough to render me the service of going to Clara Vestra, Kyrkogata 13 or 25. I am not sure which of these numbers is the right one, but after you have crossed the Clara churchyard, and when you arrive at the gate on the Vestragatan, turn to the left, then it is the first door on the right-hand side, on the ground floor. Ask for Bruhn, the painter, a poor sick man ill in bed these last fourteen years; I forgot to bring him his monthly allowance, before coming away; will you be good enough to give him, on my behalf, 8 r. d. banco, and to tell him this is for the months of July and August. Greet him much from me, as also his wife, and pardon your friend who troubles you in this way.

"JENNY."

A note is here struck, which is to sound on through her life. It expresses one of the most vital instincts of her nature—an instinct which roots itself deep down in her artistic impulses—this instinct which bids her dedicate her gift to the cause of the poor, and the unhappy. That in her which made her an artist, made her also charitable.

It was the sense of possessing a gift which prompts the giving. That which had flowed in, must flow out. She was responsible for her great possession; she held it in trust; she must put it out to use. It was no mere liberality of disposition; it was no mere genial beneficence; it was an obligation, binding, and urgent; a joyful duty; a holy privilege which it would be a sin to neglect. Everything in her which made her recognise the powers lodged in her to be a divine endowment, made her, by a like impulse, recognise her duty to give away what she gained. No one will understand her, who does not see how closely her charity was interwoven with her art; and how it was that, in after days, in deciding the question of marriage, she made it the prime necessity that her husband should leave her free in her charities. It is because it was so interwoven, that it seemed to her to be no work of merit; it was done by a plain law of right; it was spontaneous, natural, inevitable. So it is that already, at twenty, in the flush of youth and personal success, her nature is at work with instinctive security; she has found out the poor sick painter; and, quite modestly apologising for the trouble, just as if she were giving a commission to buy something at a shop, she begs her friend to see to it that he gets what he had the right to look for from her.

Back to Stockholm she got in August, where she was singing in *Lucia di Lammermoor*, on August 19th; and all through the autumn, and spring, she is hard at work, fulfilling her bond to the Directors, though, owing to her concert-tour, she had had no holiday whatever. No wonder, that her voice was left fatigued and strained after such unintermittent work, with all the weariness of incessant journeys, and the anxieties that beset new appearances in unfamiliar rooms. It was in this effort to raise funds by which to reach Paris, that she ran so near to doing irreparable damage to her vocal powers. Twenty-three times

does she perform in *Lucia*, between August 19th when she
returned, and June 19th, when she closed her engagement.
Fourteen times did she give "Alice," in *Roberto ;* and
nine times she repeated her former *rôle* of "Agatha" in
the *Freischütz*. And, besides these, there were incidental
appearances ; in the *Zauberflöte* as "Pamina"; in *The Swiss
Family* as "Emmelina"; and, seven times, as "Alaida" in
Bellini's *Stranierà*. And, moreover, there were concerts at
the theatre, in which she sang, on August 27th, and October
17th, and November 14th, and on January 11th and 20th.
And, finally, for the closing nights in May and June, came
her first seven performances of *Norma*. At the last of
the concerts, she had sung, as her piece, a duet from *Norma*,
with Mme. Gelhaar, her old playmate in the school. And, on
May 19th, the full opera was produced, in which her own
people recognised, and greeted, one of her most brilliant and
impressive impersonations. They loved to see her in this
character ; and they prize as their favourite memorial of
her, the picture taken of her by Södermark, as "Norma," of
which a print is given in our second volume.

With *Norma* she ended, on June 19th; it was her 447th
appearance on the boards of the Royal Theatre, since, as a
tiny child of ten, she played "Angela" in *The Polish Mine*,
on November 29th, 1830. The Directors had, indeed, been
justified by the venture they made with the little creature,
whom they sent on the stage to dance and sing before she
had been many months at the school. She had well repaid
them. For her sixty-nine performances in the year 1840,
she is only receiving, besides the regulation play money,
1100 r. d. banco—about £95 a year. Her voice is fatigued,
and worn ; she has done more work than she could rightly
afford. But her spirit is not looking back, but ahead. She
is not calculating her present gains ; but is all on fire with
the great hope, that is astir within her, at the bidding of

which she will wander out, a pilgrim of Art, seeking the better country, sure that there is a vision to be seen, a victory to be won, to which as yet she has not even come nigh.

She has found her opportunity; and has made her resolution. Some good, kind friends, M. and Madame Von Koch in whose house she found constant friendship and affection have arranged for her journey, and have lent her a maid, as a companion. A safe road is thus laid open for her to Paris. So, on June 21st, she gave, in the Ladugårdslands Church, a final concert on her own behalf, singing an aria from *Anna Bolena*, and another from *Norma;* winding up with a 'Lyrical Farewell,' written and composed, for the occasion, by Lindblad; and, in July, she leaves the Lindblads' house, and enters on the pilgrimage which was to mean so much. Home has been gracious to her; she loves her country which has loved her so freely; her one desire is to return to Stockholm, worthy of the enthusiasm which it has poured about her. But home cannot tell her the great secret. Somewhere else it lies, far off; she must seek it, and find it, even though, on its behalf, she sacrifice "youth, health, comfort, labour, and savings."

BOOK II.

ASPIRATION.

CHAPTER I.

On Thursday, the first of July, 1841, after taking leave of Herr and Madame Lindblad, Mr. Edward Lewin, and her friends in Stockholm, Mademoiselle Lind embarked, on the steamship *Gauthiod*—Captain Nylén—for Lübeck; in company with His Excellency, Count Gustave Löwenhielm, the Swedish Minister at Paris, Signor Belletti, and one or two less intimate acquaintances; and attended by a trusty female companion, recommended to her by Madame von Koch.

"The dear little girl," wrote Madame Lindblad, "was almost crushed. I never thought that it would cost her so much. On the last night she never slept, but wrote letters the whole night through, coming occasionally into our rooms to have a good cry. On the first of July she left, at 11 o'clock, A.M."

On reaching Travemünde, Count Löwenhielm disembarked, and proceeded by land, to Hamburg. Mademoiselle Lind and Signor Belletti continued their voyage to Lübeck; and thence travelled to Hamburg by post. On arriving there, they rejoined Count Löwenhielm, who introduced Mademoiselle Lind to the Swedish Minister in Hamburg, and left nothing undone which could make her short sojourn in the old Hanse-town agreeable.

It was a pleasant little episode—a delightful holiday, on the road to hard work.

After these few days of rest and enjoyment, she proceeded with her companion to Hâvre by the steamboat; and thence, by diligence, to Paris.

To a nature so sensitive, the change from the natural simplicity of domestic life in Sweden, to the restless activity of the French capital, with its crowded streets, its ceaseless craving for pleasure and excitement, its passion for amusement, its caprices of fashion, above all, its splendid theatres, its art-collections, and priceless opportunities for mental cultivation and improvement—to such a nature, all this, so new, so unexpected, and, in many respects, so strangely incomprehensible, must have been fraught with an all-absorbing interest.

And we must not forget, that the Paris of eight-and-forty years ago was a city, very different from, and, in many respects, very much more interesting than, that in which it delights us to spend our holidays to-day.

Eight-and-forty years ago, there was no Boulevard Hausmann; no Temple of the Muses worthy to be compared with the new home of the *Grand Opéra* which excites our envy and admiration, every time we indulge ourselves with a *loge* in its goodly *salle;* no sign of the new streets, and squares, and palaces, which were destined to spring up, as it were, in a night, under the influence of the 'Second Empire.' But in place of these, there were sights, infinitely more pleasing to the sense of the artist, and the poet. Whole streets, like the Rue du Tourniquet-Saint-Jean, described by de Balzac, were so little changed since the dark days of the *Terreur,* that it needed but little effort of the imagination to re-people them with the *sansculottes,* and the *tricoteuses,* who had whirled through the giddy mazes of the *carmagnole,* or yelled the *Marseillaise,* within their time-stained precincts, in the days of Robespierre and Danton; streets which formed part of an older Paris, as different from the Paris of to-day, as the

Hamburg of to-day is, from the Hamburg that suffered in the conflagration of 1842.

It was to this older Paris that Mademoiselle Lind repaired, in the summer of the year 1841, in the hope of perfecting herself in the technicalities of the Art she so dearly loved—that Art of Singing, of whose mysteries she knew so little, and longed to know so much ; and the details of which she found it so impossible to acquire satisfactorily in Stockholm.

For her advancement in Dramatic Art, she trusted to herself alone. No one could teach her to act, and she sought no teacher ; for her method was part of herself, based upon her own natural impulses, idealised by the deep and noble romance which, in all that appertained to the stage, was her never-failing guide, an inward light, by aid of which she was enabled to identify herself with every character she cared to impersonate, and even to "create," anew, many famous parts, which she interpreted in a manner peculiarly her own. She needed no help for this. But her need of a competent *Maestro di Canto* was a very pressing one, indeed ; and she had long been convinced that one, and one only, could teach her what she so much desired to know. But it will be readily understood that the assistance and hearty co-operation of such a master as she needed were not to be had for the mere asking ; and some little time elapsed before her desire was accomplished.

On first reaching Paris, Mademoiselle Lind found a comfortable home with a family named Ruffiaques, who kept a boarding-house, in a street near the Rue Neuve des Augustins.

Here, she was visited by Madame Berg, the wife of her former singing-master, who was then staying in Paris, with her little invalid son, Albert; and, also, by Herr Blumm, a Swedish gentleman of kindliest disposition and infinite *bonhomie,* who held the appointment of *Chancelier* to the

Swedish Legation, in the Rue d'Anjou,* and to whom she was indebted for innumerable acts of courtesy and kindness, during the period of her residence in Paris.

On leaving Sweden, she had brought with her letters of introduction, from Queen Desideria,† to her relative, the Duchesse de Dalmatie (Madame la Maréchale Soult); and, soon after her arrival in Paris, she was invited by this lady to an afternoon reception. Among the guests present at this little *réunion* were Count Löwenhielm, and the Comtesse de la Redortes (Maréchal Soult's married daughter). It was understood that Mademoiselle Lind would be asked to sing: and, by invitation of the Duchesse, Signor Manuel Garcia, the brother of Madame Malibran and Madame Viardot, and the most renowned *Maestro di Canto* in Europe, came to hear her.

She sang some Swedish songs, accompanying herself on the pianoforte; but, either through nervousness, or fatigue, she does not appear to have done herself justice, and her singing seems to have produced no very favourable effect upon the assembled guests. Her voice was worn, not only from over-exertion, but from want of that careful management which can only be acquired by long training under a thoroughly competent master. Such training she had never had. She had formed her own ideal of the difficult *rôles* that had been entrusted to her—all too soon for her welfare, if those in office at the Royal Theatre in Stockholm had but known it!—and had tried to reach that ideal by the only means she knew of—means, very pernicious indeed. The result was, that the voice had been very cruelly injured. The mischief had been seriously aggravated by the fatigue

---

* Then called Rue d'Anjou St. Honoré. The street still exists, but not the house formerly occupied by the Swedish Legation.

† The wife of Maréchal Bernadotte, who became King of Sweden and Norway, in the year 1818, under the title of Karl XIV. Johann.

consequent upon her long and arduous provincial tour; and the result was a chronic hoarseness, painful enough to produce marked symptoms of deterioration upon the fresh young voice, which had never been taught either the method of production, or the cultivation of style necessary for the development of its natural charm.

Signor Garcia was not slow to perceive all this; and he afterwards told a lady, who questioned him upon the subject, that Mademoiselle Lind was, at that time, altogether wanting in the qualities needed for presentation before a highly-cultivated audience.

Soon after this, Mademoiselle Lind called, by appointment, upon Signor Garcia, who then occupied a pleasant *deuxième étage*, in a large block of houses in the Square d'Orléans, near the Rue Saint Lazare; a handsome residence, built around a turfed courtyard, with a fountain in the centre, and a large tree on each side of it.* As, on this occasion, she formally requested the great *Maestro* to receive her as a pupil, he felt it his duty to examine her voice more carefully than he had been able to do at Madame Soult's afternoon party; and, after making her sing through the usual scales, and forming his own opinion of the power and compass of the vocal registers, he asked her to sing the well-known scena from *Lucia di Lammermoor*—"*Perche non ho.*" In this, unhappily, she broke completely down—in all probability, through nervousness, for she had appeared in the part of "Lucia," at the Stockholm Theatre, no less than thirty-nine times only the

---

* The house is still unchanged. The Square, now called the Cité d'Orléans, is situated midway between the Boulevard des Italiens, and the Barrière Montmartre, and forms No. 80 of the Rue Taitbout, near a spot formerly called the Rue des Trois Frères. Chopin, and Professor Zimmermann—the father of Madame Gounod—once lived here; the latter keeping a 'pension' for musical students, in which Garcia's pupil, Mademoiselle Nissen (of whom more detailed mention will presently be made), for some time resided.

year before, and the music must, therefore, have been more
than familiar to her. However, let the cause have been what
it might, the failure was complete; and, upon the strength of
it, the Maestro pronounced his terrible verdict—" It would
be useless to teach you, Mademoiselle; you have no voice
left "—" *Mademoiselle, vous n'avez plus de voix.*" *

The effect of this sentence of hopeless condemnation upon
an organisation so highly strung as that of Mademoiselle
Lind may be easily conceived. But her courage was equal
to the occasion, though she told Mendelssohn, years afterwards,
that the anguish of that moment exceeded all that she had
ever suffered in her whole life. The shock must have been
a cruel one, indeed; yet her faith in her own powers never
wavered for an instant. She could not forget the triumphs
of the past. Her success in Stockholm had been so genuine,
and so brilliant, that many a *prima donna* would have been
satisfied to accept it as the final reward of a long and
honourable career, the just recompense of a life devoted to
the service of Art. But she herself was far from satisfied.
She knew that she was capable of greater things, and meant
to accomplish them. She knew what Garcia could not
possibly know—that there was a power within her that no
amount of discouragement could ever subdue.

Instead, therefore, of accepting his verdict as a final one,
she asked, with tears in her eyes, what she was to do. Her
faith in the *Maestro's* judgment was no less firm than that
which she felt in the reality of her own vocation. In the full

---

* It is necessary that these words should be very distinctly recorded;
for, their frequent misquotation, in the newspapers, and elsewhere, has
led to a very false impression, equally unjust to master and pupil. The
Maestro's exact words were, " *Mademoiselle, vous n'avez plus de voix* "—
not, " *Vous n'avez pas de voix.*" Mademoiselle Lind had once possessed
a voice; but it had been so strained, by over-exertion, and a faulty
method of production, that, for the time being, scarcely a shred of it
remained.

conviction that, if she could only persuade him to advise
her, his counsel would prove invaluable, she did not hesitate
to make the attempt; and the result fully justified the
soundness of her conclusions. Moved by her evident distress,
he recommended her to give her voice six weeks of perfect
rest; to abstain, during the whole of that time, from
singing even so much as one single note; and to speak as
little as possible. And, upon condition that she strictly
carried out these injunctions, he gave her permission to come
to him again, when the period of probation was ended, in
order that he might then see whether anything could be done
for her.

CHAPTER II.

THE MAESTRO DI CANTO.

To any really earnest aspirant, six weeks of enforced idleness would have been a martyrdom. For Mdlle. Lind, such a period of inaction was simply impossible. Disobedience to the *Maestro's* orders was, of course, out of the question. But, if she was forbidden to sing, or to speak, she was, at least, permitted to read, and write. Never doubting, for a moment, of her ultimate success, she knew that she would, one day, have to sing in Italian, and possibly, also, in French. She therefore spent the six weary weeks in the diligent study of those languages; and there are actually in existence, at this moment, no less than sixty-one large foolscap pages, in her own handwriting, closely filled with exercises in Italian grammar, and twenty-three similar pages in French, the greater part of which appear to have been completed during this trying period; not mere notes, or scattered memoranda, but systematic declensions of nouns, conjugations of verbs, long lists of exceptions, and other methodical work, such as would have been executed by an industrious student on the eve of a severe critical examination.

But, the time was a weary one, nevertheless. Her nerves were excited to the last degree of tension, and never did she forget the exasperating effect of the cries which, day after day, reached her, from the street, as the long dull hours dragged on. Two of these, repeated with a persistence truly *agaçant*, she imitated, sometimes, when speaking of her Paris

life, in the presence of her daughter, who thus noted down
the "words and music."

Ha - ri - cots, ha - ri - cots verts !

Ah !   le   vi - tri - er !

The first of these street-melodies speaks for itself. The
second is the cry of a wandering glazier ; and may still be
heard, in the poorer streets of Paris, sung by men who carry
panes of glass on their backs, to mend broken windows.

Intense indeed must have been the relief, when the time of
probation—hard enough to bear, in spite of the conscientious
labour by which it was lightened—expired, at last. Once
more, Mdlle. Lind sought an interview with the master, in his
pleasant *deuxième*, in the Square d'Orléans ; and, this time
her hopes were crowned with success. Signor Garcia found
the voice so far re-established, by rest, that he was able to
give good hope of its complete restoration, provided that the
faulty method of production which had so nearly resulted in
its destruction was abandoned ; and, with the view of attaining this important end, he agreed to give her two lessons,
regularly, every week—an arrangement which set all her
anxieties at rest, and for which she was deeply grateful, to
the end of her life.*

* The exact date of these two interviews with Signor Garcia cannot
now be ascertained. The account given in the text rests upon information
furnished by Signor Garcia himself, many years afterwards, to a lady who
questioned him upon the subject, and to whom he narrated the circumstances, as nearly as he could then recollect them. No doubt, the account
he gave was, in the main, correct; but, it is not easy to reconcile it with
the date of some of Mademoiselle Lind's letters. In a letter, dated the
15th of August, 1841, she told her friend, Louise Johansson, that she

The delight of the artist, at being once more permitted to sing, may be readily imagined. Though discouraged, sometimes, by the immense amount she had to learn—and, with still greater difficulty, to un-learn—she never lost heart; and so rapidly did the vocal organs recover from the exhaustion from which they had been suffering, that, before long, she was able to practise her scales and exercises for many hours daily.

To the uninitiated, this amount of study may seem excessive, for a voice that had so narrowly escaped destruction through over-exertion. But the experienced teacher well knows that the danger lies, not in the amount of work accomplished, but in the manner in which it is accomplished. A vicious method, a want of due attention to the management of the breath, attempts to produce extreme notes in an unsuitable register, and a hundred other fatal habits well understood by those who have carefully studied the subject, exert a more deleterious influence upon the voice, and injure it more seriously, and far more surely, than any reasonable amount of honest and well-directed practice.

---

was then practising her scales, from three to four hours a day, without a master, not wishing to take lessons until after Herr Berg's departure from Paris: in another, dated the 19th of August, she told Madame Lindblad that she sometimes delighted Madame Ruffiaques' boarders, after the day's practice was over, by singing to them some of the Swedish songs which she afterwards made so famous: and, in a third letter written on the 10th of September, she told Fröken Marie Ruckman that she had already taken five lessons from Signor Garcia. This leaves no time for the compulsory silence, of six weeks' duration, prescribed, by Signor Garcia, as the condition of her admission to the privileges of his instruction. That the condition really was prescribed, on the one side, and loyally observed, on the other, we know, on her own authority; for, she herself—as the writer perfectly well remembers—related the circumstance to Mendelssohn, in the winter of 1845-6. But we have been unable to collect any evidence tending to fix the exact time at which the occurrence took place.

Under the vigilant supervision of Signor Garcia, it was impossible that Mdlle. Lind could relapse into the errors which had already cost her so dear; for she had now a guide upon whose experience she could unhesitatingly rely. Signor Garcia's claim to rank as the greatest singing-master of the present century, was, even then, and still is, incontestable. In fact he fills, in the vocal school of the nineteenth century, the place that was so nobly filled, in that of the eighteenth, by Niccolo Porpora. Not only do many of the greatest vocalists of the age owe their mastery over the art, and their brilliant and well-earned reputation, to his judicious training; but many more, unable to benefit by his personal instruction, have nevertheless benefited largely by his experience. For, his researches into the mechanism of the human voice, his discoveries with the laryngoscope, and the clear-sighted intelligence with which he has turned those discoveries to account, have placed the art of singing upon a sounder physiological basis than it has ever previously been able to claim. The vocalist can now study, with certainty, phenomena which, at the beginning of this century, were either totally misunderstood, or, at best, regarded as mysterious possibilities; and the advantage accruing to technical science from the knowledge thus patiently acquired, and intelligently utilised, is incalculable.

The lessons appear to have begun about the twenty-fifth, or twenty-sixth of August; and to have been continued, twice a week, from that period, until the month of July, 1842.

Mdlle. Lind thus describes her first introduction to the new system, in a letter to her friend, Fröken Marie Ruckman :—

" I have already had five lessons from Signor Garcia, the brother of Madame Malibran. I have to begin again, from the beginning; to sing scales, up and down, slowly, and with great care ; then, to practise the shake—awfully slowly ; and, to try to get rid of the hoarseness, if possible. Moreover,

I 2

he is very particular about the breathing. I trust I have
made a happy choice. Anyhow, he is the best master;
and, expensive enough—twenty francs for an hour. But,
what does that signify, if only he can teach me to sing?
Mdlle. Nissen has been his pupil, now, for two years, and
has made immense progress." *

A fortnight later, she writes to Madame Lindblad :—

"I am well satisfied with my singing-master. With
regard to my weak points, especially, he is excellent. I
think it very fortunate for me that there exists a Garcia.
And I believe him, also, to be a very good man. If he
takes but little notice of us, apart from his lessons—well!
—that cannot be helped; but I am very much pleased,
nay! enchanted with him as a teacher." †

And, again, to Herr Expeditionschef Forsberg :—

"Paris, February 1, 1842.

"Garcia's method is the best, of our time; and the one
which all here are striving to follow."

And, it is pleasant to know that the *Maestro* was
equally well pleased with his pupil, who, in a still later
letter, writes :—

"Paris, March 7, 1842.

"You know, to-day, four years ago, I made my *début* in
Der Freischütz.—No! five years ago, I mean. No! it is
four, I think.—Well! yes! I do not know.—Anyhow, it
was on the 7th of March." ‡
"My singing is getting on quite satisfactorily, now. I

* From a letter to Fröken Marie Ruckman. (Paris, September 10,
1841.) For the rest of the letter, see Chap. V., page 134.
† Letter to Madame Lindblad. (Paris, September 26, 1841.) From
the collection of letters in the Lindblad family, kindly furnished by
Madame Grandinson (*née* Lindblad).
‡ The *début* really took place on March 7, 1838; *i.e.* "four years ago."
See pp. 55–57.

rejoice heartily in my voice; it is clear, and sonorous, with more firmness, and much greater agility. A great, great deal still remains to be done; but the worst is over. Garcia is satisfied with me."

We may readily believe that Signor Garcia was more than "satisfied" with a pupil so apt to learn, and so well able to profit by the instruction she received. So swift was her comprehension, that she learned without knowing it. In all save that which concerned the mechanical basis of her art, her unerring musical instinct taught her far more than the greatest of living masters could impart to her. Of the management of the breath, the production of the voice, the blending of its registers, and a thousand other technical details upon which the most perfect of singers depends, in great measure, for success, she knew nothing—and, but for Signor Garcia, in all probability never would have known anything. But, of that which concerned the higher life of her art, neither Signor Garcia nor any one else could teach her anything at all. She evidently felt this, herself; for, long years afterwards, she wrote :—

"The greater part of what I can do in my art, I have myself acquired, by incredible labour, in spite of astonishing difficulties. By Garcia alone have I been taught some few important things. God had so plainly written within me what I had to study; my ideal was, and is, so high, that I could find no mortal who could in the least degree satisfy my demands. Therefore I sing after no one's method—only, as far as I am able, after that of the birds; for, their Master was the only one who came up to my demands for truth, clearness, and expression." *

But, though thus dependent upon her own natural genius for the high qualities which placed her above the greatest of her contemporaries in everything which concerned her

* From the letter to the Swedish *Biographical Lexicon* already quoted. See pp. 17-20.

loftiest aspirations in the realm of Art, she was none the less grateful to Signor Garcia for the "few important things" which gave her her first practical insight into the *technique* of singing—an insight, without which, as she herself felt, she would never have been able to bring her own great artistic ideal to perfection.

CHAPTER III.

THE STUDENT.

FOR some few weeks after her first interview with Signor Garcia, and her subsequent entrance upon a course of regular study under his guidance, Mademoiselle Lind continued to reside with Madame Ruffiaques. She found the society of her fellow *pensionnaires* very pleasant; and she was treated with unvarying kindness by the whole circle, during the time that she remained with them. But she soon awoke to the conviction that a boarding-house was scarcely a fitting place for continuous and undisturbed study; and—a still more serious consideration—she found that the terms for board and lodging were too high for her slender means. It was really necessary that she should go to a cheaper and a more convenient home; but the removal was not effected without tears on either side. The Ruffiaques had been so kind to her, and had liked her so much; and she felt that their good will had been of real service to her. Madame Ruffiaques cried bitterly when she left, saying that they had all "hoped for a longer stay on her part," and "could scarcely have believed such dignity of conduct possible in a young person coming alone to Paris;" * speaking with such evident emotion that it was impossible to doubt her truthfulness. But it was indispensable that the step should be taken. Towards the close of October, therefore, she removed to the house of Mademoiselle du Puget; a lady, who, though not a Swede by

* From a private letter.

birth, had, at any rate, been educated in Sweden, was thoroughly
Swedish in all her thoughts and habits, and had familiarised
the French with the literature of Sweden by her excellent
translations of many well-known Swedish works—circumstances of no small importance in the eyes of an exile whose
heart was continually yearning for her beloved country, and
who seemed incapable of being thoroughly happy while
absent from it.

Though a pleasant, and, in many ways, a sympathetic
companion, Mademoiselle du Puget was not free from certain
amusing peculiarities which Mademoiselle Lind occasionally
described with genuine good humour. In a letter to Madame
Lindblad, dated, 'Paris, November 26, 1841,' she narrates an
amusing little episode :—

"You must know that I am beginning to be an ape—a
fact of which I was not aware until yesterday. I was singing
to Mademoiselle du Puget, and she seemed a little bit
surprised when, just once or twice, I displayed all my powers
—*you* know what I mean—and she looked at me as if she
had not given me credit for this. (Mademoiselle du Puget—
you must know—is a person who has heard all the great
artists, and is herself musical.) First, I sang 'in Persiani's
style,' and then 'in Grisi's'; and she was kind enough to say
it was excellently *imitated*—'could not, in fact, be better.'
The compliment was rather hard to digest. I was so ashamed,
that, for a long while, I could not look up. But, after a
considerable pause, I asked, 'Do you really think so?'—with
a feeling of pride which my look—even the look of my back
—must surely have reflected. God help me! I am so proud
that I cannot bear people to tell me I 'imitate.' I loathe
the very word to such an extent that I cannot conceive what
its inventor was thinking of! It seems to me, that to take
what is another's, and use it for one's self, and then to make
believe that it is one's own, is positively to steal. But, I
seize so quickly the impression of what is good, or bad, that
I should not feel surprised if I have caught something from
the Italian Opera, which I have already visited pretty frequently. But be this as it may, the reminiscences I am
carrying away from the Italian Opera here are much better

than those connected with Stockholm and the school and
style that prevail there ? " *

But Mademoiselle Lind was not deprived of the companionship of critics better able than Mademoiselle du Puget
to appreciate her talents at their true value. Her most
intimate friend, at this period, was Mademoiselle Henrietta
Nissen,† who was also a pupil of Garcia, and a great favourite
with the master. The two talented young vocalists frequently
sang together; and, before long, a feeling of generous rivalry
sprang up between them, which must have been of infinite
advantage to both. Mademoiselle Lind thus describes her
young friend in a letter to Madame Lindblad :—

        " Paris, August 19, 1841.

" Yesterday I went to see Mademoiselle Nissen, to whom
I go pretty often; and we sang to one another. She has
a beautiful voice. Still, I think I agree with what
Adolf‡ once said—'it is getting a little thin in the upper
notes.' But, notwithstanding this, it is a splendid voice.
In future we are going to have music together at Herr
Blumm's." §

The meetings at Herr Blumm's became an institution. A
month later, she writes :—

        " Paris, September 19, 1841.

" I am just expecting Philippe— ‖ not King Philippe !—
who is going to take me to Herr Blumm's, where Mademoiselle Nissen is waiting for us, with an old relative of hers ;
and we four are going somewhere into the country for the

---

 * From the Lindblad letters.
 † Afterwards, Madame Siegfried Saloman.
 ‡ Herr Lindblad.
 § From the Lindblad letters.
 ‖ Philippe was an old servant of Herr Blumm's, who, with his characteristic kindness and courtesy, sent him to attend Madame Lind to and
from her lessons with Garcia. Philippe was said to be the model of an
old French servant of the period, and it was said of him, *Tel maître,
tel valet.*

day. She is a very sweet girl. I am really glad to have made her acquaintance. The divine song draws us to each other." *

And, again :—

"Paris, September 26, 1841.

"Mademoiselle Nissen, whom I have already mentioned to you, is an extremely nice sweet girl. She lives in the same house as Garcia; so I look in upon her, every time I take my lesson." †

But there were other bonds of sympathy between them, besides those cemented by their mutual love for " the divine song." When Christmas drew near, Mademoiselle Lind's heart was torn by yearnings for home. As the time approached she wrote to Madame Lindblad :—

"Paris, December 9, 1841.

"Do you know what I am doing, besides writing to you? I am munching away—at what ?—just guess?—at a bit of genuine Swedish *Knäckebröd*,‡ which Herr Blumm has brought me. . . . . Ah! think of me, when you go to the *Julotta*,§ for it is the most glorious thing your poor Jenny knows of." ‖

And again :—

"Paris, December 16, 1841.

"Ah! who? who will light the Christmas Tree for my mother? No one; no one! She has no child who can bring her the least pleasure. If you knew how she is ever before me! how constantly she is in my thoughts! how she gives me courage to work! how I love her, as I never loved her before!" ¶

* From the Lindblad letters.
† *Ib.*
‡ A kind of rye bread, baked in large thin round cakes, with a hole in the middle, by which they are hung up in bundles, and thus kept crisp and fresh for a long time.
§ The early service, on Christmas Day. *Jul* means Christmas (Yule), and *otta*, 8 o'clock.
‖ From the Lindblad letters.
¶ *Ib.*

And, in the midst of this cruel burst of home-sickness, good Mademoiselle du Puget bethought her of an expedient, of which we hear in another letter, written four days after Christmas :—

"Paris, December 29, 1841.

"Christmas Eve passed off better than I expected ; for, Mademoiselle du Puget went to fetch the dear sweet Nissen, and, all of a sudden, as I was standing in my room alone, she came creeping in to me. We sang duets together —but my thoughts strayed homewards." *

It is beautiful, as the time progresses, to mark the utter absence of jealousy which characterised this rare artistic friendship between two young students, each of whom had a reputation to ensure, and a name to render famous. Though Mademoiselle Lind had already established a brilliant reputation in Sweden, Mademoiselle Nissen was, nevertheless, far in advance of her on the road to European honours—or, at least, it must have seemed so to both of them. On the 26th of November, 1841, Signor Garcia gave a "grand *soirée*" in her honour. She was to be the star of the evening. Several hundred people were invited to meet her ; and it was arranged that she should sing not only alone, but also with the support of a chorus. Mademoiselle Lind was among the invited guests, and, it was arranged that Mademoiselle du Puget should accompany her ; but, not one thought of envy passed through her mind. She spoke of nothing but her friend's success. Four months later, her generosity was put to a still sterner test. On April 3, 1842, she writes :—

"Do you know that Nissen is just upon the point of concluding an engagement for three years at the Italian Opera ? For the first year, she is offered four thousand riksdaler banco ;† and, when the three years are over, she will, no doubt, be able to command from sixty to seventy thousand

* From the Lindblad letters.
† Equal to 8,000 francs ; or £320 sterling.

riksdaler banco * per annum.   Ah, yes ! God help her ! She
is a nice good girl.   Yet, notwithstanding all this, I am
contented with my own lot, and would not change with
any one, though my prospects for the future are poor, and
dark." †

And again on May 1 :—

"I am not depressed on Mademoiselle Nissen's account.
Ah, no ! Besides, how foolish it would be not to stand aside
for a merit greater than my own—and this I do.   Thank
God ! I feel no jealousy, and—shall I tell you ?—it is true
that I can never get her voice ; but I am quite satisfied with
my own.   And, furthermore, I shall be able, in time, to learn
all that she knows ; but she can never learn what I know.
Do you understand ?   She is a nice girl ; and, with all my
heart, I wish her every happiness.   Her stay here is of great
advantage to me, for she spurs me on." ‡

In truth, every brilliant manifestation of real talent served
only to spur Mademoiselle Lind on to still greater exertions
on her own account.   She was a constant attendant at the
Italian Opera ; and recorded her impressions of the principal
performers with the most perfect frankness.   In one letter
she writes :—

"Oh ! if you could have heard Madame Persiani sing in
La Sonnambula, yesterday !   Oh ! oh ! it was beautiful !"

Of Grisi, though she admired her greatly as an actress, she
spoke less enthusiastically ; and, especially, of her shake,
which, she said, was not good.   The shake was certainly not
one of Madame Grisi's strongest points.   Indeed, this particular grace was then but very little cultivated in the Italian
School,   from   an   idea—entirely   fallacious,   though   very

---

* It is possible that this may be a *lapsus calami,* for "six to seven
thousand"—*i.e.* 12,000 to 14,000 francs, or £480 to £560.   The larger sum
seems improbable, to the last degree.

† From the Lindblad letters.

‡ *Ib.*

generally entertained—that its frequent practice was deleterious to the voice.

But Mademoiselle Lind's observations were not confined
to the Italian Opera, or to singing alone. She was a great
admirer of Mademoiselle Rachel; and studied her performances with peculiar interest. In one of her letters she
writes :—

"Paris, October 24, 1841.

"There is a remarkable dearth of good actresses here.
Mademoiselle Rachel is the only one—after her, Grisi." *

And again :—

"Paris, November 20, 1841.

"Shall I tell you my thoughts? The difference between
Mademoiselle Rachel and myself is, that she can be splendid
when angry, but she is unsuited for tenderness. I am
desperately ugly, and nasty too, when in anger; but I think
I do better in tender parts. Of course, I do not compare
myself with Rachel. Certainly not. She is immeasurably
greater than I. Poor me!" †

It is evident from this, that, while striving, with all her
might, to master the technical difficulties of singing under
the guidance of Signor Garcia, Mademoiselle Lind never, for
a moment, forgot the importance of the dramatic element.
Indeed, her letters prove that, though she sought no instruction in this from any one, she was for ever endeavouring to
perfect her own ideal; observing others, but always thinking
for herself, and trusting to herself alone for the final result.
Her correspondence teems with observations which show
how constantly her thoughts were dwelling upon this important point. In one more than ordinarily interesting
letter, she writes :—

"Paris, October 24, 1841.

"I am longing for home. I am longing for my theatre.
I have never said this before, in any of my letters. I know
I am contradicting myself, but I rejoice over it. Oh! to

* From the Lindblad letters.
† *Ib.*

pour out my feelings in a beautiful part! This is, and ever
will be, my continual aim; and, until I stand there again, I
shall not know myself as I really am. Life on the stage has
in it something so fascinating, that I think, having once
tasted it, one can never feel truly happy away from it,
especially when one has given oneself wholly up to it, with
life and soul, as I have done. This has been my joy, my
pride, my glory! True, it is a great thing to be free from all
the worries connected with it; but, when I return home, I
know not what people could have to reproach me with.
Then the die will be cast; and I shall not change very much
for the better after that, I suppose—and, consequently things
will be different." *

Later on she writes :—

"Paris, March 7, 1842.

"Sometimes I act by myself; and it seems to me that I
have gained more feeling, more *verve*, more truth in my
rendering; at least, I feel, now, better than I used to do,
what life really is. It is just possible that I may not act as
well as before; but I do not think so. Nobody acts as I act.
What do you say to such language as this? But, you will
not misunderstand me." †

But there were moments of doubt, bordering sometimes
almost upon despondency. On one occasion she says :—

"Paris, May 30, 1842.

"Then Garcia pretends to believe that I shall never more
act in tragic parts! ‡ What do you think of that? I leave
him to say what he pleases. In the meantime, may God
preserve me from being altogether bewildered! I do not
think there is any danger. I acted ' *Norma*,' this morning,
and it was not much worse than at Stockholm." §

In the midst of these alternations of hope and anxiety, the
studies were interrupted, for a moment, by a sudden shock

* From the Lindblad letters.

† *Ib.*

‡ Possibly, Mademoiselle Lind's idea of tragedy may have differed from
Signor Garcia's. On such a point, the Scandinavian and the Keltic
temperament were scarcely likely to be in very close accordance.

§ From the Lindblad letters.

—a merciful escape from an accident so full of horror and death, that one almost shudders, even now, at the imminence of the danger, after reading the letter in which it is described.

On the 8th of May, the Baroness Schwerin accompanied Mademoiselle Lind on an excursion to Versailles.

Herr Blumm was anxious that the party should return to Paris by a train which would give them an opportunity of passing through some very beautiful scenery on their way home. But, that very morning, the Préfet de Police offered the Baroness a box at one of the theatres. In order to render this available, the plans were changed at the last moment; and it was not until after their return, that the little party of friends learned that the train by which they intended to travel had been wrecked by the bursting of the boiler, and that, of the four hundred persons who were injured by the explosion, one hundred were either scalded to death or cut to pieces, in a manner too horrible for description.

Mademoiselle Lind's account of the occurrence shows that it affected her, very deeply indeed. But her nature was not of the weak type which is rendered unfit for exertion by a sudden fear, however great may have been its effect at the moment; and her subsequent letters show that after the first burst of thankfulness was over, she was at work again as heartily as ever, thinking no amount of labour too great for the attainment of the end she had in view, and upon which she felt that all her hope of future success depended. She had come to Paris to work; and she left nothing undone which could, even in the slightest degree, tend to perfect her in the art to which every energy of her life was uncompromisingly devoted.

CHAPTER IV.

WITHIN SIGHT OF THE GOAL.

MDLLE. LIND's course of study, under Signor Garcia, lasted
ten months, from the 26th or 27th of August, 1841, to the
end of June 1842—by which time she had learned all that
it was possible for any master to teach her.

The result for which she had so ardently longed, so
patiently waited, so perseveringly laboured, was attained at
last. Her voice, no longer suffering from the effect of the
cruel fatigue, and the inordinate amount of over-exertion
which had so lately endangered, not merely its well-being,
but its very existence, had now far more than recovered its
pristine vigour *—it had acquired a rich depth of tone, a
sympathetic *timbre*, a birdlike charm in the silvery clearness
of its upper register, which at once impressed the listener
with the feeling that he had never before heard anything in
the least degree resembling it. No human organ is perfect.
It is quite possible that other voices may have possessed
qualities which this did not; for voices of exceptional
beauty are nearly always characterised by an individuality
of *timbre* or expression which forms by no means the least
potent of their attractions. The natural flexibility of the
Contessa de' Rossi's voice was phenomenal. Mdlle. Alboni's
involuntary *vibrato* breathed a languid tenderness of
passion which could never have been attained by any

---

* The last mention of the chronic hoarseness is found in a letter,
written on the 1st of May, 1842.

amount of study.   But, the listener never stopped to analyse
the qualities of Mdlle. Lind's voice, the marked individuality
of which set analysis at defiance. By turns, full, sympathetic,
tender, sad, or brilliant, it adapted itself so perfectly to the
artistic conception of the song it was interpreting, that
singer, voice, and song, were one.   Time had been,
when, from sheer lack of technical knowledge, she had
been unable to give expression to her high ideal; when
her method was as yet too unformed for the utterance
of her grand conception of the parts of *Agatha* and
Euryanthe, of *Pamina* and *Donna Anna*, of *La Vestale* and
Alice, and *Amina* and *Norma* and *Lucia ;* all of which
she had already sung, in Stockholm, and felt deeply, and
made her hearers feel, by resistless force of sympathy
alone, though every one had fallen short of the perfect
artistic interpretation which can only be attained when
the poetry of the mental conception is supported by an
amount of technical skill equal to its demands.   But this
time had passed away, for ever.   Her voice was now so
completely under command, that its obedience to every
changing phase of the singer's thoughts, to every demand of
the composer's genius, was absolute, and instantaneous.   All
the technical perfection that could be attained by unlimited perseverance, under the guidance of an enlightened
teacher, she had gained since her arrival in Paris; the
rest she had always possessed, for it was part of herself.
She was born an artist; and, under Garcia's guidance, had
now become a *virtuosa*.   The scales, sung "slowly up and
down, with great care," and the "awfully slow shake," had
borne abundant fruit.   Followed by exercises of a more
advanced character, they had resulted in producing a facility
of execution which serves materially to strengthen our faith
in the legendary stories told of Farinelli and " Il Porporino,"
Signore Strada, and Cuzzoni, and Faustina, the Cavaliere

Nicolini, and other marvellous vocalists of the eighteenth century, whose feats of skill have been described by admiring contemporaries in such terms of rapture, that one class of modern critics has been tempted to reject the whole story as a gross exaggeration, while another school would have us believe that the art of vocalisation, as practised in that golden age, is lost beyond all possibility of recovery. There is no logical necessity for the acceptance of either of these trenchant theories. The music written for, and sung by, those giants of a bygone age proves that the stories told of their marvellous power are in nowise exaggerated.* And, the assumption that the art has been lost is absurd. The method may have been neglected, and temporarily forgotten. We do not deny that. But there is not—or ought not to be —the possibility of such a thing as a "lost art." What has been done once can be done again. And it would be difficult, in the face of the *Cadenze* given in the Appendix contributed to this work by Mr. Goldschmidt, to imagine any *tour de force*—whether involving difficulty of intonation, or rapidity of execution, prolonged sustaining-power, or contrasts

---

* Handel wrote passages, in *Riccardo Primo*, for the Cavaliere Nicolini, which no singer now living could execute; and scarcely less trying divisions, in *Ariadne*, and other Operas, for Carestini, and Signora Strada, and Senesino. The Operas of Porpora, and Hasse, abound with similar passages for Farinelli, and "Il Porporino," Faustina, and their great contemporaries of the Italian School. No one now attempts to grapple with these monstrous *tours de force*; but Mdlle. Lind proved them to be still attainable by exceptional talent, supplemented by equally exceptional perseverance. Had Edison's Phonograph been invented, in the time of Farinelli, we should have been left in no doubt as to our estimate of the powers possessed by the leading singers of the eighteenth century, as compared with those of the nineteenth. When the instrument is brought to absolute perfection, this question will be one of very easy solution; since the critics of the twentieth century will be able to report upon the performances of vocalists now living, as clearly as the musical reporter is able, now, to describe them on the day after they have taken place.

obtainable by apparently unlimited exercise of the *messa di voce*—of which Mdlle. Lind was incapable after the completion of her course of study. One great secret—perhaps the greatest of all—the key to the whole mystery connected with this perfect mastery over the technical difficulties of vocalisation—lay in the fortunate circumstance, that Signor Garcia was so "very particular about the breathing." For the skilful management of the breath is everything; and she attained the most perfect control over it. Gifted by nature with comparatively limited sustaining power, she learned to fill the lungs with such dexterity, that, except with her consent, it was impossible to detect, either the moment at which the breath was renewed, or the method by which the action was accomplished. We say, "except with her consent," because, on the stage, there are moments when, for dramatic effect, the act of breathing has itself a rhetorical, or, in extreme cases, even a passionate significance; when the correct delivery of the words demands that breath should be taken, without any attempt at disguise, in accordance with the grammatical punctuation of the text; and of this means of expression she fully appreciated the value. But, where pure vocalisation was concerned, and unbroken continuity became an imperious artistic necessity, the moment at which the lungs were replenished remained as profound a secret as it did in the performances of Rubini—who, fortunately for him, possessed a much greater natural capacity for abundant inspiration, and had therefore a less amount of difficulty to overcome in bringing his art to the ineffable perfection he so well succeeded in attaining. The result was the same in both cases; but, in the one, it was materially aided by a happy physical organisation, while, in the other, it was wholly the effect of art—an art which, though possible to all, is so difficult to acquire, that, through want, in most cases, of the necessary perseverance, not one singer out of a hundred succeeds in attaining it, even in a moderate degree.*

With these rare powers at command, Mdlle. Lind was able, without effort, to give expression to every phase of the artistic conception which she had formed by the exercise of innate genius. Her acting, as we have seen, in former chapters, had grown up with her from her infancy, and formed part of her inmost being. She had found no one in Paris capable of teaching her anything that could improve that, though she thought it necessary to take lessons in deportment; Dramatic Art she had studied for herself; she had gained experience by observation of others; with fearless modesty, she had measured her own powers against those of Mdlle. Rachel, and dared to tell herself what she believed to be the truth, with regard to their comparative merits; she had acted the part of *Norma* to herself, and calmly passed judgment upon her own performance; she had carefully thought out the matter, and the acting and the singing had

---

* Signor Frederic Lablache once told a friend of the writer, that, when singing, on one occasion, with Rubini, in the *Matrimonio Segreto*, he held the great tenor's hand in his own, during a passage in the famous duet, and, at the same time, looked him full in the face, without being able to detect the act of breathing in the least degree. This wonderful power of concealment led the vulgar to believe that Rubini could sing, during the act of inspiration! Of course, it was simply the triumph of consummate art, misunderstood only by those who were ignorant of the first principles of singing. An absurd story was even invented, to the effect that he, who never forced a note, and whose vocal registers were more perfectly equalised, more delicately blended into one than those of any other tenor that ever existed, once broke his collar-bone in the attempt to deliver a mighty *Si de poitrine* by aid of a violent effort of clavicular breathing! He was just as likely to have broken his neck; much more likely to have displaced the odontoid process of the axis vertebra, and fallen dead on the spot. Yet, to this day, the story is cited as an instance of the dangers of a vicious method of filling the lungs: a proof that the study of breathing is still recognised as a necessary part of the singer's education, though few understand its value as it was understood by the two great artists of whom we are speaking.

become so closely interwoven with each other, that they naturally united in the formation of one single conception. Each part as she interpreted it to herself was a consistent whole, dramatic and musical, breathing poetry and romance from beginning to end; yet, as true to nature as she was herself, and no longer fettered by the fatal technical weakness which had so long stood between the ideal and its perfect realisation. There was no weakness now. The artist was complete.

CHAPTER V.

UNDER WHICH KING?

AND now arose the crucial question—should the finished
artist make her *début* in Paris?—or, should she return, at
once, to Sweden, and reappear, in all the glory of her newly-
acquired powers, in her beloved Stockholm?

There were arguments to be brought forward, on both sides.
The problem was no new one. It had frequently been discussed; but her own feeling on the subject was very strong
indeed. She could not reconcile herself to Paris. She
despised its frivolity, its selfishness, its restless love of
excitement, and its lust for gold; and recoiled, with horror,
from its shameless vice. From the very first, she had
suspected the hollowness of its social organisation. As
early as the 10th of September, 1841, she had written to her
friend, Fröken Marie Ruckman :—

"MY BEST FRIEND,—

"There might be much to say about Paris, but I put
it off until I am better able to judge. This much, however,
I will say at once, that, if good is sometimes to be found, an
immeasurable amount of evil is to be found also. But, I
believe it to be an excellent school for any one with discernment enough to separate the rubbish from that which is
worth preserving—though this is no easy task. To my mind,
the worst feature of Paris is, its dreadful selfishness, its greed
for money. There is nothing to which the people will not
submit, for the sake of gain. Applause, here, is not always
given to talent; but, often enough, to vice—to any obscure
person who can afford to pay for it. Ugh! It is too dread-

ful to see the *claqueurs* sitting at the theatre, night after
night, deciding the fate of those who are compelled to appear
—a terrible manifestation of original sin !"

To Madame Lindblad, some six weeks later, she writes :—

" Paris, October 24, 1841.

" All idea of appearing here in public has vanished.   To
begin with—I myself never relied upon it ; but people said
so many silly things about ' just one peformance,' that, at
last, I began to feel as if I were in duty bound to try.   But,
monstrous and unconquerable difficulties are in the way.   In
any case, I want to go home again.   But, if I can arrange to sing
at a concert, before leaving, I will do so ; in order that I may
not return home without having at least done something." *

Three months later, in a letter dated February the 1st,
1842, and addressed to Herr Expeditionschef Forsberg (who
controlled the Dramatic School attached to the R. Theatre
at Stockholm at the time at which Jenny was numbered
among its pupils), we find her dwelling touchingly on her
desire to consecrate her talents to her native country.

" I came hither," she says, " because I felt my talent too
insignificant.   I knew, indeed, that it was not really so.
But, having no one to consult but my dear Herr Berg—who
was miserable at his inability to help me through with my
incessant work—I resolved simply to break off, and to take
two years' leave of absence.

" I am gifted by Nature ; and to that I am indebted for a
certain amount of success : but, Art, I did not know, even
by name.   I felt this bitterly ; and it made me receive the
applause of the public with sorrow, rather than with joy : for,
I felt that I did not deserve it.   I knew that I had not made
myself worthy of it, through my own work.   Ah ! I was
right !   I was perfectly right !   God does all for the best ;
that I know.   I was guided by a Higher Hand, when I embarked on the *Scithiod* † *en route* for Paris.   I am working on,
now ; have made progress ; and—need I say it—if they want

---

* From the Lindblad letters.

† This is a slip of the pen.   It was the *Gauthiod*.   See p. 105.

to hear me again, in my Sweden, with what joy will I not hasten thither! I have only made these sacrifices, in order that I may become worthy of the public; and, if I do not succeed, I shall, at all events, have satisfied my artist's conscience.

"Therefore, Herr Expeditionschef, if I can only learn to sing, and if my presence is not felt to be quite superfluous, I shall certainly return, in a year and a half—quite certainly—but, not if I meet with coldness, or am regarded as altogether unnecessary. I am almost afraid of that. Elma Ström has everything in her favour, which I have against me. She has a much softer and better voice to work with than I ever had, during the whole time of my working period. She ought, therefore, to sing very well. The actress, probably, will come later on. I do not wish to stand in her way, or in the way of any one. Rather than that, I would settle down here to give singing-lessons; for Garcia's method is the best of our time, and every one, here, is striving to follow it. But, in any case, I shall come home, in order that people may hear what progress I have made—if I really have made any. Will they accept me, and give me a suitable engagement? If so, I shall remain. If not, I shall go abroad again. And yet!—my Sweden! my Stockholm! All that is dearest to me on earth is there—two people, for whom I would give my life, if they asked for it, and apart from whom I could not spend an entire lifetime. But, my stay here has cost both money, and trouble. I have sacrificed everything, in the hope of acquiring a 'talent.' I hope, therefore, that I shall not be misunderstood; that people will not imagine that I have gone abroad with foolish conceited ideas about this little self of mine; but, that they will rather meet me with confidence and good-will. I shall then have no higher wish, than to go back to my dear theatre, and pour out my heart in song, to a beloved public.

"The Italian Opera! Oh! how lovely it is! What a rich time of enjoyment for me! and the concerts of the Conservatoire! *Mon Dieu!* They are the best of all! They are perfectly divine! But, apart from them, there is much here that is very far indeed from divine. And this is well. For, we human creatures might possibly be unable to bear it, unmixed. I dare say it would be so.

"But, ah, me! what a long letter I am inflicting upon you. Shall I be pardoned? I will finish directly: but, I

wanted to tell you that I am living with a certain Mdlle.
du Puget, who was educated in Sweden, and is Swedish,
to the heart's core; and, that I am doing well. I have
had my crying days, and many longing moments; but I
am fairly wise, and work with a will.

"Herr Blumm is quite indefatigable in his goodness to
me, and takes care of me, like the kindest brother; so that I
have nothing to complain of, except—where is my Sweden?
Where are my friends? Do they still remember me? Shall
I be welcome, when I return? What do you think, Herr
Expeditionschef?

"May the future for yourself and your family be as happy
and prosperous as is the most sincere wish of

"Your ever grateful,

"JENNY LIND."

When the time for arriving at a decision began to draw
near, she wrote to Madame Lindblad:—

"Paris, April 3, 1842.

"I dare not tell you how I long for home! I dare not tell
you how far from happy I feel, here! but, there is one thing
in your letter that really frightens me. You say, that, if I
come back, without having previously appeared in public,
here, they will say I was not fit for it, however well I may
sing. Ho! ho! what will happen, then? It might, perhaps,
be better for me to engage myself somewhere as nursery-
maid; for it is a very difficult thing to appear, here, in public.
On the stage it would be out of the question. It could only
be in the concert-room: and there I am at my weakest point,
and shall always remain so. What is wanted here is—'admirers.' Were I inclined to receive them, all would be
smooth sailing. But there I say—STOP!

"To sing, without a name, is difficult; for, here, everything
depends upon the accessories. It matters not how little
talent there may be. My position is, indeed, a hard one!
If only I belonged to a country having more self-confidence
when passing judgment on its own artists, then, all would be
well. But, the misfortune is, that they never believe in
themselves. However, I have never said that I should appear

in public, though others have. Besides, God will certainly
help me! I needed a course of exercises—and the rest I
leave in the Lord's hands.

"With regard to my acting, I can compete with any one
out here. But, there are many other things that I lack.
Should there be any who think it worth while to envy me,
how contented will they not be, when they see me quietly
disembark at the Stockholm Skeppsbro, while Nissen will
soon be *prima donna* at the Italian Opera. I do not understand how it is that this takes no effect upon me! For my
part, I only want to go home."*

A week later she wrote to her father:—

"Paris, April 10, 1842.
"GODE PAPPA!—

"So many thanks for your last letter. I see, from it,
that you and Mamma are well. It gives me no slight comfort to know this; and I should be even better satisfied, if I
were also to learn that you prosper in your country home.

"As yet, my dear Pappa, I have not grown particularly
stout; but, what I shall be, when I grow old, I cannot tell.
However, I trust the Lord will save me from being obliged
to sing on the stage, until my life's end; and then, I shall
rest tranquil.

"Apropos of the Opera! I wonder when I shall next be
allowed to show myself 'on the boards,' as the term is. I
clearly see—yes, I do see, Pappa—that I am born to stand
on them. God grant that I may always stand 'on firm feet,'
as Gelhaar said.† In one respect, Pappa knows that I do.
In the other, I am in God's hands. Think only, if, when I
come home, I find no engagement!

"Yes, yes. 'Comes time, comes counsel.' Perhaps I may
have to sit on the Djurgårds Common, with a little money-
box in front of me, to gather in small contributions, and sing
while the day lasts—for, says the proverb, 'There is no day
so long that it has not its evening'—and, after that, I go to
my Father's bosom, to awake in a better land. And this is
surely the highest aim. It does not matter how one gets
there, so that one only does get there, somehow, and, 'he that

---

* From the Lindblad letters.
† Herr Gelhaar was a member of the Royal Orchestra at Stockholm.

humbleth himself shall be exalted,' says the Scripture.—But, be this as it may!

"I was obliged to act as I did; otherwise, the whole thing would have remained at a standstill with me. Perhaps I have not yet been quite forgotten—though I have some doubt about it: and, in that case, and if I have also made some progress, people may perhaps find pleasure in listening to me, when I come back again. I wish for nothing better than this.

"A concert was to have taken place, yesterday, at the Italian Opera. Rossini's *Stabat Mater*—his latest composition—was to have been given; and Nissen was to have sung in place of Grisi, who is away in London. But, the President of the Chamber of Deputies gave a concert instead, and, as this was attended by all the great people, nothing came of it—a very annoying thing for Nissen, for it would have been a good opportunity for her.

"*Adieu, lille Fader.* Write, if occasion offers, to your

"AFFECTIONATE DAUGHTER."

A letter addressed, on the same day, to Madame Lindblad, announces still greater indecision with regard to the future :—

"Paris, April 10, 1842.

"I am really anxious to see how a life, begun like mine, will end. Oh! what emptiness beyond description there is around me! An unwonted amount of courage is necessary, for prolonging my stay here for another year. But I need this, for several reasons. This journey has altogether changed me. The foundation of the building was tolerably safe, and needed no pulling down. But, the superstructure! —this has crumbled away, through not having been better put together." *

The spirit which pervades these letters is unmistakable; and clearly shows Mdlle. Lind's own feeling, with regard to the critical question, on the settlement of which her artistic destiny seemed now mainly to depend.

But, she was not, and could not possibly be, the only, or

* From the Lindblad letters.

even the best judge, of what was best for her. From the very nature of the case, she was placed very much at the mercy of others, who, moved by feelings of friendship, or self-interest, as the case might be, took an active part in the discussion; and it was mainly through their intervention that the question was solved with the results which we propose to describe in our next chapter.

CHAPTER VI.

THE RETURN.

On the 24th of May, 1842, while Mdlle. Lind was still tortured by doubts as to the best course to follow, in this difficult crisis, the Directors of the Royal Theatre at Stockholm sent her the offer of a definite and official engagement— or rather re-engagement—at the Opera-House in which her early triumphs had been achieved. It must be confessed, that the terms proposed by the *Direktion* were more in accordance with her former *status* at the Royal Theatre, than with that which was the just due of the great artist she had now become. The engagement was to last either one, or two years; from the 1st of July, 1842, to the same date, in 1843, or 1844—the longest period for which an engagement was legally possible. The salary was fixed at 1800 *riksdaler banco, per annum*—equal to about £150, in English money; with the privilege of an extra "benefit"; and "extra service-money, according to the regulations of the Royal Theatre," for each appearance; the necessary "silk costumes and bridal gowns" being provided at the expense of the management. In return for these emoluments, Mdlle. Lind was engaged to submit, in all things, to the regulations laid down for the direction of the Royal Theatre, in the year 1839; but she was permitted to extend her stay abroad, until September, 1842, without diminution of salary, as a compensation for the expenses connected with her home journey.

To this not very tempting offer, she replied, as follows :—

" Paris, June 6, 1842.

" I have had the honour to receive the Royal Direction's flattering offer of an engagement, for one or two years, from the 1st of July, 1842, at the Royal Theatre of Stockholm, and hasten to submit my humble answer.

" Although the period which I intended to devote to my studies abroad does not terminate until next year, and, therefore, an earlier return home will either interrupt these studies, or entail redoubled efforts for the accomplishment of the course on which I have entered, I feel not disinclined to accept the offer of the Royal Direction, for two years ; but, well remembering the rather too heavy service to which I had to submit in former times, at the Royal Theatre, and from the evil consequences of which I am still suffering, I am compelled to attach the following conditions to my engagement, viz. :—

" (i.) That, while enjoying the salary, benefices, and other advantages proposed by the Royal Direction, I shall not be obliged to appear in more than fifty representations during the season.

" (ii.) That an extra fee of 66 *Rdr.*, 32 *sk.*,* *Banco,* may be granted to me for each representation over and above the said fifty, during the season.

" (iii.) That the representations be so arranged, as not to compel my appearance more than twice during the week

" (iv.) That leave of absence be granted to me, from the 15th of June, to the 1st of October, in each year.

" I trust that the Royal Direction will appreciate the fairness of the above-named conditions, and will consider them as pardonable forethought with regard to my health and future, both of which are particularly uncertain, and difficult to ensure, by a dramatic artist, in Sweden.

" JENNY LIND." †

On the same day, she thus confided her difficulties to Madame Lindblad :—

---

* Rather less than £5 10s.

† Letter to the " Direction " of the Royal Theatre at Stockholm, kindly furnished by Herr Bureau-chef Alfred Grandinson.

"Paris, June 6, 1842.

"I have been offered an engagement at the theatre in Stockholm, and this has somewhat altered things. There is much to be said for, but much also against it. It seems to me that my demands are not exaggerated, when I propose to appear fifty times during the season, for 1800 *Rdr. Banco* in the form of salary, with extra money, etc.; while, for other evenings, beyond that number, they will have to give me, each time, 66 *Rdr.*, 32 *sk.*, *Banco*—the same as to Belletti. I shall not do it for less; so, if they do not agree to this—well and good!

"Adolf wished me to limit the number to forty; but I am dreadfully afraid of appearing presumptuous.

"So, it may happen that I come home in the autumn. What do you say to that? I rather long for home; and this offer, on the part of the Direction, will furnish a good opportunity for closing the mouths of those who might feel inclined to say something about my incapacity for another theatre." *

Herr Lindblad, who was in Paris, at this time, wrote to his wife :—

"Paris, June 1, 1842.

"Jenny has had an offer, from the Direction of the Royal Opera, to come home; and she seems inclined to accept it. If so, she will return, in the autumn. She does not care, at all, to appear here; nor are the circumstances tempting. She is bound up with Sweden, and asks for nothing better than to make her living there, and thus to give enjoyment to our people." †

This seems to imply that Herr Lindblad took no unfavourable view of the arrangement; yet when, in consequence of a letter from the Direction, dated June 20th, 1842, and agreeing to all Mdlle. Lind's conditions, the engagement was finally concluded, he wrote to Madame Lindblad :—

* From the Lindblad letters.
† *Ib.*

" Paris, July 4, 1842.

" Jenny has engaged herself at too small a salary. This she regrets, now, but it cannot be helped. Her love for Sweden, and the kind letter from the Director of the Opera, have dimmed her vision." *

And again :—

" Paris, Friday, July 15, 1842.

" I conducted Meyerbeer to Jenny, when she sang for him airs from *Roberto, Norma,* and several of my songs. He thought much of her voice, and wishes to take her to the Grand Opera-House, in order to hear how it would sound on the stage there ; for he believes that its carrying power would grow in the large room. †

And, again : —

" Paris, July 18, 1842.

" So it is, however, that, had Meyerbeer arrived here before Jenny accepted the engagement at Stockholm, she would probably not—unless tempted by home-sickness— have returned so soon to Sweden, for Meyerbeer was not against engaging her for Paris or Berlin. Not a soul has here done the least towards making her known. She has been living as in a convent.

" Still, she is not sorry to return home ; for, the greatest stage reputations are here won only through sacrificing honour and reputation. While the world is resounding with their praise, every *salon* is closed to them ; and this, even in easy-going Paris. Such homage as Jenny met with in Sweden, no foreign artist ever received. This, she feels ; and it is for this vivifying atmosphere that she is longing." ‡

As may well be supposed, Meyerbeer's influence was no unimportant factor in the arrangements which concerned the future. He had come to Paris, for the purpose of making preparations for the production of *Le Prophète*—which, however, through an accumulation of difficulties, was not really produced until the year 1849 ; he had there heard of Mdlle. Lind—probably, from Herr Lindblad ; and—as we gather from that gentleman's letter of the 15th of July—

* From the Lindblad Letters.   † *Ib.*   ‡ *Ib.*

had already heard her sing, in private. But he seems to have entertained doubts as to whether her voice was powerful enough to fill the *salle* of the Grand Opéra ; and, in order to satisfy himself on this point, he wished to hear her sing on the stage of the theatre itself. Whether, or not, Signor Garcia felt any doubts upon the subject, we do not know. On the 13th of June, Herr Lindblad had written :—

" On Saturday last, I met Garcia, and spoke to him about Jenny. He has found out that she has much *esprit*, and feeling ; but considers her voice still somewhat *fatiguée.*"

But, whatever Signor Garcia may have felt, it is quite certain that Meyerbeer was determined to carry his point ; and, that he made the necessary arrangements with M. Leon Pillet, then the Director of the Grand Opéra, for the gratification of his wish ; for, on the 22nd of July, he wrote (in German) to Herr Lindblad :—

" Honoured Sir,—

" I was unable to answer your kind letter, yesterday, as I found it impossible to speak to the Director of the Opéra. But I have since seen him, and have arranged that, to-morrow, Saturday, at two o'clock in the afternoon, precisely, a well-tuned pianoforte, and an accompanist, shall be in readiness, on the stage of the Opera, to accompany Mdlle. Lind in her songs.

" I have told the Director, that Mdlle. Lind wishes to bring with her six or eight persons with whom she is acquainted ; and orders have been given to the porter to admit them. The entrance, however, will not be from the Rue Lepelletier, as in the evening ; but, in the Rue Grangebatelière, No. 3, through the great gateway, on the left hand of the court.

" Begging you, honoured sir, to make my compliments to Mdlle. Lind, and in the hope of seeing you again to-morrow, at the Opéra, at two o'clock,

" Yours most sincerely,

" Meyerbeer." *

* From the Lindblad letters.

Of the proceedings which took place at this probationary meeting, no detailed account has been preserved. M. Castil-Blaze * tells us, that the pieces sung were, the three grand scenes from *Der Freischütz, Robert le Diable,* and *Norma;* but, as we shall presently see, his account of the occurrence is so glaringly incorrect, in other respects, that it is not safe to accept any part of it. Herr Lindblad, however, has described his impressions; briefly enough, it is true, but, in language which may be accepted as thoroughly trustworthy. His account of the effect produced is thus recorded:—

"Paris, July 25, 1842.

"Nothing worth mentioning happened, in the course of last week, except that Jenny appeared at the Grand Opéra, here; † but, without the lights, and with no other listeners than Meyerbeer, the Hiertas, Herr Blumm, Branting, the Director of the Opéra, and myself. It was in order to hear how her voice would tell, in the immense *salle.* Jenny was unusually nervous; and, you know, she never does herself justice until she is in full action on the stage. But, notwithstanding this, she sang well; though it seemed pale in comparison with what she can do. Meyerbeer said the prettiest things: ' *Une voix chaste et pure, pleine de grâce et de virginalité,*' etc., etc. Yesterday, I breakfasted with him; and, in the presence of Berlioz, and some other Frenchmen, he spoke of her with an enthusiasm so great, that I almost felt inclined to question its sincerity—for, Jenny had not sung nearly so well as she is capable of doing.

"In the meantime, she is coming home, for which she longs with her whole heart. May the Swedes receive her well, now, and not soon get tired of her! Otherwise, we shall take her to Berlin, and get her an engagement there, in accordance with Meyerbeer's wish. He maintains that she ought to appear there." ‡

This proves, clearly enough, that, after hearing the effect of Mdlle. Lind's voice, in the *salle* of the Grand Opéra, Meyer-

* *Histoire de l'Académie Royale de Musique.* (Paris.)
† The date of this letter establishes Saturday, July 23, 1842, as the day on which the trial took place.
‡ From the Lindblad letters.

beer was of opinion that Berlin would offer a better field for the exercise of her talents than Paris; and subsequent events proved that his judgment was perfectly correct. Neither the style, nor the tastes of the singer, would have found a congenial home, on the stage of the Grand Opéra; and it would have been a miracle indeed, if the pronunciation of any foreigner, though never so accomplished, could have perfectly satisfied a Parisian audience. There was, in all probability, no difference of opinion between any of the parties concerned, on this point; and, for the moment, this probationary performance passed off, without any practical result. But, in after years, the circumstance was brought before the public, in a distorted form which entirely changed its import, by giving a glaringly false account of the circumstances under which the trial took place.

It was said, that "Mdlle. Lind had vowed a profound artistic dislike to France, in remembrance of the check which she had there experienced, and for which she retained a lively resentment;" that "she constantly refused the engagements offered to her from Paris, because she had been heard there, without success, at the beginning of her career, by the Direction of the Opéra;" that she had even "made a *début* at this theatre;" that "this *début* had not been a happy one;" and that it was this "that provoked her resentment." *

These false reports were publicly contradicted, in November, 1887, by M. Arthur Pougin—the author of the Supplement to M. Fétis's well-known *Biographie Universelle des Musiciens*—who, in an article communicated to 'L. Ménestrel,' related the circumstances, precisely as they are here recorded, with the addition of some farther details furnished by M. Léon Pillet, the Director of the Grand

* See *Le Ménestrel*, (Paris, November, 1887, pp. 372, 373); also *The Musical World*, (London, November 12, and 26, and December 3, 1887).

Opéra under whose auspices the trial performance took place upon the unlighted stage.

These reports appear to have originated, or, at least, to have reached their culminating point of falsehood, in the year 1846, when the management of M. Léon Pillet was severely criticised, both by the public, and the press.

M. Pillet published, in his defence, a *brochure*,* in which he alludes, in no uncertain terms, to the circumstances in question. In answer to the accusation, that he had neglected more than one opportunity of engaging so famous a vocalist, he says :—

"It has been pretended: (i) That Meyerbeer himself presented Mademoiselle Lind to me, four years ago, and, that I rejected her.

(ii) That, after her success in Germany, he again pressed me, in vain, to engage her.

"Some have even gone so far as to say, that Mademoiselle Lind offered herself; and the exact amount of the salary that I refused her has actually been published, in some of the theatrical journals.

"These were so many fables, on the value of which it is necessary that I should enlighten you.

"Four years ago, when Meyerbeer was in search, not of a soprano, but a tenor, for *Le Prophète*, he came, on the evening before his departure,† to ask me for permission to hear, on the stage, a young person of whom he had heard a very good account. 'It is not for you,' he hastened to add; 'it is a voice which is described as pretty, but too weak for the Grand Opéra. I want to see whether I can make use of it, for Berlin.'

"I gave Meyerbeer all the facilities he demanded; placing at his disposal, not only the theatre, but an accompanist— M. Benoist. Finally, I myself escorted Mademoiselle Lind to the stage, where I prepared to listen to her, when I was told that the Commission, which was then assembled at the Opéra, was waiting for me.

---

* *Académie Royale de Musique. Compte rendu de la gestion, depuis le 1ᵉʳ Juin, 1840, jusqu'au 1ᵉʳ Juin, 1846, par Léon Pillet.* (Paris, 1846.)

† It will be remembered that Meyerbeer, in his letter, mentions details which confirm the microscopic correctness of M. Pillet's account.

" I excused myself to Mademoiselle Lind, and to Meyer-beer, and left them, without hearing a single note.

" On the next day, I asked what Meyerbeer had thought of his singer.

" He had said—I was told—that she was not without talent, but had still much to accomplish.

"This did not indicate that she had made any very great impression upon him; and, in fact, he thought so little of her, for the Opéra, that he did not even speak to me about her. It was only last year, when talking about Mademoiselle Lind, at Cologne, that he recalled the circumstances that I have had the honour to relate to you.

" As to the other assertion, that, after this period, Meyer-beer vainly pressed me to engage Mademoiselle Lind, it is as inexact as the preceding. Meyerbeer did indeed tell me, last winter, that he had the highest opinion of this *artiste's* talent, and that, if it were possible to engage her, and Madame Stolz, at the same theatre, it would be an admirable thing. But, he hastened to add, that he believed this to be impossible; that it would probably be with them, as with Nourrit and Duprez; that, both being strong enough to take the first rank at the theatre, neither the one nor the other would be content with the second; that Mademoiselle Lind's pecuniary demands would also be very considerable; and that, so far as he himself was concerned, he would be quite content with Mademoiselle Brambilla, or Madame Rossi-Caccia, for the part of *seconda donna* in *Le Prophète*.

" On my own account, however, in order to satisfy my mind, I begged him to ask Mademoiselle Lind whether she would quit the country of her triumphs, for Paris. But, he refused to undertake the commission.

" I was about to take this step, myself, when M. Vatel—the then Director of the Théâtre Italien—who entertained the same desire, sent me the following letter, which he had just received:—

" ' Berlin, December 9, 1845.

" ' Monsieur Le Directeur,

" ' I have had the honour of receiving your letter of November 13, and I must ask your pardon for having left it so long unanswered. But, before replying to you, it was necessary that I should reflect.

" ' I have decided, Monsieur, to remain in Germany, for the little time that I shall continue on the stage, and there to pursue my artistic career.

" 'For, the more I think of it, the more I am persuaded that I am not suited for Paris, nor Paris for me.

" 'I shall quit the stage, in a year from this; and, until that time, I shall be so much occupied in Germany, that it would be impossible for me to accept any other engagement, either at Paris or in London.

" 'Permit me, nevertheless, to express my thanks to you for having thought me worthy to appear before the first audience in the world. But, rest assured, also, Monsieur le Directeur, that I do you less wrong by not running the risk of bringing a failure upon you.

" ' JENNY LIND.' "

" 'One can see from this,' says M. Pougin, ' what to think about the pretended resentment of Jenny Lind against the public of Paris; and, also, about the unfortunate *début* she was said to have made, either at the Opéra, or the Théâtre Italien. This famous *début* never took place; and, if Jenny Lind was never heard in Paris, it was undoubtedly because she felt too much distrust of our public, persuaded as she was—as she herself says, in her letter—that she was not for Paris, nor Paris for her.' " *

We have thought it necessary to reproduce this correspondence, *in extenso*, because, of late years, the subject has been discussed, both in England, and in France, in terms calculated to give Parisian audiences a very false idea of the esteem in which they were held by an Artist, who, during the time she spent in Paris, derived such intense delight from the performances she witnessed at the Grand Opéra, the Théâtre Italien, and the Conservatoire, as well as those of Mademoiselle Rachel.

When the great singer—then, Madame Goldschmidt—gave a concert, at Cannes, in 1866, for the benefit of the hospital,† *Le Phare du Littoral* announced:—

---

* *Le Ménestrel.* (Paris, November, 1887.)

† The concert took place in the rooms of the Club [*Cercle Nautique*], at Cannes, on the 7th of April, 1866; and, after all expenses were paid, produced, for the Hospital the sum of 3300 fr. A full account of the performance, and the enthusiastic reception accorded to the singer, is contained in the *Revue de Cannes* for April 14, 1866.

" Jenny Lind will sing in France !!! It is true, that it will
be at Cannes : and, for the benefit of a charity. It is not yet
at Paris. But, it is still a concession of the celebrated
vocalist, who had declared that she would never sing in
France."

She never made any such declaration. But it is strange
that she should have been accused of this, on the one hand,
and, on the other, of having actually sung in France,
and failed. Both Mendel, * and La Rousse, † assert
that she sang at the Grand Opéra, without success; while
M. Castil-Blaze, in the work already quoted, gravely tells
us, that, " strongly recommended by Garcia, under whom
she had been studying, and by Meyerbeer, who had heard
her sing, Jenny Lind applied in 1840, for an engagement
at the Grand Opéra, but was refused, after a private
hearing, through the influence of Madame Stolz with M.
Léon Pillet;" and Mr. Sutherland Edwards, commenting
upon this, in the *Musical World*, for December 3, 1887,
says, that, " justly susceptible, Jenny Lind did not forget the
slight; and when, seven or eight years later, after her
brilliant success in London, an engagement was offered her
at the Paris Opera-House, she refused it, without assigning
any definite reason."

We have seen, from the letters of Meyerbeer and Lindblad
that these statements are without a shadow of foundation—
so baseless, that, but for the deductions drawn from them,
with equal unfairness to the *débutante*, to the Director
of the Opéra, and to the Parisian public, we should not have
thought this long digression necessary for their refutation.
Mademoiselle Lind was not in Paris, in 1840. Never having
sung before a Parisian audience, she could have had no
possible cause for resentment against it ; and, at no period of

---

* *Musikalisches Conversations-Lexicon.*
† *Dictionnaire du Dix-neuvième Siècle.*

her life did she ever entertain so unworthy a feeling. Moreover, when the trial performance took place, in 1842, she was
not open to an engagement, either in Paris, or elsewhere ; for,
the contract with the "Direction" of the Royal Theatre at
Stockholm had already been signed and ratified.   The die
was cast.

" Paris, July 25, 1842.

"Jenny is now returning home," wrote Herr Lindblad,
"and longing for it, with her whole heart.   She will accompany the Hiertas.   There is a question of returning by way of
England, and staying there until the 11th of August, when
the steamer leaves for Stockholm.   If this is possible, we
might all be back, by the 14th of August, or the 15th, at the
latest." *

And it was possible.   The journey to Paris, with its hopes
and fears, its long hours of diligent study, its cruel alternations of confidence and despondency, dominated by a firm
and righteous determination to achieve success in spite of every
obstacle, at the cost of every sacrifice of personal ease and
comfort that the nature of the case might demand—the
eventful journey to Paris, so carefully planned, and so
bravely brought to its conclusion, had accomplished all, and
more, far more than ever was expected from it.   And the
second phase of the great Art-life was at an end.

* From the Lindblad letters.

BOOK III.

ACHIEVEMENT.

CHAPTER I.

" LAND of my birth! Oh, that I could one day.show how
dear thou art to me!" That had been the deep desire of
Jenny Lind, as she toiled in Paris. And, indeed, it had
seemed as if the Fates were set on fulfilling her desire.
Back to Stockholm it was decreed that she should go.
Paris, in one way or another, failed to open its doors to her.
Berlin, in the shape of Meyerbeer, had hovered about her,
but had let her slip. The Continent remained passive as
yet; it suffered her to come and go, without any positive
sign. She had made her pilgrimage; and now, at its close,
she was, it would seem, to return to her familiar boards—to
put herself under the old yoke. At home, then, lay her
mission; not in the open field of European drama. That
great Italian Opera, with its famous heroines of song,
was to remain a vision of what was doing in the big world
outside. She was not to enter, it would seem, on that
magnificent scene. Enough for her to carry out her bond
with that Theatre, which had been her nursery and her
home, in her beloved Stockholm, at a humble salary of
1800 r. d. banco, *i.e.*, £150 a year. Very happily, so far as
we can see, she set to work; though inwardly conscious of
the immense increase of knowledge and power which had
become hers since she had begun again with Garcia " at the
beginning of the beginning," and had learnt what " Art "

meant. She arrived in August, 1842, and rented rooms for herself and Annette, the maid, on the upper floor of the same Bonde Palace, where the Lindblads still lived. With them she had the delight of feeling at home, and all the comfort of domestic affection; but, in the following year, she found it well to establish herself in an independent position, and she took rooms in another house, whither she invited her old friend, Louise Johansson, to come, and be her companion.

On October 10th she opened, at the theatre, with a performance of *Norma*—the very Opera in which she had closed her appearances on June 19th, 1841. It must have been a direct challenge to the critical world of Stockholm, to recognise the change that had intervened between the two performances. What that change was, we learn from an estimate which has been kindly supplied us by a most competent and judicious critic, himself a musician, who sang with her often, both before and after her visit to Paris. We give his own words :—

" So much has already been written, concerning Mdlle. Jenny Lind's artistic career, that farther discussion of its details may possibly be regarded, by some of your readers, as needless. Those, however, who enjoyed the opportunity of intimate acquaintance with this rare apparition in the world of Art, and were gifted with the insight necessary for true appreciation of its significance, well know that the subject is far from being exhausted.

" Among many things still remaining untold, the following are worthy of notice, as characteristic of the Artist's extraordinarily rapid powers of perception.

" When, during the years 1838, 1839, and 1840, Jenny Lind enraptured her audience, at Stockholm, by her interpretation of the parts of ' Agathe,' ' Pamina,' ' Alice,' ' Norma,' or ' Lucia,' she succeeded in doing so solely through her innate capacity for investing her performances, both musically and dramatically, with truthfulness, warmth, and poetry.

" The voice, and its technical development, ·were not,

however, in sufficiently harmonious relation with her intentions.

" In proof of this, it was noticed that the Artist was not always able to control sustained notes in the upper register —such, for instance, as the A flat, above the stave, in Agathe's cavatina, ' *Und ob die Wolke*'—without perceptible difficulty ; and, that she frequently found it necessary to simplify the *fioritura* and *cadenze*, which abound in florid parts like those of Norma and Lucia.

" Nay !—there were not wanting some, who, though they had heard her in parts no more trying than that of Emilia, in Weigl's *Swiss Family*—a *rôle*, which, in many respects, she rendered delightfully—went so far as to doubt the possibility of training the veiled and weak-toned voice in a wider sense.

" Jenny Lind, however, went to Paris, fully determined to cultivate her Art more fully, under Garcia's direction.

" Garcia, finding the voice fatigued, enjoined three months' absolute rest; and the period of twelve months originally set apart for study was thus reduced to nine.

" Yet, in spite of this, Jenny Lind, when resuming her sphere of action at the Stockholm Theatre, proved to have not only acquired a soprano voice of great sonority and compass, capable of adapting itself with ease to every shade of expression, but to have gained, also, a technical command over it, great enough to be regarded as unique in the history of the musical world.

" Never have the walls of the Royal Theatre at Stockholm —so famous for their excellent acoustical properties—echoed to a more finished, more enchanting song than that of Jenny Lind, in the part of ' Amina,' in *La Sonnambula*, after her return from Paris. What exquisite sonority ! What mastery over the *technique !* Her *messa di voce* * stood alone —unrivalled by any other singer. As the awakening 'Amina,' in the last scene of the above-named Opera, she made a long-sustained G (above the stave) express, first, her surprise, bordering on consternation, at the sight of ' Elvino,' penitent, at her feet ; then, doubt, as to whether it were really he ; and finally the blissful rapture of receiving back

---

* A technical term, applied to the art of swelling or diminishing the tone of the voice, by imperceptible gradation from the softest attainable *piano*, to the full volume of its utmost power, and *vice versa*.

again him by whom she believed herself to have been abandoned.[*]

"In like manner, in her shake, her scales, her *legato* and *staccato* passages, she evoked astonishment and admiration, no less from competent judges than from the general public: and the more so since it was evident, that, in the exercise of her wise discrimination, the songstress made use of these ornaments, only in so far as they were in perfect harmony with the inner meaning of the music.

"The incredibly rapid development of Jenny Lind's voice and *technique*, caused many people to question the value of the instruction she had originally received. Such doubts must, however, be dismissed, as unjustifiable. The true reason why Jenny Lind's singing, before she went abroad, could not be said to flow in the track which leads to perfection, is undoubtedly to be found, in the first place, in the fact that she was a so-called *Theaterelev*—a pupil educated at the expense of the Directors of the Theatre itself—and, as such, was unable to escape from the necessity of appearing in public before her preparatory education was completed—a proceeding no less disastrous to the pupil than contrary to the good sense of the teacher.

"To the impartial critic, it must, indeed, be evident, that, though the technical development of Jenny Lind is to be traced, in the main, to her quick reception of Garcia's training, she was nevertheless greatly indebted, with regard to several important details, to her first teacher,[†] for the high rank she subsequently occupied in the world of song."

Such, then, was the transformation that had come over her rendering of *Norma.* She had sung it before, with a thin

* This wonderful G, in the extended form here described, forms no part of Bellini's score. The germ from which Mdlle. Lind developed it is to be found in a short phrase of exceedingly common-place recitative :—

Ah! gio - ja!　　Ah! gio - ja!

The first *Ah! gioja!* was an agitated whisper; after which, the singer prolonged the minim G—here marked with an asterisk—to a length almost incredible, with the effect described in the text. This beautiful, and altogether original conception, was entirely due to the genius of Mdlle. Lind; not to that of Bellini.—ED.

† I. A. Berg.

voice, in a "provincial" style, with a throat fatigued, using bad methods of *technique*. She sang it now with a voice that, besides its new tone and sonority, had become capable of a vocalisation which placed her among the phenomenal singers of European history. No wonder that Stockholm was wild with enthusiasm.

She sang in seven performances of *Norma*, and in six of *Lucia*, besides giving some scenes from Rossini's *Semiramide*, and in January, 1843, repeated her favourite "Alice," three or four times.

She took up several new characters — "Amazili," in Spontini's *Ferdinand Cortez*, the second act of which was given eight times during the spring; "Valentine," in the *Huguenots*; "Minette," in *La Gazza Ladra*; "La Contessa," in Mozart's *Nozze di Figaro*; above all, "Amina," in the *Sonnambula*—one of her representations which was to become so famous in after-years, and which she sang, for the first time, on March 1st, 1843. Altogether, before the nine months of the year's engagement were out, she had made, between October 10th, 1842, and June 21st, 1843, one hundred and six appearances in thirteen different parts.

But, besides her normal work, those nine months were chiefly memorable for two main incidents, one, personal and domestic; the other, national and dramatic.

The personal event formed the last crisis in her home-relations. These relations were still strained; for we must remember that she has never gone back on that first decision to leave her parents' home, which landed her in the Lindblads' household. She is still living apart from them; and this is all the more marked, now that she is independent of the Lind-blads, and living in her own hired rooms, with the sole companionship of the faithful Louise. A woman, by Swedish law, at that time, was bound to be under guardianship until she married. Yet it must have been as difficult as ever for her to remain under the guardianship of parents, who cared, indeed, for her, and valued her highly, but who, yet, could not possibly enter into her motives and aims, which were beyond the range both of the easy-going conscience of her father, and of the embittered temperament of her mother. We have only to recall her deep and peculiar sense of the obligation she was under, to devote her art and its rewards to the service of God and man, to see how tough a difficulty this desire would prove to Herr Lind, who had never taken life very seriously, and to Fru Lind, who had fought her own way along, with sturdy resolution, under the ugly burden of poverty, and who had seen no good cause to be over tender towards a world which had dealt hardly enough with her.

In view, then, of this radical difficulty, Jenny Lind took a step, which, with characteristic generosity, put an end to the long and tangled story. Out of her earnings, scanty though they were, she managed to secure a little home in the country, in which she established her father and mother. And, then, she won their consent to transfer a guardianship, which they could not well exercise at a distance, to an official guardian, duly appointed by law, to whom they would hand over all parental responsibilities. This they did; and the transference was a marked moment in her life. Not only did she thereby put a total end to all the domestic troubles which had so darkened her young days; not only did she set free her natural affection for her mother, by releasing it from all the aggravation of jarring wills; but also she did something towards securing for herself what she, always, most sorely needed—needed, indeed, with all the innermost necessities of her being—a strong and steady personal influence at the back of her life, to calm her agitations, to control her uncertainties, to abide constant throughout her reactions, to correct her self-mistrust, to dissipate her suspicions, to fix her emotions, to anchor her conscience. She

had all the fervour and the lapses, the starts and the recoils,
of a dramatic genius ; and, firm and high as was her moral
ideal, its very force brought it into confused collision with the
bewilderment of circumstances, and it was as liable to perplex
and distress her, as to cheer and impel.   This made her passionately feel for something which could from without
buttress and reassure her spiritual intentions, which so often
found themselves sadly at fault in a world that would not
correspond with them.   Shaken, as she herself often was, by
the strong emotions which swept across her soul, she needed
an external mark, a sign, a symbol, of the unshaken security
of that moral End in which she trusted.   Some one ought to
be near at hand, from whom she could receive the profound
assurance that " all was well "—that her belief in goodness
had not played her false.   This is what her home had sadly
omitted to give her : and for this loss nothing could now
compensate.   But it was, at least, a profound relief, under
such a strain, to have obtained a guardian whose presence
abode with her, from then to his death in 1880, as a
permanent pledge of all that was wise, and kindly, and
excellent, and of good report.   Herr Henric M. Munthe,
Judge of the Court of Second Instance, the guardian
chosen, was a man of high character and distinguished
position ; she could confide in his judgment with absolute
confidence, while she could also rely on his appreciation of her art, as he was himself a cultivated musician,
and took his part in the best amateur quartette in Stockholm.   His portrait suggests a benignant and benevolent
" Thackeray "—a face full of fatherly interest and mild good
humour, yet with the discreet wisdom of one who knows the
Law.   He looks compact with honesty, of unqualified worth,
charged with measured advice, sober and yet not unsympathetic.   And, indeed, with the shrewdness of a councillor, he
combined true sympathy with all that was most deeply im-

planted in her heart. She wrote to him constantly and freely ; and she found in him one who could understand her, even in those respects in which a legal trustee is most apt to fail. For it was he who directed and managed for her, so long as his guardianship lasted, those abundant charities which she showered upon her native Stockholm. About these she could pour out her mind to him, sure of intimate comprehension. And his open recognition of her ideas in all this, is evidenced by the fact that he stored up her letters to him, and left them at his death inscribed with this description, "the mirror of a noble soul"; though, according to her own words to his son, these letters were almost entirely occupied with the distribution of her charitable gifts. She declares this, in a letter written, in June 1880, to Carl H. Munthe, the son of the Judge, after she had learned from him of the existence of these letters, on the father's death in April, 1880. Her letter throws so much light on her character that the main portion of it is printed here. It shows her own instinctive feelings about her gifts, and how natural she thought them. And it shows, also, how entirely the old man had acquiesced in her designs, and how faithfully and loyally he had set himself to the task of carrying them to a wise issue, without raising objections, or hampering her with cautions ; while, by his preservation of the letters, he evinces his recognition of the special nobility of the soul which he was serving.

This letter to Carl Munthe has an interest, also, that belongs to the present memoir, for it will be noticed that she here mentions her intention of writing an autobiography ; and, above all, of recording her artistic experience. Though this purpose was utterly abandoned (or, rather, was never put in action), yet her words lend a sanction to the effort made, in these volumes, to give some record of her career as an artist. In her last years, she was prone to justify her abandonment of the autobiography by indignant remonstrances

at the hopeless failure of the public to understand Carlyle's
'Reminiscences.' Her experience of the cruel stupidity with
which a mighty character like his could be maltreated and
misinterpreted, made her put the thought utterly away. "If
they could so treat him, who was so great, what respect would
they pay me?" she said. "No! let the waves of oblivion
pass over my poor little life!"

But we must go back to our letter: here it is:—

*Extract of a Letter from Fru Jenny Lind-Goldschmidt to
Hofrättsrådet Carl Munthe.*

"1 Moreton Gardens, June 15th, 1880.

"The letters from me, left in your charge, my dear brothers
and my sister Emma, can contain only dispositions for distribution of pensions and purses to different people. What good
would there be in exhibiting these letters to the curiosity of
the public, long after that the writer thereof is decayed and
forgotten? To me, the most acceptable course would be the
burning of those letters after you all are gone. There is nothing
I have shunned more, during my life, than praise for the assistance I have been fortunate enough, through the grace of God,
to render to my fellow-men as far as lay in me, and it can
never be a merit to give of that which has been given to us.
These are my views—and if I am not much mistaken about
you, brother Carl, you will say I am right.

"Moreover, I intend to write an autobiography. My life—
especially as an artist—has furnished material for a biography
in such abundance, that I almost look upon it as a duty to
produce something of the kind, before leaving a world where
I had been called upon to take so active a part. That in such
a biography, written by myself, my beloved guardian should
take his well-deserved place, is only natural; that the help
he gave me with the distribution of my little bounties in my
fatherland, was of the greatest importance for those who
received them, is a fact nobody can dispute, and, consequently, his part in this page of my life must be clear and
unmistakable. Alas! in my letters to him, he does not by
any means occupy the place to which he is entitled, consequently they would be only interpreted to my advantage;
and still, had he remonstrated against my urgent commis-

sions—which he was much too noble and much too discreet ever to do—I should most probably have listened to his objections."

Such was the kind and fatherly guardianship which she won for herself, under a legal sanction obtained from His Majesty's Lower Town Court on the 30th of January, 1843, under the chairmanship of the Sous-Préfet, Chamberlain, and Knight of the Order of the Royal North Star, M. Kuylenstjierna, when the following request was presented :—

" Having decided to leave Stockholm for good, and consequently being unable to bestow due attention to the guardianship of my dear daughter, the Court-singer, Jenny Lind, I hereby beg that I may be relieved from this duty, and that Herr H. M. Munthe, Judge of the High Court, may be appointed in my place to the guardianship."

This is signed by N. J. Lind, with the title of "Fabrikör," *i.e.*, manufacturer, to which he was entitled through having acquired ownership of a weaving-loom. After that Herr Munthe has formally signified his consent, the Royal Court agrees to the request, and Judge H. M. Munthe " is herewith appointed guardian of the Court-singer, Jenny Lind, in accordance with regulations provided by the law."

So happily closes a long and chequered chapter of domestic history. The parents contentedly enjoy the fruits of their daughter's generosity. Their discomforts, and their anxieties are over. They seem to have been very fond of one another; and henceforward, the days seem to have begun of which their daughter speaks in her letter from America, on her mother's death—days of quiet and kindly peace in which the natural affections found free way.

The second great event of that spring was the National Jubilee, to celebrate the twenty-fifth year of the reign of

King Carl Johan. The Royal Family of the Bernadottes, in spite of their abrupt introduction into the country, have succeeded in attracting about them the national associations ; and the Jubilee was to be celebrated by appeals to everything that was native, and popular, and Swedish. The Royal Theatre set itself to the task by the production of a " Divertissement National,"—a medley of national scenes, with words and dances by Böttiger, Tegner's son-in-law, and himself a poet ; and with music by Berwald, the conductor at the Theatre Royal. In this, Jenny Lind sang, in the character of a peasant girl from Wermland. This piece ran for twenty-seven nights, all through February, and March, into April ; and it was followed in May, by another *Pièce d'Occasion*, of the same type, with national melodies and dances, called *A May Day in Wärend*—full of Swedish customs, and melodies, and dresses ; in which she sang the part of "Märtha," the heroine, riding in, at one part, on horseback on to the stage, and singing as she rode. This ran for fifteen nights before June was over. She was capitally supported by the barytone, Belletti, in the character of an itinerant Italian. We can imagine how her Swedish blood would tingle, as she threw herself, with her whole heart, into the delight of rendering the native peasant life which was so dear to her, and which she so instinctively interpreted. She would pour her soul out in melodies which touched the very fibres of her being, as they spoke to her of the sounds and sights which make Sweden what it is to Swedish hearts. She must have felt that the opportunity was indeed come to put out all the new powers, which she had gained abroad, to prove to her own people how dear they were to her.

We find that, from this time on, the Court began to take delight in showing her both favour, and friendship ; and especially kind to her was the Queen, Desideria, wife of Bernadotte. We are allowed to use the interesting notes from the diary of a lady-in-waiting on Queen Desideria, which belong to this, and the following years. This lady, Fröken Marie von Stedingk, had, in quite early days, predicted a great future for Jenny Lind, when she heard of her wonderful dramatic gifts, as a child of eleven or twelve. And, now, after the return from Paris, it was " her greatest treat" to witness the fulfilment of her prophecy; and to hear "Our nightingale, the charming Jenny Lind," both in the *Divertissement National,* and in her great parts, " *Norma,*" "*la Sonnambula,*" etc. She had, also, "often the advantage of hearing her, through the winter, in private houses, where one and all treated her with distinction. Her behaviour, and her reputation are faultless ; her manners pleasant and modest. Without being pretty, she has an expression of purity and genius, which, combined with her youth, and her charming figure, is exceedingly prepossessing." This is a delightful picture of her at the time—the simple modest girl, with her light, graceful, quick-moving figure ; and, then, the last, the crown of all—"a look of purity and genius !" We shall hear more of this diary in the years 1844 and 1845.

So the first year of the home engagement ended—prosperous, happy, secure. But, after all, was it to be possible that this great gift of hers should be left to be the private possession and prize of her Swedish home? Could it be so hid ? Was no rumour to creep about of this strange singing 'mid the northern seas? Was the "Nightingale" caught, and caged for ever?

It could not be ; and we have, now, to follow her first flights outside the home-limits, and to watch her, as she discovers that her voice has that in it which can overleap all the barriers set up between people and people, and can speak to the souls of those whose tongue is unknown to her, and whose

eyes have never seen the woods and waters of Sweden.
There was a little experiment first, in Finland, in the summer
of 1843, which met with overwhelming response. A graceful and pathetic record of the visit is given us in the verses
of the aged poet of Finland, Topelius, written for a festival in
1888, on the news of Jenny Lind's death. The old poet is
carried back to recall the days when he first heard her sing
so long ago; and we venture to give, in a free translation, a
few of the opening verses, which describe, with delicate
accuracy, the effect she then made on all—the effect of one,
who, using all the subtlest resources given her by skill and
training, still spoke straight home, from soul to soul, with the
natural direct ease with which a bird sings its heart out, in
sheer simplicity and joy :—

> " I saw thee once, so young and fair,
>   In thy sweet spring-tide, long ago ;
> A myrtle wreath was in thy hair,
>   And, at thy breast, a rose did blow.
>
> .   .   .   .   .   .
>
> " Poor was thy purse, yet gold thy gift ;
>   All music's golden boons were thine :
> And yet, through all the wealth of Art,
>   It was thy *soul* which sang to mine !
>
> " Yea ! sang, as no one else has sung,
>   So subtly skilled, so simply good !
> So brilliant ! yet as pure, and true
>   As birds that warble in the wood ! "

So it went well in Finland.

But yet another step outward was to be made that
summer—a step into a country, near enough to be familiar,
yet remote enough to be almost foreign. Once before, she
had just looked in at Copenhagen, in the middle of her provincial tour, in 1840 ; and, now, she visited it again. It was
in connection, again, with a provincial tour which she made ;
and of which we have some happy records in the life of the
musician, Jacob Axel Josephson.

This name is so closely linked with these years of Jenny
Lind's life, that we must pause upon it before going on
with our story.　Josephson was a Swedish composer—
born in 1818, and died in 1880—whose songs have become
widely famous in Sweden.　In these songs he has proved
himself a faithful successor to Geijer, and Lindblad; he
has much of their spirit; on the other hand, he reproduced less of the national type of music than they did,
and showed more of the influence of the great German
song-writers of his own day.　The event of his life
was a tour through Germany and Italy, for the study of Art;
it was this which brought him under the full sway of classical
culture in music; and it was with this tour, as we shall see,
that Jenny Lind was so personally and deeply concerned.　He
returned from it in 1847, and was appointed Musical Director
of Upsala University in 1849.　He devoted himself with
indefatigable perseverance to producing the great works of
the great masters, especially the oratorios of Handel, Haydn,
and Mendelssohn.　Through these efforts, as well as through
his lectures on the 'History of Music,' given at Upsala, he
has done much to kindle and to purify, by the power of
music, the minds of the present generation in Sweden.　All
his compositions, and they were many, including one
symphony, prove him to have been an earnest and highly-
trained musician.

Now, in 1843, Josephson was just at the critical point in
his musical education; he was longing to get abroad; he had
no sufficient funds.　Here was a situation which Jenny Lind
would thoroughly understand; for it had been her own.　We
shall soon see how she dealt with it.　They met, in the
August of this year, at this town, Linköping, whither
Josephson had gone, on the occasion of an annual concert,
to be given under the direction of Concert-Master Randel, in
aid of the fund for the widows and orphans.　It was a

most pleasant surprise, as he tells us in his Diary,* to
meet with a number of old acquaintances and friends, and
among others Jenny Lind and Günther, who had come to
give a concert of their own, and joined in this preliminary
entertainment.   Crowds were present from all parts of the
country, partly owing to the presence of some of the royalties ; and the heat and the crush in the church, where the
concert was given, were intolerable, and he did not enjoy it
so much as he expected—"even Jenny Lind was less successful than usual." This was on the 18th August ; but, at her
own concert, in the evening of the following day, she was
in excellent voice, and he was enraptured ; "she sang in
a manner unsurpassed.   What brilliancy of delivery, side by
side with that grandeur which is so characteristic of her !
What energy and pathos, even in the very *fioriture !*   What
classical finish in her cadenzas !" In the evening she was
serenaded.   And on the following day, at the concert given
by her and Herr Günther, he heard her sing, in costume,
a scena from the *Freischütz.* "She is incomparable !" is his
verdict.   "The beautiful gentle calm during the first part of
the scene ; her fine attitudes, full of feeling, when listening
for the horns ; her rapture and glowing prayer at the supposed victory of her beloved—all this is so glorious, so true,
so enchanting, that in reality, nothing can be said, while the
full heart feels all the more from the lack of words." She
sang one of Josephson's own songs, at this concert, "Believe
not in Joy !" After this musical feast at Linköping, the
friends separated.   Josephson and Günther went on a tour of
their own, giving musical soirées, while Jenny Lind took the
opportunity of a run across to Copenhagen. Before the three
meet again, we must see what happened to her there.   She
had intended only to make a visit ; but there was in Copenhagen, an eager, and enthusiastic friend who was not to be

* 'Gedenkblätter an Jakob Axel Josephson :' von N. P. Ödman, 1886.

denied. This was Mr. A. A. Bournonville, of whom we have
already spoken as being delighted with Jenny Lind's operatic
singing as far back as 1839, when he was indignant at the
pittance at which she was rendering such magnificent service
to the Royal Theatre. He was eminent, both at Copenhagen
and at Stockholm, as a composer, and master of ballets; he
was made knight of the Danebrog in Denmark, and of the
Wasa in Sweden; he was greatly respected and beloved, and
it was at his house that Jenny Lind usually stayed, on her
visits to Copenhagen. He urgently pleaded that she should
give them "her incomparable Alice" in *Roberto*; and suggested
that she should sing her part in Swedish, while the rest sang
in Danish, as the languages were so nearly akin.

"All the theatre showed the greatest good-will," he writes
in his memoir of his theatrical life; "but the one obstacle
was the fear of Jenny Lind herself; she dreaded a foreign
stage. And when she saw Fru Heiberg act in the *Son
of the Desert* she felt such enthusiasm for her, and, at the
same time, such depression for herself, that she begged me,
with tears of anguish, to spare her the pain of exhibiting her
own insignificant person and talent, on a stage which had, at
its disposal, the genius and the beauty of Fru Heiberg. In
addition to this, my counter-arguments excited her to such a
degree that she began to reproach me for having laid a trap
for her. This both frightened, and wounded me; and I promised to cancel all. But now the 'woman' came to the
front; for as I began to doubt, she waxed firm."

An admirable episode, as amusing as it is natural! So
long as it is only her *own* doubt, it is only due to nervousness, however real its anguish; but if another doubt her
powers, it constitutes an attack, a challenge; and "the
artist," as well as "the woman," is up in arms to repel it.
Bournonville seems to have seen how to reap the advantage of
this mode of argument with her; he must have deepened his
doubts to the point which secured complete conviction in her.
For, certainly, he obtained her consent. She sang; and the

success was tremendous, was overpowering. "Jenny Lind gained in Denmark a second Fatherland," writes Bournonville. And, after deploring the slackness which failed to secure her services for the Danish Opera, he speaks, significantly enough, of the impression which the event made on her—of the discovery which she made for herself. "The ice was broken. Jenny Lind discovered that she could get her living out of Sweden; and also she learned that the Artist, in reality, should not settle down on the native-soil, but, like the bird of passage, should go there only in search of rest." The words are those of the theatrical master, who has made the drama his world. They are singularly unlike what she would have used, at any time. But they may describe, in his language, an effect which she would have differently expressed, if indeed she could have expressed it at all, but which did take place within her secret self. She must have experienced a sense that the doors were being flung open, and that she might pass out through them, if she would. There was a world, she now knew for certain, out and away beyond the range of home, where she would find that her powers would tell, her gifts be welcomed, her genius be met with the warmth of sympathy. There were worlds which she could conquer, elsewhere. This must have, indeed, been something like a revelation, to one who, as we have just seen in the scene with Bournonville, was terribly susceptible to self-mistrust. There can be no doubt that Copenhagen marked an eventful hour in her destiny. It was the omen of what was to come. Bournonville records what so shortly followed, with a touch of justifiable pride in his own anticipatory judgment. "Her name soon became of European fame; gold and praise were showered upon her; princes and nations vied with one another in their offerings to her; poets sang of her; in the midst of winter, she never wanted flowers."

She only sang twice in the theatre, on September 10th and 13th: and in one concert, in the large hall of the Hôtel d'Angleterre, on September 16th. The Opera, on each occasion was *Roberto*. The following words from a History of Danish Dramatic Art, by Th. Overskou, form an admirable comment. After stating that, in her case, it was not a single party of admirers, excited into ecstasy by some one or other brilliant quality, but that it was the entire public which was moved to enthusiasm by all the harmonising elements of true artistic beauty, it goes on :—

"It was said about Jenny Lind, that in her everything is combined to make the perfect dramatic singer; a clear, full, sonorous voice of large compass; an easy and charming method of singing, which she never overburdens with inappropriate ornament: a style, in the highest degree expressive and enchanting: and an extraordinary dramatic talent. Added to this, there lies diffused throughout the whole personality of this admirable artist, a peculiar charm, a naturalism rare on the stage, which makes an immediate appeal to the goodwill of the audience. And, after all, this eulogy, however detailed and true, can only give but an imperfect account of the gifts by which, without dazzling through beauty, she fascinates all by her appearance, her singing, and her speech; or her power derives its origin and its life from a loveliness altogether characteristic and individual, such as it is impossible to describe, and which banishes all disturbing influences, and collects all her rare and precious advantages, so as to create an irresistible impression of grace and purity of soul."

No words could be more delicately chosen, to convey the effect which Jenny Lind invariably produced. It is most interesting and curious to note how all attempts to describe this effect, whenever they come from elevated and sympathetic observers, fall into the same language. "Genius and Purity," said the Lady of the Court at Stockholm. "Grace and Purity of Soul," says the Danish History. "A noble Nature," said the Upsala Journal. The same phrases come

to the surface again and again : and all of them testify to the
intensity of the personal character, which fused all the varied
gifts of Art and Nature into a vivid, and irresistible unity.
It is she herself who lends the wonderful bewitchment to the
voice, and to the action : and the impression, so received,
though without the aid of physical beauty, has always (as
they tell us) all the character of that which we call
"beautiful," so that they cannot but speak of her possessing
" charm " and " loveliness."

Nor was it only the possibility of a wider public, which
opened upon her at Copenhagen. She also found that here,
as at Stockholm, she won, in a peculiar manner, the admiration and the friendship of eminent men, such as the artists
Jensen and Melbye, the poet Œhlenschläger, and, above all, of
Hans Andersen, who was absolutely fascinated, and who for
a long time after, paid her a devotion, which had in it all
that delightful mingling of simplicity, and childishness,
which was so characteristic of him. In his ' Story of my
Life ' he tells in beautiful words how he was called in by
Bournonville, to take part in the work of persuading her to
sing :—

"Except in Sweden," she said, "I have never appeared in
public. In my own country all are so kind and gentle
towards me ; and if I were to appear in Copenhagen, and be
hissed ! I cannot risk it ! " "When she appeared in *Alice*,"
he writes, "it was like a new revelation in the domain of art.
The fresh young voice went direct to the hearts of all. Here
was truth and nature. Everything had clearness and
meaning. In her concerts, Jenny Lind sang her Swedish
songs. There was a peculiar, and seductive charm about
them : all recollection of the concert-room vanished : the
popular melodies exerted their spell, sung as they were by a
pure voice with the immortal accent of genius. All Copenhagen was in raptures. Jenny Lind was the first artist to
whom the students offered a serenade : the torches flashed
round the hospitable villa, where the song was sung. She
expressed her thanks by a few more of the Swedish songs,

and I then saw her hurry into the darkest corner, and weep
out her emotion. 'Yes, yes,' she said, 'I will exert myself;
I will strive ; I shall be more efficient than I am now, when
I come to Copenhagen again ! ' "

This is the remarkable note of her character—so natural,
yet so rare—that every triumph, instead of satisfying her with
her skill, spurs her to further efforts to be more worthy of
its joy. Hans Andersen goes on :—

" On the stage, she was the great artist, towering above all
around her ; at home, in her chamber, she was a gentle young
girl, with the simple touch and piety of a child. . . . The
spectator laughs and weeps, as she acts : the sight does him
good : he feels a better man for it : he feels that there is
something divine in Art. One feels, at her appearance on
the stage, that the holy draught is poured from a pure vessel."

We will close this visit to Copenhagen with the graceful
and touching words in which Mr. Bournonville has clothed
an incident which seemed to him to embody the secret of
Jenny Lind's significance at that time. In translating the
words from their congenial French, we must, we fear, strip
them of half their charm : but here they are :—

" Again and again have the delights of Nature, the glory of
Art, the enthusiasm for the true and the beautiful, inspired
in me some attempts at verse. How, then, is it that, to-day,
the sweet singing of Jenny Lind has left my lyre mute ?
How is it that I fail to find even an echo within me which
might pass on into the distance the sound of that music which
laid open to my soul a world as yet unknown ? Alas ! To
paint in words the tones of a voice steeped in all the utter-
most tenderness of the human heart, is as vain as to seek
shadows in the darkness ! Moreover, the sound of my voice
would be lost in the thunders of a people's praise. The little
flower that alone I could offer to the artist, in the midst of
her triumphs, would be crushed under the feet of the crowds
that press round her. No ! Rather let me treasure up the
memory of her gifts, and of her story within my home, and
let me leave, as a legacy to those that come after, one trait of
her life, which will serve to bring her honour in the day when

the loud applause will have died away, and when the poets
will be singing the praises of other, and newer names.

"I had a friend who enjoyed all the privileges of happy
comfort, of public esteem, of cultivated taste, of the affection
of his family, of the love of his fair, young wife. A cruel
sickness brought him down to the very edge of the grave ; but
by God's mercy, he was saved. He was lying, still weak and
faint, in his bed, when the thrill of excitement which Jenny
Lind had kindled in Copenhagen, reached even to his sick-
room ; and bitter were the regrets of the young wife, at the
sick man's loss of that which would have been to him such a
delight. Jenny heard of her desire, and offered, at once, to
sing to the invalid : and so, in the very heart of her triumphs,
when the Court, and the Town were anxiously craving to
know whether they could yet keep her one day more, she
found time to charm, with her heavenly voice, the hearts of
the two young people. It was on a Sunday, the 16th of
September, 1843, at the hour when all the churches were
filled with the praises of God, that Jenny, without any
strangers to observe her, without any public notice, did this
act of charity ; and the tears of gratitude which flowed from
the eyes of Mozart and Mathilde Waage Petersen were the
waters in which they christened her with the name of 'Angel.'
The emotion, and the pleasure of the visit served to help the
recovery of my friend.

"May God ever bless Jenny Lind !

"May she receive the reward of her charity, if, one day, she
be wed !

"And if God grant her children, may it be given them to
know of this, their mother's act."

This kindness of hers was not forgotten, we shall find,
when she returned to Copenhagen about two years later ; for
on the back of the picture then presented to her—a picture
of white roses by Jensen—appear the names of this happy
little couple, Mozart and Mathilde.

It may be further noted, that she went to sing to the sick
man in spite of having to appear, on the afternoon of that
same day, in the large room of the Hôtel d'Angleterre, at her
great concert, at which she sang two songs from *Norma*, and
Swedish Ballads, and National Melodies.

So ended the first flight outside the house, the first brief act of achievement beyond her native stage. She crossed back to Sweden, to continue her series of concerts; and on reaching Westerwik about the 25th of September, by the steamer "Scandia," she found herself once again in company with Günther and Josephson, who had lingered on in the town, after a successful musical soirée. The friends joined together at the hotel in the evening. "I greatly rejoiced," writes Josephson, "to meet her again after the brilliant triumphs she has achieved at Copenhagen."

"Her genial modesty had lost nothing through her success. Her Nature wins more and more harmony; and in consequence there is more equanimity in her disposition and in her friendliness, than before she went abroad."

Josephson was just parting with Günther, at the close of their tour; so, while Günther went straight home to Stockholm, Josephson decided to tack himself on to Jenny Lind and her companion, now on their way to give a concert at Norrköping, where he might be able to help. So, on the 28th, he started after her in a light cart, caught up her carriage at Vida, and, after that, took his seat alternately on his own trap or on the box of her carriage, while she read aloud to him some of Hans Andersen's poems, from a book presented to her by Hans himself. At the country inn they improvised a rough dinner, which they enriched with the music of an old barrel organ, by chance discovered on the premises. They arrived at Norrköping that night; and spent the next day in arrangements and rehearsals, while, in the evening, Jenny was serenaded by singers from Upsala.

"After the rehearsal," Josephson goes on, "I spent a pleasant evening with the ladies, partly at the tea-table, partly at the piano. Jenny sang many of Lindblad's newest and unpublished songs. Like the earlier ones, they are marked by genius; and he clearly, in the *Lied* gains more

and more a character of calm development in the melody.
The mysticism which envelopes most of his earlier songs with
peculiar fascination, has now somewhat diminished; the
melody is more flowing, though not more captivating; the
whole has gained in transparency and sweetness. . . . . .
Through the great development Jenny's song and voice have
attained, through the grandeur which gives colour to her
diction, the *Lied*, as rendered by her, has lost much of the
unconscious inspiration of the moment. She sings the
Lied better than nearly everybody else, as a matter of
course; but still, not as ——. In that case, the character of
the *Lied* never gets lost, just because the voice has, not
arrived at any developed power of execution. Such a power
always must imply reflection upon its own use; the natural
devotion to the subject is not any longer so independent.
The strength and sonority developed in the voice have, with
Jenny Lind, received every kind of noble grandeur, which,
perhaps, ought to draw her, chiefly, to compositions of a
grand character. In the meantime it is always interesting
to hear her sing; her genius always shines through in full
glory." *

This most interesting personal criticism seems to show
that, just at this period, before her own inherent spontaneity
had wholly absorbed her new-trained technical development,
she was apt to prove too overpowering for those lighter and
simpler effects of song, which, a year or two later, when the
mastery over her art was matured, she could render with
such exquisite delicacy of tone, and effect, that she made
those very songs of Lindblad speak with wonderful direct-
ness, to the first musicians of Germany.

On the 30th of September she gave her concert, singing
airs from *Figaro*, *Norma*, *Roberto*, and *Niobe*. At supper
that evening at General Cronhjelm's she was again serenaded,
and next morning was off to Stockholm.

She returned, for another year's work, at her old salary;
in the course of which, between October 4, 1843, and
July 5, 1844, she made sixty-six appearances, in sixteen

---

* N. P. Ödman in *op. cit.*

different characters, six of them being wholly new. She
reached her sixtieth performance of " Alice "; her forty-ninth
of " Lucia "; her thirty-sixth of " Agatha "; her twenty-
sixth of *Norma;* her eighteenth of the *Sonnambula.* The
jubilee play, *The May Day in Wärend,* ran on to within a
few days of the National mourning for the King Carl Johan,
whose death closed the theatre from March 4 to May 2. Her
new parts were " Thyra " in *The Elves,* an opera, by a Dutch
pianist of mark, residing in Stockholm, called Van Boom:
" Fiorilla " in Rossini's *Turco in Italia:* " Armida " in
Gluck's famous work: and " Anna Bolena " in Donizetti's
opera of that name. Of *Armida,* she wrote a characteristic
note to Judge Munthe, on February 17, 1844 :—

> " I send you some seats for my 'benefit' on the 19th in
> Gluck's *Armida.* I trust that you will greatly enjoy the
> music. Both the music, and the piece, are so grand, that my
> smallness will be shown out, thereby, in its true light. But
> I am so thrilled by the sublime spirit of the music that I am
> only too ready to risk my own personality."

During the opening of this year, 1844, she was, in concert
with Günther, interesting herself greatly in the fortunes of
Josephson. Günther had begun to scheme on behalf of his
tour abroad, during their trip together in the autumn; and
had already in November written to him about a proposal to
give a concert to raise funds for this, in Stockholm. " Jenny
Lind," he had then reported, " knows all; and has besides
received an anonymous letter from Upsala on the matter."
On the 12th of January, 1844, Josephson received, with
rejoicing, a kind letter from Jenny Lind, confirming the news
of the concert which she and Günther were to give for his
benefit.* On the 6th of March, he spent the morning arrang-
ing with them the details; but, towards the close of April, the
concert, to his great joy, was shifted from Stockholm to Upsala,
and was fixed for Whit Monday. It succeeded beyond all

* 'Biography of J. A. Josephson,' p. 100. ·

expectations. "All have come forward in the most generous, spontaneous manner, and the result has, by God's grace, turned out for the best. My journey is now guaranteed." So he writes on the 30th of May: "If hitherto I have belonged to Art privately, I am now challenged to work more generally for the holy cause. This gift from my friends ought to bring with it a blessing on my way, for their sympathy has had the largest share in bringing it about. I am all round besieged with kindness. How remain faithful and grateful!" * So loyally and generously had she worked to fulfil the dream of another, who shared in her own profound aspiration after the highest ideal, and was beset by the same obstacles. For two long years, Josephson had been yearning for this opportunity, and now it was given him. It was a good work, which proved well rewarded.

As to the Season, it must have passed much as usual. She wrote to Hans Andersen, at the time of the national mourning :—

"Stockholm, 19th March, 1844.

"MY GOOD BROTHER:

"Mr. Bournonville mentioned in his last letter to me that you have been shedding tears because of my silence. This, naturally, I take to be nonsense, but as my conscience does reproach me in regard to you, my good brother, I hasten to recall myself to your memory, and to ask my friend and brother not to be angry with me, but rather to furnish me soon with a proof that I have not forfeited my right to his friendship and goodwill. A thousand, thousand thanks for the pretty tales! I find them divinely beautiful to such a degree as to believe them to be the grandest and loveliest that ever flowed from your pen. I hardly know to which of them I should concede the palm, but, upon reflection I think *The Ugly Duckling* the prettiest.—Oh, what a glorious gift to be able to clothe in words one's most lofty thoughts; by means of a scrap of paper to make men see so clearly how the noblest often lie most hidden and covered over by wretchedness and rags, until the hour of

* *Ib.*, p. 124.

transformation strikes and shows the figure in a divine light! Thanks, from all my heart, thanks for all this—as touching as it is instructive. I long now very much for the moment when I shall be allowed to tell my good brother by word of mouth how proud I am of this friendship, and with the help of my *Lieder* to express—if even in a trifling degree—my gratitude! only that you, my brother, are surely better fit than any one to comprehend our Swedish proverb: 'Every bird sings according to his beak.'

"This country is now in mourning—peace to those who are gone! After all one is happiest when once well out of the way. Our theatre is now closed for about seven or eight weeks, and this is not pleasant, but meanwhile, we are busy, studying new things. I must tell you, my good brother, that I have here quite a cozy little home. Cheerful, sunny rooms, a nightingale and a greenfinch :—the latter, however, is greatly superior as an artist to his celebrated colleague, for, while the first remains on his bar grumpy and moody, the other jumps about in his cage, looking so joyous and good-natured, as if, to begin with, he was not in the least jealous, but, instead of that, supposes himself created merely for the purpose of cheering his silent friend! And then he sings a song, so high, so deep, so charming and so sonorous, that I sit down beside him and, within, lift up my voice in a mute song of praise to Him whose 'strength is made perfect in weakness.' Ah! it is divine to feel really good. My dear friend! I do feel so happy now. It seems to me I have come from a stormy sea into a peaceful cottage. Many struggles have calmed down, many thoughts have become clearer, many a star is gleaming forth again and I bend my knee before the Throne of Grace and exclaim: 'Thy will be done.' Farewell! God bless and protect my brother is the sincere wish of his affectionate sister

"JENNY."

This peace in the "cosy little home" is to be quickly broken up. A flight abroad is now to be taken, which will carry her further afield than Finland, or Copenhagen. It is no less a place than Berlin that has begun to take note of this wonderful singing, and is preparing to capture it for its own service and joy. Meyerbeer is there, engaged in bringing out a work, which is to celebrate all the glories of the

Prussian kingdom : and he is anxious to secure all the talent
open to him.   He had heard her sing, as we know, in Paris,
and had felt, then, that Berlin was her proper sphere: and,
now, his memory and his zeal are kindled anew by the enthusiasm of an artist of no mean ability, who arrived at
Berlin from Stockholm, with a fervent admiration for what
he had seen and heard there.   This artist was M. Paul
Taglioni, a brother of the famous *danseuse*, a descendant,
on the mother's side, of the Swedish tragedian Karsten, and
well known both in Paris and Berlin, not only as a graceful
dancer, but, also, as a skilful composer of Ballets, and a
ludicious and competent critic.   During the course of a
conversation with her son, many years afterwards, Madame
Goldschmidt spoke of the visit of M. Paul Taglioni to
Stockholm as having undoubtedly revived Meyerbeer's
recollections of what he had heard of her singing, at Paris,
in the month of July, 1842 ; and to M. Taglioni's report of
the successes he had witnessed at the Royal Theatre she
attributed Meyerbeer's marked anxiety to engage her at Berlin
in order that she might take the principal part in the new
opera—*Das Feldlager in Schlesien*—which he was composing
for the opening of the new Royal Opera House in the
Prussian capital.

The records of the proposals made by Meyerbeer are lost ;
but, some time in that summer, they reached sufficient
definiteness to induce her to determine on a visit to Dresden
in July, in order that she might work up her German to the
level demanded by an appearance, on such an historic
occasion, in the Opera House at Berlin.   Off to Dresden she
resolutely went, as soon as her season was over, ending, as it
did, on July 5, with eight performances of the *Turco in
Italia*—an almost forgotten opera of Rossini's—in which she
played the part of Fiorilla.   Mdlle. von Stedingk tells us
how she stole off to the Theatre, *incognita*, owing to the

Court being still in mourning, and heard her in this Opera, in which, as she says, "she made even the unpleasant part of Fiorilla graceful and womanly. But I prefer *Norma*, which is her greatest triumph."

Her enthusiasm breaks out in the record of a tea-party which she gave. "In honour of Jenny Lind, previous to her departure for Germany; Carl and Charlotte* were the other guests. It was to me an indescribable enjoyment, when she sat down at my piano, and sang to us. From that moment, my little room became dearer to me, and more harmonious than ever.

"The Queen Dowager was extremely kind to Jenny, at the farewell audience, presenting her with portrait medals of herself and the late King, and with a watch, which, she said, is 'To remind you not to forget the time of your return to us.'"

So the time came for the new venture. She had thought herself escaped "into a peaceful cottage from out of a stormy sea." So she had written to Hans Andersen in March. But a greater voyage into a wider sea is now before her. The wind is up: the sails are set: she must go. The first note that she sings in Berlin will have sealed her fate. There will be no withdrawal possible for her after that. Out into the deeper floods the strong currents will sweep her. The great European world, its peoples, its kings, its musicians, its heroes, will close in round her;—will claim her with irresistible insistence. Her returns to Stockholm — her "beloved Stockholm"—will become rarer, and rarer: at last, she will come back only to enrich it with endowments, and to bid it "Good-bye"!

---

* *I.e.* Count and Countess Carl Björnstjerna.

BOOK IV.

MASTERY.

CHAPTER I.

AND now, once more, the Curtain rises on a new Act in our Drama—a new phase in the great Art-life which we are endeavouring to depict, as faithfully as we may, by aid of the records that have been preserved to us, and the memories of some whose recollections are even more precious than written evidence or printed criticism.

Now, for the second time, we find Mademoiselle Lind leaving home and friends and all that lay nearest to her heart, and departing, in obedience to the call of Art, to seek new fortunes in a country utterly unknown to her; and we, who followed her earlier venture, must once more accompany her on a journey, undertaken, not as in the former case in the character of a timid student in search of knowledge, but in that of a profoundly cultivated and highly accomplished mistress of her Art, distrustful as ever of her own artistic power, yet quite capable of displaying that power to the wonder and delight of the most exacting critics in the world.

The opportunity was a splendid one, and might well have tempted any aspiring artist. But there was the terrible home-sickness in the way—the aching void which, in her case, seemed almost to verge upon physical malady, the cruel *nostalgia* of the medical schools.

Still, we may fairly believe that, to a nature so thoroughly

Scandinavian, German thought and German habits would
seem less unsympathetic than those of France. For France,
in temper, manners, and associations, stands curiously alone
among the nations of Europe; while between the Teutonic
and the Scandinavian peoples there exist, indubitably, many
ties and bonds, which continue to exercise a vital influence
such as is recognised and felt in the most intimate departments of life.

No bond exists of stronger tenure than religious conformity. Now, religious thought was no less deeply affected
in Sweden and Norway than in the northern provinces of
Germany by the doctrines set forth in the religious teaching
of Luther and his disciples, and the affinity thus established
when those doctrines were first preached to the world was
certainly not weakened by the terrible experiences of the
Thirty Years' War.

Again, the touching pictures of Scandinavian home-life,
painted in such glowing and natural colours by Frederika
Bremer and Hans Christian Andersen, find a ready response
under many a German roof-tree, and are in living sympathy
with practical home-life on the banks of the Elbe and the
Weser.

Here, then, are two points which may be fairly looked upon
as connecting links between the two races—to say nothing of
others which it would be manifestly beyond our province to
notice in our present chapter.

We may hope, therefore, if we give due weight to these
considerations, that Mdlle. Lind did not feel herself quite so
much a stranger in Germany as she had previously done in
France, though her attachment to her own country was so
deep and passionate that it seemed as if she could never be
truly happy in any other.

But it rarely falls to the lot of genius to choose its own
sphere of action. Events had shaped themselves·irrevocably.

The die once cast, nothing remained but to submit to the necessities of the case; to press forward on the only path that still remained open, while all side issues were hopelessly barred; and to determine that, come what might, it should lead to success; and this is what Mdlle. Lind did.

Her farewell to Sweden had been, as we have already seen, a touching one.

The reader will not have forgotten the incidents mentioned in connection with it by Fröken Maria von Stedingk, who supplements the account in her Diary with the words, " I was also present at the farewell representation, and felt that I had never seen anything so superior as Jenny Lind."

She was indeed "superior" in every sense of the word. It was time that the Germans should know this; but it needed careful preparation.

It had never been her wont to trust to genius alone for results which, she well knew, could be attained only by the union of genius with conscientious industry. As a cultivated musician, a singer, an actress, a sympathetic interpreter of the master-pieces of the greatest dramatic composers of the modern schools, she had nothing more to learn. She did not even need experience ; for, after forming her method in Paris, she had already had ample opportunity for testing its excellence in practical connection with the stage. But in order to ensure her success at Berlin it was necessary that she should add to these high qualifications an intimate acquaintance with the pronunciation, at least, of the German language, if not, indeed, a thorough mastery of its grammatical construction. We have already witnessed the zeal with which, in Paris, she strove to overcome the difficulties of two languages—French and Italian—the necessity for studying which then presented itself to her for the first time. She

now found herself placed in precisely the same position with
regard to German; and, far from attempting to evade the
difficulty, she adopted the best possible expedient for over-
coming it. She determined to set apart a sufficient time for
quiet and regular study, not in the city in which she was to
appear for the first time before a German audience, but
in Dresden, where she would not only be able to obtain
without difficulty the best possible instruction, but could
also usefully supplement it by attending the performances
at one of the best Opera-Houses in Germany. And here,
too, Meyerbeer had arranged to meet her, for the purpose of
consultation with regard to the principal part in the important work—*Das Feldlager in Schlesien*—which he was
preparing for the reopening of the Grand Opera House in
Berlin.

To Dresden, then, she repaired, accompanied by her aunt,
Fröken Apollonia Lindskog — familiarly known by her
relatives as Tante Lona—arriving there on the 25th of
July, three weeks only after her last performance in Stockholm. Truly, it was not her habit to waste much time in
" needful rest."

By the luckiest of chances she was welcomed at the very
moment of her arrival in the Saxon capital by her trusty and
valued friend, Herr Jakob Axel Josephson, who was then,
through her generous assistance, prosecuting his studies in
Germany, and who, while accidentally crossing the Alte
Brücke, the grand old bridge over the Elbe, passed a crowd
of carriages conveying passengers into the town from the
terminus of the Leipzig Railway, and, peeping into one
of these, saw Mdlle. Lind with Tante Lona sitting by her
side.

"I hailed the driver immediately," he writes in his Diary.
' The carriage stopped; and, as soon as I could force my way
through the crowd, I paid my respects to the travellers; ar-

ranged to call on them, later in the day, at their hotel, and
left them to continue their journey."[*]

After paying his visit, and finding her "happy and contented," he resumes :—

" It was, in fact, to Jenny that I was indebted for the
means of coming here myself. I had therefore a great deal
to say to her, but I found it difficult to express my meaning,
and she herself seemed to turn a deaf ear to me. Between
old friends there is no need of many words." [†]

The evening was pleasantly spent in a walk on the
Brühl'sche Terrasse by moonlight, followed by a friendly
supper at the hotel ; and after devoting the next morning to
an exhaustive exploration of the town in search of private
apartments for the ladies, a pianoforte for Mdlle. Lind, and
another for Herr Josephson, the three friends walked together,
at six o'clock, to the fine old Opera-House,[‡] to hear Wagner's
Rienzi, which had been produced there, with great success, in
1842, and had furnished the first stepping-stone to its
composer's subsequent reputation.

It will naturally be understood that, having visited Dresden
for purposes of study only, Mdlle. Lind lived a life of comparative seclusion, residing in the private lodgings found for
her by Herr Josephson, and very rarely going into society.
She was furnished however, as a matter of course, with
letters of introduction to the Swedish Consul, Herr Karl
Kaskel—who happened to be a personal friend of Meyerbeer
—and Herr Josephson's sympathetic pen has furnished us
with an account of her appearance at an evening party given,
during the last week in July, at the country house of that

---

[*] ' *Aus dem Leben eines Schwedischen Componisten ; Gedenkblätter an
Jakob Axel Josephson*,' von N. P. Ödman (Stockholm, 1886), vol. ii.
[†] *Ibid.*
[‡] Long since burned down, and rebuilt on a still grander scale.

gentleman's father. Making due allowance for the somewhat highly coloured language of a young man just entering
upon an artist's life and determined to employ his critical
faculties to the best possible advantage, we shall find the
narrative a very interesting one.

"It is just a month," he says in his Diary, "since I left
Sweden. This short time has already been rich in experiences, and brought me into contact with many interesting
acquaintances. I have heard a great deal of music, and
made various discoveries in connection with its condition in
Germany at the present time. Although the love for music
of the best kind, as it has been fostered in Germany for more
than a century, is more at home there than in other countries,
one must confess that it is only instrumental music that is
thus encouraged, while the Art of Song lacks representatives
everywhere. It is therefore not to be wondered at that a
talent so genial as that of Jenny Lind, awakening great and
unusual interest wherever it is brought into notice, should
now, like a lightning flash, illumine the darkness of the
singer's night in Art-loving Germany, penetrate the overflowing mass of German music and kindle the flame of
enthusiasm.

"The beginning of this was effected this evening, and
though only in a private *soirée*, still in such a way that its
repetition on a larger scale can scarcely be delayed. Consul
Kaskel had, in addition to some music-loving residents
in Dresden, invited Fräulein Lind, Fröken Lindskog,
Herr Beskow and family, Pastor Ödberg with his
pupils, and myself. We were really however the guests
of Consul Kaskel's father (the head of a rich and influential
banking firm), who lives in a pleasant country house on the
Elbe.

"The evening began, as usual, with conversation, for the
polite and true-hearted Saxons are well known as excellent
hosts and the Saxon ladies as entertaining hostesses. But
after a little time they begged Jenny Lind to sing; and,
sitting down to the piano, she began with Berg's *Fjerran i
skog*.* Scarcely had she ended it before a cry of satisfaction

---

* *Herdegossen*; a Swedish song, by Herr Berg, containing some long-
sustained notes concerning which we shall have more to say in a future
chapter.

rang through the room. She repeated the song, followed it
up with *Tro ci gladjen*, sang *Fjerran i skog*, for the third
time, and finished with the Romance from Winter's *Das
unterbrochene Opferfest*, which flows so sweetly and lovingly
on the true classical stream. As Jenny, later on, sang the Aria
from *Niobe** in her grand style, and adorned it with her most
beautiful *fioritura*, the general delight burst forth into loud
applause, and all remained throughout the rest of the
evening simply enchanted, for God knows how long a time
had elapsed since any one had heard anything like it.

"For us Swedes the meeting was a truly brilliant inauguration of Jenny's entrance into Germany, and an
especially joyful one, though only in so small a house ; and
we remarked with pleasure how anxious the good Germans
were to hear her in public, whether on the stage or in the
the Concert-room."†

Apart from the sensation she created on the occasion
to which Herr Josephson alludes, she lived, in company
with Fröken Apollonia, in strictest privacy during the
whole of the time she remained in Dresden. She had
indeed but little time permitted to her, even for consultation
with Meyerbeer or for the purpose of study; for on the
28th of August—one month and three days only after her
arrival at the terminus of the Leipzig Railway—she was
recalled to Stockholm, to assist, in her character of "Court
Singer," at the festivities which graced the Coronation of
King Oscar I.

Queen Desideria's watch had already marked the hour for
the wanderer's return, ‡ though on this occasion it was to
be represented by a very brief visit.

The Court was now out of mourning, and all Stockholm in
festal attire to do honour to the approaching ceremony.
Unfortunately, Fröken Marie von Stedingk, being in close

---

* ' *Il soave e ben contento*,' from Pacini's *Niobe*, with its brilliant
caballetta—' *I tuoi frequenti palpiti*'—in B♭.

† N. P. Ödman, in *op. cit.* vol. ii.

‡ See page 182.

attendance on the Queen Dowager, was prevented by the
imperious demands of Court etiquette from attending the
performances at the Royal Theatre, and her Diary therefore
furnishes us with no account of Mdlle. Lind's appearances.
But we know, from the archives of the theatre, that they
were ten in number—viz., three of *La Sonnambula ;* three of
Norma ; one of Gluck's *Armida ;* and three introducing
single acts of *Der Freischütz, Norma, Lucia di Lammermoor,*
and *Anna Bolena.**

So well prepared were the Swedes to appreciate their
talented countrywoman at her true value that they could
not endure the idea of losing her. In the hope of preventing her from singing in Germany, Count Hamilton, the
then Director of the Royal Theatre, offered her an engagement as principal singer, for eight years, at an annual salary
of five thousand dollars,† which was to be continued to her
after the termination of the contract as a pension for life.
To this offer she felt very much inclined to agree, though
her best friends tried hard to make her see that, by so
doing, she would deprive the rest of Europe of all participa-
tion in the advantages derivable from her exceptional talent.
For a long time her resolution remained immovable. But
one day a trusted friend bethought himself of a curious
method of persuasion, which could only have occurred to one
who understood her nature thoroughly. After leaving her,
as he feared on the point of signing the dangerous contract,
he encountered in the street a certain Consul General who
prided himself upon an intimate knowledge of everything
connected with music. To this gentleman he narrated the
circumstance, with many expressions of regret as to the turn

---

* The dates were:—Sept. 18, 20, *La Sonnambula ;* Sept. 24, *Der
Freischütz* (act ii.) ; Sept. 26, *Norma* and *Anna Bolena* (single acts) ;
Sept. 27, *Der Freischütz,* and *Lucia* (single acts) ; Sept. 30, *Armida ;*
Oct. 2, *La Sonnambula ;* Oct. 4, 8, 9, *Norma.*

† About £420 sterling.

affairs were taking. But to his great surprise the Consul General took the opposite view, maintaining that, notwithstanding her successes at home, the artist herself must have known that her powers were unequal to the attainment of a similar result in a more extended sphere. Well knowing the effect which this absurd misrepresentation of the true state of the case could not fail to produce upon Jenny's mind, her friend lost no time in making her acquainted with it; and then and there he had the satisfaction of seeing her tear up the fatal contract and thus put an end to the discussion for ever.

Retreat was now impossible, and as soon as practicable after the last performance of *Norma*, on the 9th of October, she took leave of her friends and started on her trying journey —a journey now forced upon her by her refusal to accept the engagement offered to her at Stockholm, but none the less trying on that account, and rendered painful, moreover, by those fears for the unknown future which her constitutional diffidence forbade her to shake off.

CHAPTER II.

NOTWITHSTANDING the temporary interruption of her linguistic studies at Dresden, Mdlle. Lind was far from being unprepared for her approaching trial when the appointed time drew near.

Of the severity of that trial and the gravity of its inevitable though as yet wholly uncertain consequences it would have been difficult to form an exaggerated idea. The successes achieved by the young artist in her own country counted as nothing when considered in connection with the ordeal that awaited her in Berlin. That a native singer of rare and undoubted talent should have been received with acclamation by her own admiring countrymen, that her reappearance on the stage she had trodden as a child should have been regarded by the audience assembling at the Royal Theatre as a national triumph, that the critics of Stockholm should have been ready to endorse, in its fullest significance, the verdict pronounced, in a moment of enthusiasm, by the general public; all this was naturally to have been expected, and might indeed have been easily foreseen by any one with discernment enough to read the signs of the times, as Fröken Marie von Stedingk's account of the circumstances sufficiently proves. But would the critics of Berlin endorse the verdict pronounced by those of Stockholm? That was indeed another and a very different question. Stockholm was not, and never had been, a centre of artistic

progress, even of the second order. The Royal Theatre, at
its best, gave but a dim reflection of glories which in the
more famous European Opera Houses were of too common
occurrence to excite any extraordinary amount of astonishment.   On the other hand, though for very different reasons,
the triumph at Stockholm could not be dismissed as an
altogether unimportant factor in the coming crisis. And
here lay the gravest difficulty in the situation—an almost
unprecedented paradox, which the future alone could solve.
Though, in so far as her European reputation was concerned,
Mdlle. Lind was really preparing to make, at Berlin, her
true *début* in the great world of Art, she had been preceded
by rumours which rendered it imperative that she should
appear there, not in the character of an unknown *débutante*,
but in that of a finished and recognised artist of the first
order; of a *prima donna*, to be judged, not by the measure of
her own merit, but by the achievements of the greatest
prime donne who had appeared before the world since the
beginning of the century. For however limited might have
been the experiences of the Stockholm critics, there were
critics in Berlin who were familiar with the performances
of Mesdames Malibran and Pasta, and Mara and Sontag and
Schroeder Devrient, and even of the famous Madame
Catalani herself, to say nothing of Mesdames Grisi and
Persiani and other brilliant stars in the contemporaneous
operatic firmament; and it was absolutely certain that
with the performances of these bright luminaries of past and
present years would the performances of Mdlle. Lind be
mercilessly though, it was to be hoped, not unjustly compared.

We hear people wonder sometimes why she was
so modest, so diffident, so distrustful of her own powers.
But surely she had reason on her side a thousand times.
She was not blind, could not possibly have been blind,

to the perfection of her own ideal; but she did not know, and had no means of informing herself, how far the greatness of that ideal was likely to commend itself to the severely critical audience before which she was about to appear. She had never heard either Catalani or Pasta, or Sontag or Malibran, yet circumstances had placed her in rivalry with them all. Was her ideal really greater than theirs? Was it even as great? How could she tell! She must have seen the difficulties of the situation; must have felt that her position was, in many respects, an altogether exceptional one. Yet, for all that, she did not shrink from the ordeal, and when the time of trial came she was ready to meet it.

After her last performance at Stockholm, on the 9th of October, she made instant preparation for her journey, and, accompanied by Mdlle. Louise Johansson, arrived, in the third week of October, at Berlin, where she made arrangements for residing, during the winter, in the house of Madame Reyer, No. 43, in the Französische Strasse.*

While preparing for her first appearance on the stage, she passed her time in complete retirement from public life, but her reception by the circle of private friends to whom she was introduced was of the warmest character. Meyerbeer was, of course, unremitting in his attentions. His position towards her was, indeed, an almost painfully responsible one. He alone was answerable for her presence in the Prussian capital, and her success or failure were matters of scarcely less importance to him than to her. His taste, his experience, his artistic judgment were staked upon her fitness to sustain the position to which he had introduced her. Through him she was privately presented to the Royal Family, the members of which, and especially Queen

---

* Madame Reyer (sister to the Baroness von Ridderstolpe) appears to have been the wife of a schoolmaster in Berlin.

Elizabeth, received her with a grace and courtesy which did much to render her visit more than ordinarily agreeable. On one occasion—memorable as the first on which she was called upon to display her talent in the presence of the Court —she was invited to a reception given by the Princess of Prussia * one evening during the last week in November. Concerning this she thus wrote to her guardian, Judge Munthe—

" Berlin, Dec. 2, 1844.

" I have sung at Court, and been so very fortunate as to please greatly. This may sound somewhat conceited, but I do not mean it so. The Countess Rossi (Sontag) was present, and my modesty prevents me from telling you what she is reported to have said. I am meeting with extraordinary success everywhere. I go out much into fashionable society, because this gives the first entrance into the world of Art; and—do you know ?—I am already known by all Berlin, and people talk of me with an interest so lively, and so flattering to me, that I begin to think I must be in Stockholm!

" Forgive me! dear M. Munthe, for thus openly speaking of things as they occur. I promise not to become proud or conceited; only glad and happy when things go well."

Among the guests present at the reception thus playfully described were the late Earl and Countess of Westmorland. Lord Westmorland was at that time the English Ambassador at the Court of Prussia; and, through the kindness of a member of His Excellency's family, we are able to present our readers with a vivid picture of the impression made by Mdlle. Lind's singing upon the Countess of Westmorland, who, it must be remembered, was no unenlightened or inexperienced listener; for Lord Westmorland was himself an ardent student of music, an excellent violinist, the composer of no less than one English and six Italian Operas, and the founder of the Royal Academy of Music in London.

* Afterwards the Empress Augusta.

When released from his political duties he lived in an atmosphere of Art; and Lady Westmorland's testimony is the more valuable since she was in the constant habit of hearing at home the best music of the time. The lady to whose kindness we are indebted for our information writes thus:—

"It was, I think, in 1844 that Meyerbeer brought Jenny Lind to Berlin, to come out at the new Opera House there in the part he had written for her in his Opera of *Das Feldlager in Schlesien.*

"He had told all his friends (amongst whom were my parents *) about this wonderful voice, and predicted that she would be the greatest singer-artist the century had produced. There was great curiosity about her, and Meyerbeer talked of her as '*un vrai diamant de génie.*'

"Before she appeared on the stage he was asked to bring her to sing at a small musical party at the Princess of Prussia's (the late Dowager Empress Augusta) arranged for the purpose. For some reasons, my father was prevented from going; my mother went alone. She went in, full of curiosity, and saw sitting by the piano a thin, pale, plain-featured girl, looking awkward and nervous, and like a very shy country school-girl. She could not believe her eyes, and said that she and her neighbours—among whom was Countess Rossi (Henriette Sontag), whose fame as a singer and a beauty was then still recent—began to speculate whether Meyerbeer was playing a practical joke on them, and when he came up to speak to them my mother asked him if he was really serious in meaning to bring that frightened child out in his Opera. His only answer was '*Attendez, Miladi.*'

"When the time came for her song—I do not know what it was—my mother used to say it was the most extraordinary experience she ever remembered. The wonderful notes came ringing out, but over and above that was the wonderful TRANSFIGURATION—no other word could apply—which came over her entire face and figure, lightening them up with the whole fire and dignity of her genius. The effect on the whole audience was simply marvellous, and to the last day

* His Excellency and Lady Westmorland.

of her life my mother used to recall it vividly and its effect
upon her.

"When she reached home, my father asked her—

"'Well, what do you think of Meyerbeer's wonder?'

"She answered—

"'She is simply an angel.'

"'Is she so very handsome?'

"'I saw a plain girl when I went in, but when she
began to sing her face simply and literally "shone like that
of an angel." I never *saw* anything or *heard* anything the
least like it.'"

"This first effect did not wear off when she appeared on
the stage. My mother used to say that she thought her
dramatic power was quite as great as her musical genius,
and that if she had had no voice she might still have been
the greatest of living actresses. And there was this
peculiarity about her acting—that it was entirely part of
herself. It seemed not so much that she entered into the
part as that she became, for the moment, that which she
had to express. For this reason her acting was unequal.
She could not render anything in which there was a suggestion repugnant to her own higher nature. But in a part
that suited her—such as the *Sonnambula*—she expressed
every varying emotion of the character perfectly because
she really felt it. And, for the same reasons, she never
acted the same scene twice precisely alike, just as in real
life no one does the same thing twice precisely in the
same way. In her gestures and tones there were little
unconscious variations, which the people who acted with
her and went through their own parts with mechanical
precision often found disconcerting.

"In these early days she was very careless of outward
appearances—her Art possessed her and left her no time to
think of herself. She disliked the artificial adjuncts of
rouge, &c., which are a necessity of the stage, and as a
natural result was often unbecomingly dressed. My mother
herself and her friend Madame Wichmann remonstrated
with her about this and made her attend more to these
details, and in the end she learned to dress for her parts
becomingly and gracefully, though never conventionally.

"On looking back I cannot help being struck with one
thing. My parents lived a great deal in musical and
theatrical society of all kinds, and I recollect, from my
earliest childhood, hearing musicians and actors talked of

and often praised. But even quite as a little girl, in Berlin, long before I was old enough to know anything about it, or even to be taken to the Opera, I can distinctly remember having the impression that Jenny Lind was something quite different from the ordinary people I heard discussed. And there has always been a sort of reverence in the way they spoke of her—as they would have spoken of a very beautiful and very sacred picture or poem. I suppose it was the intense purity of her nature that made her very acting religious. I cannot exactly express it, but I very distinctly recollect, as a child, associating her name with a sort of mysterious reverence. And even now the same childish feeling seems to come back to me mixed with the remembrance of my mother's enthusiastic love for her." *

These interesting recollections prove conclusively that even before her first appearance in public Mdlle. Lind had completely won the hearts of a brilliant and influential circle of private friends, many of whom remained in affectionate intercourse with her to the last day of her life. Their kind sympathy must have encouraged her to face the coming trial with the resolution and fortitude it so imperatively demanded; for, strong as was her determination when the crisis arrived, the time of anticipation was always one of terror and depression.

At this period also an event took place which exercised a marked influence on the artistic phase of her professional career, though less perhaps in connection with the Stage than with the Concert-room.

She had been invited, on the 21st of October, to a *Soirée* at the house of Professor Wichmann in the Hasenheger Strasse. At the moment of starting Meyerbeer called to pay her a visit; and having, no doubt, many important matters to discuss with her, stayed so long that she arrived at the evening party under the escort of Madame von

---

* From a private memorandum written by the Lady Rose Weigall, by whose kind permission it is inserted here.

Ridderstolpe some hours after the appointed time. However, late as it was, she did arrive there, and in a letter dated October the 22nd she thus describes the great event of the evening :—

"Last night I was invited to a very pleasant and elegantly furnished house, where I saw and spoke to Mendelssohn Bartholdy,[*] and he was incredibly friendly and polite, and spoke of my 'great talent.' I was a little surprised, and asked him on what ground he spoke in this way. 'Well !' he said, 'for this reason, that all who have heard you are of one opinion only, and that is so rare a thing that it is quite sufficient to prove to me what you are.' "

This first meeting between the two great artists was a memorable one for both, and formed the foundation of a friendship which terminated only with the death of the beloved composer in 1847.

That Mdlle. Lind stood in sorest need of all the help and consolation that friendship could afford during the period of suspense that preceded her introduction to the general public is evident from private letters, in which she expresses herself in terms of almost hopeless despondency with regard to her capacity for fulfilling the expectations that had been formed of her. Her anxiety had, in fact, become almost intolerable—so deep that it prompted her to write, in agonised insistence, to her friends in Sweden, even before she had any decisive intelligence to communicate to them either of good or evil.

That the true nature of the intelligence she was really justified in sending has long since been anticipated by our readers we cannot reasonably doubt; but though the coming triumph seemed assured, we shall see presently that the path to the Stage was not exactly strewn with roses.

---

[*] Mendelssohn was at that time residing at Frankfort, but he frequently came to Berlin, either in his character of General Musik Director to King Friedrich Wilhelm IV. or for the purpose of visiting his family.

CHAPTER III.

BEFORE narrating the events connected with Mademoiselle Lind's first appearance at the Court Theatre at Berlin it is desirable that we should say a few words in explanation of the more than ordinary interest attached to the reopening of that splendid Opera-House, so famous in the history of Art and so closely interwoven with that of the Hohenzollern dynasty.

One of the first acts of King Frederick the Great, after his accession to the throne of Prussia,* on the 30th of May, 1740, was the foundation of an Opera-House, designed on a scale sufficiently splendid to eclipse the glories of every other theatre in Europe.

The scheme was worthy of its author, who was one of the most enthusiastic patrons of Art then living—a "Royal Musician" in every sense of the word; and the promptitude with which it was carried out gave early proof of the decision which formed so prominent a feature in his character.

The preparation of the design was nominally committed to the Freiherr von Knobelsdorf, the Court architect; but, if tradition may be trusted, its most important features were suggested by the King himself.

The building was completed in the winter of the year 1742, and on the 7th of December its inauguration was celebrated with extraordinary pomp by a magnificent performance of

* Under the title of King Friedrich II.

Graun's *Cesare & Cleopatra*, at which the King and all the
Court were present. The fitness of the theatre for the high
purpose for which it was designed was pronounced by those
best able to form a judgment upon the subject to be perfect;
and, fortunately for the history of Art, an eye-witness of no
small experience who visited Berlin in 1772—just thirty
years after its completion—and was present at a performance
at which the King himself assisted, has left us the following
eloquent description of its then appearance: a description
which we quote in preference to a more modern account,
because it furnishes an exact and graphic picture of the theatre
in which Mademoiselle Lind was to make her *début*, for
after the calamitous fire of 1843 the present Opera-House was
reconstructed so exactly upon the model of the old one that
one and the same description will serve for both.

"The theatre is insulated," says Burney, " in a large square,
in which there are more magnificent buildings than I ever
saw, at one glance, in any city of Europe. It was constructed
by His present Majesty soon after his coming to the Crown.
The principal front has two entrances: one on a level with
the ground, and the other by a grand double escalier. This
front is decorated with six Corinthian pillars, with their
entablature entire, supporting a pediment ornamented with
reliefs, and with this inscription upon it—

"FRIDERICUS REX APOLLINI ET MUSIS.

" This front is decorated with a considerable number of the
statues of poets and dramatic actors, which are placed in
niches. The two sides are constructed in the same manner,
except that there are no pillars.

" A considerable part of the front of this edifice forms a
hall, in which the Court has a repast on *ridotta* days. The
rest is for the theatre, which, besides a vast pit, has four rows
of boxes, thirteen in each, and these severally contain thirty
persons. It is one of the widest theatres I ever saw, though
it seems rather short in proportion.

" The performance of the Operas begins at six o'clock; the
King, with the Princes and his attendants, are placed in the

pit, close to the orchestra; the Queen, the Princesses, and other ladies of distinction sit in the front boxes. Her Majesty is saluted at her entrance into the theatre and at her departure thence by two bands of kettle-drums placed, one on each side of the house, in the upper boxes.

"The King always stands beside the *Maestro di Cappella*, in sight of the score, which he frequently looks at, and indeed performs the part of *Director-General* here as much as that of *Generalissimo* in the field." *

The building thus described by Dr. Burney stood almost intact, with but slight modifications suggested from time to time to suit the conveniences of the age, for more than a hundred years. But a fate hangs over theatres which it seems impossible to evade. On the night between the 18th and 19th of August, 1843, it was burnt to the ground, in the hundred and second year of its existence; and, following the example of his illustrious ancestor, King Frederick William IV. commanded its immediate reconstruction almost exactly upon the lines of the original design. The task of rebuilding the edifice was, on this occasion, entrusted to Baurath C. Ferd. Langhans, jun., who departed from Knobelsdorf's design only in narrowing the elliptical form of the interior, the irregularity of which had attracted Dr. Burney's notice more than seventy years previously; in re-arranging the boxes upon a more convenient plan; and in making some indispensable changes in the disposition of the staircases. The modern building, therefore, with the inauguration of which we are now concerned, was almost an exact reproduction of that described by our learned and genial musical historian in 1773.

The new theatre was completed towards the close of the year 1844, and opened in the presence of the Court on the evening of the 7th of December.

* 'The Present State of Music in Germany, the Netherlands, and United Provinces'; by Charles Burney, Mus. Doc. (London, 1773, vol. ii. pp. 94, *et seq.*)

It was naturally to be expected that on an occasion so deeply interesting to the leading members of the House of Hohenzollern care would be taken to present a piece in harmony with the spirit of the festival.   To this end Meyerbeer had been commanded, as we have already seen, to compose the music for an Opera the *libretto* of which was founded upon an episode in the history of King Frederick the Great, and had arranged the meeting with Mdlle. Lind, in Dresden, for the purpose of accommodating the principal part to the style of her performance.   The piece was to be called *Das Feldlager in Schlesien,** and the *libretto,* carefully prepared by L. Rellstab, brought into prominence an incident in the history of that famous campaign in Silesia, through which the world first learned to appreciate at its just value the military genius of the redoubtable " Vater Fritz." This piece was a good one, full of highly dramatic situations, though entirely free from violence or exaggeration.   Meyerbeer's music was of his best.   Fired by the splendour of this opportunity, he had thrown his whole soul into the work, and it was in response to his desire that the principal *rôle* should be performed by the most finished artist who could be persuaded to undertake it that Mademoiselle Lind had been invited to Berlin.

But the intrigues of the stage are inscrutable, and cannot be foreseen even by the most experienced directors.   Meyerbeer's cherished project was opposed by a local interest.

Fräulein Tuczec, who had for years sung at the theatre as *prima donna,* claimed the right of appearing in the principal part, on the reopening of the house, on the ground

---

* The full title of the Opera was, ' *Das Feldlager in Schlesien. Oper, in drei Aufzügen, in Lebensbildern aus der Zeit Friedrich des Grossen, von L. Rellstab. Musik von Meyerbeer. Tänze von Hoguet.*' ' *The Camp of Silesia. Opera, in three acts, in Life-pictures from the time of Frederick the Great,*' by L. Rellstab. Music by Meyerbeer. Dances by Hoguet.'

that she, being a permanent member of the company, enjoyed privileges of which it would be unjust to deprive her in favour of a stranger engaged for " guest performances " only ; * and for the perhaps still stronger reason that, when it had appeared doubtful whether Mademoiselle Lind, after having been recalled to Stockholm for the coronation of King Oscar, would arrive in Berlin in time to undertake the part, she herself had been requested to study it.

The case was not without its difficulties. On both sides there was a show of justice with respect to the conflicting claims.

Meyerbeer was perfectly justified in urging that not only had he written the part expressly for Mademoiselle Lind, but that she had been invited to Berlin for the express purpose of singing it,† while on the other hand he could not conceal from himself the fact that, since the part had been given to Fräulein Tuczec for study, when doubt arose as to the probable date of Mademoiselle Lind's arrival in Berlin, her chagrin when she found that it had been withdrawn from her was far from unnatural. The moral strength of her claim was patent to every one. Whether or not she had talent enough to justify her in forcing that claim on the present occasion was another question, which the event only could decide. Meyerbeer, no doubt, foresaw the result of her determination ; but with that result Mademoiselle Lind was in no wise concerned. We have written to little purpose if our readers have not already obtained sufficient insight into her character to feel convinced that she would be the last person in the world either to infringe upon a lawful privilege or to take advantage of an untoward accident.

---

* *Gastrollen.* In the German theatres, performers not belonging to the regular company, and employed for a limited number of performances only, are called ' guests ' (*Gäste*), and engaged on special terms, without a formal contract in writing.

† See page 188.

When Meyerbeer endeavoured to persuade her to take his view of the circumstances, she even went so far as to appeal to the authority of the Haus Minister, Prince Wittgenstein, in support of what she considered to be Fräulein Tuczec's just claim; and it was actually through the Prince's intervention, imported into the case at her earnest request, that Fräulein Tuczec was able to fight with any prospect of success against the enormous weight of Meyerbeer's influence at Court.

But even before the case was decided, and while Fräulein Tuczec's claim was still in abeyance, a false account of the circumstances had already found its way into the newspapers; and to correct this Mademoiselle Lind wrote the following letter to her friend, M. Lars Hierta, at Stockholm:—

"Berlin, Nov. 25, 1844.

"Herr Königl. Secretär,

"Kindly excuse me if, for a few moments, I beg to encroach upon your valuable time.

"Having seen, in an article in the 'Aftonblad,' reproduced from the 'Frankfurter Ober-Postamt-Zeitung,' that my friends in Stockholm are incorrectly informed about my position in Berlin, I venture, Herr Königlicher Secretär, to call your attention to the following lines.

"I came to Berlin under the impression that the principal *rôle* in the new opera * had been assigned to no other than myself; but I found that it was also given for study to Mademoiselle Tuczec, under the apprehension that my detention in Sweden might otherwise have rendered it necessary to delay the opening of the new Opera-House. On my arrival in Berlin, however, Meyerbeer took it for granted that I, for whom he had composed the part, should undertake to sing it at the first representation. He therefore called upon Mademoiselle Tuczec, and—perhaps with some temper—informed her that I had now arrived, that the part was mine, and that it was consequently my duty to sing it for the first time.

"Mademoiselle Tuczec, who is very nervous, was altogether

* *Das Feldlager in Schlesien.*

beside herself, and wrote a petition to the King begging
His Majesty to permit her to appear at the opening of the
new theatre.

"When this came to my knowledge I was greatly surprised,
for I had not heard a single word of it, and did not even
know that the *rôle* had been given to Mademoiselle Tuczec.
And as I am not fond of strife and understand nothing whatever of intrigue, I ceded my place with pleasure—the more
willingly because I considered that Mademoiselle Tuczec was
right, since she had had the part for some time, and was,
moreover, a great favourite with the public here, while I am
quite unknown and a foreigner also.

"In addition to this there remains the question of the
foreign language. It surely would be very unfavourable for
me, under these circumstances, to make my first appearance
in connection with dialogue and melodrama!

"It is I, then, who have really arranged the whole
matter, and Mademoiselle Tuczec seems quite satisfied
with me.

"I hope, Herr Königlicher Secretär, that you have been
able to understand my disjointed phrases, and that you will
be good enough to say a few words in my behalf in your
paper in order that my friends in Stockholm may be aware
of the true state of the matter—and also of this, that, though
I am a poor sensitive lonely girl, in a foreign land and
surrounded by cabals and intrigues, I am none the less
possessed of a heart that beats high at the thought of Sweden,
and am consequently not always in a cheerful mood; and this
I know, that the pleasure I have been happy enough to give
my countrymen—at times, perhaps, when my mind was most
oppressed—would be forgotten, beyond all doubt, if at any
moment I appeared here without success, even though my
talent remained undiminished. But rather than involve
myself in law-suits I would renounce everything; and as
long as I have my two hands to work with I would rather
earn my bread, under such circumstances, away from the
stage.

"I trust, Herr Königlicher Secretär, that you will be good
enough to excuse this long epistle, which now draws to an
end; and should you find anything in it worth writing about,
I venture to rely on the kindness you have always shown me,
and hope you will place me on this occasion in the light I
really deserve.

"Begging you to convey my kind regards to your wife and

the other members of your family, I take the liberty of signing myself,

" Your obedient servant,

" JENNY LIND." *

As the reader will, no doubt, have already foreseen, her intervention on the side of simple justice produced a marked reaction in Fräulein Tuczec's favour; and, to Meyerbeer's intense disappointment, the part of "Vielka," in the new Opera, was officially confided to the privileged *prima donna*.

The inauguration of the new Court Theatre was celebrated with the utmost possible splendour on the 7th of December, in presence of the Royal Family, the foreign ambassadors, and a brilliant gathering of all the rank and fashion of Berlin. The general success of the festival was, of course, assured beforehand; but though *Das Feldlager in Schlesien* contained some of the best and most attractive music that Meyerbeer had as yet produced, it was evident that it failed to make the desired impression upon the public—for the simple reason that the principal *rôle* was unsuited to the style of the performer who had undertaken to interpret it. The part of "Vielka" had not been written for Fräulein Tuczec. It bristled with difficulties with which but very few of the best singers of the day would have been able to contend; and to add to the embarrassment of the situation, the music, expressly written for Mademoiselle Lind, had been so exactly adapted to the quality of her voice and the style of her execution that, deprived of the individuality which she was prepared to communicate to it, it would necessarily have lost its greatest charm if it had been entrusted to' any other singer than herself, however highly accomplished. As it was, the new piece could scarcely have been regarded as having

---

* Letter from Mdlle. Lind to Herr Königl. Secretär, Lars Hjerta, dated, Berlin, Nov. 25, 1844; and inserted by permission of his family.

fallen very much short of a failure, and Meyerbeer's chagrin
at the cold reception of his long-cherished work was very bitter
indeed.   It is true that Fräulein Tuczec appeared in it
altogether five times,* but after Mademoiselle Lind's *début*,
on the 15th of December, the two last performances were
treated by the public very much after the manner of "off-
nights."   It was an unfortunate mistake, and the more to be
regretted because it placed a really clever singer and actress
—which Mademoiselle Tuczec undoubtedly was—in a cruelly
false position.

* On Dec. 7, 10, 13, 17, and 22, 1844.

CHAPTER IV.

THE DÉBUT.

SINCE Mdlle. Lind had been prevented, by untoward circumstances, from taking an active part in the festival with which the new Opera-House was inaugurated, there clearly remained no reason why she should not make her first appearance before a German audience in one of her own favourite parts; and she herself felt it to be eminently desirable that an Italian opera should be selected for the occasion.

Her choice fell upon *Norma*, in which she had already achieved immense success, notwithstanding the well-known fact—or perhaps by reason of it—that her interpretation of the *rôle* differed in every one of its most striking characteristics from that adopted by every *prima donna* of note who had undertaken to impersonate the unhappy priestess from whom Bellini's master-piece takes its now familiar name. And what *prima donna* of note had not undertaken that most difficult impersonation? It was a part in which all the greatest soprano singers of the age had striven to shine; and though Mdlle. Lind chose it for her *début* simply because it was one of her favourite parts, and without a thought of constructive rivalry, she really, by that bold and, as it turned out, most happy choice, unconsciously staked her reputation against that of every *prima donna* who had charmed the public, from Madame Pasta, for whom the part was written, in 1832, to Madame Grisi, who was

P 2

nightly playing it in London and in Paris in the self-same
year 1844.

The *début* was fixed for Sunday the 15th of December,
and its success exceeded the warmest expectations of all
concerned. The public was in raptures—the critics were
disarmed. The heroines of the past and present were
forgotten. The new reading of the part commended itself to
all. Madame Pasta had rendered it with a noble energy,
a fiery power, worthy of high admiration, though, it must be
confessed, more remarkable for its vigour than its womanly
tenderness. Madame Grisi, inheriting the *rôle* directly from
her great predecessor, in company with whom she had, in
the original cast, played the secondary part of *Adalgisa* *
—Madame Grisi, with even less of tenderness and more
exaggerated energy, delineated a Pythoness—a passionate
savage, with whom none but a savage could have fallen in
love. But *Pollio* was not a savage. He was a true Roman,
voluptuous, inconstant, ready to sink weakly into the arms
of a new mistress without a thought of remorse, when his
passion for his first *inamorata* began to cool, but incapable
of yielding to the violence of a Mænad. He might reasonably have fallen in love with Madame Pasta's *Norma*, but
not with Madame Grisi's.

Upon these two primary interpretations of the part all
later ones were based, until, for the first time in its history,
Mdlle. Lind presented the impassioned Druidess before the
world in the character of a true woman. The critics of
Berlin, familiar with every tradition of the Stage, early
or recent, yielded at once to the logical consistency of this
beautiful though unfamiliar conception, and accepted the
new ideal as the highest impersonation of the character of
Norma that had as yet been presented to the public. One

* At the Teatro della Scala at Milan, during the carnival of 1832.

of them,* writing in the leading journal of the day, gives us the following account of the impression it made upon him both from a musical and a dramatic point of view, After some preliminary remarks of no general interest, he begins his critique proper with a description of the artist herself:—

"Her voice," he says, "not without fulness, but more pleasing than powerful, moves within the two soprano octaves, from the once to the thrice-marked C,† with charming lightness and certainty; though the middle register is sometimes shaded by a soft veil which serves to bring out the upper notes in clearest and most silvery contrast. This beautiful natural gift is supplemented by a groundwork of most diligent study. Her pronunciation—though the German language is not familiar to her—is pleasing, clear, and distinct. She possesses that sustaining-power of tone which in the best Italian school lends so peculiarly tender a colour to Recitative. Her melodies she accentuates in truest measure throughout. But the high cultivation of her style most strikingly manifests itself in the clearness and pearly evenness of her passages. We have heard such passages sung with greater rapidity, but never with greater perfection.

"So much for the Singer.

"And the Actress—especially in the elasticity of her motions—is of fully equal excellence.

"All her movements have a womanly charm, which gives a beautiful expression to her voice, while, at the same time, it shows no lack of character, or energy, or majesty.

"One might not unnaturally suppose, from these general features in the portrait of our artist, that *Norma*, at least, ruled by demons of darkness, would give her some trouble. But it is exactly here that her conception reconciles us with this fearful character. She bases it throughout upon the element of love, that one day changes this proud priestess into a humble slave; love, that thenceforth vanquishes the sombre flames of rage and vengeance with its soft and rosy rays. Pasta presents a "Norma" *before* whom, our artist a

---

* Herr Ludwig Rellstab, critic and poet, the author of the *libretto* of *Das Feldlager in Schlesien.*

† That is to say, from the notes known to English pianists as "middle C," to the C two octaves above it. But Mdlle. Lind's voice really extended far beyond this in the upward direction.

"Norma," *with* whom, we tremble. The art of the one is broader, more astonishing; that of the other more sweet and enthralling. Upon these essential peculiarities the part depends for its culminating point of interest.

"Until now no singer has ever sung the cavatina, *Keusche Göttin*,* as we think it ought to be sung. Our actress is the first who has satisfactorily performed this apparently easy task. She clothes the melody in that pale romantic moonlight under the influence of which it was conceived, and she knows so well how to sustain this colouring throughout the difficulties of the mechanical passages—in themselves less beautiful—that the highest triumph of her thrilling delivery is achieved in the clear execution of the chromatic runs. The singer here obtained a mark of recognition which has never before been witnessed within the experience of any of us—the air was encored, and the artist called forward in the middle of the act! May such barbarous applause, which destroys all the dramatic propriety of the work, never become naturalised among us! The singer herself seemed to feel it in its true light ; for her demeanour was so modest, as the affair proceeded, that on her part, at least, no interruption was noticeable.†

"We should be carried much too far were we to dilate upon every beautiful detail of the performance. The singer was charming from the first note to the last, and proved thereby that which we have so often vainly striven to impress upon many other performers, that the true beauty of Art, as well as its most powerful effect, lies in the skilful economisation of the means at command. There was nothing of that tormenting *piangendo*, that ceaseless wailing, that destroys all beauty of tone ; yet everywhere there was inmost spiritual expression, even in passages which are treated by others as

---

* "*Casta diva*" in the original Italian.

† It is not, we believe, generally known that the opening movement of the well-known cavatina—*Casta diva*—was originally written for Madame Pasta in the key of G. It stood thus in the MS. score formerly used at Her Majesty's Theatre, and destroyed in the conflagration of December 6th, 1867, but the only printed edition with which we are acquainted in which it appears in the original key is the complete one published some years ago by Messrs. Boosey & Co. in the series entitled 'The Standard Lyrical Drama.' Mdlle. Lind sang it in the softer and far more appropriate and congenial key of F, in which it is now almost universally performed and printed.

accessories introduced merely for the purpose of attesting to the brilliancy of a finished execution. The singer firmly associates each passage with the nature of the situation, and thus employs, as a necessary living feature indispensable to the perfection of the whole, that which would otherwise appear as a dead or superfluous ornament. A proportionate measurement of many of the *tempi*, of which expedient Pasta also availed herself—for instance, in the duet, '*Empfange diesen Schwesterkuss*' *—served materially to enhance the beauty of the changeful expression, whether of feeling or passion.

"When, however, we say that the artist attains in the cavatina the purest and most inspiring effect that we have ever heard produced by any representative of the part of "Norma," the reader would grievously misunderstand us were he to suppose that she has reached the summit of her ideal. Oh, no! She well knows how to rise from weak and yielding moments to passionate ones, and increases in power from scene to scene. She is as much mother as lover; and especially in the closing scene, when she remembers her children and the fate that awaits them after the sacrifice of their parents, both acts and sings with inimitable beauty and power of expression.

"The summons of the singer before the curtain after the first act and at the close of the performance is a theatrical accessory which speaks for itself. Among the public there was not one single dissentient voice: its verdict truly represented the expression of its thanks for the gift received." †

Warm as is this eulogium, those who are fortunate enough to remember her impersonation of the part of "Norma" will confess that it is in no degree exaggerated. "Norma" was certainly one of her most perfect creations, comparable only to her interpretation of the *rôles* of " Alice " in *Robert le Diable* and " Amina " in *La Sonnambula*. Even in the master-pieces of Mozart, her vocal powers were scarcely

---

* " *Ah! si fa core e abbracciami* " in the original Italian.

† *Königliche privilegirte Berlinische (Vossische) Zeitung*. (Berlin, Dec. 15, 1845.) *Vide* also, ' *Gesammelte Schriften* von Ludwig Rellstab.' (Leipzig, 1861, vol xx. pp. 388–91.)

displayed to greater advantage, and as an actress she could not have won higher and purer praise, even in a classical tragedy.

From the moment of this first performance, the reputation she had already attained, in Stockholm, was more than confirmed, and her position in Berlin assured. She appeared in *Norma* for the second time with equal success on Friday, December 20th; and again, for the third time, on Wednesday the 25th. Then followed a few days of retirement from the turmoil of actual publicity, concerning the employment of which we are furnished with an interesting account from a sympathetic pen.

On the 23rd of December her young friend, Herr Josephson, arrived in Berlin on an invitation to spend Christmas with her. After calling upon her at Madame Reyer's he writes in his diary :—

"I have seen Jenny again, now that she also has been abroad—and winning laurels. When we parted, four months ago, in Leipzig, we little thought that we should so soon meet again. Fate, however, shapes our paths in a way we cannot foresee; and here we were pleasantly associating again as in Dresden last summer.

"Jenny seemed satisfied with her reception here—which, indeed, is as splendid as it can possibly be; and I found her in a calm and fairly cheerful mood.

"On the following morning I called on the Swedish Minister, and again heard what the Baroness Ridderstolpe—Madame Reyer's sister—had already told me on the previous evening; viz., that every one in Berlin has been in raptures ever since Jenny's appearance.*

Josephson spent Christmas Eve with her at Madame Reyer's, and on his return home made the following entry :—

"I have spent a merry Swedish Christmas Eve with Jenny and the Reyers. The Baroness Ridderstolpe was there, and

* N. P. Ödman, in *op. cit.*, vol. ii.

some Swedish ladies who were here on a visit had been assisting our hostess to arrange everything in true Swedish fashion. Amidst joyful friendly faces, cheering and beautiful gifts, and a profusion of lights, a harmonious tone pervaded the whole, despite a few passing clouds over the sky of the Swedes when thinking of the dear ones left behind. If we were to be so far away from home we could not wish for anything better or happier ! " *

The homely little Swedish festival recalls a similar one which took place in Paris in 1841, at the house of Mdlle. du Puget.†

But how different the circumstances. Then Mdlle. Lind was labouring to acquire the technical knowledge and power of execution, with which she hoped one day to accomplish something worthy of the high mission which in her heart of hearts she felt certain had been committed to her. Now she had accomplished it. The most severely critical people in the world in matters of the highest Art, admitted that they had never seen her like. It might well have been said, without presumption, that her reputation was already made and her fortune assured. There was hard work before her, it is true ; and it was not her wont to neglect anything that she believed to be her duty. Still, it was familiar work and there could be no reasonable doubt as to its results.

* *Ibid.*
† See pages 122–123.

CHAPTER V.

DAS FELDLAGER IN SCHLESIEN.

MDLLE. LIND's triumph was but a few days old when she began to devote herself to the exercise of that boundless charity in which, throughout the whole of her life, she took infinitely greater interest than that which she bestowed upon her own advancement in the world.

On Sunday, the 29th of December, Herr Josephson—who had been reading one of Pastor Lindgren's sermons to her early in the morning at Madame Reyer's—accompanied her, later in the day, to the house of Madame Birch-Pfeiffer, a lady under whose superintendence she had resumed her study of the German language so inopportunely interrupted in Dresden.

"She had just returned," says Herr Josephson in his Diary, "from the Intendant of the Theatre, Herr von Küstner, who had offered her an engagement for six months, with an honorarium of six thousand thalers and a benefit.* She had, of course, not yet given her answer; but she felt grateful and happy that such a sum should have been offered to her without any suggestion whatever from herself.

"'I feel bound,'" she said, "'in one way or another, to prove in a practical way my thankfulness to God, who has given me so much prosperity. You remember—do you not?—something that I once spoke to you about when we were at Dresden? I myself have good reason to remember it, for now you will be able to go to Italy whenever you like.'†

---

* Six thousand thalers equal about £900 in English money.

† A sojourn in Italy, for purposes of study, had been the dream of Herr Josephson's life; and it is evident that he must have spoken to her about it in Dresden during the previous summer.

"We had only a short distance to walk. There was no time for long explanation. I only replied, therefore, that I thought it was too soon to think of this, and that, moreover, in accepting her proposal I should always consider myself her debtor, as even I might hope for more success in the future.

"Every day reveals to me some new trait in her character; and I know not which is greatest, my gratitude to, or my admiration for, her. I stand daily on a more and more intimate and brotherly footing with her, and am therefore able to accept gladly and thankfully from her that which from many others I could not take without a certain reservation of feeling. I can only pray that, in her restless life, peace may one day obtain the victory." *

Of the result of this conversation we shall have to speak more fully hereafter. For the moment we must follow Mdlle. Lind in the fulfilment of her own career.

No record of the contract mentioned by Herr Josephson has been found among the archives of the Berlin Opera House, and that for the very good and sufficient reason that it is customary for the royal intendancies to issue contracts in writing only in connection with engagements offered to members of the permanent staff, and not to draw them up in favour of visitors engaged for *Gastrollen* only.† It is therefore impossible now to ascertain whether the arrangement was actually concluded or not; though, as the duration of Mdlle. Lind's first visit to Berlin was limited to four months, during which period she sang twenty times only for the directors—her own "benefit" taking place, as a matter of course, as an extra night—it is evident that, if six continuous months were intended, the engagement could not have been completed.

But however this may have been, the strength of her position, founded singly and solely upon the brilliancy of her

---

* N. P. Ödman, in op. cit.
† *Vide* page 206.

success, was incontestable; and we may well believe that she might have obtained any terms she herself felt justified in demanding. She was accepted as the greatest singer and actress then living. Meyerbeer was in raptures with her, and his desire that the principal *rôle* in his new Opera should be assigned to her grew stronger and stronger every day. Though he had, *bon gré, mal gré,* suffered Fräulein Tuczec to appear in it on the opening night, he had never relinquished his long-cherished project. He had written the part of "Vielka" expressly for Mdlle. Lind, and was quite determined that the task of interpreting it in accordance with his own idea should be confided to her. It was due to his artistic position that Fräulein Tuczec should resign into more masterly hands the duty she had so imprudently undertaken to fulfil, and fulfilled so imperfectly that the success of the Opera was more than endangered by the un-fitness of the *rôle* for her. To this compromise Mdlle. Lind was quite willing to assent, but some little time and a great deal of very hard study were needed in order to secure a perfect interpretation of the *rôle*. For, after the manner of the time-honoured German *Schauspiel,* the new Opera con-tained, in place of classical recitative, long passages of spoken dialogue, and it was chiefly for the sake of attaining a more perfect accent in the delivery of these that she had resumed her studies in German under the direction of Madame Birch-Pfeiffer.

She could scarcely have made a better or a more fortunate choice, for the lady—of whom we shall have to speak again more particularly hereafter—had herself been well known as a clever and intelligent actress, and under her maiden name—Charlotte Pfeiffer—had appeared on the stage with success in Munich, Vienna, Berlin, and many other import-ant German capitals. In middle life, she retired from the stage, married Dr. Christian Birch, of Copenhagen, the

son of a late Danish Minister of State, and, uniting his
name to her own, devoted herself thenceforward to dramatic
authorship, producing at different times nearly seventy plays,
some of which—such as the well-known dramas *Die Marquise
von Villette* and *Die Frau Professorin*—have kept their places
on the German stage to the present day.*

Under the superintendence, then, of Madame Birch-
Pfeiffer, Mdlle. Lind made such rapid progress in the German
language that within less than a fortnight after her third
performance of *Norma* she was ready to appear in the new
part.

The gifted composer was delighted with her interpretation
of his music, which, as was his wont, he altered, re-wrote,
improved, and not unfrequently injured, with microscopic
attention to every minutest detail till the very last moment.
Herr Josephson was present at two of the last rehearsals, on
the 3rd and 4th of January, which he thus describes in his
Diary :—

"January 3, 1845, Meyerbeer was altogether enchanted
with Jenny's singing, and embraced her at the end of the
rehearsal. January 4th. Rehearsed again, in the morning.
I drove back with Meyerbeer and Jenny. I begged the
maestro that I, too, might be allowed to express my thanks
for his beautiful Opera, and he answered me in a very
gracious manner. He is a most polite man ; something of
the courtier ; something of the man of genius ; something of
the man of the world ; and has, in addition, something fidgety
about his whole being. Before re-producing the Opera with
Jenny Lind he called upon her, to the best of my belief, at
least a hundred times, to consult about this, that, or the
other. He alters incessantly, curtails here, dovetails there,
and thus, by his eagerness and anxiety, prevents the spontaneous growth of the work, and imparts a fragmentary
character to its beauty." †

* Madame Birch-Pfeiffer died on the 25th of August, 1868; and her
husband, Dr. Birch, four days later, on the 29th.

† Josephson, *op. cit.*, vol. ii.

In this fastidious desire to secure the most perfect finish
in every insignificant detail Meyerbeer was only following
out his own invariable custom—and, after all, his crowd of
after-thoughts was not greater than that which haunted
Beethoven until his works were actually in print.   However,
he was satisfied at last; in conformity with previous announcement, *Das Feldlager in Schlesien* was duly performed,
with Mdlle. Lind in the principal part, on the 5th of January,
1845; and its effect upon the audience was even more
striking than that produced by the great performance of
Norma exactly three weeks previously.

The constitutional diffidence of her character tempted her
to distrust her own powers up to the very moment of
performance.   Herr Josephson, who saw her in the morning,
evidently thought she was no less " fidgety " than Meyerbeer
himself.

" Jenny was extremely successful," he says, " in her *début*
as ' Vielka.'   Her singing was beautiful, her acting full of
genius, life, and fire.   The applause was spontaneous and
enthusiastic.   Her nervousness, which had kept her practising
the whole afternoon and again before the beginning of the
Opera, was not noticed by any one ; neither did it prevent her
either from singing or acting her very best.   The public was
enchanted, and Meyerbeer happy.   On comparing it with
what I have seen and heard in Germany, I am amazed
at the difference.   With her the moving principle is the
nobility of art—with others, less worthy motives are always
apparent.   The public sees this, and is astonished and fascinated.   How she will be missed when she is gone." *

The verdict of the critics, far warmer than this, was recorded without reserve.   The most influential journal of the
period gave an account of the performance no less generously
enthusiastic than that which had appeared after the first
representation of *Norma*.

* Josephson, *op. cit.,* vol. ii.

"Through her second *rôle*—'Vielka,' in the *Feldlager*—Mdlle. Lind has proved," says the critic,* "that her talent fulfils the highest conditions not only in one direction, but in many.

"With unerring sensitiveness, with the clearest knowledge of the heart, she has based the groundwork of the character upon a conception of its inner life, by which it can, through its forebodings, its childlike faith, and its pure intentions, soar into the regions of marvel. Vielka's faith gives her the power to interpret character. Such insight she would be logically bound to possess; but to display this power of hers, as our artist does, in a living picture is a rare and a wonderful gift.

"The deep earnestness with which she entered upon the first part of her task, when she first delivered the *Romanze* in musical form in tones full of ominous foreboding, might well have given rise to the presumption that she would bring the light and more pleasing part less prominently forward. But she justly recognised true earnestness and true cheerfulness as perfectly compatible emotions, clothed them in the natural loveliness and grace of womanhood, impersonated the loving maiden no less truthfully than the inspired prophetess, and thus in her ideal fulfilled the later conditions as perfectly as she had fulfilled the earlier ones in those more exalted moments in which she was brought into contact with the weightiest concerns of inner life and external history.

"An ever-living commentary on her inward conception is furnished by her dramatic and imitative expression, both of which are richly employed in the scene in which, by the exercise of her magic art, she terrifies, tames, charms, cajoles the wild country-folk. Nothing can equal the grace with which, in most modest, most gentle gyrations, she shakes the tambourine in her dance, and puts in practice all the magic of her loveliest allurements. The action was irresistible; and one could not only foresee that the wild warriors would obediently follow her, but could feel that they had no choice but to do so.

"From this scene forward the liveliest and most enthusiastic bursts of applause were accorded to her until she was called before the curtain.

"Our task would never come to an end were we to notice every striking detail, every truthful charm, with which

* Herr Rellstab.

throughout the entire *rôle* she illustrated her delineations. Her outward expression rendered every inward feeling with the veracity of a mirrored picture. Fear, love, hope, joy, all imprinted themselves with equal ease and truthfulness to nature upon every gesture and every significant movement. She set before us earnest, tragic, joyful, lively surprises, in endless variety. We remember, for instance, the manner in which she rendered the little phrase, 'He is saved! He is hidden!' in the finale to the first act; how, in the third act, she dragged Conrad to the writing-table; and—more beautiful than all—how she sang the little added recitative at the close as she retired backwards from the royal cabinet.

"Some passages allotted to the artist in the dialogue had been changed into recitative, and many others excised or assigned to other performers, as she was too diffident to make use of the foreign language unaided by the music. We venture, however, to give her the positive assurance that this precaution was unnecessary, for her fulfilment of even this part of her task was more than pleasing. Indeed, the soft foreign accent seems rather favourable than the reverse, and may well be accepted as a happy characteristic of the *rôle*, since the alien 'Vielka' might well have retained some trace of her nationality in her speech.

"But are we to busy ourselves, then, only with the acting? Have we nothing to say concerning the singer?

"Yes, indeed! to repeat everything that we said after her first appearance. The singer is here exactly what she was then. The mild *timbre* of the voice, the clearness of the finished passages, the colouring of the tones through their ever-changing expression, are here, as everywhere, apparent. In a host of piquant cadences introduced by the composer, no less than in the duet with the two flutes in the third act,[*] the art of the singer asserts itself in its most powerful form. And thus a picture is presented that, through the romantic conception of the whole no less than through the charm of its multifarious details, imprints itself indelibly upon the soul."[†]

---

[*] This famous piece, in which the voice is accompanied by two flutes (*obbligati*) was afterwards transferred, by Meyerbeer, to *L'Etoile du Nord*.

[†] *Königliche privilegirte Berlinische (Vossische) Zeitung.* (Berlin, Jan. 7, 1845.) A second and equally enthusiastic critique of *Das Feldlager in Schlesien* appeared in the same journal on January 13, and a second critique of *Norma* on January 24.

It was in all probability this highly favourable critique which Mademoiselle Lind sent to her friend, Fru Lindblad, in a letter dated January 8, 1845, from which we reproduce the following extract:—

"Everything seems to go well in hand. It would be impossible to imagine a greater success than I have made here in Berlin. Sontag herself had not so brilliant a triumph. Last Sunday, the 5th, I appeared in Meyerbeer's new Opera,* and I herewith enclose a critique.

"I do feel so happy about Meyerbeer's exceeding satisfaction. And I feel easier in my mind, for having been able to put his Opera into better relief; for through Mdlle. Tuczec's unequal rendering of my part it very nearly came to grief. I almost think I achieved a greater triumph than in *Norma.*

"Last night Josephson and I were at Frau Bettina Arnim's,† and I cannot conceive how the time passed so quickly. We did not return till after twelve! The old lady is divinely child-like sometimes. When she is in her right element, and creeps up in her chair, with all those sweet girls dispersed around her on the floor, one can only envy their light-heartedness and independence of the narrow judgment of the world.

"Nowadays the world is influencing me very considerably, and just now I cannot say that creeping is my principal pleasure. It looks, however, as if I might become independent some day; for I am now invited to go to London, and it will be curious to see where all this will land me. This evening I am invited to Tieck's."

Continued on the 9th of January, 1845:—

"Last evening was one rich in enjoyment. The talented old man, with that frail body of his, was a touching sight. I had the honour of taking turns with him; for, when he had recited a poem, I had to sing a song. And in this way the evening flew by very quickly indeed." ‡

* *Das Feldlager in Schlesien.*
† Goethe's 'Bettina.'
‡ From the Lindblad letters.

Though she speaks thus modestly of the possibility that
she may some day "become independent," it was evident
that her future was now assured.   The demonstration
that accompanied her first appearance in *Das Feldlager in
Schlesien* proved to be no evanescent burst of enthusiasm.
The Opera was repeated on the 10th, 14th, and 19th of
January, with raised prices and undiminished success; and
succeeded by four performances of *Norma* on the 21st, 23rd,
28th, and 31st of the month, after which Meyerbeer's Opera
was resumed, for one night only, to be succeeded by Weber's
Euryanthe.

Every one of these performances was a veritable triumph,
and so strong was the popular feeling that, after the fourth
performance of *Das Feldlager in Schlesien* on the 21st of
January, she was publicly greeted with a serenade, which is
thus described in the journal from which we have already
quoted :—

"After the Opera, in which, as always, Mdlle. Lind
had achieved the most brilliant success, a number of
singers and young musicians greeted the artist at her
residence with a vocal serenade. Four poems, by Messieurs
Förster, Kopisch, Schnackenburg, and Rellstab, had been
set to music for the occasion by Messieurs Rungenhagen,
Commer, Lührs, and Wichmann. The artist received
this expression of homage to her talent in the modest
manner which so greatly enhances the value of her artistic
gifts, and seemed deeply moved by this acknowledgment of
them. The poems were brought to her printed upon a white
satin fillet, and presented, with a laurel crown, upon a satin
cushion." *

The white satin fillet was preserved by Madame Goldschmidt. The following is the list of the poems :—

---

* *Königliche privilegirte Berlinische (Vossische) Zeitung.* (Berlin,
Jan. 21, 1845.)

I. '*Das Land der Tapfern und der Treuen.*' (Words by Förster. Music by Rungenhagen.)

II. '*Ach! wie lieblich ist das Leben.*' (Words by Kopisch. Music by Commer.)

III. '*Woher erschallen jene Wundertöne.*' (Words by Schnackenburg. Music by Lührs.)

IV. '*Die durch Töne uns beglückte.*' (Words by Rellstab. Music by Herrmann Wichmann.)

CHAPTER VI.

WE called attention in our opening chapter to the fact that, notwithstanding a very wide-spread belief to that effect, Mdlle. Lind's artistic reputation was neither confined to nor even made in the country of her final adoption—England.

Nor was it the special property of Germany—though, for the world in general, it certainly originated there.

Before she had appeared five times on the stage in Berlin it had spread so far that an attempt was made to induce her to visit London.

She alludes to this, as we have seen, in her letter to Fru Lindblad, written two days after her first appearance in the part of " Vielka."

The matter was brought about in this wise.

Mr. Alfred Bunn, the then lessee of Drury Lane Theatre, went to Berlin in the hope of securing Mdlle. Lind, for his approaching season of English Opera. He was an experienced manager, well acquainted with the public taste, and past-master in all that concerned the business aspect of theatrical affairs. No one knew better than he how to draw up an agreement, to tempt an aspiring *débutante*, or to turn to good account the talent of a popular favourite. He had done something for Art, but not for Art of a high order. He had revived Weber's *Oberon*, brought out a number of popular Operas, and written a multitude of *libretti*, original and translated, some of which had been severely satirised by

unfeeling critics. Moreover—and it is with this point that
we are now chiefly concerned—he had attained, by long
experience, the power of predicting, with absolute certainty,
whether or not an artist was likely to find lasting favour
with the public; and by prudent exercise of this precious
faculty he had succeeded, not only in engaging Madame
Malibran, but also in bringing into notice a goodly number
of fairly capable singers of the second order, many of whom,
having done well, both for themselves and for him, under his
management, remained faithful to him to the last.

Mr. Bunn's visit to Berlin took place at a period ante-
cedent to that at which the difficulty of obtaining tickets for
the Opera became almost insuperable; he was, therefore,
fortunate enough to hear Mdlle. Lind, and to be thus enabled
to judge for himself how far the rumours he had heard were
well founded. To a man of his long experience one hearing
was more than enough to decide the question. He saw at a
glance that, if he could only succeed in attaching her to his
company at Drury Lane Theatre, his fortune would be made.

He was a man of prompt action, and lost no time in
making an offer which, to a young singer, seemed not
illiberal. But how could she form a fair judgment upon it,
she who was utterly ignorant of everything connected with the
stage except in so far as its artistic aspect was concerned?
She knew that it was to be the stepping-stone towards the
independence she had mentioned in her letter to Fru Lindblad, but in what way she knew not. She stood in urgent
need of an experienced and impartial adviser, but where was
she to look for one? She stood alone. A mere child, whose
interest was pitted against that of one of the most acute and
enterprising speculators in the then theatrical world. What
could she do? How was it possible for her to solve the
problem?

Mr. Bunn pressed for an immediate answer. Naturally

enough, she hesitated. He was urgent. It was manifestly
to his interest to allow her the least possible time for reflection, and still less for taking advice ; for the intervention of
a thoroughly disinterested and business-like friend might ruin
everything—for him. Not a word could be said against his
position from a business point of view. He was perfectly
justified in endeavouring to secure the services of the most
splendid dramatic artist he had ever met with on the lowest
possible terms. But it was hard upon the artist, who was
probably less able to form a true estimate of her own value
in the theatrical market than any one in Berlin. She knew
what she was worth to Art; but the manager alone knew
what she was worth to him. And, as a man of business, he
was certainly not bound to enlighten her on a subject in
which her interests were diametrically opposed to his own.
The danger was that some one else might enlighten her at
any moment. And to prevent this he pressed his offer upon
her with the utmost possible urgency. It would be unfair
to blame him for it. Any other manager would quite
certainly have done the same. Yet our readers must surely
feel, with us, that it was very hard upon her.

On the 10th of January the matter came to a crisis.

On that evening—a most unlucky Friday in so far as Mr.
Bunn's proposal was concerned—Mdlle. Lind was to play the
part of "Vielka" for the second time, and so great was the
excitement with which the announcement of the coming event
was received that Herr von Küstner, the Intendant of the
Opera House, finding it impossible to supply the demand for
places, determined to raise the prices of admission. At any
other time this proceeding would have given rise to serious
dissatisfaction, but on this occasion the public was prepared
to make any sacrifice rather than miss an opportunity of
hearing the new *prima donna*. And the excitement was no
ephemeral outburst of popular feeling. As the season ad-

vanced the demand for tickets increased to such an " extraordinary and unaccustomed extent," that the number of
applications frequently amounted to twice, and even thrice,
the number of places at the disposal of the Royal Intendantur,
who found it necessary to issue elaborate instructions as
to the form in which preliminary application for tickets
was to be made.   Even with these safeguards the number
of final disappointments, when the season came to a close,
was enormous; and so great was the pressure that no
less than four clerks were kept constantly employed in
answering the letters of application in the order of their
arrival.*

In the midst of this excitement Mr. Bunn was fortunate
enough to obtain a seat in the box of the British Ambassador.
We have already had occasion, in a previous chapter, to
speak of Lord Westmorland's deep interest in everything
connected with the Art, of which, during the whole of his
long and useful life, he was so generous and munificent a
patron.   He was no less enthusiastic in his admiration for
Mdlle. Lind's talent than Lady Westmorland, whose opinion
on the subject we have already learned; and his personal
regard for her was sincere and lasting—so lasting that he
remained her friend until the end of his life.   He had been
informed that an engagement for London had been proposed ;
and, for the credit of his country's taste, he was anxious
that so great an artist should be heard and duly appreciated there.   It is more than probable that she had,
before this, asked his advice upon the subject; but what
could he say ?   He was as ignorant of managerial business
and managerial terms as she was, and was an absolute
stranger to the manifold intrigues which seem to be inseparable from the destiny of a " Child of the Drama."   To him

* See the notice issued by the *General-Intendantur der Kyl. Schau-
spiele,* and published in the play-bills of the day.

the proposal seemed an advantageous one, and there seems no doubt that he said as much to her.

Our information concerning the events of this memorable evening is very far from complete. In after life Madame Goldschmidt could rarely be induced to speak of the occasion, the disastrous results of which she could never recall without pain. We have, however, been favoured with a MS. sketch of her early life, written in 1855–57 by the late Mrs. George Grote (*née* Lewin), the sister of her old and valued friend (Madame von Koch,* of Stockholm), from which we extract an interesting passage tending to throw some welcome light upon the subject, notwithstanding the inaccuracy of its dates and some other self-evident slips of memory.†

"It was during her engagement in Berlin that Mr. Alfred Bunn, the manager of Drury Lane Theatre, London, conceived the hope of alluring Jenny to his theatre, for the winter season of 1845–6.

"In this view he repaired to Berlin in the month (I think) of March, 1845; and laying close siege to the fair *cantatrice*, induced her to contract an engagement to sing, in English, at his theatre in the winter of 1845–6.

"Jenny (she often assured me) was not willing to form the engagement, and hung back for some time; and at the last moment was, as it were, surprised into putting her signature to the bargain.

"The occasion on which she was persuaded to sign was this—

"Between the Acts of an Opera in which she was performing, the Earl of Westmorland—the British Ambassador at the Court of Berlin—invited her to his *loge* in the *salle,*

---

* See page 105.

† The late Mrs. Grote—widow of George Grote, the historian of Greece —left, among her unpublished MSS., an incomplete 'Memoir of the Life of Jenny Lind,' carried down to the year 1848, and filling between fifty and sixty closely written pages. This Memoir, which was written between the years 1855 and 1857, has been committed, through the kindness of Mrs. Grote's literary executrix, to Mr. Goldschmidt.

attached to which was a small private *salon*. Jenny complied, all 'stage-attired' as she was, and on entering the *loge* found Mr. Bunn along with His Excellency awaiting her. The former urgently conjured Jenny to complete the contract in question, pleading that pressing business compelled him to leave within a few hours for London. He of course endeavoured to inspire her with a belief that her appearance at his theatre would pave the way to permanent advantages in England, and it is but fair to add that the sum which he offered her for her services was both liberal and unusual in amount, and that, considering the conditions on which she was then acting in Berlin, it bore the appearance of a handsome and advantageous engagement.

"The Ambassador warmly seconded the entreaties of the manager; and thus beset, and anxious not to lose what appeared a respectable and lucrative offer—having nobody to consult with, and wholly ignorant as she was of the state of theatrical matters in England, Jenny allowed herself to be persuaded, chiefly (she afterwards said) confiding in the judgment of Lord Westmorland—she took the pen, signed the treaty, and returned to her part, not however without grave misgivings as to the prudence of the step she had taken. Away sped Manager Bunn, contract in pocket; the said 'contract' being destined to entail a concatenation of difficulties, embarrassments, and wearisome contests for the three years following upon this transaction." *

In explanation of the grave anachronisms involved in this account it would be unfair to the writer to omit her own confession that "her memory respecting the exact dates of their occurrence was not complete."

And it must also be remembered that Mrs. Grote did not write at Madame Goldschmidt's dictation, but simply introduced into her narrative the record of events which to the best of her recollection had been mentioned by her friend in the course of casual conversation.† In presence of these elements of doubt it seems not unnatural to believe that His Excellency may well have expressed his opinion on

---

* From Mrs. Grote's MS. 'Memoir.'
† *Vide supra*, 'she often assured me' (page 232.)

the matter without resorting to actual persuasion ;* and we
now know with absolute certainty that he was at first inclined
to regard the proposal in a favourable light, but afterwards
entirely changed his mind, and rejoiced greatly that it was
never put into execution.

Passing from the discussion of the incidental circumstances here related, we proceed to put our readers in possession of a literal translation of the now famous "Bunn
contract," the text of which was originally drawn up in
French to the following purport :—

"Mr. Bunn † director of Drury Lane Theatre London
makes the following offers to Mdlle. Jenny Lind and engages
to execute them entirely at his own risks and perils if Mdlle.
Lind accepts them :

"(1) Mr. Bunn engages Mdlle. Lind to sing twenty times
at Drury Lane Theatre either from 15th June to 31st July
1845 or from 30th September to 15th November 1845.　It
depends upon Mdlle. Lind to decide which of these two
different epochs is most convenient to her, but she engages
herself to make known her choice to Mr. Bunn not later
than the end of the month of March.

"(2) Mr. Bunn engages to pay to Mdlle. Lind the sum of
fifty *Louis d'or* ‡ for each of these twenty representations and
allow her also the half of a benefit (gross receipts).

"(3) Mr. Bunn engages to pay to Mdlle. Lind the
stipulated price of fifty *Louis* always twenty-four hours after
each represention.

"(4) Mdlle. Lind will sing three times a week and not
oftener except during the last week.　She will never sing on
two following days and Mr. Bunn engages to leave an
interval of at least one day between one representation and
the next.

"(5) Mdlle. Lind will make her *début* in the part of
"Vielka" in the opera *Ein Feldlager in Schlesien* by Meyer-

---

* A letter, written some months later, proves that whatever amount
of 'persuasion' may have been used, it came from a very different
quarter. The moving spirit was undoubtedly Meyerbeer.

† *Sic,* without the Christian name Alfred.

‡ Equal to about £40 in English money.

beer and she will afterwards sing also the *rôle* of " Amina " in
La Sonnambula by Bellini if Mr. Bunn requires it.   It is
understood * that Mdlle. Lind will only sing in two *rôles*
during the whole course of her representations.

"(6) Mr. Bunn will find at his cost the costumes for the
two *rôles* of Mdlle. Lind.

"(7) Mdlle. Lind accepts these conditions but as she has
not time to consider sufficiently the contract which Mr. Bunn
presents to her to-day and as Mr. Bunn must depart
to-morrow she reserves the right of introducing additions and
changes into this contract if that appears to her necessary
but she must make them known to Mr. Bunn by the
1st of March at the latest.   Meanwhile it is well understood
that such additions and changes as Mdlle. Lind may introduce
must never apply to the first or second articles which must
remain fixed as they are now.

"It is agreed equally that if the changes and additions are
not agreeable to Mr. Bunn he shall have the right to reject
them but if this be done the treaty shall be revoked and
regarded as null and of no effect.

"Executed in duplicate at Berlin the 10th January
1845." †

It has been said that taking into consideration the
difference between the terms demanded by the popular
operatic " stars " of the present day and those received by
the great singers of forty or fifty years ago, those offered to
Mdlle. Lind were both liberal and unusual in amount, and
that the proposed engagement was " a handsome and an
advantageous one "—but it was nothing of the kind.

Some fourteen or fifteen years previously Mr. Bunn
himself had engaged Madame Malibran, for nineteen nights,
at £125 a night, payable in advance; in 1833 she had sung
forty nights at Drury Lane, for £3,200, with two benefits,
which produced an additional sum of £2,000—thus raising
the *honorarium* for each night to the sum of £130; and in

* ' *intendu* ' (*sic*).

† Translated from the somewhat questionable French of the original
document.

1835 she had received, at Her Majesty's Theatre, £2,775 for twenty-four performances—that is to say, £115 12s. 6d. a night.

Surely, after such a *début* as she had made at Berlin, Mdlle. Lind's services were worth more than half as much as those of Madame Malibran.

However, be this as it may, it was in the terms above mentioned that the contract between Mdlle. Jenny Lind and Mr. Alfred Bunn was duly signed and ratified, in the presence of the British Ambassador, and in His Excellency's box at the Berlin Opera-House—and therefore, in the political sense of the term, within British territory—on the 10th of January, 1845. That is to say, 'duly signed' by Mdlle. Lind; but, as we shall hereafter be able to show, the 'duplicate' given to her was not signed by Mr. Bunn.

As we shall have occasion to recur to the history of this remarkable document more than once during the course of our narrative, the reader will do well to bear in mind, not only the facts we have recorded, but together with these the doubts we have expressed and the suggestions we have ventured to place before him.

The subject is a very difficult one, and for the present we must leave it, to follow the course of our history in other directions.

CHAPTER VII.

AFTER performing seven times in *Norma,* and five in *Das Feldlager in Schlesien,* Mdlle. Lind was announced to appear, on Tuesday the 7th of February, in *Euryanthe.*

She had been familiar with this remarkable Opera in Stockholm, where she had appeared in it, for the first time, on the 1st of December, 1838. But she had not revived the part since her return from Paris, nor had she, as yet, attempted it in German ; and the occasion for which she was now preparing to do so was a more than ordinarily interesting one.

Carl Maria von Weber died, in London, at the house of his friend, Sir George Smart, in Great Portland Street, on the night between the 4th and 5th of June, 1826. He had been laid to rest, on the 21st, far away from home and friends, in a vault beneath the floor of S. Mary's Chapel, Moorfields. But, in the autumn of 1844, the surviving members of his family, aided by a few devoted friends and admirers—foremost among whom were his pupil, Mr. (afterwards Sir Julius) Benedict,* and the then almost unknown Richard Wagner—made a vigorous effort to treat his memory with the homage which had been denied to him by his ungrateful fellow-citizens during his life-time, and, at their expense, his remains were exhumed, transported to Dresden, and, on the night of the 14th of December, deposited in a vault in the Cemetery of Friedrich-

* See his "Life of Weber," in 'The Great Musicians.'

stadt in which his son Alexander had been buried only a fortnight before. His widow and surviving children, supported by Madame Schrœder-Devrient and a crowd of sympathising fellow-artists, covered his coffin with laurels and flowers, and it was proposed to erect over it a monument worthy of his fame. Great efforts were made to collect sufficient funds for the execution of this project, and a grand performance of *Euryanthe* had been promised at the Berlin Opera House in aid of the pious purpose.

It was on this solemn occasion that Mdlle. Lind sang the part of "Euryanthe" for the first time in the language in which it was originally produced.

A prologue, written for the occasion by Herr Rellstab, was spoken by Fräulein Charlotte von Hagen, and no pains were spared for the purpose of rendering the performance worthy of its high intent. The whole musical world took a vivid interest in the proceedings. Dresden had nobly expiated the long course of neglect which had terminated so sadly, and so fatally, eighteen years before. And now Berlin had taken up the good cause, in the name and with the full consent of the whole Fatherland.

The task assigned to her, in connection with this solemn festival, was, beyond all doubt, the most difficult one that had ever been, or was ever destined to be entrusted to her, during the whole of her artistic career. And she inherited the difficulty from Weber himself.

From first to last, *Euryanthe* had never been understood, either by the critics, or by the public. The scope and purpose of its design had escaped them all. In *Der Freischütz* Weber had spoken, for the first time, heart to heart with the great German people; and they had understood him as he had understood them, on the evening of its first performance, without one instant of doubt or hesitation. With *Euryanthe* it was different. As a direct inspiration of creative genius—not worked out, but flashed in upon the composer's heart and brain—*Der Freischütz* stands alone in the history of the Romantic Opera. *Euryanthe* is no less clearly impressed with the stamp of inspiration than *Der Freischütz:* only, in this case, the idea is carefully and elaborately worked out with consummate skill and truest artistic instinct; with richest development of musical form and exhaustive employ-ment of all available technical resources in one direction; and in the other—involving the æsthetic aspect of the subject—with intensest sympathy, with virgin purity, with knightly loyalty, with pomp of chivalry, and, above all, with the powerful element of the supernatural. It was in con-nection with this last-named point that Weber was so fatally misunderstood. He made it the leading characteristic of his conception, both in his treatment of the music and in the conduct of the story, which was worked out by the librettist entirely under his direction; and it was utterly ruined by the critics, who, mistaking Lysiart's infamous wager for the true *animus* of the plot, abused the *libretto* for its inanity while overlooking the motive upon which its whole romantic interest depended.

When the Opera was first produced at Vienna, in 1823, it soared so high above the heads of the audience, that the brainless wits of the period nicknamed it *L'Ennuyante*, and the stupid joke was accepted as a miracle of *esprit*. When Madame Schrœder-Devrient afterwards undertook the interpretation of the principal *rôle*, she sang the music superbly, but treated the part as one needing the expression of pure passion only —a characteristic in which not one of her German con-temporaries could approach her—and missed the super-natural element entirely. Mdlle. Lind seized upon it as the leading motive of the whole impersonation. She penetrated Weber's meaning, though the critics did not. They could not withstand the power of her conception—it would have been impossible to have done so, but they utterly failed to comprehend its moving spirit.

The following quotation from a critique which appeared in the *Berlinische Zeitung* on the 13th of February will explain this clearly enough :—

"In the first act, the singer presents before us all that she possesses of loveliness and grace. The duet with Eglantine*—Madame Palm-Spatzer—and the finale † are pearls of finished execution. But for us, the greatest achievement in this act is the narrative of the apparition of Emma, which, in dramatic and vocal expression, fulfils the highest demands of an Art-ideal.

"In the second act, the artist impresses us with the most perfect form of womanly innocence and purity. Her task here fulfils itself by the force of its fidelity to nature. Yet she would, perhaps, have succeeded in expressing contrasts more richly varied still if she had seen some of her great predecessors. For instance, we can scarcely doubt that, if she had been acquainted with Wilhelmine Schrœder-Devrient's rendering of the passage, '*Den Blick erhobt Ihr nicht zu mir,*'‡ she would joyfully have availed herself of it for use in her own representation without losing anything of her individuality. That which she sets before us is beautiful, womanly, but not creative—no fitting climax to the long chain of beauties in her performance.

"The emotional problem, as propounded in the third act, is solved by the artist from the depths of a pure soul. But her features exhibit too much morbid bodily fatigue. Perhaps an atom of rouge might remove this slight defect.§ The dizzy, almost maddened, rapture of the Aria in C major ‖—one of the composer's grandest creations—forms a crown to the rich treasures of the performance.¶

* '*Unter ist mein Stern gegangen.*'

† That is, the quartet, '*Fröhliche Klänge,*' with which it concludes.

‡ In the finale to the second act.

§ We have already had occasion to notice Mdlle. Lind's dislike to such stage-accessories. See page 199.

‖ '*Zu ihm! zu ihm!*' An air filled with enormous technical difficulties.

¶ *Kgl. priv. Berl. Zeitung.* (Feb. 13, 1845.)

The reader cannot fail to notice that, warm as it is, this *critique* is the first that has expressed a doubt as to the truthfulness of Mdlle. Lind's conception of her *rôle.* The critic had formed a conception of his own, founded on that of Madame Schrœder-Devrient, and the new one did not accord with it. But unconsciously, as it would seem, he calls attention to a point, in the new interpretation, which proves both its correctness and the keen intelligence brought to bear upon it in connection with the composer's own intention.

He tells us that, for him, " the greatest achievement in the first act is the narrative of the apparition of Emma "— that is to say, the precise point at which the supernatural element, to which he makes no direct allusion whatever, is first introduced, and he confesses that Mdlle. Lind's conception of the passage "fulfils the highest demands of an Art-ideal." *

The importance attached by Weber himself to this passage, and to all else that concerns the episode of Udo and Emma, with its ghostly sequel, is—or ought to be—made unmistakably evident before the curtain rises on the first act. For, though the design is very rarely carried out in practice, the overture was intended by Weber to serve the purpose of a prologue and to fix the attention of the audience in a marked manner upon the narrative so highly praised by our critic.

At the hundred-and-twenty-ninth bar of the overture— where Weber introduces the wonderful *Largo,* with its weird unearthly harmonies, its long-drawn wail, sustained by the scarcely audible tones of the four *violini con sordini,* intensified, now and again, by the broken *tremolo* of the *viole* shuddering beneath them — at this most striking point Weber directed that the curtain should rise upon a gloomy tableau, intended to prepare the

* See page 240.

spectator for the secret which forms the mainspring of the plot.

The stage represents a sepulchral vault, in the centre of which lies Emma's coffin, surmounted by a medieval herse. Upon the coffin is seen the ring which plays so fatal a part in the story, behind it is a monumental figure in the style of the twelfth century, at the foot of the sarcophagus kneels Euryanthe in prayer, the traitress Eglantine crouches in the shadow beyond, and in the vaulting of the groined roof hovers Emma's restless spirit, condemned to haunt the scene of its unexpiated sin.

This highly suggestive tableau having been exposed to view for a few moments only, the curtain slowly descends again, and the overture proceeds with the contrapuntal treatment of the bold subject which follows.

The audience is now fully prepared to understand the secret of Eglantine's treachery; and when, in the first act, Euryanthe narrates to her the story of the ghostly apparition, the connection is kept up by the recurrence, in the accompaniment to her recitative, of the weird harmonies and wailing orchestration already heard in the *largo* of the overture.

Whether this tableau was exhibited or not at the Berlin Opera-House we cannot say; but however that may have been, it is certain that Mdlle. Lind penetrated the composer's idea, seized upon this salient point in his conception, and brought it out so clearly that even Herr Rellstab, though so strongly prepossessed in favour of another reading of the part, pointed to this very scene as "fulfilling the highest demands of an Art-ideal." And it is worthy of remark that, original as her conceptions invariably were, pervaded as they were, through and through, by the marked individuality which enabled her to make each part her own, she never attained her own ends at the sacrifice of the composer's meaning.

Her ideal, however new it might seem to superficial observers, rested always upon an esoteric basis, in closest connection with and logically inseparable from the very heart and life of the dramatic poem she was illustrating. It is precisely upon this same basis that every really great composer—and we speak of no others—builds up his own ideal; and thus it was that, by following the same path as the composer, Mdlle. Lind always succeeded in attaining the same end by the same means.

Euryanthe was announced for repetition on the next Opera night (February the 9th), but in consequence of the illness of Madame Palm-Spatzer, *Norma* was substituted for it; it was however repeated, with the same cast, on the 11th, and with Mdlle. Marx in the part of "Eglantine," on the 14th, after which Mdlle. Lind was announced to appear, on Tuesday the 18th, in *La Sonnambula*. In this ever-welcome Opera she created so profound a sensation that, when a repetition of the performance was announced for the 2nd of March, the price of the boxes rose to fifty, and even eighty thalers, and no places could be obtained for less than three thalers,* even in the pit—a price which was said, in in the German theatrical world, to be absolutely unprecedented.

It is—or, at least, was at the time of which we are writing —the fashion, among German reviewers, to speak very contemptuously indeed of the music of *La Sonnambula;* but Mdlle. Lind, by her delightful interpretation of the *rôle* of "Amina"—which was always a special favourite with her, —seems to have disarmed the critics and obtained a free pardon for the sins of poor unfortunate Bellini. The leading journal thus speaks of one of her later appearances in the part:—

* That is to say £7 10s., £12, and 9s. in English money.

"She raises the art of singing to a glorious level. Everything that the most cultivated instrumentalist can accomplish
the scatters amongst us, in richest profusion, in lavish pro-
digality. The singer's arpeggios move through closely combined chords which even the player would find it needful to
treat with the greatest possible care, and which, in addition
to this, create for the voice difficulties which only become
graceful and beautiful by the ease with which they are
overcome. The first act is the field in which these blossoms
more especially flourish. For the actress it furnishes an
opportunity for displaying the most maidenly gentleness,
the most charming *naïveté*, and the merriest laughter of
love. Earnestness is reserved for the second act, in which
dramatic and vocal expression melt inseparably into each
other. In the first half, until she falls asleep, the singer
avails herself only of the indescribable beauty of the
softer tones she has so easily at command : all is sweetness
and stillest enchantment. In the latter half, when the
weight of undeserved sorrow falls upon her, she adds the
strongest colouring of dramatic and changeful expression to the
wailing tones that, in her song, sink so deeply into the soul.
Here she comes out more strongly than before ; yet we
almost venture to think that the bonds within which she had
previously confined her expression led her into the realms of
a purer beauty. But in the effect she produced upon the
public she evidently won a more brilliant victory, for
the storm of applause burst out in a veritable explosion.
In the third act, in which the sun of blessed joy alternates
with the darkest clouds of grief, tragic elevation with elegiac
abandon and rapturous joy, the effect rises to its culminating
point. Here we see the artist in full command of the whole
range of many-sided feeling, and the rich picture, which is
thus illuminated by the dramatic completion given to the
poem, leaves nothing more to be unfolded." *

We have thought it desirable to insert these long quotations from Herr Rellstab's transcendental critiques, since they
exactly represent the feeling produced by Mdlle. Lind's per-

---

* *Kgl. priv. Berlinische Zeitung.* (October 19, 1847.) See also
'*Gesammelte Schriften von Ludwig Rellstab.*' (Leipzig, 1861, vol. xx.
pp. 408, *et seq.*)

formances at the time they were written. In reading them
we must remember that, however extravagant or "high-
flown" their language might appear in an English critique
at the present day, it was not thought "high-flown" in
German critiques in 1844. Moreover, Herr Rellstab was a
poet as well as a critic, and wrote his reviews from a
modern German poet's point of view. It was only natural
that he should adopt a glowing—nay, even an ecstatic tone.
And yet, however glowing his phrases, they were but the
echo of those that passed from mouth to mouth, in the theatre,
in the salon, in the street, in every corner of Berlin in which
the discussion of artistic topics was possible. He only gave
utterance to the opinions that were openly expressed, on
every side, by every one capable of forming an opinion upon
the subject.

But the long chain of successes suffered a temporary
interruption.

After appearing twice, in the part of "Amina," on the
days already mentioned, Mdlle. Lind was announced, on the
23rd February, to sing for the fourth time in that of "Euryanthe," but was seized with sudden indisposition at the close
of the first act, and compelled to omit a considerable portion
of her *rôle* as the Opera proceeded. The audience, however,
showed the greatest sympathy throughout the evening with
the beloved artist."*

The indisposition continued for more than a week, to the
unspeakable disappointment of the public. During this
trying time the patient was overwhelmed with visits of con-
dolence, but prudence forbade the admission of more than a
few intimate friends, and these only at favourable moments.
Meyerbeer seems to have been unfortunate in his choice of
days or hours, and expressed his disappointment, on the
28th of February, in the following letter :—

* *Kgl. priv. Berlinische Zeitung.* (Feb. 25, 1845.)

" Berlin, Feb. 28, 1845.

' MY DEAR MADEMOISELLE,

"Though I have called on you several times since
your indisposition, I have not been so fortunate as some of
your other friends in seeing you.

"It only remains, therefore, for me to express in writing
my congratulations and good wishes on the anniversary of
your *fête*, which Madame Reyer tells me occurs to-day, and
to beg you at the same time kindly to accept these few
flowers, modest and pure as yourself.

"But what remains for your friends to wish, to-day, for
you whom Heaven has so richly endowed ! It has given you
that great and sympathetic voice which charms and moves
all hearts ; the fire of genius, which pervades your singing,
and your acting ; and, in fine, those indelible graces which
modesty and candour and innocence give only to their
favoured ones, and which bring every enemy into sub-
jection.

"One can, therefore, ask nothing more for you from
Heaven, than relief from those doubts in the power of your
talent which turn even your days of triumph into days of
anxiety ; the removal of that indecision and irresolution
which throw you into such continual agitation ; and, finally,
the disappearance of that diffident temperament, which, rendering you distrustful of the source of the sympathies you
inspire, may perhaps, in the end, deprive you of that most
beautiful consolation of human life, friendship.

"But whether Heaven grants you or not this little supplement to your other precious qualities, you will always be, for
me, my dear Mademoiselle, one of the most touching and
noble characters that I have ever met with during my long
artistic wanderings, and one to whom I have vowed for my
whole life the most profound and sincere admiration and
esteem.

"Your

"Ever devoted,

"MEYERBEER." *

It will be seen from the closing paragraphs of this most
kind and sympathetic letter that Meyerbeer, like so many

* Translated from the original autograph, which is written in French.

others at this period, was sincerely grieved, and even pained, by the diffidence for which Mdlle. Lind's character was so remarkable. We shall have more to say on this subject hereafter, but at the moment at which the above letter was written more than one cause of uneasiness was at work of which neither Meyerbeer nor any one else in Berlin entertained the slightest suspicion—more than one element of anxiety quite serious enough to have originated the illness which the world, and probably the doctors themselves, mistook for the natural result of over-study and fatigue.

For instance, the reader will readily understand that, since the unhappy moment in which the " Bunn contract " was signed in the box of the British Ambassador, Mdlle. Lind had never failed to reflect upon it, in secret, even at a time when her mind was so fully occupied with her work upon the stage.

She had, in fact, written to Mr. Bunn, informing him that, for reasons which to her appeared quite unanswerable, she found it impossible to fulfil the terms of her engagement with him ; and by a coincidence which it is difficult to believe accidental her letter is dated on the 22nd of February— the day previous to that on which she was so suddenly taken ill in the middle of the fourth performance of *Euryanthe.*

The letter, originally written by Mdlle. Lind in French,* ran thus :—

" Berlin, Feb. 22, 1845.

" MONSIEUR,

"I have delayed until to-day to give you the required information concerning the time of my visit to London (the decision of which was left to me until the 1st of March), because I wished very much to fulfil my promised contract.

* The original draft of the letter was drawn up for Mdlle. Lind, in German, by her friend, Madame Birch-Pfeiffer. She herself only transcribed it, in French, from the copy thus supplied to her, and now in the collection of Frau von Hillern (the daughter of Madame Birch-Pfeiffer), by whose kind permission it is inserted here.

" Unfortunately, weeks of continued study and fruitless effort have proved to me that it is impossible for me to learn the English language in the short time allowed to me, for which reason, if I were to come to London in October, I should not be ready to appear in English Opera.

" I am therefore compelled to tell you that I cannot come to London, and that I look upon the engagement as null and void, because I cannot fulfil the principal condition. Moreover, the great exertion I have suffered here has so shaken my health that the doctors have recommended me, if I wish to preserve my voice, to take complete and continued rest during the whole of the summer.

" On this account my guardian at Stockholm *—without whose consent, and signature, none of my engagements are legal—has quite forbidden me to undertake the fatiguing enterprise in London.

" Do not believe the report that I count upon going to the Italian Opera in London. On my word of honour, which I pledge to you, I will no more sing, this year, at the London Italian Opera House than at the English one. And I assure you I regret very much that I am obliged to disappoint those hopes the fulfilment of which exceeds my physical strength and capability.

" With the greatest respect,

" Yours obediently,

" JENNY LIND." †

To this certainly not very " business-like " letter Mr. Bunn replied in language which rendered anything like a release from the conditions of the contract almost hopeless. Nor was the style of his communication any more encouraging than its substance—and it was in all probability for this reason that she left it for some considerable time unanswered. Mr. Bunn, however, insisted upon his right to a reply, and some weeks afterwards demanded it in no uncertain terms.

---

* Judge Munthe.

† The letter is dated, Berlin, Feb. 22, 1845; and was published, in *The Times*, in the form of an English translation, on the 23rd of February, 1848.

We subjoin his letter, without attempting to soften the "business-like" tone of the language in which it is couched.

"Theatre Royal, Drury Lane, March 20, 1845.

"MADEMOISELLE,

"You have not replied to my last letter, and I therefore address you again.

"I am well aware of your great progress in the English language, and am also aware that you are deterred from fulfilling your contract with me by the falsest misrepresentations; and I know the parties who have made them; and I know likewise the overtures which have been made to you to sing at our Italian Opera.

"If you have any doubts as to the payment of your money, I will lodge it in a banker's hands before you leave Berlin,* and if there be any other obstacle I will also remove it.

"The public here would be ready to hear you sing in German as well as in English, and there is no question of your having immense success. All I want is, for you to keep faith with me and for me to keep faith with the public. I therefore again call upon you to fulfil your contract with me, or to make me such ample remuneration as will justify me in releasing you from it.

"I have the honour to be,

"Your obedient servant,

"A. BUNN."

It will be observed, that, while Mdlle. Lind cautions Mr. Bunn not to believe the "report" that she intended to sing at "the Italian Opera in London," Mr. Bunn tells her that he knows she is "deterred from fulfilling" her contract "by the falsest misrepresentations," and then goes on to say that he knows of "the overtures which have been made" to her, "to sing at our Italian Opera."

After having made the most minute and diligent researches in every direction in which it seemed possible that light

---

* She had left Berlin, for Hanover, some days before this was written.

might be thrown upon the question, we do not hesitate to say that no such "overtures" were made to her until long after the period of which we are now treating. That false "reports" were current there can be no possible doubt; but the "falsest misrepresentation" of all was that which accused Mdlle. Lind of accepting another engagement in London while she left unfulfilled that contracted with Mr. Bunn. How or where these reports originated no one has ever been able to discover. But there is ample evidence to prove that they were extensively propagated, at a very early period, both in England and in Germany; that they reached her ears as well as those of Mr. Bunn; and that they tended to exacerbate, with fatal effect, the tone of the resulting controversy.

The coincidence of dates leaves no reasonable doubt that the worry of this miserable controversy was a primary cause, though not the only one, of the alarming attack which prevented her from finishing the part of "Euryanthe" on the 23rd of February—that cruel worry which, to sensitive natures, is a far more potent source of illness than any amount of predisposition or even of actual infection.

For a whole week the indisposition continued, to the equal disappointment of the subscribers and the public.

On the 28th of February a performance of Donizetti's *La Figlia del Reggimento,** with Fräulein Tuczec in the principal part, was substituted for the serious opera. Mdlle. Lind was, however, able to reappear in *La Sonnambula*, on the 2nd of March, with undiminished powers. On the 4th she sang, for the last time, in *Das Feldlager in Schlesien;* repeated the part of "Amina" on the 7th and 9th—the last two nights of her engagement—and on the 11th made her last appearance for the season in *Norma*, on the occasion of her

---

* It was not until some months after this that Mdlle. Lind herself appeared for the first time in this popular opera at Stockholm.

own benefit. She speaks of her reason for choosing that
Opera, in preference to another which had been suggested, in
a letter to Madame Birch-Pfeiffer :—

"Berlin, March 7, 1845.

"DEAR MOTHER,

"I hesitate no more. All is settled, and I adhere to
Norma for my benefit, and sing on Sunday in *La Sonnambula*. Why? do you ask? Because I have no time for
reflection, and I cannot and will not appear before the public
in a state of uncertainty. So I have begged to be let off *Der
Freischütz*, and to sing the part of "Agathe" on my return;
and all has been conceded. Only, dearest, kindest, best Frau
Mutter, do not be angry with me; but—I am really delighted
not to be obliged to sing, act, and talk in *Der Freischütz*,
on Sunday. Greetings, a thousand times (what lovely
German !),* to the Aunt, and my best-beloved little sister,
and two tickets for Nanni, from

"Your heartily devoted,

"JENNY." †

The announcement of this was followed by so frantic a
demand for places that, long before the performance took
place, it was found necessary to issue an official notice to
the effect that no more tickets could be given out; and it
was agreed, on all hands, that on the evening itself she
surpassed herself in the part she had already made so
famous.

"We followed 'Norma,' in her love, grief, wrath, despair,
magnanimity, and self-sacrifice," says the Berlin journal,
"with the irresistible sympathy she had wrung from us at
her first performance; nay, with more! At certain moments
the artist seemed to us to have reached a higher level than

---

* The original is—*Tausend Mal Grüsse!*

† Translated from the original autograph, in the possession of Madame
Birch-Pfeiffer's daughter, Frau von Hillern, who has kindly given us
permission to quote largely from her valuable collection of letters. In
future cases, these quotations will be acknowledged as, "From Frau von
Hillern's collection."

before; as, for example, in her resolution to make known her
fault, in the remembrance of her children, in the abandonment of her humility when she threw herself at her father's
feet.   Her art possesses the property of rising, with so clear
a success, into a higher sphere, that, in her interpretation,
she always brings with her something that touches us
supremely, as in those burning passions of the woman's soul,
which, while thus disclosed, are purified, like asbestos, in
their own flame.

"After all the effect and triumph that necessarily followed
the artist throughout the series of her dramatic interpretations, she reached, at the close, the highest point that had
been yet attained.   The stage was covered with flowers and
wreaths thrown from the boxes in the proscenium; even the
ladies, carried away by the enthusiasm of the moment,
heightened the meed of applause with eyes, hearts, and hands.
The wreath that they gave her was not of laurel, but of roses;
a sister's gift for the artist, who, among the difficulties
of her calling, appears as so fit a guardian of the Palladium
of Womanhood and Purity.   As for her thanks, the threefold
summons before the curtain could win no word from the
firmly closed lips; but the eye overflowed and blotted out
the faults of the mouth.

"The artist appears to-night for the last time.   She
leaves us—but we shall see her again, and we hope in
the full possession of her gifts; yes, in fresher, richer un-
folding of their spring-blossoms!   And may the mild sun
of this spring be the omen of a long, long continuance!" *

And with this touching *Auf Wiedersehen* the Berlin public
took leave of the actress.   But the singer was yet again to be
heard in the Concert-room.

* *Kgl. priv. Berl. Zeitung.* (March 11, 1845.)   See also, Rellstab's
'*Gesammelte Schriften*,' vol. xx. pp. 394–396.

CHAPTER VIII.

WE have recorded, in a former chapter, the impression produced upon the Countess of Westmorland by Mdlle. Lind's singing at a reception which took place in the apartments of the Princess of Prussia not long after her arrival in Germany.

This, however, was not the only concert in which the young singer took part during her first visit to Berlin.

On Thursday, the 13th of February, 1845, she made her first public appearance in the Concert-room at a *Soirée* given by the brothers Ganz ; and, if we may accept the verdict pronounced by the critics of the day as a fair and unbiassed one, her triumph on this occasion was not a whit less brilliant than that which she had achieved two months previously at the Opera-House.

"Our reporter," says the leading journal, "entered the room at the exact moment at which the first note of the air from *Niobe* * was sung by Mdlle. Lind. It was also the first note that the artist had uttered in the character of a concert-singer ; and, whether it was that the hall resounded with peculiarly happy effect to the tone of her voice, or that this very effective air was especially effective for *her*, it seemed to us that the splendour of the concert-singer exceeded even the brilliancy of the dramatic artist—though, of course, in a subordinate sphere. The tones were of such pearly clearness, the words were so closely united with the tones ; *piano, forte, crescendo* shaded the expression so tenderly, and

---

* ' *Il soave e len contento,*' from Pacini's *Niobe.*

yet so certainly, that we never remember having been so
delighted with a concert-singer. We noticed especially the
charm of the little passages of *fioritura* executed with
absolute certainty in the highest register, the smooth descend-
ing chromatic scales, and some shakes, with which the singer
adorned the tasteful and fascinating brilliancy of the air." [*]

The same high praise was awarded to the accomplished
vocalist on the occasion of her next appearance, at Herr
Nehrlich's concert on the 10th of March.

"Mdlle. Lind," says the reviewer, "sang the air of
Donna Anna, in F major,[†] with womanly depth of expression
and with strict adherence to the text. On the stage we
might perhaps have wished for a little more power in certain
passages, but for the concert-room she exactly reached the
happy medium. The individuality of the artist was still
more captivatingly displayed in her delivery of three
German songs. Each of these little compositions deserves a
word of praise. The first, by Josephson, was perhaps the
most worthy of remark, though the low *tessatura* of the vocal
part rendered it the least welcome. To the second—' *Vergiss-
meinnicht* '—by Herrmann Wichmann, we ourselves should
feel inclined to give the preference, for its simple natural
expression, which the singer brought out with full earnestness. The third, by F. Weiss, was the most successful of
the three. Certain it is that, so interpreted, these three
songs touched the inmost chords of artistic sympathy." [‡]

Of the Court-concerts in which she took part about this
time the journals gave, of course, no published account.

Apart from the private reception given by the Princess of
Prussia, and already described, she sang, on the 18th of
December, 1844, in company with Herr Bötticher and
other artists, at a Court performance, in memory of which the
King and Queen presented her with a valuable bracelet.
And again, soon after the beginning of the new year, she

---

[*] *Kgl. priv. Berlinische (Vossische) Zeitung.* (Feb. 15, 1845.)

[†] ' *Non mi dir,*' from Mozart's *Il Don Giovanni.*

[‡] *Kgl. priv. Berl. Zeit.* (March 12, 1845.)

assisted at two more Court concerts—the last of the season. The impression made upon the Royal Family by these performances and the personal interest taken in her by Queen Elizabeth, were well known in Berlin, and it is pleasant to know that the feeling was a lasting one and not the result of a mere evanescent burst of artistic enthusiasm.

The actual farewell for the season took place on the 13th of March, at a concert given, in the hall of the *Sing-Akademie*, in aid of the "Asylum for Blind Soldiers." The room was so crowded that not only was the space usually devoted to the orchestra filled by the audience, but it was only with great difficulty that room could be found for the artists and the accompanying pianoforte. It is pleasant to find Fräulein Tuczec highly praised on this occasion.

"The most piquant charm," says the journal we have so frequently quoted, "was produced by the duet from *Sargino*,* sung by Mdlles. Lind and Tuczec, and followed by a storm of applause, called forth by their zealous efforts to do their best. Every artist, indeed, contributed his part with the best possible good will, and thus deserved the liveliest thanks of the public. Before all, however, these thanks were won by the beloved and modest Singer who took leave of us in this concert. She sang the grand air, '*Robert, toi que j'aime*,'† from *Robert le Diable*, with expression as intense as her execution was brilliant, rising to the high D flat in the upper register; and completed the cycle of her artistic achievements in our capital city by the performance of some of those simple Swedish songs, which overcame us with so irresistible a charm. The first—'*Am Aarensee rauscht der viel grüne Wald*'‡—she sang in German; the two others—one a very tender one, dying away in the softest scarcely audible

* An *Opera buffa*, by Paer.

† This famous air belongs to the part of "Isabelle"; not to that of "Alice," which Mdlle. Lind always impersonated on the stage.

‡ A strikingly original song by Adolph Lindblad, composed to German words by Graf von Schlippenbach, and printed, in the general collection of his songs, without a Swedish translation.

tones *—in the original Swedish; so that her last notes
seemed already vanishing in the distance.

"Amidst the loud outbreak of applause which followed
place was found for a silent sign of acknowledgment. While
Mdlle. Lind was singing, a lady had deposited a wreath and
a garland of flowers upon the pianoforte. The artist now
took them up, with a look of eloquent thanks, and, retreating
backwards, greeted the audience repeatedly, while the shouts
of applause continued until she had vanished beyond the
last steps of the platform.

"Many heartfelt blessings accompany her into her retreat,
where she needs must take with her the rich satisfaction that
she has done so much and been so thoroughly appreciated." †

And many heartfelt blessings most certainly did accompany
her, not only from the grateful public, but from dear ones
with whom she had found true and, as later events proved,
lasting bonds of friendship.

King Frederick William IV., Queen Elizabeth, and the
various members of the Royal Family, behaved to her as
true friends, not only then but in after years also.

By Lord and Lady Westmorland she was never forgotten,
and among the members of their family her memory is
still held precious.

She has told us, in her own words, of her pleasant intercourse with the aged poet Tieck, and the innocent little
family party at Frau Bettina von Arnim's.‡ Madame Reyer
and her sister, Baroness von Ridderstolpe, were kind and
home-like friends; and through their acquaintance with the
family of Herr von Waldenburg, a gentleman of position in
Berlin, she was first introduced to the well-known sculptor,
Professor Ludwig Wichmann, who, with his wife and family,
received her, a little later on, into bonds of closest intimacy.
Professor and Madame Wichmann had been delighted with

* Probably, Berg's '*Fjerran i skog.*'
† *Kgl. priv. Berl. Zeit.* (March 15, 1845.)
‡ See page 225.

her first performance in *Norma*, and had begged Madame von Waldenburg to bring her to their house, in the Hasenheger Strasse, which was then a favourite resort for artists and persons of culture; and this first interview led to the formation of so intimate a friendship between herself and Madame Wichmann that their affection for each other never afterwards cooled for a moment. The reader will not have forgotten that it was at Professor Wichmann's house that she first met Mendelssohn on the 21st of October, 1844; and here also, in March, 1845, she met for the first time Herr Heinrich Brockhaus, the then head of the great publishing firm of that name in Leipzig, a man of high cultivation and great influence, of whom we shall have occasion to speak again.

Most of these kind friends were intimate with each other, and many pleasant little *réunions* took place within the charmed circle. It was at a party at Madame von Arnim's that, on the 7th of January, Herr Josephson first had the pleasure of hearing two of his songs sung by Mdlle. Lind in the presence of Meyerbeer; "and," says he, in his journal, "they won the approval both of the *maestro* and of the other listeners—but then, Jenny sang them in excellent style." *

But notwithstanding the sympathy she met with on every side, the great artist seems—if we may trust Herr Josephson's opinion—to have been rather dazed than rejoiced, rather bewildered than delighted, with her almost miraculous success. He speaks with evident anxiety of her unrest, and the sudden transitions of her moods.

" She is oscillating," he says, " between heaven and earth, not knowing, as yet, on what terms she is with either. In the meantime my friendship for her is growing stronger every day. Daily do I call down blessings on her artist-soul, so great, so loving, so deep, so enthusiastic. May God send her all the peace and consolation of which she stands

* 'Aus dem Leben eines Schwedischen Componisten,' vol. ii.

in need; and grant that, in days of storm, she may not forget the treasures of grace offered her." *

The "unrest" which caused Herr Josephson so much anxiety may perhaps be partly accounted for by the home-sickness to which, as we have known from the very beginning of her wanderings, she was so constantly subject.

She herself justifies us in arriving at this conclusion in a letter written to her guardian, Judge Munthe, just before the first performance of *Euryanthe* :—

"Everybody is so kind to me," she says, "that it is only through my unbounded love for home that, in the midst of all these splendours, my whole soul goes out, all the same, in longing for Sweden. There is an inexplicable home-sympathy in the depths of my soul, and I look upon its possession as an unspeakable happiness; for to feel so warmly as this for one's country is a divinely elevating sentiment.

"The next Opera will be *Euryanthe*, which is now being diligently rehearsed. *La Sonnambula* will probably follow, and after that *Iphigenia in Aulis*. But I must make haste, if I am to get through my twenty appearances. Hitherto I have only reached the sixth. During the last weeks I shall have to hurry on and sing a little oftener." †

Surely this is a sigh of longing—not of bewilderment. And surely this, added to the ceaseless worry of the Bunn-contract, may have done a good deal in producing that "unrest" that gave Herr Josephson so much concern, and may, possibly, furnish a key to the mysteries of changing humour which seemed to puzzle him so cruelly.

Let us bear this last sad sigh for home carefully in mind, while we take leave, for a time, of the turmoil of Berlin, and accompany her on a tour which certainly brought her nearer to her beloved Sweden.

---

* ' Aus dem Leben eines Schwedischen Componisten,' vol. ii.

† From a letter written by her to her guardian, Judge Munthe, dated ' Berlin, Jan. 13, 1845.'

CHAPTER IX.

ON Thursday, the 13th of March, 1845, as we have already heard, Mdlle. Lind's last notes died softly away in Berlin at a concert given for the benefit of the "Hospital for Blind Soldiers."

On Wednesday, March the 19th, she made her first appearance at the Court Theatre at Hanover in her favourite character of "Norma." The Opera was repeated on Tuesday, the 25th, and immediately afterwards she left for Hamburg.

We do not propose, during the rapid transitions from city to city upon which we are now entering, to dilate in detail upon performances which have already been sufficiently criticised at Berlin. It will suffice therefore for the present if we say that the now famous songstress was received by the public with enthusiastic plaudits, and at Court with a kindly consideration which, during the reign of the succeeding King and Queen, ripened into undisguised attachment on both sides. Years ago, in the days of the Electress Sophia and her descendants, the Georges, Hanover had ranked with Dresden and Berlin and Hamburg as one of the principal centres of Art in the north of Germany. Under the direct influence of the Abbate Steffani, and the shadow of the giant Handel, the Lyric Drama had prospered exceedingly in the fine old Theatre. The Electors had thoroughly appreciated the work of these great Masters, had patronised them liberally, and treated them with marked consideration and

s 2

respect; and the last scions of the old Electoral Dynasty
proved faithful to the traditions of their House to the end.

The visits to Hanover were always pleasant ones; but on
this occasion a disquieting communication from the manager
of Drury Lane cast its ominous shadow over the otherwise
happy scene, as we learn from the following sentence contained in a letter to Madame Birch-Pfeiffer, dated Hanover,
March 24, 1845 :—

"I have received a letter from Mr. Bunn, who speaks of
dishonour and ingratitude, etc., etc. Dreadful! (*Schreck-
lich !*)" *

But *that* shadow fell everywhere. Let us try to forget it
as long as we can.

On leaving Hanover, Mdlle. Lind proceeded at once to
Hamburg, where, on the 29th of March, she made her first
appearance at the Stadt Theater, in the Opera in which she
had already won so many well-earned laurels for Bellini as
well as for herself.

And new laurels were won that night.

The following account of the first visit to Hamburg is
rom the pen of a careful and conscientious German Art-
historian.

"The 'guest-performances' began on the 29th of March,
1845, with *Norma*, and created a positive *furore*.

"It would be impossible to give any idea of the state of
ecstasy into which the whole of Hamburg was thrown. More
than twelve times during her visit she sang, at raised prices,
to houses so crowded that the aid of the police had to be
called in to regulate the crush. The celebrated Swede did
not produce this effect merely by aid of splendid natural
gifts supplemented by diligent study, but also through an
ever-winning personality, shown in little details, which
atoned for the somewhat narrow changes of a not very exten-

* From Frau von Hillern's collection.

sive *répertoire*,* while the artist enchanted every one with her
pure and virgin loveliness.

"Jenny Lind was the first in Hamburg whose whole figure
was so completely bestrown with flowers that she stood upon
an improvised carpet of blossoms. The critics were moved
to exhaust the whole circle of laudatory expressions: 'Her
scales are pearls;' 'In her *mezza voce* was a charm like the
tone of an Æolian harp;' 'While the ear is delighted, the eye
sees poetry alone before it.'

"The serenade which was sung to the artist in front of
her hotel—the old Stadt London—after her last performance
was quite a popular festival. With this ovation was combined a torch-light procession, a display of fireworks on the
Alster, and other demonstrations, which lasted until long
past midnight." †

During this visit to Hamburg she sang in *Norma* five
times, including her own benefit, on Tuesday, the 6th of
May; five times in *La Sonnambula*; twice in *Lucia di
Lammermoor* (for the first time in Germany); and once (also
for the first time out of Stockholm) in *Der Freischütz*.

She also assisted on the 14th of April at a concert
in Altona,‡ at which she sang the aria from Pacini's *Niobe*
—'*Il suave e ben contento*'—in which she had created so profound a sensation in Berlin, and her own favourite Swedish
melodies. On the 21st of April she sang the same pieces at
a concert given by Herr Kapellmeister Krebs—the father of
the celebrated pianiste, Fräulein Marie Krebs—in the theatre

---

* Although she sang in such an endless variety of characters at
Stockholm—*Fidelio* being almost the only great operatic *rôle* that she
never attempted—the persistent desire of the public to hear her in certain
special parts, after her first great triumph in Berlin, and the labour
also of learning new parts in a foreign language, prevented her from
appearing in others in which she was equally great.

† '*Ein Beitrag zur Deutschen Culturgeschichte;*' von Dr. Hermann
Uhde. (Stuttgart Cotta, 1879.) The reader will observe that, in this
case, the transcendental language does *not* proceed from the pen of Herr
Rellstab. If he was under the spell in 1846, surely Uhde was not in 1879.

‡ The town of Altona forms a suburb of Hamburg, which it almost
joins, though it was formerly within the Danish territory.

at Hamburg. And on the 25th of April she sang at the
Court Theatre of Schwerin, in *Norma*, followed by *La Sonnambula* on the 28th, after which she immediately resumed
her duties in Hamburg, as above described, concluding with
the "benefit" on the 6th of May.*

And now, after the anxieties and fatigues of this most
trying season—trying and fatiguing in direct proportion to
its success—came the moment of its rich reward.

On the doors of the Royal Theatre at Stockholm was
affixed a play-bill announcing that Mdlle. Lind would reappear in her native town on the 16th of May, in *Norma*.

It needs but little effort of the imagination to picture the
joy with which the lonely exile—for lonely she had been,
even amidst the glories of her most splendid triumphs; lonely
while critics, finding conventional terms too weak to express
their admiration, were exhausting the hendecasyllabic licence
of German idiom in the fabrication of new ones; lonely,
while she stood upon the carpet of flowers in Hamburg;
lonely, beyond all loneliness, even in company of the devoted
friends whose affection she returned with ten-fold warmth—
it needs, we say, but little effort to imagine the joy with
which this lonely exile prepared to stand once more upon the
boards of the theatre in which she had sung and acted as a
child, to sing and act, in presence of a Swedish audience, in
that same part of "Norma" which she had already impersonated upon those very boards no less than thirty times,

* The dates were, March 29, 31, and April 2*, *Norma*; April 5*, 7*, 10*,
La Sonnambula; April 12*, 15*, *Lucia*; April 18, *La Sonnambula*;
April 30, *Der Freischütz*; May 2*, 4, *La Sonnambula*; May 6, (Mdlle.
Lind's benefit), *Norma*. Twelve performances, in all, besides the benefit.
The asterisks denote raised prices, which were not charged on the benefit
night.

and in which she had in the meantime excited the wonder
and admiration of the most critically exacting nation in
Europe.

Such joy as that is not to be described in words, and we
must perforce leave it to the reader's imagination to paint the
pleasant picture—bearing in mind, however, that it was
distinctly a double one. The Swedes were as glad to welcome
home their great national artist as she was to return to them
—as proud of her as she was of her country. And not
without good cause! She had left Stockholm the idol of
Sweden, she returned to it the idol of northern Europe.
The Swedish critics had accepted her as the greatest singer
known to them; the German critics had endorsed and
confirmed—nay, glorified the verdict passed by their
northern brethren. It was no small thing for the credit of
Scandinavian Art that its representatives should find their
opinion so triumphantly vindicated. And here we must beg
the reader to remember the position we assumed in the very
first chapter of our history, and have ever since maintained,
that the reputation with which we have to deal was not a
Swedish, nor a German, nor an English, but an European
one. This great fact, which might have been anticipated from
very early times, was made more and more clearly apparent,
as each successive capital expressed its opinion; and, by the
time of which we are now treating, there could be no reasonable doubt as to its ultimate acceptation. The Swedes did
not doubt it, at any rate; and all Stockholm went forth to
greet the national heroine, with songs of joy and gladness.

"Jenny Lind's return to Sweden caused general delight
and jubilation," says Fröken Marie von Stedingk, "and the
first reception was a very cordial one. The steam-boat, with
the celebrated artist on board—our 'Northern Nightingale'—
did not arrive until midnight; but notwithstanding this the
port and neighbouring streets were so packed that I could

only with difficulty find a tiny corner for myself and maid
on a ship close by.

" A rocket gave the signal for the liveliest shouts of delight,
and a boat went out to meet the steam-ship with the most
beautiful music on board.

" When the crowd began to disperse I was able to get
home safely, but without having caught so much as a
glimpse of Jenny Lind, who probably went straight to her
home as quickly as possible.　Her stay at Berlin, and her
progress through Germany, had been a long succession of
triumphs, and her modesty and great eminence combined
had won friends for her everywhere."*

It was the old, old story.　Wildest excitement on the one
side, feverish yearning for retirement on the other.　It was
the quiet of home that the wanderer longed for—not the
shouts of the admiring multitude.

During the course of this short visit to Stockholm,
she sang eighteen times: twice in *Norma,* twice in *Der
Freischütz,* three times in *La Sonnambula,* twice in *Lucia di
Lammermoor,* eight times in Donizetti's *La Figlia del Reggimento,* and once in Rossini's *Il Turco in Italia.*†

The terms under which these eighteen performances were
secured by the direction were laid down in a special contract,
drawn up with the consent of and duly signed by Judge
Munthe, her guardian.

Among the Operas mentioned the reader will observe the
names of several which we have not hitherto critically
noticed.

Rossini's *Il Turco in Italia* (first produced at Milan, in
1814, as a companion piece to *L'Italiana in Algeri*), is a
delightful *Opera buffa,* full of genial melody and true Rossinian
freshness.　The part of " Fiorilla " abounds with passages of

---

* From the Diary of Fröken Marie von Stedingk.

† The dates were: May 16, 19, *Norma;* 23, 26, *Der Freischütz;* 28, 30,
La Sonnambula; June 2, 4, *Lucia;* 6, *La Sonnambula;* 9, 11, 13, 14,
16, 18, *La Figlia del Reg.;* 20, *Il Turco;* 21, 25, *La Figlia.*

most delicate *fioritura*, furnishing constant opportunities for the introduction of those inimitable *cadenze* in the charm and variety of which Mdlle. Lind stood unrivalled. And thus it was that the part, though not in all respects a pleasant one, became a favourite with her audience at Stockholm, where she had first introduced it in the previous years, and now sang it, on the 20th of June, for the ninth and last time.

Of *Der Freischütz* we shall prefer to speak in connection with its performance in Berlin, where it was in the following year received with unbounded admiration. Our notice of *Lucia di Lammermoor* and the world-famous *La Figlia del Reggimento* we shall reserve until we meet with them in London.

One circumstance, however, connected with the last-named Opera, in which she appeared for the first time on the 9th of June, we must not omit to notice here, since its interest is entirely centred in Stockholm.

The reader will not have forgotten the "historic fanfare" mentioned in our account of the little Jenny's childhood; how delighted she had been when she heard the soldiers playing it in the street, or how cleverly she had afterwards imitated it on the little old family pianoforte. Military music had always delighted her, and the sight of a regiment of soldiers gave her scarcely less pleasure in after life than it had done in her infancy. *La Figlia del Reggimento* had therefore a special charm for her quite apart from its claim for consideration as a work of Art, and she threw so much spirit into her interpretation of the part of the little *vivandière* that the Swedish soldiers were wild with enthusiasm about it. In a letter to Madame Birch-Pfeiffer, dated 'Stockholm, June 26, 1845,' she describes her eighth and last performance of the part, on the previous evening, as a veritable military triumph :—

" I am free," she says, "and I mean to rest myself right well.

" Yesterday, the performance of *Die Tochter des Regiments* was given entirely for officers and soldiers. The King had invited them all, and I was never so much amused in my life. All was cheerful and good-humoured. The soldiers laughed awfully, and applauded me so furiously that I really felt quite sorry for their hands. All was enthusiasm, and it all looked splendid. The whole house was filled with uniforms. It was beautiful indeed!

" This evening I am going to sup with my beloved widowed Queen—to my unspeakable pleasure, for she is so very gracious to me." *

Yes, 'beautiful indeed'! The mischievous little *vivandière* was evidently as much delighted with the gallant warriors who applauded her so furiously as they were with her. What a treat the performance must have been! and how the King must have enjoyed it!

Besides these operatic performances, she assisted, on the 7th of June, at a concert given by F. Prüme, on which occasion she sang an air from *Il Turco in Italia* and a duet (with Herr Günther) from *Das Feldlager in Schlesien.*

It was a happy time, and the return to home-life and home-scenery inexpressibly refreshing. The first part of the visit was indeed too much occupied with professional engagements to deserve the character of a holiday; but after the performances at the Opera were over she spent a few weeks in pleasant retirement at the country-home of her friends, Herr and Madame von Koch, of whom mention has already been made in previous chapters.† The eventful episode was however broken in upon, for the second time within the space of little more than twelve months, by a Royal summons—this time requiring her presence at the Court of Prussia.

---

* From Frau von Hillern's collection.
† See pages 105, 232.

King Frederick William IV. was preparing to entertain
Queen Victoria and the Prince Consort, first at Brühl, and
afterwards at Schloss Stolzenfels, the restored Castle on the
banks of the Rhine; and it was his wish that Mdlle. Lind
should add to the interest of the festivities by singing to
his Royal guests.

When the time of departure drew near she received
some touching marks of affection and esteem.

" The Queen Dowager," * says Fröken Marie von Stedingk,
" was exceedingly friendly to her, and gave a little *soirée* to
which the Royal Family alone were invited, and at which
Jenny sang some operatic airs splendidly to a pianoforte
accompaniment. I prefer, however, to hear her on the stage.

" Before going to the Queen Dowager she came to tea
with me, in company with the two maids of honour, Lotten
Mörner and Lotten Skjöldebrand; and we spent together an
hour that seemed too short to all of us.

" After this I went to see her several times; my last visit
being paid for the purpose of taking her a bracelet sent by
the Queen Dowager.

" Jenny Lind resided at that time, in some very comfortable apartments, in Norra Smedjegatan.

" Donizetti's *La Figlia del Reggimento* had been brought
out that season, and universally admired. To me it was a
real happiness to see and hear her. Both her acting and her
singing were exquisite, especially in the scene at the piano
and the farewell to the regiment. Still, in *La Sonnambula*, I
admired her even more. Never had she appeared to me in
such perfection—nature, gracefulness, expression—everything! It was thus a matter of deep regret to me when she
left, first, for the country to take some rest, and, afterwards,
to continue her triumphal progress abroad." †

* The late Queen Dowager Desideria, was the widow of King Karl
XIV. Johann (Bernadotte).

† From the Diary of Fröken Marie von Stedingk.

CHAPTER X.

THE month of August, 1845, witnessed festivities of unusual interest on the banks of the Rhine.

Between five and six o'clock on Saturday evening, August the 9th, the Queen and Prince Consort started down the river from Woolwich in the royal yacht *Victoria and Albert*, commanded by Lord A. Fitzclarence ; and, escorted by the *Black Eagle* and the *Porcupine*, arrived at Antwerp on Sunday evening, *en route* for Brühl, in response to an invitation from King Frederick William IV. and the Queen of Prussia.

The occasion was especially interesting, as this was the first time that the Queen of England had visited the Continent since her accession to the throne, and the highest legal authorities were somewhat cruelly exercised as to the constitutional etiquette of the proceeding. In this case, however, fact overpowered theory, and on Monday evening the Royal party was received at Brühl, about six miles from Cologne on the road to Bonn, by the King and Queen of Prussia, and entertained at half past eight with a grand military concert in the brilliantly illuminated courtyard of the Palace, where seven hundred performers officiated, beginning the programme with ' God save the Queen ' and ending with ' Rule Britannia,' supplemented by the famous Prussian ' tattoo '—a kind of quick march, for drums and fifes, composed about the year 1720, during the reign of King Frederick the Great.

But it was not in the Military Concert that the chief interest of the musical performance offered to the Queen was centred. Her Majesty's visit was designedly coincident with the inauguration of the bronze statue erected in honour of Beethoven, which was to take place at Bonn on the following day.

Accordingly, at one o'clock on Tuesday, the 12th of August, the monument was unveiled, amidst the firing of cannon, the flourish of trumpets, and the shouts of the multitudes gathered together from every quarter, not only of Germany, but of every other music-loving nation in Europe, and in the presence, not only of the Royal Families of England and Prussia, but of more Royal and Princely lovers of Art than we have space to mention.

Among the great musicians present at the unveiling of the statue were Spohr, Meyerbeer, Moscheles, Sir George Smart, Fétis, Liszt, Berlioz, Rellstab, Lindpaintner, Staudigl, Madame Viardot-Garcia, Miss Sabilla Novello, with a host of singers and instrumentalists of the highest order. And Mademoiselle Lind was also invited—not to the festival, but to sing privately to King Frederick William's Royal and distinguished guests at Brühl and the restored old feudal fortress of Stolzenfels on the Rhine.

Herr Heinrich Brockhaus, of Leipzig, who, it will be remembered, had visited Berlin in the month of March,* makes the following entry in his Diary for the 7th of August :—

"(1845. Leipzig, August 7.) Eduard's † birthday was celebrated in quite an exceptional way ; namely, by the presence of Jenny Lind.

"She had begged us to take post-tickets for her to Frank-

---

* See page 257.

† Herr (afterwards Dr.) Eduard Brockhaus, then a bright enthusiastic youth of sixteen.

fort on the Main, as she had been summoned by the King of
Prussia, to Stolzenfels. on the Rhine, where Queen Victoria
is to be received with great splendour; and I took this opportunity of inviting her to spend with us the few hours between
her arrival and departure.

"I met her at the station, and she seemed pleased with my
invitation. Her Swedish companion,* who speaks but little
German and no French, and Herr Berg, who, I believe, was
her first teacher, came with her, and we spent a few hours
very pleasantly together.

"She is still in every respect the dear, sensitive, modest
girl whom I learned to know in the spring; and it seems as
if the usual consequences of the excitement and jubilation
that she everywhere creates pass over her. Art is, to her, a
veritable religion, of which she is, herself, a pure and chaste
priestess. I have known but few womanly natures that have
made so wholly favourable an impression upon me as that of
Jenny Lind.

"We accompanied the travellers to the post-carriage, and
our farewell was a very hearty one indeed." †

A touching little episode connected with the journey is
told in a letter written to Madame Birch-Pfeiffer from
Frankfort, and dated August 10, 1845 :—

"I have not much to say; since, as I told you, we spent
most of our time in the *diligence.* But I had one sorrow.

"When we left Leipzig the conductor took with him a
little dog—a Spitz—as they are always obliged to do, for the
protection of the luggage. The little dog was engaging, and
every time we came to a station I kissed him, but soon
afterwards the poor little animal fell under the wheels, and
was run over. Ah! it made me so unhappy." ‡

The English correspondents of the various London journals,
while giving detailed accounts of the " Beethoven Festival "
at Bonn, were, of course, necessarily silent on the subject of

* Mdlle. Louise Johansson.

† Translated, by kind permission of his sons, from ' *Aus den Tagebüchern
von Heinrich Brockhaus* ' (Leipzig, 1884), Band i. p. 56. Privately
printed, for friends only.

‡ From Frau von Hillern's collection.

the private performances at Court; but, fortunately, we are able to supply, from a private source, some valuable information of a very interesting character concerning the occasion on which the Queen and Prince Consort heard Mademoiselle Lind sing for the first time.

The late Mrs. Grote, in her unpublished 'Memoir of the Life of Jenny Lind,' from which we have already made more than one valuable quotation, gives the following account of the circumstances :—

"The Queen and Prince and their suite having arrived at the Château of Brühl—not far from Bonn—Mademoiselle Lind was invited thither, and took part in the musical entertainment offered by the Royal host to his guests.

"An English nobleman *—then Lord Steward of the Household—who attended the Queen to Brühl, and who related to me not long afterwards all that passed there, said that the expectations raised in the Royal minds by the reports current in Germany respecting Jenny Lind's singing were very high indeed. He himself—an amateur of great experience, and familiarly acquainted with the stage and its votaries all his life—was rather disposed to be prepared for a disappointment. King Leopold of Belgium, who was of the party at Brühl, and aware of My lord Liverpool's scepticism, smilingly said to him, 'I expect, that you will be satisfied, when you have heard the Lind ; she is something extraordinary.'

"Whilst 'the Lind' was singing her first aria, King Leopold amused himself by watching the effect produced upon his English friend ; and it was not long before Lord Liverpool, turning his head round, made a gesture sufficiently expressive to satisfy the King that he surrendered.

" 'It was,' said Lord Liverpool, 'a combination of style, vocal skill, and quality of voice, which absolutely took one by storm.'

"The Queen and Prince Albert were, both of them, enchanted with the treat provided for them ; insomuch that the King of Prussia pressed Jenny to favour him with a farther visit, at Stolzenfels, another schloss belonging to him, near Coblenz. Again Jenny obeyed the Royal mandate, and

* The late Lord Liverpool.

again Lord Liverpool was captivated by her incomparable powers, as were indeed the whole courtly circle there assembled.

"The Queen of England paid her the most cordial compliments, expressing a 'hope of seeing her, one day, in England.'

"Jenny was very much pleased with the whole week's excursion; and being afterwards at liberty to follow her own bent, she accepted an engagement to perform a couple of nights in Frankfort, where the utmost impatience was felt to see and judge one who was beginning to make so strong a sensation among the whole musical world." *

The Queen and Prince Consort left Stolzenfels, in the *Fairy*, on Saturday, the 16th of August, and proceeded thence to Mainz. On Monday, the 18th, they quitted the Rhine Provinces, passed through Frankfort on their way to Coburg and Gotha, reached the first-named town on the 19th, and the last on the 28th; re-embarked at Antwerp, on their homeward journey, on the 6th of September, and returned to Osborne on the 8th.

After the departure of the Royal party from Stolzenfels, Mademoiselle Lind descended the Rhine again as far as Cologne, where, on the 26th of August, she was serenaded by the company of the theatre, who presented her with a poem beginning, ' *Wohl beherrscht Gesang die Geister!* ' beautifully printed on a white satin filet, and addressed to her by "Die Mitglieder des Kölner Stadt-theaters, Köln, den 26 August, 1845."

On the following day she bade farewell to the Rhine Provinces, and started on her journey to Frankfort, where she was announced to appear, in *Norma*, on the 29th.

It was during this visit to Frankfort that Mademoiselle Lind first actually met Mr. and Mrs. Grote, of whom she had frequently heard, through Madame von Koch, and Mr. Edward

* MS. ' Memoir of the Life of Jenny Lind ; ' by Mrs. Grote.

Lewin ; and the acquaintance thus formed soon ripened into
closer intimacy. Mr. Grote was a man of business-like
habits and experience, while Mrs. Grote was almost equally
well versed in the ways of the world ; and when, feeling sure
of their integrity and confidence, Mademoiselle Lind entrusted
to them the secret of the nightmare which had for so many
months oppressed her, Mrs. Grote offered to do all that lay in
her power, when she returned to England, to induce Mr.
Bunn to rescind his contract, though she did not expect to
obtain this eminently desirable result without to a certain
extent indemnifying the manager for his disappointment—a
condition to which Mademoiselle Lind readily agreed,
" adding," says her friend, " that she would ratify any terms
which I should deem it desirable to arrange, in the way of
délit, or ' smart-money ' as the old phrase used to be." *

Before leaving Frankfort, on her return to England,
Mrs. Grote held another confidential communication with
her, which she thus describes in the MS. sketch already
quoted :—

"Among the things Jenny said to me during those two
days," she writes, " one was that her earnest desire was to
have done with the Stage, and to retire into private life as
speedily as was consistent with pecuniary independence.

" I manifested some surprise at hearing her speak of her
profession with such dislike.   She went on to say that it was
the Theatre, and the sort of *entourage* it involved, that was
distasteful to her: that at the Opera she was liable to be
continually intruded upon by curious idlers and exposed to
many indescribable *ennuis;* that the combined fatigue of
acting and singing was exhausting : that the exposure to cold
coulisses, after exertions on the stage in a heated atmosphere,
was trying to the chest: the labour of rehearsals, tiresome to
a degree : and that, altogether, she longed for the time to
arrive when she would be rich enough to do without the
Theatre—adding, ' My wants are few—my tastes simple—a

* MS. ' Memoir,' by Mrs. Grote.

small income would content me.' She would sing occasionally, she said, both for charity and for her friends, as well as for the undying love she felt for the musical Art; but not act, if she could help it.

" I mention this to prove how consistent her language was all through the subsequent phases of her artist-life. I must also say that her modesty and distrust of her own powers, at this period, showed me that she cherished a lofty standard of ideal excellence, and was far from thinking herself what every one who heard her thought her—a singer of the highest order." *

This however was certainly the opinion of the inhabitants of Frankfort, whose enthusiasm was scarcely less remarkable than that of the audience at Berlin.

The engagement at Frankfort was for nine nights, from the 29th of August to the 15th of September, and included three performances of *Norma*, four of *La Sonnambula*, one of *Der Freischütz*, and one of *Lucia di Lammermoor*.† The 'Frankfort' correspondent of one of the leading London journals thus speaks of her appearance and reception :—

" Rather above the middle height, Jenny Lind is slender, but peculiarly graceful in figure and action. She is very fair, with a profusion of beautiful auburn tresses; but it is entirely in the expression of her eyes that the truly great *artiste* will be identified : the feeling and intelligence of those bright orbs are unmistakable.

" The lessee of Drury Lane Theatre went expressly to Berlin to engage her, and she signed an agreement with Mr. Bunn for twenty performances, either for last May or the present month of October.

" Most liberal offers have also been tendered to her by Mr. Lumley's agents, for Her Majesty's Theatre; but we repeat the expression of our belief that, whenever her *début* takes place in this country, it will be on the Drury Lane boards.

" The writer of this little narrative had the good fortune to

---

* MS. ' Memoir,' by Mrs. Grote.

† The following were the dates of the performances: Aug. 29, 31, *Norma* ; Sept. 3, 5, *La Sonnambula* ; Sept. 7, *Der Freischütz* ; Sept. 10, *Norma* ; Sept. 12, *Lucia* ; and Sept. 14, 15, *La Sonnambula*.

hear Jenny Lind at Frankfort, last month, in Bellini's *La Sonnambula.* The house was crowded to excess, and even the side-scenes were filled with auditors disappointed of places in front of the curtain. The sensation that she created in the part of 'Amina' can only be compared to that which was wont to attend the delineations of Malibran in the same part, and that is awarding the highest possible praise to the Swedish Siren.

"Jenny Lind has a voice of extraordinary compass, the only defect in which is a deficiency of volume in the medium register. Her upper notes are delicious, as clear as a bell; and she warbles with the facility of a nightingale. Her execution is of the most brilliant kind, and nothing can approach the exquisite propriety and aptness of her *cadenzas.* They always come in at the right moment: she never sacrifices sense to sound. Her simplicity of style is, indeed, most rigid; but this charming naturalness it is which goes so home to the hearts of her hearers. Her shake is perfect—truly marvellous—proving that she must have an intuitive knowledge of her Art as well as the best culture. Her style is full of impulse; or, as the French call it, *abandon.* In the absence of all stage-trickery or conventionalism may be distinguished the child of genius. Her opening *Cavatina,* in the presence of Amina's friends, and her finale were contrasted with the highest skill. In the first was the modest subdued expression of joy—in the last, the triumphant outbreak of rapture at being restored to Elvino.* The untiring energy of this last vocal display, after two encores, electrified the band as well as the audience. Never shall we forget the amazement of the conductor, Professor Guhr, a first-rate musician. Throwing away his *bâton,* after the exhibition of this wondrous power on the part of Jenny Lind, he clapped his hands furiously over the stage-lamps." †

It was about this time that a proposal was sent from Vienna, by Herr Pokorny, the lessee of the Theater an der Wien, for some performances at that famous Opera-House during the coming winter. It was a great opportunity, but the idea was not at all pleasing to Mademoiselle Lind, who

* See also p. 158.

† From the *Illustrated London News* for October 11, 1845. (Pages 232–233.)

thus wrote about it to her friend, Madame Birch-Pfeiffer, through whom the engagement had been offered to her :—

> " Frankfurt-am-Main,
> " 4 Sept. 1845.

" DEAR GOOD MOTHER BIRCH,

" What do you think of me, and my obstinacy ? For Heaven's sake do not be angry !—only let me tell you honestly all about it, and then you will quite certainly be— more angry than ever !

" Everything goes splendidly with me, and even better than that ! and yet I have such anxiety about Vienna that I scarcely believe I shall dare to go there. They have such excellent singers in Vienna ; and what can I do there ? And, besides that, I gain just as much money by the journeys I am now making—though Vienna is the chief thing, on account of the renown.

" My good master * is now away, so I must judge for myself. I have had the privilege of speaking to the Prince and Princess Metternich, here in Frankfort, at Baron Roth-schild's, and they have both advised me to go to Vienna. And yet—only think !—what if I lose my whole reputation ! If I do not please ! And this anxiety grows so much upon me ! And all through next winter the thought of my first appearance in Vienna will follow me like an evil spirit. Ah, yes ! I am very much to be pitied !

" Tell Herr Pokorny that I am very grateful to him for the offered half-receipts and quite satisfied on the score of money ; but—that he must engage some other singer ; for he cannot reckon on me, as I cannot accept the engagement, and cannot believe that I should be able to carry it out in Vienna. Break it off, good mother. I am contented with very little, and shall perhaps sing no longer than till next spring, as I can then go home, by Hamburg, and afterwards live in peace. For, you see, mother Birch, this life does not suit me at all. If you could only see me—the despair I am in whenever I go to the theatre to sing ! It is too much for me. This terrible nervousness destroys everything for me. I sing far less well than I should, if it were not for this enemy. I cannot understand how it is that everything goes so well with me. People all take me by the hand. But all this helps nothing ! Herr Pokorny would not be very well

* Herr Berg.

pleased, for instance, if I were to sing there once only and, that once, fail. For the money he offers me he can get singers anywhere who are not so difficult to satisfy as I am, and who, at least, wish for something, while I wish for nothing at all !

" Mother ! what do you say to this—that I have so mislaid your letter to Madame—yes ! what is her name ?—that I cannot find it anywhere ? It is certainly hidden away somewhere ; but where, I cannot tell. For Heaven's sake, do not be angry ! On the day on which your letter arrived, I received so many, that it was possibly put aside. I beg you, above all things in the world, not to be vexed with me and not to lose your confidence in me.

" To-morrow (*La Sonnambula*) the Queen of England is coming to the Theatre, and the King and Queen of Bavaria, and all the royalties of Darmstadt ; that is what they believe here—but I do not ! Is not that lovely ?

" Greet the Aunt, my dear Sister, and all,

> " From your ever grateful and devoted
>
> > " JENNY." *

The picture is not a cheerful one. But we shall hear more of Vienna later on.

* From Frau von Hillern's collection.

CHAPTER XI.

WITH THE DANES.

THE short visit to Frankfort had been a genuine success, but a far more brilliant one was at hand.

After singing two nights at Darmstadt, at raised prices, and to crowded houses,* Mdlle. Lind prepared to renew her acquaintance with the kindred spirits with whom she had entered into so close an intellectual communion in the autumn of the year 1843.

With the delights of her first visit still green in their memory, the grateful and appreciative Danes went forth to meet her with demonstrations of enthusiastic welcome.

For the moment their hopes were held in abeyance, under the circumstances narrated in the following communication,

---

* In *Norma*, on the 17th of September; and *La Sonnambula*, on the 19th. In memory of the impression produced by the performance of *Norma*, an anonymous poem, beginning, "*Einst war's, dass tief vom Norden*," was privately printed, on a pink card, and circulated among the art-loving inhabitants of the town. We subjoin the first two stanzas:—

> "Einst war's dass tief vom Norden, im Siegesjubelklang,
> In deutsche Herzen stürmte der Schweden frommer Sang;
> Der grosse Gustav Adolph zog kämpfend mit seinem Heer,
> Als Sieger durch Deutschlands Gauen, zum Schutze und zur Wehr.

> "Und nach zweihundert Jahren tönt wieder Schwedenschall,
> Doch strömt er aus der Kehle der Schwedischen Nachtigall;
> Sie singt so süss und innig, so mächtig und so stark,
> Ihr Ton schwillt an zum Sturme, durchzittert Herz und Mark.

>   *   *   *   *   *   *

"Darmstadt, den 19ten September, 1845."

addressed by Herr Schoeltz von Schrœder, the Prussian
Envoy at Copenhagen, to His Excellency Graf von Redern,
in charge of the Hofmusik at Berlin :—

"YOUR EXCELLENCY,

"The fêted heroine of the day, Mdlle. Jenny Lind,
was expected here yesterday by the steam-packet said to
be arriving from Hamburg. Expectant worshippers without
number were assembled on the strand; there was no lack of
wreaths and flowers ; the poet Andersen had prepared a
beautiful 'Welcome'—but, alas! all fell through ; and
instead of the Singer came an apologetic letter, which
destroyed all hopes of seeing her here . . . .

"&c., &c., &c.,

"SCHOELTZ VON SCHRŒDER.*

"Copenhagen, September 25, 1845."

"Destroyed all hope"—the writer should have said—"for
that particular day;" for she was positively announced
to appear, three days afterwards, and arrived in ample
time to fulfil her engagement. Her appearances were necessarily few in number, for her time was limited, and on
one of the appointed nights the theatre was unavoidably
closed, on account of her indisposition. But her stay was
sufficiently prolonged to create a profound and lasting
impression among all classes of society.

She sang three times in *Norma*, twice in *La Figlia del
Reggimento*,† and also at four concerts. ‡

The effect of these performances upon the public is thus
described :—

* From information kindly supplied by the *General-Intendantur der
kgl. Schauspiele zu Berlin*, who courteously submitted the Archives of the
Royal Opera and Hofmusik to Mr. Goldschmidt's examination for particulars without which these chapters could not have been written.

† Sept. 28, Oct. 3, and Oct. 5, *Norma*; Oct. 8, 15, *La Figlia del Regg.*

‡ The concerts took place on Sept. 16 and 30, and Oct. 10 and 16.

"Then came Jenny Lind, whose few special *Gastrollen* raised a tremendous enthusiasm among the public, and every time drew such crowds that the tickets were immediately sold for four times their usual price. This, however, was of no particular benefit to the theatre, considering that she was paid two hundred Danish rixdollars for every performance.

"The reception she had met with two years before was extraordinary, yet it counts for nothing when compared with the homage now offered to her in so unprecedented a manner. On the occasion of her first visit she merely brought from her own country a distinguished artist-name, supported by the rare talent by aid of which she was destined to acquire European fame. This fame she had now earned in fullest measure. In Berlin and Paris * she was now admired and praised, no less by the first musical authorities than by the enchanted public.

"Everything she did produced a thrilling effect, leaving behind an impression far more lasting than the most marvellous execution. Endowed with a mellow, flexible voice, of large compass, great power, and delightful sonority; with a noble style of acting, in the comic as well as the pathetic parts; with a personality which, though lacking regularity of features, was rendered charming to the last degree by its womanly dignity; with eyes capable of the deepest expression ; with the highest finish of vocal *technique ;* with the most refined taste in the use of these musical and dramatic gifts; with spiritual conception and feeling, even in the most varied compositions—endowed, we say, with these precious qualities, she carried everything before her.

"The public had been wondering whether she was really able now to produce anything more beautiful than that which had already been so much admired as the highest form of perfection. But at the very beginning of the first representation it became evident, from the lofty calm and clearness, the grace and power with which the notes streamed forth, that she actually had advanced still farther in vocalisation, in precision, and in taste.

"Her 'Norma' had not the wild and glowing passion which most singers impart to it, but there was such deep feeling, such energy in the acting as well as in the singing, such unpretending greatness, such graceful harmony in look, in

---

* This, of course, is a mistake.

motion, in *plastique*, and in diction, that the public was
transported by the poetry of the personification; and after
the first act, amidst interminable plaudits, the artist was
called before the curtain and received with a gentle shower
of flowers. At the end of the performance the same act of
homage was repeated in a still higher degree; and from the
theatre a great crowd rushed on to her residence, in order to
greet her with cheers on her return home.*

"Her performance of the part of ' Marie' in *La Figlia del
Reggimento* was received with no less rapture. Here, again,
she did not interpret the part in accordance with the usual
conception, but in a way which suited her temperament to
perfection. There was so intimate and marvellous a union
of good-nature, poetical feeling, jesting humour, and amiable
naïveté in the delivery of her dialogue that, with whatever
apparent lightness she threw her words about, they all, in
accordance with the needs of the moment, teemed with a
brightness of fun of which she herself appeared wholly
unconscious. The effect of this was to constantly call forth
a burst of applause the spontaneity of which was self-
evident; and yet the chief interest of the performance really
lay in her singing, which, whether the intention was grave or
merry, had in every simplest phrase, in every minutest
ornament, no less than in the most brilliant *bravura*
passages, a fulness of soul and a perfection of *technique*
which, combined with the truthfulness to nature which
everywhere pervaded it, held the public in a condition of
never-failing enthusiasm."†

The reader will bear in mind that this is no ephemeral
critique, culled from the pages of a daily journal, but the
deliberate verdict of a sober art-historian; and it is impossible to read his glowing narrative without a feeling of
surprise, that he should have permitted himself to indulge in
a display of enthusiasm so little in accordance with the
traditions of his order; yet his language is certainly no
stronger than that to which we have already become accus-

* As on the occasion of her first visit to Copenhagen, Mdlle. Lind was
the guest of her friends, Monsieur and Madame Bournonville.

† From ' Den danske Skueplads;' a History of Danish Dramatic Art,
by T. Overskou. (Copenhagen, 1864, vol. v.)

tomed, in the accounts of the performances at Berlin contributed to the *Berliner Zeitung* by Herr Ludwig Rellstab,
whose reviews are regarded by German journalists as examples
of genuine criticism, second only in value and interest to
those of Schumann and Rochlitz. What can we infer from
this but that a talent capable of inspiring experienced
critics with a fire of enthusiasm so foreign, not only to their
practice, but to their fixed and habitual principles, must
necessarily be a very remarkable one—a talent of an order
with which they had not been previously accustomed to deal?
And the progress of events proved this to be the truth.

Besides the dramatic performances thus favourably noticed,
Mdlle. Lind sang at a concert given, on the 16th of September,
in the large hall of the Hôtel d'Angleterre; at another, given
in the Ridehus (or Hippodrome) of the Royal Palace at
Christiansborg, on the 30th of September; and at a third,
given on the 10th of October at the Court Theatre, in the
palace at Christiansborg, in aid of the Association for the
Rescue of Neglected Children.

So great was the success of this charitable entertainment
that, on the following day, the governors of the Association
sent her the following gratifying address :—

" MADEMOISELLE,

　　" During the years that the under-mentioned Association has carried on its work, the object of which is the
prevention of crime through the education of children in need
of moral training, the aid received from private persons has
never represented a richer contribution than that for which
the Association begs permission to express to you its heartfelt
thanks.

　　" By using the rare talents you possess in such abundance
for the benefit of the Association, at last night's performance
at the Court Theatre, you have procured for it an income
which will render possible a considerable development of its
means of doing good.

　　" On leaving Denmark you will take with you the pleasant

consciousness of having rescued, from dens of vice, many a
child, who now, through your active charity, will be brought
up to a useful and virtuous life, the blessings of which will
follow you wherever you go."

(Here follows a long list of signatures.)

"Association for the Rescue of Neglected Children,
        " October 11, 1845.

  " To Fröken Jenny Lind."

Truly, this was a worthy beginning of the work which, not
so very many years afterwards, reached so noble a consum-
mation at Brompton, at Norwich, and Manchester, and
now evokes a blessing from the lips of every loyal and
patriotic Swede in Stockholm itself.

The last concert at which she assisted, during this visit
to Copenhagen, took place, on the 16th of October, in the
Ridehus; and the records of the period prove that these
purely musical performances were no less successful than
the dramatic representations. Mdlle. Lind herself—though
she caught a serious cold—was delighted, not only with her
reception by the Danish public, but by the hearty and able
co-operation of the artists with whom she was associated in
her arduous duties. Writing to Madame Birch-Pfeiffer, on
the 14th of October, she says :—

"Ah! people are here more than ordinarily kind to me.
The ladies of the chorus have decorated my room so beautifully; and the whole orchestra and chorus have been so
friendly. On my birthday they brought me a *Vivat!* and a
serenade. Ah, yes! I am quite at home here !

"But the weather has been frightfully bad; so stormy
that, up to this time, I have not dared to venture upon a
voyage by sea, for several ships have been lost. However, as
I am giving concerts here to four thousand people—for they
have so large a room—I have stayed on a few days longer.
But—alas!—I have caught a horrible cold; had to put off
the performance the day before yesterday; and feel myself
so much knocked up that I can only sing in my farewell

concert, and dare not risk any more singing this month, if I wish to preserve my voice; and, as I shall have to use that voice for another year, I have been obliged to write to Hanover, Bremen, Cassel, and Leipzig, to say that I cannot come—to my very great regret, for nothing in the world grieves me so much as not being able to keep my promise.

"It was particularly unfortunate with regard to Hanover, as the King had evidently looked forward to it. I have promised to go there as soon as my engagement in Berlin expires, and my *répertoire* will then be more extensive. But it would really not have been right of me to sing any more now, as I must so soon be in Berlin; for, as you know, mother, I need all my strength there." *

But, the remembrance of the artistic tone which had made her visit to Copenhagen so thoroughly enjoyable, remained long after the cold, and the loss of voice, and the stormy weather had been forgotten. Many years afterwards she wrote to Madame Bournonville :—

"I shall never forget the joy with which I sang at Copenhagen; for never since have I found more cultivated artists anywhere." †

It was a happy time, in spite of the threatened loss of voice; but it owed its brightest charm far less to the applause of a genuinely appreciative public than to the atmosphere of poetry and high intellectual culture with which the young priestess of Art found herself surrounded on every side. With all that was best and greatest in the mind-world of the North, she was admitted to closest and most unreserved communion. Poet and painter, romancist and historian, vied with each other in paying homage to her genius. Thorwaldsen, whom she had known on her first visit to Copenhagen, had died in the previous year; but her "brother," Hans Christian Andersen—as she delighted to call

* From Frau von Hillern's collection.
† From a letter from Madame Goldschmidt to Madame Bournonville, dated London, June 11, 1877.

him, in obedience to the homely Scandinavian custom—was
there to greet her with the 'Welcome' mentioned in the
letter of Herr Schoeltz von Schrœder.   An album which she
kept at the period, and which is still fortunately preserved,
is filled with the contributions of her most valued friends.
Andersen wrote in it a poem, dated, " Copenhagen, October 12,
1845 "; and Anton Melbye, the painter, illustrated it with
a beautiful little etching, executed with a reed-pen, and
representing the steam-packet surrounded by the shipping
in the harbour. Œhlenschläger wrote a poem also, and
Geheimrath Jonas Collin. Music was represented by Niels
W. Gade, the friend of Mendelssohn and Schumann, and the
composer of *Comala, Im Hochlande,* and many other works
of undoubted merit.*   Ed. Lehmann was there also.   And
Jensen, not contented with drawing in the album, and
unwilling that the " gentle shower of flowers " which had
fallen upon her in the theatre should fade without remembrance, drew an inspiration from Van Huysum, and painted
a lovely wreath of white roses, which was presented to her
as a testimonial, and is now the property of her daughter.
The picture was painted at the desire of a few friendly
subscribers, among whom we find the names, not only of
her genial host and hostess, M. and Madame Bournonville,
but also those of M. Mozart and Madame Mathilde Waage-
petersen, the touching story of whose sickness was related in
a former chapter.†

The poems of Œhlenschläger and Andersen are of so
great an interest that we have thought it desirable to reproduce them in the original Danish, for no translation
could possibly have done justice to their strong national
colouring.

* Herr Gade filled the post of Hof Kapellmeister in his native city,
Copenhagen, until his recent (lamented) death.

† See page 175.

JENNY LIND.

Folkesangen har en Werden inde,
Du har kaldt den frem til Liv paa nÿ ;
Sangens Muse kom, en Nordisk Qvinde,
Snillet sèlv og dog som Barnet blÿ !

Sèlv dù ei Din bedste Ynde kjender,
Sjelens Reenhed ùbevidst ùdtalt;
Hellig for Din Kunst Dit Hjerte brender,
Gud er Dig dog Stjernen over Alt.

I Krystal-Skal Nectar-Dricken bÿdes,
Norden har ved Dig een Stjerne meer,
Ved Din Sang vi lùttres, rôres, frÿdes,
Gud med Dig!—Hans bedste Willie skoer !

med broderligt Sind

H. C. ANDERSEN.

Kjòbenhavn, 12 Oct., 1845.

PHILOMELE.

En lille Fugl i Busk og Dal,
Soedvanlig kaldet Nattergal,
Om den de gamle Sagn os sige
At allerförst den var en Pige.

Og Philomele hendes Navn !
(: Hvad i Stockholm og Kiòbenhavn
Hun hedder, skal jeg strax berette ;
Dog först maa jeg fortaella Dette :)

Formodenlig af Jalousie,
Fordi hun sang sin Melodie
Saa södt, en Trold det Barn fortrylled,
Og i en Fuglcham indhÿlled.

Nu qvad hun—Trylleri til Spot—
Som Fugl vel ikke mindre godt,
Og hver en Vaar i Blomsterdalen
Hun qviddred södt som Nattergalen.

For Elskerne var hendes Sang
Til Kildens Accompagnement
Saa kioer som för. Hunselv, bedrôvet,
Beskeden sad i Skyggelôvet.

Saa gik det mange hundred Aar,
Da vaagned hun engang en Vaar
Igien som Pige. Hendes Stemme—
Hvo den har hört kan den ei glemme.

Thi Fuglens Triller, Örets lyst,
Med Hiertet i et oedelt Bryst
Forened denne hulde Pige,
Saa aldrig för man hörte lige.

Nu stod hun der med Smil paa Kind—
Med Taareblik—som Jenny Lind!
Om Philomele, Nattergalen,
Var der slet ikke mere Talen.

Men ak! vor Gloede var kun kort—
Som Fugl hun flyver atter bort.
Dog tröst dig Hierte, stands din Klage,
Hun kommer snart igien tilbage.

A. ŒHLENSCHLÄGER.

MELPOMENE OG THALIA.

Thalia stred med Melpomene
Om förste Rang paa Digterscene,
Apollo skulde fælde Dom,
I strid de hidsigt til ham kom.
Sanggudeu i det Musamöde,
Som ingen af dem vilde stöde,
Ved Harpen hilste dem og loe.
At begge vandt og ingen tabte
Til Jenny Lind han dem omskabte.
I hende see vi beggeto!

A. ŒHLENSCHLÄGER.

Kiöbenhavn, 21 Oct., 1845.

The two visits to Copenhagen seem to have made a deep impression upon the mind of Hans Christian Andersen, for not only did he celebrate them in verse, but in the autobiographical sketch entitled '*Das Mährchen meines Lebens*,' he speaks of them at considerable length and in a very enthusiastic tone indeed.

"The youthfully-fresh voice," he says, "forced itself into every heart. Here reigned Truth and Nature. Everything was full of meaning and intelligence.

" ' Yes, yes,' said she, ' I will exert myself; I will endeavour; I will be better qualified, when I come to Copenhagen again, than I now am.'

" ' There will not be born, in a whole century, another being so gifted as she,' said Mendelssohn, in speaking to me of Jenny Lind; and his words expressed my own full conviction.

" There is nothing which can dwarf the impression made by Jenny Lind's greatness on the stage except her own personal character at home. An intelligent and childlike disposition here exercises its astonishing power. She is happy—belonging, as it were, no longer to the world. A peaceful quiet home is the object of her thoughts; yet she loves Art with her whole soul, and feels her vocation in it. A noble, pious disposition like hers cannot be spoiled by homage. On one occasion only did I hear her express her joy in her talent and in her sense of power. It was during her last visit to Copenhagen. Almost every evening she appeared, either in the Opera or at concerts. Every hour was in requisition. She heard of a society the object of which was to assist unfortunate children and to take them out of the hands of their parents by whom they were ill-treated, and compelled either to beg or steal, and to place them in other and better conditions. Benevolent people subscribed annually a small sum each for their support; nevertheless, the means for this excellent purpose were small.

" ' But have I not still a disengaged evening?' said she. ' Let me give a performance for the benefit of these poor children, and we will have doubled prices.'

" The performance was given, and its proceeds were large. When she was told of this, and that by this means a large number of poor children would be benefited for several years, her countenance beamed and her eyes were filled with tears.

" ' Is it not beautiful,' she said, ' that I can sing so?'

" I feel towards her as a brother, and I think myself happy that I can know, and understand, such a spirit. God give to her that peace, that quiet and happiness, that she desires for herself.

" Through Jenny Lind I first became sensible of the holiness of Art. Through her I learned that one must forget one's self in the service of the Supreme. No books, no men, have had a more ennobling influence upon me as a poet than Jenny Lind; and therefore have I spoken of her so fully and so warmly." *

"She is happy," says the Danish poet, "belonging, as it were, no longer to the world." In the world—as the holy ones have ever lived—but not of it. Living among its people, to help them, wherever help was possible, but withdrawing from contact with all that was mean, and base, and sordid. And happy, thrice happy, in the voluntary isolation.

Yes, it was indeed a happy time—but even then the world intruded itself into the happiness of the moment, however little the "sensitive young girl" belonged to it. The nest of the "Swedish Nightingale" was overshadowed—or, at least, seemed to her to be so—by a "sable cloud," which obstinately refused to "turn forth its silver lining on the night."

* 'Das Märchen meines Lebens,' von H. C. Andersen (Leipzig, 1880).

CHAPTER XII.

THE "BUNN-CONTRACT" (*continued*).

NOT even her intercourse with the master-minds, in communion with whom she spent so many pleasant hours during her second visit to Copenhagen, could free Mdlle. Lind from the nightmare of her dreadful London engagement. The remembrance of it haunted her everywhere, and in the midst of her brightest triumphs, oppressed her sensitive and unsophisticated nature with a quite unreasonable terror, which, as time wore on, sensibly undermined her health and caused her a world of unhappiness.

On the 14th of October she wrote to Madame Birch-Pfeiffer, in a letter which has already been partly quoted in an earlier chapter :—

" What do you say to Mr. Bunn, who has lately announced that I must make my *début* at Drury Lane on the 19th of October! ! otherwise I shall have shamefully broken my contract ?   Ah ! ah ! mother !   More foul weather is in store !   But he can do me no harm, for I shall never in my life go to London.   And—is it true ?—have I dreamed it ?— or was not the contract signed with my name only, and his name not appended to it ?   Was it not so ?   I do not know where that horrid thing (the contract) is.   Is it with you ? or is it in Sweden ?   In either case, give me comfort !   Dear mother, give me comfort, and write to me once more before I return to Berlin, as I shall stay a few days in Altona with Madame Arnemann.

" Your truly loving and grateful,

" JENNY." *

* From Frau von Hillern's collection.

Strange as it may seem, this suspicion as to the omission
of Mr. Bunn's signature was found to be perfectly justified.
Why the manager did not append his own name to a
document so important it is difficult to understand; but he
certainly did not append it—at least to the copy left in
Mdlle. Lind's possession—as we learn from another letter
written by her to the same lady, from Nienstädten, on the
28th of October, 1845 :—

" I have, only to-day, found the English contract; and I
was quite right—the name of Mr. Bunn is wanting, and
therefore, I am told, the contract is not valid. Altogether,
since I received the letter from my good mother, I have been
much easier; and I am easier still now, in every way, than
I was. And for that I have to thank my firm determination
to leave the stage. *Mon Dieu !* This happiness will be too
much for me.

" Your ever grateful,

" JENNY." *

Meanwhile, on the 18th of October, a few days only before
she took leave of her friends in Copenhagen, she wrote to Mr.
Bunn an unfortunate letter, which was afterwards fraught with
the most disastrous consequences. Knowing nothing at all of
business matters, she expected that Mr. Bunn, when her
difficulties were explained to him, would treat her with the
generosity which she would most certainly have accorded to
him had he been similarly circumstanced. A more ill-
advised step could scarcely have been imagined, for Mr.
Bunn was emphatically " a man of business"; but, in most
unbusiness-like terms, she wrote to him thus :—

"Copenhagen, Oct. 18, 1845.

" M. DIRECTEUR,

   " The interest that you have deigned to show for
my trifling talent, the obliging offer that you have made
me in London—in short, the facility that you have wished to

---

* From Frau von Hillern's collection.

grant me relative to the *début* you are preparing for me at
the National Theatre of Drury Lane, entitles you to my
gratitude and my highest esteem.   How can I thank you
sufficiently ?   I shall exercise towards you the greatest
frankness, and you shall judge me, not as a director, but as
a gentleman *par excellence.*

"It is impossible for me to come to sing in London. Not
that other engagements prevent me—for I have not contracted any—but I do not feel that I possess sufficient
capacity to fulfil properly the expectations of a public
accustomed to the most remarkable abilities of the period.
The success that I have obtained, up to this time, does not
give me courage as to the fate which might await me in
England.   I neither possess the personal advantages, the
assurance, nor the charlatanism of other *prime donne ;* and
I feel, with fear, that a check experienced in London would
be fatal to the rest of my theatrical career.

"Another obstacle, no less serious, is my ignorance of the
English language, the pronunciation of which is so contrary
to my powers.   Even supposing that, during six months, I
were to sacrifice all my other occupations and to give myself
up entirely to the study of the English language, it would
still be indispensable that my organs should acquire the
flexibility necessary to enable me to perform in a manner that
would not expose me to the laughter of the audience.   All
the objections which I made, in the first instance, to the
proposals you offered at Berlin, and which M. Meyerbeer
endeavoured to combat, in order to attach me to the destiny
of his Opera, *The Camp of Silesia,** are still farther fortified
by a succession of fruitless efforts.   In fact, the execution of
the project of the celebrated composer has been stopped.
Consequently, the primitive cause of my plan for a journey
is practically annulled.   I find myself in the most isolated
position, without a knowledge of the language and without a
hope of success.

"I have, then, no other resource but to beg you, as a
favour, not to consider my signature as a contract, and to be
generous enough to disengage me from an unconsidered
promise.

"You know, yourself, under what influence I have been
persuaded, not to say surprised, into taking a step so contrary

* It was naturally Meyerbeer's wish that Mdlle. Lind should make
the Opera as popular in England as she had already made it in Germany.

to my interests.   It is not a question of money, but simply
of my existence as an artist, which would be compromised
by my appearance in London, and perhaps annihilated by
my *début* at Drury Lane.

"I know nothing of chicanery; but I am of good faith,
and I know the respect I owe to your undertaking.   I do
not count on taking any other engagement in England.   Will
you give me back my agreement?   And I promise you, that,
even although it does not contain any article of *délit*, if I
should resolve to sing at the Italian Opera in London, I will
pay such indemnification as the laws of your country may
impose upon me.

"In eight days, I shall be in Berlin, where I shall await
your reply, and the release which I expect from your
humanity and generosity.

"Will you, in the meantime, receive the assurance of my
highest consideration, and believe me,

"M. Directeur,

"Your very humble servant,

"JENNY LIND." *

To this appeal, Mr. Bunn replied, on the 30th of October,
in the following terms :—

"Theatre Royal, Drury Lane, Oct. 30, 1845.

"MADAME,

"In reply to your letter, dated 18th inst., I beg to
observe that the matter in question being purely a business
transaction can only be answered in that light.

"The sole object of your appeal to me is, to get rid of
your liability to this theatre that you may engage at the
Italian Opera ; on which subject I am aware of all the
representations which have been made to you and of the
parties who have made them.

"The pretext of your inability to learn the English
language, taking into consideration the wonderful facility
you have already evinced, and the great effects produced by
your predecessors, Madame Schrœder-Devrient, Madame

---

* From a translation of the original letter, which appeared in *The
Times* on the 23rd of February, 1848.

Malibran, * &c., cannot be listened to.   When you state that
your contract '*ne contient point d'article de délit*,' I am led
to suppose that you omitted it in order to evade it.   But
you will find yourself subject to damages more than any
délit, and those damages I shall contend for.

"I went at great expense to Berlin purposely to engage
you.   I employed an author to re-write and translate *The
Camp of Silesia*; and I incurred the heavy cost of painting
scenery for the two first acts.   I incurred this heavy outlay
on the faith of your signature, witnessed by the British
Ambassador.   Can you suppose that I will now accept a
promise, when you violate a contract which you have
formally signed?   I tell you I will not.   You have accepted
an enormous salary at Berlin, and are there at the very time
that, by law and honour, you ought to be here; and you
must fulfil your contract with me, or fully indemnify me
for my expenses and my losses.

"On giving me an undertaking that you will not appear
at the Italian Opera House in London before the 15th of
August next, and on paying me such a sum as will cover all
my heavy expenses, and in some measure compensate me for
my anticipated gains, I will annul the contract existing
between us and violated by you; and, if you fail so to do, I
shall carry the whole matter to be laid before His Majesty
the King of Prussia, who is too good to suffer an English
subject to be defrauded by any one paid by the Prussian
Government.

"I shall also commence an action-at-law in Berlin,
where the contract was made, and another in England,
whenever you land here.   This is my fixed determination.

"Oblige me, therefore, with an immediate reply, to say
whether, by an honourable offer, we are to remain in amity,
or, by a refusal, we are to be at war; and, in either case, I
have the honour to be

                    "Madame,

                         "Your obedient servant,

                              "ALFRED BUNN (*Directeur*)."†

---

* Madame Malibran spent two years and a half in England during her
youth, and spoke the language fluently long before she was ready to
make her *début* upon the operatic stage.

† From the transcript, published in *The Times* for Feb. 23, 1848.

In order to judge this letter fairly, it is necessary to entirely separate the *brutalité*—we use the word strictly in its French sense—of its tone from the subject-matter of Mr. Bunn's complaint.

It is impossible to deny that Mr. Bunn had the right to complain—or, rather, that he had the right to refuse the request. No doubt, he had been put to a certain amount of expense, and still more disappointment; but the letter did not contain a threat to violate the contract—it simply asked, as a favour, that it might be cancelled. And though no one with the least idea of business matters could for a moment suppose that Mr. Bunn would accede to that request, the fact that it had been preferred did not justify him in imputing to the writer motives which she most certainly never entertained. She had no desire whatever to sing at the Italian Opera in London, and had entered into no negotiations with any one on that subject. The difficulty of which she complained with regard to the pronunciation of the English language was a real one—so real that, to the last day of her life, even after a residence of so many years in this country, her accent would have sounded strangely foreign in spoken dialogue—and the English version of *The Camp of Silesia* would have been full of spoken dialogue. Equally real was the modesty which led her to dread a failure in London, which would " be fatal to the rest of her theatrical career." She doubted her own powers on the eve of her greatest victories, and that long after her experiences of the past should have assured her that the victory was certain. From the first word to the last her letter was written in the most perfect good faith, and no one whose eyes were not blinded by self-interest would have failed to see that this was the case. Mr. Bunn, however, preferred to assume that an attempt was being made to hoodwink him, and appealed to the Law in what he considered a necessary case of self-defence.

We have said, in a former chapter, that Mrs. Grote had promised to act as *intermédiaire* with Mr. Bunn in this case. She did actually enter into negotiations with him immediately after her return to England, and indulged in the hope that she might have the happiness of seeing the contract annulled, in return for the payment of a sum of £500 by way of forfeit-money, or £300 if Mdlle. Lind would consent to sing one night for Mr. Bunn, for nothing. But at the very time that Mrs. Grote was expecting an answer to this proposal Mr. Bunn's agent (Mr. William Sams) called upon her, armed with the unhappy letter of October the 18th, on reading which Mrs. Grote, without enquiring " in what terms Mr. Bunn replied to Mdlle. Lind," wrote to her, saying that " her interposition had entirely set her aside, and leaving it to her to deal henceforward with the case after her own fashion." *

In the meantime the most unfounded rumours were spread on every side. It is doubtful whether Mr. Bunn, even now, gave up all hope of securing his prize. One section of the English public, at any rate, did not give up all hope of hearing the coveted *prima donna* at Drury Lane, while another felt equally certain of enjoying that pleasure at Her Majesty's Theatre. For the idea that Mdlle. Lind contemplated the acceptance of an engagement at the last-named house—which at that period, she most certainly did not—was by no means peculiar to Mr. Bunn. It was mentioned everywhere—and, of course, after the manner of reports in general, and utterly unfounded ones in particular, it was mentioned with the assurance that it was absolutely and most incontrovertibly true. Each repetition was based on "certain private intelligence" which no one but the narrator possessed, and in process of time the story was

* From the MS. 'Memoir of the Life of Jenny Lind,' already quoted.

told so well that no one dreamed of questioning its
veracity.

It is scarcely ever possible to trace a rumour of this kind
to its veritable source.   How this one originated no one
ever knew.   In all probability it first found utterance in
the mysterious *on dit* of some imaginative journalist.
But it is quite possible that it may have obtained increased
consistency from the fact that, in the hope of doing the
best she could for her friend, Mrs. Grote asked advice on the
subject from Mr. Lumley—who was her great friend also.
If—as is more than probable—Mr. Bunn discovered this, the
step between giving advice concerning one engagement and
proposing another one in its place would have seemed to
him so microscopically small that, although Mr. Lumley did
not really propose an engagement for Her Majesty's Theatre
until long after this,* it would have been difficult to convince
the manager of Drury Lane that no sort of intrigue had ever
been introduced into the business.   For intrigue is the
natural atmosphere of the Theatre, in England, as on the
Continent; and in this case Mdlle. Lind, who was ignorant
of its simplest rudiments, was accused of being its instigator
when she was in reality its victim.

Ignorance is not always bliss.   It was her ignorance of
the machinations to which the Stage is chronically subject
that caused her so much needless anxiety.   She did not
know that Mr. Bunn's threats were absolutely nugatory;
that an appeal to the King of Prussia would have furnished
the best possible opportunity for her full and complete
justification; that damages could no more be claimed from
her in Berlin than they could be claimed, at this present
moment, in Paris, from a French composer against whom

---

* A year, *minus* one day, elapsed after this before she could be
persuaded to sign an engagement for Her Majesty's Theatre; and she
did so then chiefly by the advice of Mendelssohn.

they had been awarded in England; that she was as safe in Prussia as if the contract had never been signed.

She was as inexperienced in all such matters as a child. Had she been less so she would never have written her unfortunate letter. But she had a reason for this which at the time seemed to her imperative. She never spoke of it to Mrs. Grote, but, in a subsequent conversation with Mr. Grote she said that she did not at that time possess £500 in the world. Mr. Bunn taunted her with the "enormous salary" she had "accepted at Berlin," yet she assured Mr. Grote that, up to the moment of her engagement at Frankfort, her earnings had been entirely absorbed by her expenses —including, be it fully understood, the maintenance of her parents and her munificent gifts to Herr Josephson and others *—and that consequently she was "in absolute want of pecuniary means to fulfil the conditions proposed." †

This, then, was the state of affairs when, in the last week of October, 1845, she took leave of her friends at Copenhagen, and returned to Berlin to fulfil her renewed engagement at the famous Opera-House.

---

* We shall see, later on, that she had sent Herr Josephson a cheque about the middle of June.

† From Mrs. Grote's MS. 'Memoir.'

CHAPTER XIII.

THE RETURN TO BERLIN (*Don Juan*).

THE entries in the album kept by Mdlle. Lind at Copenhagen extend to the 22nd of October, 1845. On the 23rd, or 24th, she quitted Denmark and went to stay with her friend Consul Arnemann, and his wife and family, at Nienstädten, near Altona; and on the 28th she wrote from thence to Madame Wichmann, the wife of the sculptor, at whose house—No. 1, in the Hasenheger Strasse *— she had been invited to spend the coming winter at Berlin.

The letter, written in French, and the first of a long and interesting series from which we shall have frequent occasion to quote, ran thus:—

"Nienstädten bei Altona, 28 Oct. 1845.

"DEAR AND AMIABLE MADAME WICHMANN,

"I am very grateful for the kind letter which I had the honour to receive from you, and more enchanted still to find that you retain for me the kindly feeling which makes me so pleased and happy.

"I have been unwell for some time. I caught cold at Copenhagen, and was therefore unable to go either to Hanover or to Bremen or anywhere else. It is because of this indisposition that I am now staying with a very good friend, Madame Arnemann, near the town of Altona, where I am getting quite well, and resting myself.

"But in the meantime it is necessary that I should start for

* Now called the Feilner Strasse, in honour of Madame Wichmann's father.

Berlin, and it is for this reason, dear Madame, that I take the liberty of informing you that I leave this place to-morrow morning—or on the 30th; and I expect to be in Berlin on the 31st.

"I go from here to Zelle, and from thence I hope to reach Berlin, by railway, in a day. To-day is Monday, and on Friday I hope to have the pleasure of seeing you again.

"It will be very nice to have my maid there. I only feared, Madame, on your account, that it would not be agreeable to .you to have so many strange faces about you. I hope to find you in good health, and your family also; and, until then, good-bye, dear, good, and kind Madame Wichmann.

"I am,

"Your very grateful and devoted

"JENNY LIND."*

We have spoken in a former chapter of the sincere friendship which sprang up, during the winter of 1844–45, between Mdlle. Lind and Frau Professorin Amalia Wichmann, née Feilner—the lady to whom the foregoing letter was addressed. The attachment thus formed proved to be a lasting one. The young artist stood sorely in need of a trusty friend and counseller, in whose good faith and loyalty she could place unbounded confidence, and upon whom she could lavish the wealth of affection with which her own true heart was overflowing. To an ardent and impulsive nature like hers the love of such a friend was priceless, and Madame Wichmann proved herself well worthy of the confidence she inspired. She was a woman of marked ability, unvarying discretion, amiable and prepossessing to the last degree, and beloved by all who knew her.

---

* Translated from the original autograph, contained among the letters written by Mdlle. Lind to Frau Professor Amalia Wichmann, by whom they were carefully preserved. These letters are now in the possession of one of Frau Wichmann's sons, who has kindly permitted us to furnish our readers with numerous extracts, which in future we shall acknowledge as "From the letters to Frau Wichmann."

THE WICHMANN ROOM, AT BERLIN. [To face p. 301.

Her husband, Professor Ludwig Wilhelm Wichmann, Knight of the Red Eagle,* the friend of Thorwaldsen and the favourite pupil of Schadow, was at this period, though much her senior, a vigorous and energetic man of sixty-one, of much general cultivation apart from his own noble calling. His house in the Hasenheger Strasse was the familiar resort of the most distinguished artists and men of letters in Berlin, and one particular room in it became afterwards consecrated by the recollection of many happy evenings spent in company with the Wichmann family and Mendelssohn, and a host of kindred spirits, never to be forgotten. A little sketch of this room, painted in oil colours by one of the Professor's sons, the late Herr Otto Wichmann, was treasured by Madame Goldschmidt among her choicest relics, accompanied by the following inscription (in English) in her own handwriting :—

" A room in Professor Wichmann's house in Berlin, where we oft were sitting till late in the night conversing with Mendelssohn and Taubert."

As the reader will, no doubt, be glad to picture to himself the scene of so many pleasant *réunions* we have obtained permission to present him with an engraving of the pretty *salon*.

The approaching winter season promised to be a brilliant one. Mdlle. Lind took part in it for five months, from the 9th of November, 1845, to the 2nd of April, 1846, during which period she sang twenty-eight times, including her own benefit. As her second engagement was, like the first, for *Gastrollen* only, there exists among the archives of the Opera-House no written contract from which we might ascertain the amount of the *honorarium* she received. All we know is that on Saturday, November the 1st, 1845, the play-bills, after announcing the first performance of Men-

* Ritter des Rothen Adler Ordens.

delssohn's *Œdipus in Colonos* in the theatre attached to
the New Palace at Potsdam, added, in a foot-note, that
application for tickets for Mdlle. Lind's first two operatic
performances would be received on Monday, November the
3rd. On the 4th of November the advertisement was repeated, and on the 5th appeared a notice to the effect
that no more tickets for the first two performances
remained unsold, though—as during so great a part of
the former season—the prices were raised, to all parts of the
house.

The series of *Gastrollen* began on the 9th of November
with *Norma*, which was repeated on the 13th; and the
journals of the day criticised these revivals with no less
enthusiasm and no less minuteness in detail than they
had imported into their notices of the original performances
in 1844. The Berlin journal laid great stress on the fact
that the artist had "learned nothing and forgotten nothing."
That she had passed through the fiery trial of a long succession of triumphs without once yielding to the temptations
with which it is invariably associated, and had returned to
Berlin bringing back her own lofty ideal in all its original
purity. We will not, however, follow the critics in their
prolonged analysis of works already fully discussed, but
pass on, at once, to the *rôles* produced this season for the
first time.

The first of these was Mozart's *Il Don Giovanni*—the
greatest by far of his dramatic works—in which she
appeared, for the first time in Berlin, in the character of
"Donna Anna," on the 19th of November, repeating the part
on the 21st and 25th.

Up to this period it had been the custom when this
great work was sung in German to suppress Mozart's
Recitativo secco in favour of spoken dialogue. Moreover,
since Mozart's death, the Opera had been brought to a con-

clusion—not only in Germany, but wherever else it was performed—with the descent of its hero to the depths below; an arrangement which curtailed the *Finale* to the second act of three important movements absolutely necessary to the perfection of its artistic and logical proportions, and this in spite of the obvious intention of the composer to concentrate in two of these movements—the *Larghetto* in G major, containing the marvellously beautiful duet passages for "Donna Anna" and "Don Ottavio," and the *Presto* in D, with its bold contrapuntal subject, which is undoubtedly the most masterly piece of choral writing in the entire work—in spite, we repeat, of the evident intention of the composer that, in this magnificent epilogue, the interest of his greatest masterpiece should culminate. To neither of these barbarisms would Mdlle. Lind consent. Undeterred by the absurd assertion—sufficiently disproved long before that time by Weber in his *Euryanthe,* and destined to be still more satisfactorily contradicted a few years later by the musical dramas of Wagner—that the German language was unfitted for continuous recitative, she caused the spoken dialogue to be expunged, and Mozart's original *Recitativo secco* to be restored, throughout the entire Opera. And, regardless of her own personal fatigue, she procured the restoration of the last three movements of the *Finale* also— an act of self-renunciation, for the sake of Art, in which no other *prima donna* of the period would probably have cared to imitate her, for there can be no reasonable doubt that the omission of these movements arises in a great measure from the unwillingness of the lady who plays the part of " Donna Anna"—to say nothing of the representatives of " Donna Elvira," "Zerlina," and "Don Ottavio"—to reappear upon the scene, in a long and elaborate concerted piece, after the triumph of their solo performances has been completed. The outcry raised against an anti-climax will not bear

examination for a moment in this particular case; for
the interest of the story culminates, not in the punish-
ment of the libertine, but in the victory of Good over Evil:
and the climax is not reached until the close of the last
*Finale.**

Two days after Mdlle. Lind's first appearance in the part
of "Donna Anna" her performance was exhaustively criticised in the leading journal at Berlin; but before we
record the critic's opinion it is necessary that we should
say a few words in explanation of the point of view
from which, in the then prevailing aspect of German literature, he would be irresistibly tempted to approach the
subject.

We have spoken, in a former chapter, of the strong pre-
possession on the part of the Germans in favour of Madame
Schræder-Devrient's interpretation of the part of "Euryanthe," and of the courage with which Mdlle. Lind undertook the difficult task of contending against it. She found
herself placed at almost an equal disadvantage with regard
to the *rôle* of "Donna Anna"; only, on this occasion, she
was brought into antagonism, not with a rival *prima donna,*
but with a literary genius of the highest order—one of the
then leading spirits of the German "Romantic school."

Heinrich Hoffmann, in his well-known 'Phantasiestücke,'
describes an imaginary performance of Mozart's *chef-d'œuvre,*
accompanied by a fantastic analysis of the plot of the story,
and embodying an interpretation of its inner meaning diametrically opposed to that which Mozart, in his music, has
expressed with a clearness too great to admit the possibility
of misconception. Starting with the assumption that Donna

---

* We have reason to believe that spoken dialogue is still substituted
in Germany for the original *Recitativo secco.* The curtailment of the
Finale was, until very lately, universal; but we believe it is now sometimes performed as Mozart wrote it.

Anna is not the pure and grossly insulted maiden depicted
in the music of Mozart, he presents her to us in the character of a guilty accomplice of the libertine: a repentant
sinner, it is true, but a sinner nevertheless: a victim—but
not an innocent one. He would have us believe that, having
yielded to the wiles of the tempter, she awakes from her
dream of passion only when she finds herself face to face
with its fatal consequences, and that then only her remorse
takes the form of vengeance for the murder of her father;
that her fancied love for the "cold and vulgar Don Ottavio"
—too poor a creature to assist her, of his own free will,
in her projects of revenge—is purest self-deception; and
that when, in the last scene of all, she begs him to defer
their marriage for a year that she may complete her term of
mourning for her father,* she knows very well that she has
not another year to live, since, for remorse like hers, the only
cure is death.

But surely this is the character that Mozart has
painted in the part of "Donna Elvira"—not in that of the
pure, though cruelly outraged, "Donna Anna," whose music
has not a shadow of affinity with that assigned to the less
heroic victim of Don Giovanni's insidious treachery. Mozart's "Don Ottavio," too, is the very opposite of "cold and
vulgar"—a loyal gentleman, the very ideal of a romantic
lover. If we accept Hoffmann's interpretation of the story
we must reject Mozart's from the first scene to the last,
and this Mdlle. Lind, at least, was not prepared to do. As
in the case of *Euryanthe*, her ideal conception and that of
the composer were one.

Bearing this difference of interpretation in mind, the
reader will now find no difficulty in understanding Herr

---

* '*Lascia o caro un anno ancora, allo sfogo del mio cor*,' in the *Finale*
to Act II. This passage is differently rendered in the German translation of Rochlitz.

Rellstab's critical description of Mdlle. Lind's reading of the part.

"When the critic," he says, "exercises his calling with relation to the achievements of Fräulein Jenny Lind, it behoves him to use a special standard of measurement. The closest adherence to this standard is needed when one sees how this gifted artist grasps a *rôle* in its totality, and carries it through from beginning to end. We are speaking to-day of her performance of 'Donna Anna,' in Mozart's *Don Juan.** It is well known that this part admits of a two-fold conception, in accordance with the sense given to the recitative '*Schon sank die Nacht herab, mit ihrem Dunkel.*' † Some critics—first among whom stands Hoffmann, in his richly imaginative '*Phantasien*'—places Donna Anna under the spell of Don Juan's fascinating influence, thereby introducing a morbidly romantic element similar to that with which some would surround the collision between Emilia and the Prince in Lessing's *Emilia Galotti.* In so far as past performances of 'Donna Anna,' here and there, are present to our memory, artists seem willingly to have inclined to this interpretation; the more so because it is the easiest and can be painted in the most gaudy colours. ‡ But none the less do we hold such an interpretation to be entirely false. In the first place, it is not deducible from the text; besides which it deprives 'Donna Anna' of an important part of her completeness as a dramatic figure; whereas the element of inward leaning towards such an inclination is admirably represented in the part of 'Zerlina.' In one word, Jenny Lind clothes the part in her own modest purity —no other conception would be intelligible to her. In corroboration of what we have said we propose to mention a few passages which were brought prominently forward, during

---

* It is by this name that Mozart's *Il Don Giovanni* has always been known in Germany.

† '*Era già alquanto avvanzata la notte,*' in the original Italian, Atto I. Scena 13. *Recitativo*, No. 9, preceding the *Aria*, No. 10, '*Or sai che l'onore.*'

‡ An honourable exception to this assertion must be recorded, in the case of Madame Grisi, whose "Donna Anna" was free from the slightest suspicion of an impure reading—which indeed it would have been impossible to have associated with the noble "Don Ottavio" of Signor Rubini, with whom she first sang the part.

the course of the performance. In the first Recitative the
Artist expressed an almost more than earthly sorrow, in the
words, '*Weh mir! mit Todtenblässe ganz bedeckt,*' * and
'*Himmel! ich sterbe!*' † and the question, '*Wo ist mein
Vater hin?*' ‡ betokened a grief so childlike, and so deeply
felt, that the daughter seemed to have forgotten all else that
surrounded her. The grandest point of the performance,
however, was exhibited from quite another side. We mean
the moment, in the first quartet, § when Donna Anna first
gains the full assurance that Don Juan is the murderer
of her father. The expression of this seems the more difficult inasmuch as the previous words—'*Höre, wie mir die
Thränenfluth tief in die Seele geht*' ‖—stand in no connection
with, though they serve to prepare it. The whole action of
the scene, the recognition of the traitor, is comprised in the
words, '*Beim Himmel! er ist der Mörder meines Vaters!*' ¶
We will not attempt to describe the tones in which Jenny
Lind here expressed so exactly the grief of the daughter.
We refrain from selecting contrasted fragments of the part for
separate praise, in order that we may show how all these
details work together for the perfection of the whole. Only
in this way can we prove how, in the Artist's mind, the
whole intention of the part is summed up in the grief of the
daughter for the father's death. This stands forth, everywhere, most clearly. It may be the expression of the strongest
determination, as in the words, '*Der Bösewicht überlegen
an Kraft, häuft seine Missethaten, da er ihn mordete.*' ** Or
it may indicate resignation in connection with the happiness
of love, as when she says, '*Liebe kann nur die Zeit mir
gewähren.*' †† We could cite many such passages from a *rôle*
so full of meaning, especially in connection with the purely

---

* '*Quel volto, tinto, e coperto del color di morte,*' in the original
Italian.

† '*Io manco—io moro!*' in the original.

‡ '*Ah! Il padre mio dov' è?*' in the original.

§ '*Non ti fidar, o misera.*' Atto I. No. 8 of the score.

‖ '*Il suo dolor, le lagrime m' empiono di pietà,*' in the original.

¶ '*Quagli è il carnefice del padre mio,*' in the *Scena*, No. 9, Atto I.,
which immediately follows the quartett.

** '*E l'indegno, che del povero vecchio erà più forte, compìe il misfatto
suo.*' In the *Scena*, No. 9, Atto I.

†† '*Abbastanza per te mi parla amore.*' *Recit. ed Aria*, No. 10, Atto
II.

musical part of the performance; though, in this case, it is difficult to separate the acting from the singing, so closely are they interwoven together. But the limited space at our command warns us that, for the present, we must bring our remarks to a conclusion." *

Three days later Herr Rellstab resumes his unfinished critique, discussing, with perfect fairness and strict impartiality, the points of difference between Hoffmann's fantastic theory and Mdlle. Lind's pure and maidenly conception of the character of "Donna Anna"; and summing up his masterly analysis with the strongest possible arguments in favour of the latter, maintaining that in presence of this lofty ideal the exaggerated poetical licence with which the subject has been so fancifully surrounded loses all its pretended consistency and must of necessity be rejected, by every thoughtful mind, as utterly false and artificial.

With this favourable verdict the frequenters of the Opera were evidently disposed to agree : for "Donna Anna" was at once accepted as one of Mdlle. Lind's most powerful impersonations; and though Hoffmann's utterances were received at that period with almost superstitious veneration, no less by the general public than by the literary and philosophical world, no sign of dissatisfaction was ever shown at this open 'and unqualified rejection of a theory propounded in one of the most charming and *spirituelle* of his imaginative pieces.

On the first occasion on which she undertook the part the performance derived an additional interest from the fact that it took place on the "name-day" of the Queen, in honour of which the Opera was mounted with new scenery of unusual splendour. The other parts were assigned to Fräulein Marx ("Donna Elvira"); Fräulein Tuczec ("Zerlina"); Herr Mantius ("Don Ottavio"); Herr Bötticher

* *Kgl. priv. Berlinische Zeitung.* (Nov. 21, 1845.)

("Don Juan"); Herr Krause ("Leporello"); and Herr Behr ("Masetto"). All did good service to the general effect; and the "Zerlina" of Fräulein Tuczec received high praise at the hands of the critics. The performance, indeed, was an exceptionally fine one in every respect; and the Opera was given five times during the season with ever-increasing interest and raised prices of admission.*

* For the dates, see p. 366.

CHAPTER XIV.

DER FREISCHÜTZ.

THE next new Opera in which Mdlle. Lind appeared, during this, her second season at Berlin, was Weber's *Der Freischütz.*

To give entire satisfaction to a German audience in this first and most famous of Romantic Operas is no easy matter. The work is so thoroughly German, so well known, so deservedly popular, and affords so many precious opportunities for the display of vocal and histrionic talent, that it is not to be wondered at that singers of other than German nationality approach it, on the national stage, with a certain amount of diffidence; nor can we feel surprised that, since the part of "Agathe" has been so often performed by native singers of the highest excellence, a German audience usually listens to its impersonation in a frame of mind severely critical and not inclined to be easily satisfied.

The Opera was first produced at the then newly opened *Schauspielhaus* in Berlin, on the 18th of June, 1821—the anniversary of the Battle of Waterloo—which Weber looked upon as a lucky day. The first performance took place under unheard-of difficulties. Spontini, who then held the post of General Musical Director to King Frederick William III., was strongly prejudiced against it. None of Weber's previous Operas had really succeeded; and his friends trembled for the fate of this. At the last rehearsal, everything went wrong. Yet the work was received by the public with an enthusiasm which bordered upon frenzy, and ever since that eventful night it has kept its place on the German Lyric stage with undiminished success, and year after year it is received in every German Opera-House with a welcome as warm as that which greeted its first presentation years ago. The Germans seem, indeed, incapable of tiring of it; and at the Royal Opera-House in Berlin it is more frequently performed than any other Opera, *Don Juan* alone excepted.

Mdlle. Lind first impersonated the part of "Agathe" at Berlin on the 30th of November, 1845; and on the 2nd of December the *Berlinische Zeitung* contained the following remarks on her performance :—

"It gives us more than ordinary pleasure to record that, through the performance of Jenny Lind, *Der Freischütz* has received a new impulse and a new birth; a new element over and above that derived from the new mounting and the careful study bestowed upon it; and the whole organism of the work is enlivened with the beat of a stronger pulse. The singer began her performance in a modest tone. In the duet with "Aennchen"—of which charming character Mdlle. Tuczec was the excellent exponent—she set before us the gentle homely element alone. One had to listen very carefully here in order to recognise the singer and actress who exercises so irresistible a power over us, and yet she rounded off the whole with many fine and varied touches. In the grand *Aria*, later on, the most heart-felt love and the tenderest breath of maidenhood were blended together and hallowed, both of them, with sincerest piety. The singer was not contented with continuing her prayer so long only as it was indicated in the music : she retained it in her soul, that it might ring forth as a thank-offering even in the ecstasy of love that occupied her to the last moment. No singer has ever before adhered so closely, or with such warmth and clearness, to the religious tone with which Weber has coloured this entire scene. If the memorable Nanette Schechner* carried us upwards, by the might of her powerful tones, to bursts of inward gladness rising ever higher and higher—so, on the other

* Afterwards, Madame Waagen.

hand, the expression of our Artist, springing from the inmost depths of the soul, hallowed the relations of earthly love, and well knew how to enthral the hearer through a higher bond of sympathy. Beyond this rendering of the entire picture, in action and expression, addressed to the eye and the ear, the artist delighted us with a wealth of musical beauties of purest worth. We well remember the ethereal breath with which she dwelt upon the so frequently misinterpreted pause, at the words ' *Welch schöne Nacht,*' * rendering it with the greatest possible correctness; the *pianissimo* with which she began the prayer, '*Leise, leise, fromme Weise,*' and which she continued to its conclusion; and the passage in the Allegro, '*Himmel, nimm' des Dankes Zähren,*' overflowing with the thankfulness of sincerest piety. That this scene produced an outburst of stormiest applause, which was only with difficulty calmed down after it had long delayed the progress of the drama, was no more than the natural effect of so beautiful a performance.

"In the third act the performance was still happier. In the second,† one felt sometimes that the ideal nature was, to a certain extent, restrained, through the necessity for accommodating it to the burgher element. But in the third, when the dreamy bride, clothed in her wedding dress, alone claims our attention, the action was entirely devoted to the manifestation of her love. In some passages in the ' Prayer '‡ her voice seemed to float upwards, like a cloud of incense—a musical glamour with which no other singer has ever so enchanted us in this composition.

For most singers the *rôle* of Agatha is comprised in two airs alone. Our Artist carried on the interest, like a golden thread, from beginning to end. And so dear to her heart was the masterpiece, *as a whole*, that in the concerted pieces she never once assumed more than the exact share allotted to her, though she must have found it often very difficult to restrain herself within the bounds prescribed by the demands of the situation.

"We need scarcely say that at the close shouts and a

---

* The pause is on the F♯, in the upper register, on the vowel *ö*, in *schöne*. It is often thoughtlessly transferred to the lower F♯, at the end of the passage, on the last syllable of the word.

† The heroine makes her first entrance on the rising of the curtain in the second act.

‡ ' *Und ob die Wolke.*'

call before the curtain resounded on every side though after having been so deeply moved by truest Art such a conclusion to the performance is rarely pleasant."*

If ever critic struck the right note in his analysis, Herr Rellstab struck it here. If ever reviewer was led, by true artistic instinct, to divine the secret of a great conception—to trace back a perfect ideal to the germ whence it originally sprang—Herr Rellstab was so led in this particular instance. " So dear to her heart was the masterpiece *as a whole*," he says—and he says well. We know, from her own words, how dear it was to her. He found it out, from the manner of her performance. He did not know, as we do, the story of that memorable 7th of March, in 1838, when she made the famous discovery recorded in one of our earlier chapters †—the discovery that she had within her the power of striking out an original conception, of forming an ideal of her own untinged by the colouring of other artists, of identifying herself with a being of her own creation, of thinking its thoughts, of speaking its words, feeling its pains, its agonies of anxiety, its pangs of cruel torture, its suspense, its hopes, its consolations, its bursts of rapturous joy. He did not know that she had discovered this—but he saw the results of the discovery, and with the instinct of a true critic he traced them to their veritable source—saw that it was not for its two great songs, but *as a whole*, that the masterpiece was so dear to her—that she had created a real character to illustrate the composer's meaning in its entirety, and that in this character she thought, and wept, and smiled, and lived, and had her being. How could it have been otherwise ? How could she, who loved all Nature with so true a love; she to whom forest, and tree, and stream, and mountain spoke with a voice so clear and sweetly intelligible

---

* *Kgl. priv. Berlinische Zeitung.* (Dec. 2, 1845.)
† See pp. 55–57 and 116.

that she had never once in her whole life misunderstood it; she, to whom the voice of the birds was as familiar as her own; how could she have failed to identify herself with "Agathe," the Forest Child? If she had actually lived in the hunting-lodge, instead of imagining that she lived there, would not every bird and beast and butterfly, every wild creature that haunted the surrounding forest, have made her its friend? She was herself a Forest Child; as true a Child of Nature as ever lived. And *Der Freischütz* was so dear to her, *as a whole*, because it was essentially the Opera of Nature. Strange as it may seem to say so, it is precisely through its marvellous truth to nature that it reaches the supernatural; through the cheery halloo of the realistic chase, that it arrives at the infernal yell of the Wild Huntsman; through the sough of the night wind among the pines so truthfully depicted in the immortal *Scena*, that it attains the demoniac storm in the terrible *Finale* to the second act. And all this ghastly conflict between the natural and the supernatural is—or ought to be if rightly understood—inseparable from the part of "Agathe." The power of the grim fiend, Zamiel; the weird influence of the Wild Huntsman; the unholy spells of the Necromancer, Caspar; all the dread forces of the supernatural are in league against her. And the Child of Nature conquers them all. The wreath of natural roses, consecrated by faith and love and purity, baffles every spell that the spectres of the forest can bring to bear against it. And in the union of this transcendental side, so to speak, of the character of "Agathe," with the natural picture of the simple-minded loving peasant girl, lay the charm which made the part one of the finest and most masterly of Mddle. Lind's impersonations, and one of her own special favourites.*

* For the dates of the three repetitions of the Opera which followed, see p. 367.

CHAPTER XV.

Μείζων δὲ τούτων ἡ ἀγάπη.

AND now, after having analysed in detail Mdlle. Lind's
ideal interpretation of some of the greatest masterpieces of
dramatic and musical Art, we may be allowed to withdraw
our attention for a moment from the Stage, with its turmoil
and its enchantment, the glamour of its poetry on the one
side and the disappointment of its cold illusions on the other,
its thunders of applause in front of the curtain and its heart-
burning cabals and conflicts of bitter jealousy and merce-
nary self-interest behind it. We may leave, for a while, this
strange scene of mingled reality and deception while we
turn temporarily aside for the purpose of refreshing ourselves
with some pictures of a different kind.

We have seen many instances of the calmness with which
Mdlle. Lind accepted the enthusiastic applause which was so
freely lavished upon her. It is scarcely too much to say
that, many and many a time, she seemed to be the one
person in the midst of the excited concourse of admiring
spectators whom one would have supposed to be the least
interested in the demonstrations made in her honour. But
it would be a great mistake to infer from this that she was
insensible to, or ungrateful for, the admiration she excited.
The secret of her outward calmness was that she accepted it,
not for herself, but in the name of the Art of which she
herself was the most fervid worshipper in the crowd. Her
standard of self-measurement was so provokingly low—if one

can venture to use the word, without disrespect—that she could never be persuaded to attribute to her own genius the results which were evidently due to it. But, she felt her responsibility keenly, and worked with untiring energy in order that she might not incur the danger of falling short of the high standard that was expected of her.

Her own state of feeling with regard to her position in Berlin at this particular period may be satisfactorily gathered from a letter written by her to Madame M. Ch. Erikson, an eminent Swedish actress, with whom she had long been on terms of intimacy, and who died, at the age of sixty-eight, in 1862.

" Berlin, Nov. 24, 1845.

" MY DEAR MADAME ERIKSON,—

　" It was with the wildest pleasure and rejoicing that I had the honour of receiving your kind letter, and I cannot thank you enough for it.

　" I use no empty words when I say that my rejoicing was intense, for I had not forgotten that it was you who first guided my sensitive young mind towards higher aims, or that it was you who saw beneath the surface and fancied that you had discovered something, overlooked by others, behind those small grey insignificant eyes of mine.

　" How changed is everything now ! What a position I have now attained ! All the musical talent of Europe is, so to speak, at my feet. What great things has the Almighty vouchsafed to me ! It gives me real pain to lose the inexpressible satisfaction of submitting the progress I have made to the judgment of one who so well understood me before there was any one else who would even believe in my capacity to do anything at all—and that one so rare and gifted an artist as yourself !

　" What a pity it is that we Swedes cannot get on in our own country ! No fame ! nothing ! nothing !

　" What a celebrity you yourself ought to have become, with that grace of yours—that charm displayed in every movement when you are before the curtain ! What a sensation ought not that, in itself, to have produced ! for grace is scarce upon this earth.

　" In seven months only I have succeeded in making my

reputation here: and, after seven years at home, not a creature knew anything at all about me. At this present moment all the first engagements in the world are offered to me! After seven months! Is it not strange?

"I have lately appeared in 'Donna Anna'; and have every reason to be more than satisfied with the reception that was accorded to me. The Berlin public is terribly critical. But, this I like; for, if I take pains, I am at least properly appreciated. They want to analyse my every gesture—every shade of expression. Indeed one has to be careful; but this certainly tends to mental cultivation.

"I am going to sing in *Der Freischütz* and the *Die Vestalin*; for Operas such as these win the greatest and most solid fame; though such *rôles* are not to be lightly approached. And, moreover, I have to sustain no trifling comparisons; for the moment I step forward I am measured with the Sontag-measure, or that of the greatest artists that Germany has produced.

"Perhaps you think that I have grown vain? No. God shield me from that! I know what I can do. I should be very stupid if I did not. But I know, equally well, what I cannot do.

"I have not yet quite made up my mind whether I go to Vienna in the spring or not. In the meantime, I wonder whether I may venture to tell you that, next autumn, I mean to return home quite quietly, and to settle down, caring nothing for the world. You will call this a crime. But please to reflect, just a little, how difficult it is to stand all this racing about—alone!—alone! with the certainty of having to rely on my own judgment in everything, and yet so absorbed at the same in my *rôles*. Oh! it is not easy. However, we will not talk of this just yet. Enough to say that connection with the Stage has no attraction for me—that my soul is yearning for rest from all these persistent compliments and this persistent adulation.

"Is not this sad news concerning Aurora Österberg!* I had always cherished great expectations with regard to her, for she really possesses charm and natural dispositions. But when they marry! Ah!

"1 wish I could hear, some day, that you were re-engaged at the so-called 'Great Theatre.' I should so rejoice. Ah!

---

* A young Swedish Artist—afterwards Madame Olof Strandberg—who died, in 1850, at the early age of 24

Do not resist the wish of the public. What a boon it would
be to have once more the chance of seeing a true Artist
perform! May this, my sincere wish, become a reality.

"I trust that I may be able to be of use to that good
fellow, Herr Ahlström.* It is hard for a stranger to manage
here in Berlin without help.

"I do hope this long letter has not quite tired you out,
dear Madame Erikson; and, in proof of this, I trust that I
may still look forward to hearing from you again. It would
make me so happy!

"And here I will finish; assuring you of my sincere
affection, and remain,

　　　　　　　　　"Your grateful pupil,

　　　　　　　　　　　　　"JENNY LIND."†

It is interesting to compare these remarks upon the style
of the Berlin criticisms with the copious extracts we have
reproduced from the writings of Herr Rellstab, the character
of which she exactly describes. And greater interest still
attaches to the comparison of what she here says concerning
her retirement from the Stage, with the description of its
"fascination," contained in the letter written from Paris to
Madame Lindblad, on the 24th of October, 1841.‡ That
description had, however, been written four years previously.
Since then she had passed through many experiences
—not all of them exhilarating; and it must be confessed
that the remarks addressed to Madame Erikson accord very

---

* Musical Director and Orchestral Conductor at several of the smaller
theatres in Stockholm, and afterwards Bandmaster of the Second Life-
Guards. Later on he was Organist of the parish church of Hedwig
Eleonara, in Stockholm, where he died, in 1857.

† Translated from the original letter, written in Swedish, and dated
Berlin, Nov. 24, 1845. Soon after Madame Goldschmidt's death the text
of this letter was printed in a newspaper published in the province of
Skania, whence it speedily ran the round of the Scandinavian press. Mr.
Goldschmidt, having had his attention drawn to it, endeavoured to establish its authenticity, and was fortunate enough to acquire the original
autograph.

‡ See page 126.

well with the expressions she used when addressing Mrs. Grote on the same subject some two months before the foregoing letter was written.*

But in any case, whether she then seriously contemplated an almost immediate retirement from the Stage or only thought of it as a desirable and extremely probable contingency, she made the noblest use of the pecuniary advantages she derived from it.

We have spoken of her offer to assist Herr Josephson in his project of carrying on his studies in Italy.†

In the month of June, 1845, he wrote, at Vienna, in his Diary :—

"Through the care of Munthe, Jenny Lind's *homme d'affaires*, I have received a letter containing a cheque which guarantees my going to Italy. And now I am looking hopefully towards the south. May it prove of real use! Not in vain must my good friend have tendered the proffered aid, accepted in the name of Art. God grant she may ever prosper! She is growing into my heart, as a sister and as a friend."‡

Mdlle. Lind did not, however, write to him herself until the beginning of December, when she sent him the following letter :—

"You poor boy! so far away in a strange country and for so dreadfully long a time, without having heard a word, directly, from your friend who is now writing to you, and who wishes you so well and has so faithfully retained her friendship for you!

"Dear good Jacob! I cannot understand how it is possible that I have left you so long without a word. But I have been travelling again nearly the whole summer, and have really not been able to write.

"I have received your letters in due course, and hasten to

---

* See page 273.
† See page 218.
‡ N.P. Ödman, in *op. cit.* tom. ii.

answer the last. My money matters are not just now in my
own hands, and as you need money only at the time of the
new year, I write this to-day before sending it. But it is
coming soon.

" And now I suppose I must tell you everything about
myself. In the first place, I am splendidly well. I am
enjoying myself very much. I am very glad and very
grateful for the kind treatment we—that is, Louise and I—
are receiving at Professor Wichmann's, and we find it very
enjoyable there. Furthermore, my voice has grown twice
as strong as it was—the middle register quite clear. My
acting is something quite different, with much more vivacity
and passion ; stout and broad-shouldered, and quite first-
rate ! If my success was great last year, it is now quite
furious. I have appeared here as ' Donna Anna,' and
succeeded well. Yesterday also I appeared, for the first
time in Berlin, in *Der Freischütz*—and that also went well.
Now guess what my next part will be ? *Die Vestalin.*
After that, ' Alice ' and ' Valentine.' Tithatschek will
probably be here at the new year. Meyerbeer is still in
Paris, but is expected here soon. But, Jacob, Mendelssohn
is here ! I see him almost every day at the Wichmanns'.
And he is quite an exceptional man. Dear ! we are going,
the day after to-morrow, to Leipzig. Now, at least, I shall
sing at a Gewandhaus Concert under his direction !

" Your letter to Gade * has been sent off in due course.

" Mendelssohn's *Œdipus* has been given here, and it was
magnificent.† To-night‡ his *Athalie* is to be produced, for
the first time, at Charlottenburg, and I look forward eagerly
to the evening.

" It is possible that I may go to Vienna next spring.
True, I feel restrained by nervousness, but the engagement
is a good one.

" All is as before at home. Art has disappeared ! Home-
life alone is pleasant, as before. Apart from that all is
emptiness. But how does that help me ? I have as much
home-sickness as ever, all the same. And my only wish is

---

* Herr Niels W. Gade was then residing at Leipzig, where he had been
invited, at the instance of Mendelssohn, to accept a Professorship in the
newly-founded Conservatorium der Musik. (See also page 285.)

† The reader will remember that it was produced in the Theatre of the
New Palace, at Potsdam, on the 1st of November, 1845.

‡ Sunday, December the 1st.

to attain repose away from the Stage. And a year hence
I shall go home, and remain at home, my friend! Oh! how I
shall enjoy life! Ah! peace is the best of all. I have never
had that as I have it now. You will come and see me
sometimes, will you not?

"Well! I am quite ready to believe that Italy must be
beautiful. God give you success and progress, my good
friend! We need you much in Sweden. It would please
me well to go to Italy next spring, but I must first earn
some money. So, God's peace and blessing be with you.
Remember me to young Wichmann. All his people are
well.

"I need not assure you that I always remain

"Your faithful friend,

"J. L." *

It is touching to see the great Artist longing for the
beauties of Italy, yet deferring the enjoyment of them until
she could "earn some money," while she was really enabling
the young student to whom she wrote to prosecute his studies
there with money she had previously earned. But she felt
that she was doing a good work for him and for Art, and
with her that consideration always overrode all others.
Her whole life was modelled on the words we have chosen
for the heading of our present chapter. She not only felt, in
her heart of hearts, the firm conviction that "The greatest
of these is charity," but she so lived that every act of her
existence was a proof of the sincerity of her convictions—a
proof that she not only recognised the truth of the law by
force of intelligent deduction, or even by grace of divinely
inspired faith, but that she herself felt personal experience
of its truth in the happiness she derived from moulding every
thought and action of her life in accordance with it.

It is touching, too, to see how her Artist-nature expands at

* Letter from Mdlle. Lind to Herr Jacob Axel Josephson, dated
"Berlin, Dec. 1, 1845," and translated from a copy kindly furnished by
Madame Josephson.

the thought of a closer acquaintance with Mendelssohn—the composer whose genius was in closer sympathy with her own than that of any other musician then living,—and to mark how she revelled in the thought of singing to the accompaniment of the orchestra he conducted, well knowing beforehand the delight she would feel in being so perfectly and so effectually accompanied. None but a really great singer can fully understand the delight of singing to such an accompaniment, whether played by the orchestra or on the pianoforte, and in this case the vocalist was certainly not disappointed.*

---

* She was always most particular with regard to her accompaniments, and was never satisfied unless they were as completely in accord with her own conception as if she herself had played them. At a later date—October 8, 1851—she wrote, from the Falls of Niagara, to her guardian, Judge Munthe, with reference to a concert tour of three months' duration on which she was then starting: " Herr Goldschmidt is our accompanist, and whether he accompanies me or I accompany myself, it is absolutely the same thing."

CHAPTER XVI.

In a letter addressed to her guardian, Judge Munthe, on the 12th of January, 1846, Mdlle. Lind writes :—

"Felix Mendelssohn comes sometimes to Berlin, and I have often been in his company. He is a *man*, and at the same time he has the most supreme talent. Thus should it be."

The words are few, but weighty enough in their relation to the social history of Art; for, taken into consideration in connection with the expressions quoted in the preceding chapter from her letter to Herr Josephson, they give us the first direct indication of a friendship which, ripening with time, continued, with ever-increasing loyalty and warmth, until the moment at which the composer of *Elijah* entered into his rest, on the 4th of November, 1847; a friendship the full value of which can be understood by those only who enjoyed the inestimable privilege of friendly intercourse, though in ever so humble a degree, with that truly remarkable "*man;*" a friendship in which the world of Art itself was interested. For it is absolutely certain that these two artistic spirits exercised a notable influence over each other in all that concerned the Art they worshipped; insomuch that the *Elijah* itself owed something to Mendelssohn's familiarity with her ideal treatment of the voice,* while her interpretation of his loveliest melodies was

* See Vol. ii.; Book VIII., Chapter vii.

undoubtedly penetrated with the spirit he infused into the harmonies with which he accompanied her on the piano-forte.

Though residing at this time in Leipzig, Mendelssohn came occasionally to Berlin, and had evidently taken such opportunities as he could of renewing the acquaintance first formed on the 21st of October, 1844, at the house of Professor Wichmann. On the 1st of November, 1845, he super-intended the production of his *Œdipus in Colonos*, at the theatre attached to the New Palace at Potsdam. A month later he came again, to conduct the first performance of his music to Racine's *Athalie*, on the 1st of December, at the Royal Theatre at Charlottenburg, and this visit he turned to excellent account in more ways than one. He was engaged, that winter, in conducting the famous Ge-wandhaus Concerts at Leipzig, which were then universally acknowledged to be the finest in Europe. Under his all-powerful *bâton* they had met with unexampled success. The best artists of the day thought it an honour to be permitted to take part in them. He, on his part, did all in his power to make them as perfect as possible, and he eagerly seized this opportunity of persuading his friend to assist him in his noble work. The Intendant of the Opera-House* seems to have granted the necessary leave of absence without difficulty, and on the 3rd of December—the day following the second performance of *Der Freischütz*—the two great Artists pro-ceeded together to Leipzig.

Though the dimensions of this quaint old town were greatly inferior, in 1845, to those of which it now boasts, it exercised a greater and far more healthy influence upon the develop-

---

* Herr C. Th. von Küstner, General-Intendant der Königlichen Schau-spiele, from June 1, 1842, to May 31, 1851, of whose genuine kindness and powerful support, during her residence at Berlin, Madame Goldschmidt spoke at all times with warmest recognition.

ment of Art than either Berlin or Vienna. The audience, at
the Gewandhaus, was being gradually educated on a system
which was already beginning to bring forth excellent fruit.
Though severely critical, it was prone to bursts of genuine
enthusiasm; and when the good burghers who dominated
the society of the town heard of the treat that was in store
for them, their excitement knew no bounds. Though the
prices of admission were instantly raised from two-thirds of
a thaler to one thaler and a third—*i.e.*, from two shillings to
four—the tickets were all sold off at once, and their lucky
possessors were able to command any price they liked to ask
for them at second-hand. The "free list" was stopped, of
course, and even the students of the Conservatorium,* who
enjoyed prescriptive right of admission, were politely told
that their prescriptive right would not be recognised on the
evening of the eighth concert.

This arbitrary resumption of vested privileges provoked an
"indignation meeting" at the rooms of one of the offended
brotherhood, at which it was resolved that a firm but
respectful protest should be addressed to the most active of
the Directors—a gentleman of severe aspect, but not it was
hoped of absolutely stony heart. The difficulty was, to find
a mouse to bell the cat. A victim was, however, selected
and sacrificed, and in the course of the day he reappeared
before the adjourned conclave with a face which distinctly
showed that he had been received with the gentle courtesy
usually accorded by College dons to students too keenly
alive to encroachments upon their privileges.†

The rush for tickets was, in fact, so great that had the
Saal des Gewandhauses been four times as large as it really
was it could have been filled over and over again. Through

---

* Founded by Mendelssohn in 1843, and then flourishing exceedingly
under his energetic personal superintendence.

† The "victim" was Herr Otto Goldschmidt.

the kindness of Herr Julius Kistner, the well-known music publisher, the writer, maddened with the excitement of the moment, was fortunate enough to obtain a seat in the front row, close to the orchestra, between the places occupied by the heroic presenter of the protest and the late Mr. Joseph Ascher, another member of the "Indignation Committee." The room was crowded to suffocation and the audience breathless with suspense.

The programme contained the following pieces:—

1. Symphonie von W. A. Mozart (D dur, ohne Menuet).
2. Arie aus *Norma*, 'Keusche Göttin' ('Casta Diva'), gesungen von Frl. Jenny Lind.
3. Adagio und Rondo für die Violine, mit Orchester, componirt und vorgetragen von Herrn Joseph Joachim.
4. Duet ('Se fuggire') von Bellini, gesungen von Frl. Jenny Lind und Miss Dolby.

———

5. Ouverture zu *Oberon*, von C. M. von Weber.
6. Recit. und Arie, aus *Don Juan*, von Mozart, 'Ueber alles bleibst du theuer' ('Non mi dir'), gesungen von Frl. Jenny Lind.
7. Caprice für die Violine, über ein Thema aus dem *Piraten*, von Bellini, componirt von H. W. Ernst, gespielt von Herrn Joseph Joachim.
8. Lieder, mit Pianofortebegleitung, gesungen von Frl. Jenny Lind.

The burst of applause which, at these concerts, was usually reserved until the *Gast* of the evening had earned her laurels, was awarded to her, on this occasion, on her entrance into the orchestra; but probably every one in the room felt, a few moments later, that it had been sufficiently earned by the veiled yet indescribably delicious sweetness of the long-drawn A with which the scena from *Norma* begins.

Herr Heinrich Brockhaus, in his Diary, describes the events of the evening in terms which exactly correspond with our own recollection of them:—

"1845. Leipzig, December 4. Jenny Lind has fulfilled the promise she made, in the summer, to sing at one of the subscription-concerts, to my great enjoyment and truly heartfelt pleasure.

"Luise * wrote to Fräulein Lind to offer her our hospitality, so I am actually living under the same roof with our charming visitor.

"The expectations of the Leipzigers—who pride themselves somewhat on their musical taste and are sometimes a little hypercritical—were raised very high indeed; but the first air, from *Norma*, at once won everything for the Singer, and the enthusiasm rose higher and higher through a duet with Miss Dolby from *Romeo and Juliet*, through a recitative and air from *Don Juan*, and, finally, through some songs by Mendelssohn and some Swedish national airs, to a quite extraordinary pitch.

"And with good reason.

"She is a most extraordinary singer: a musical nature through and through, in full command of the most beautiful means; and, besides that, so penetrated and spiritualised with the singing of everything which she renders, that a song sung by her goes straight to the heart.

"Soul and expression so intimately associated with so beautiful a voice and so perfect a method will never be met with again; the appearance of Fräulein Lind is, therefore, truly unique.

"And with all that what noble and beautiful simplicity pervades her whole being! free from all fictitious coquetry, though, all the same, she takes delight in the effect she produces. One can only wonder, and love her. And this affectionate appreciation of her is universal—the same with young and old, with men and with women. And again, there is something so thorough and consistent; a noble and beautiful nature; a manifestation of the genius of the noblest womanhood and the highest art.

"Who can sing either German or Italian music as she does? † Who is so great a mistress of National Song as she? In the case of other singers people are often influenced by a critique, and astuteness prides itself upon the discovery of some weak point. With Fräulein Lind one rejoices one's

---

* Frau Friedrich Brockhaus, *née* Wagner; a sister of Richard Wagner.

† Mdlle. Lind sang the airs from *Norma* and *Don Juan*, and two songs by Mendelssohn, in German; the duet from *Romeo* in Italian; and two Swedish songs in her own language.

self at her success, and feels with her until the applause bursts forth." *

Instead of following up her success by giving a " benefit " on her own account, and filling the room to suffocation, as she might easily have done at any prices she liked to demand, she announced her intention of singing, the next night, at the concert which she determined to give in aid of the *Orchester-Wittwen-Fond*—an institution for the maintenance of the widows of deceased members of the Gewandhaus Orchestra—for which the following programme was advertised :—

1. Ouverture zu *Euryanthe*, von C. M. von Weber.
2. Scene und Arie aus dem *Freischütz*, von C. M. von Weber, gesungen von Fräulein Jenny Lind.
3. Concert für Pianoforte, in G moll, componirt und vorgetragen von Herrn General-Musikdirektor Felix Mendelssohn-Bartholdy.
4. Finale aus *Euryanthe*, von C. M. von Weber. Die Parthie der " Euryanthe," vorgetragen von Fräulein Jenny Lind.

---

5. 'Im Hochlande.' Ouverture für Orchester von Niels W. Gade.
6. Scene und Arie aus *Figaro*, von W. A. Mozart, gesungen von Fräulein Jenny Lind.
7. Solo für Pianoforte.
8. Lieder am Pianoforte, gesungen von Fräulein Jenny Lind.

At the morning rehearsal for this concert—which took place on Friday the 5th of December—the fêted *Gast* was greeted, as she entered the orchestra, by an unpremeditated flourish of trumpets; and, while rehearsing the finale to the first act of *Euryanthe*, the pupils of the Thomas-Schule, to whom the choral portions were entrusted, were so enchanted with the delivery of the graceful scale-passages to the words

> " Sehnen Verlangen durchwogt die Brust;
> Wieder ihn sehen, O himmlische Lust ! "

---

* ' *Aus den Tagebüchern von Heinrich Brockhaus*,' (Leipzig, 1884), Band ii. p. 88. Privately printed, for friends only.

that they forgot to count their bars' rest, and Mendelssohn brought down his *báton*, at the hundred and seventh bar of the *allegretto*, amidst a ridiculous silence, which at any other time would have infuriated him, though on this occasion he joined, as heartily as any one, in the general laughter.

Herr Heinrich Brockhaus has included a minute description of this Concert also in his published Diary; but the account given in the unpublished note-book of his youthful son, Edouard, is so charmingly unaffected and natural, that we insert it in preference to the more mature remarks of the elder gentleman.

" On Friday, the 5th of December, the Lind was to sing at a concert for the *Orchester-Wittwen-Fond*. Every one was delighted, but I most of all, as I hoped that I also might get a chance of hearing her; and, luckily, at dinner-time, mother gave me a ticket, which I kept in my hand all the afternoon, for fear of losing it.* Tickets were very rare just then, and, though they only cost 1 Rthl., 10 Ngr.,† I know that some were sold for 3 Rthl., and even 5 Rthl.‡ The concert was to begin at half past six o'clock, and I was at the Gewandhaus by half-past five; it took me, however, a good quarter of an hour to get up the few steps leading to the hall. For the steps were crammed with people, including many ladies, and there was scarcely room to stand, much less to turn round. So we moved slowly forwards, and thought ourselves lucky when we mounted a single step. The hall was soon so full that not another creature could be squeezed in, and many had to stand the whole evening in the little room where the *buffet* is; but, luckily, I got a seat in the third row in the gallery, where I could see and hear everything.

" The Lind first sang the scena and air from *Figaro*,§ and I can really find no adequate expression to apply to her singing. The power of the voice, even in the highest notes, the feeling, when she sang *pianissimo*, and, above all, the perfection of her execution, cannot be described in words. The shake,

* The usual dinner-hour at Leipzig then was, and still is, one o'clock in the afternoon.   † Four shillings.

‡ Nine, and even fifteen shillings; unheard-of prices in Leipzig.

§ The places of the airs from *Figaro* and *Der Freischütz* were changed.

and all the finer *nuances,* sounded so perfectly natural,
and she sang with such life and expression, that she had
to hold back continually, to keep herself from acting.
And the people seemed as if they would never leave off
applauding.

"In the second part she sang the well-known scene and
air from *Der Freischütz,* and here again, from every gesture,
one could see that it was as much as ever she could do to
hold herself in check so as not to act it. And the expression
she gave to every word, and the swelling of the tones and
the feeling and the execution, were really unsurpassable.

"After Mendelssohn had played a beautiful solo on the
pianoforte, in the most masterly style,* the Lind sang, last
of all, three songs. The first was Mendelssohn's 'Frühlingslied,'† and the two others extremely original Swedish *Volkslieder.‡* Mendelssohn accompanied them on the pianoforte,

* This solo included a remarkable passage of improvisation which still
lives within the memory of all who had the happiness of hearing it.
Beginning with a characteristic prelude in E♭, Mendelssohn played, as
he only could play it, his own *Lied ohne Worte,* No. 1, Book VI. Then,
during the course of a prolonged and masterly modulation to the remote
key of A major, he continued the semiquaver accompaniment of the
movement for some time longer, carrying it through new and unexpected
harmonies, so arranged as to permit the reiteration of the bell-like B♭,
under constantly changing conditions, and afterwards varying it with
other notes, similarly treated, after the manner of an inverted pedal-point.
Presently a new figure made its appearance, invoking at first vague
reminiscences only, but gradually settling down into the floating arpeggios
of the *Allegretto con grazia,* No. 6, in the Fifth Book—the so-called
Frühlingslied. Every one knew now what was coming : but all were
taken by surprise by the agitated climax into which he worked up the
arpeggio-form ; first, carrying it through a stormy *fortissimo,* and then
suffering it to die gently away as it approached the long-delayed chord of
A major, until at last the lovely melody fell on the ear with a charm too
great to be expressed in words. The recollection of it returns as vividly
as if it had been played but yesterday. It was, we believe, the last time
that Mendelssohn ever played this delicious movement—now, alas ! so
remorselessly hackneyed !—in public ; and all present agreed that he had
never before been heard to play it with such magical effect.

† *I.e.* the vocal *Frühlingslied* in D ; ' *Leise zieht durch mein Gemüth.*'

‡ The first of these *Volkslieder* was the brilliant *Tanzlied aus Dalekarlien*—'Kom du lilla flicka'—sung by Mdlle. Lind in A minor, and
beginning with a bright trill on the upper A ; from which note it passed,
immediately, to the upper C. This song afterwards became extremely

and with them the Concert came, all too soon, to an end.

"The Lind had promised to spend the evening with us, and when we got home we found everything made ready for her reception. As she had begged that no company might be invited, mother * had only asked Tante Luise,† with the rest of the family, and the Mendelssohns.

"About nine o'clock our court-yard was suddenly filled with a crowd of people, mostly students, who had come, with torches, to serenade the Lind. When a circle had been formed, by torch-light, Weber's *Jubilee Overture* was first played;‡ then a song was sung; and afterwards they sang and played alternately. The Lind was quite taken by surprise, and kept on asking father what she should do and how she should thank the people.

"While she was peeping out of the window there came a pause, and a lot of Concert directors, with Concertmeister David§ and Dr. Haertel ‖ at their head, came into the room,

---

popular, both in Germany and in England. The second *Volkslied* was Herr Berg's *Fjerran i skog—'Der Hirt'* (*Herdegossen*)—in F♯ minor ; in the ninth and tenth bars of which occurred a long-sustained pause upon an unaccompanied F♯, in the middle register. While the audience were listening to this in breathless suspense, as it gradually died away, and every moment expecting it to fade into absolute silence, it gently descended to an almost equally long-drawn F♯, so wonderfully *piano* that it was all but inaudible, and yet so true and firm, that it penetrated to the remotest corners of the Concert-room. The effect was magical : it was, perhaps, the most marvellous feat of vocalisation that had ever been attempted within the memory of the oldest critic then present; a living verification of the legendary stories told of the wonderful Farinelli, the history of whose exploits has been so frequently laughed at as too extravagant for credence. Herr Berg's song will be found, in our Appendix of Music, at the end of Vol. ii.

* Frau Heinrich Brockhaus (*née* Campe).

† Frau Friedrich Brockhaus (*née* Wagner).

‡ *I.e.* by a large band of wind instruments which accompanied the students. The number of serenaders amounted, in the aggregate, to fully three hundred; and as the concert was over by half-past eight o'clock, they easily reached the house by nine.

§ Mendelssohn's friend, Herr Ferdinand David, the well-known violinist.

‖ Dr. Haertel, the then head of the well-known music-publishing firm.

and, in the name of the musicians, presented her with
a beautiful silver salver, on which were engraved the
words :—

"'To Fräulein Jenny Lind, from the grateful musicians.'

"On the salver was placed a beautiful wreath of laurel
and camellias. It was given to her by the musicians as
a mark of thankfulness, because she had sung for the
institution for the benefit of the widows of members of the
orchestra. David accompanied the gift with a few words,
and the Lind was so surprised that she could only look at
him while he was speaking, and thank him with a silent
gesture.

"During all this time I got the champagne ready, and
many healths were drunk—naturally, hers first of all.
Father then filled a great tankard and brought it to her, that
she might first taste it herself, and then send it round to the
gentlemen; but she would not do this—why, I cannot
imagine. She passed it on, however, to David, saying,
'Drink to your own health!'

"During the music she stood, for the most part, at the east
window, in the corner, and listened to it eagerly; but one
could see that the crowd of people was painful to her.
When the students had left off singing—there were two
hundred singers, besides a multitude of others—Mendelssohn led the Lind into the court-yard. I followed her,
with Tante Luise; and Mendelssohn said that the honourable task of conveying to them Fräulein Lind's thanks for
this had fallen to his lot, and that he fulfilled it with
pleasure; but that, in addition, and in his own person as
'Leipziger Musikdirector,' he wished long life to Fräulein
Lind.*

* Mendelssohn's exact words were :—

"MEINE HERREN!

"Sie denken dass der Kapellmeister Mendelssohn jetzt zu Ihnen
spricht, aber darin irren Sie sich. Fräulein Jenny Lind spricht zu
Ihnen und dankt Ihnen herzlich für die schöne Ueberraschung die Sie
ihr bereitet haben! Doch jetzt verwandele ich mich wieder in den
Leipziger Musikdirector und fordere Sie als solcher auf, Fräulein Jenny
Lind hoch leben zu lassen! Sie lebe hoch! und nochmals hoch! und
zum dritten mal hoch!"

"All joined, naturally, in shouting 'Long life to Fräulein Lind!' And we then tried to get back into the house, but found it very difficult to do so, so closely did the crowd press round, on every side, to catch a glimpse of the Lind.

"In going away, they sang the beautiful 'Waldlied.' * The gentlemen who had presented the silver *plateau* then took their leave after the Lind had duly thanked them, and the Mendelssohns did not stay very much longer.

"No sooner were the doors closed behind them than she embraced mother and Marie, and all who were standing near her, and jumped up like a child. The presence of so many people had worried her, and it was not until they were gone that her joy broke forth.

"We now sat round a table and enjoyed ourselves very much. The Lind showed us, among other things, her bracelets, two of which were particularly beautiful. One, in the form of a serpent, was given to her by the late King of Sweden, and the other, which was very splendid, by the present King of Prussia.† At the top of this last was a cover, with three real pearls as large as peas; and under this cover, which was made to lift up, was a little cylinder-watch, the size of a four-groschen piece. ‡ She looked with great pleasure at our pictures and engravings, while I held the lights for her, and at about eleven o'clock she went down to her apartments." §

The graphic and life-like picture, thus charmingly painted by the bright youth of sixteen, forms a fitting conclusion

---

(Translation.)

"GENTLEMEN!

"You think that the Kapellmeister Mendelssohn is speaking to you, but in that you are mistaken. Fräulein Jenny Lind speaks to you, and thanks you for the beautiful surprise that you have prepared for her. But now I change myself back again into the Leipzig Kapellmeister, and call upon you to wish long life to Fräulein Jenny Lind. Long life to her! and again, long life to her! and, for the third time, long life!"

* 'Lebewohl, du schöner Wald,' Mendelssohn's Part-song for four male voices, then the most popular Part-song in Germany.

† See page 254.

‡ A little larger than an English sixpence.

§ From a MS. Journal, written, at the time, by Mr. (now Dr.) Edouard Brockhaus.

to our narrative of Mdlle. Lind's memorable visit to Leipzig.

She might well have retired to her rooms, tired out with fatigue and excitement, at eleven o'clock; for on the next day—Saturday, the 6th of December—she was to return to Berlin, where she was announced to reappear, for the fourth time, in *Don Juan* on the following Tuesday.

CHAPTER XVII.

DIE VESTALIN.

HERR JOSEPHSON received Mdlle Lind's letter on the 12th of December, 1845, and on that day made the following entry in his Diary:—

"Letter from Jenny Lind.* Since I left Leipzig I had not once heard directly from her, as her constant travels during the summer had prevented her from writing quietly to friends far away. Her words are full of friendship, and she writes concerning herself with a clearness which cannot but be gratifying to her friends. She speaks of new triumphs in her artistic career. Mendelssohn has been in Berlin, and she has been to Leipzig and sung in the Gewandhaus Concerts.

"Mendelssohn and Jenny Lind together in Leipzig! What would I not have given to have been there in those days!" †

They were very delightful days indeed, as the writer himself can testify; but to no one were they more delightful than to the two great Artists to whose joint offerings at the shrine of Art they owed the charm of their enchantment.

Some months, however, elapsed before these two great Artists were again able to pursue their high task with each other's assistance. The dates of Mendelssohn's visits to Berlin were fitful and uncertain. Though the Mendelssohn family lived in the Prussian capital, and much regretted his absence

---

* See page 319 for the text of Mdlle. Lind's letter.

† 'Aus dem Leben eines Schwedischen Componisten;' von N. P. Ödman. (Tom. ii.)

from it, his duty manifestly lay in Leipzig, at the Conservatorium which he himself had founded and in the orchestra of the Gewandhaus. When summoned to Berlin, in his capacity of Kapellmeister, by command of King Friedrich Wilhelm IV., he had, of course, no choice but to obey; but no such summons seems to have been issued subsequently to the production of *Œdipus in Colonos* until long after the winter season was over. In the meantime, however, the pretty room in the Hasenheger Strasse was not deserted. Many pleasant evenings were spent in it in the company of Taubert, Professor Edward Magnus (the well-known German painter), Professor Werder, Professor Schnackenberg, Graf von Schlieffen, Concertmeister Ries, with, on rarer occasions, Lenné, (the well-known landscape-gardener, and the originator of the German royal plantations around Potsdam), Graf von Redern (the so-called *Musikgraf*, or Director of the Court Music), and other distinguished artists, men of letters and other privileged guests, on terms of intimacy with the Wichmann family, and welcomed at their little *réunions*, in virtue of their talents, their conversational powers, or their achievements in various branches of Literature, or Art. Madame Wichmann enjoyed, in fact, the envied distinction of forming a *salon* of which Mdlle. Lind was by no means one of the least brilliant ornaments, though she herself would probably have been the last to believe that her presence could have added anything to the attractions of a social gathering founded on so broad an intellectual and artistic basis.

On the 30th of December—that is to say, a little more than three weeks after her return from Leipzig—Mdlle. Lind appeared, for the first time at Berlin, in a new and very arduous and important *rôle*—that of "Julia," in Spontini's opera, *Die Vestalin*—which she had previously impersonated six times only, at Stockholm, during the whole of her long career—probably because it was found unsuited to the Swedish popular taste.

Die Vestalin had long been a very favourite Opera, in Berlin, where it had been placed upon the stage with extraordinary magnificence, and entirely under the composer's own personal direction, when he was invited to the Prussian capital, in the character of General Music Director, by King Friedrich Wilhelm III., in the year 1820. The part of "Julia" had then been sustained by Madame Milder-Hauptmann, and since then most of the great German *prime donne* had interpreted it in their turn. It was therefore no easy task to satisfy a Prussian audience with a new conception of the work, and as Mdlle. Lind had intimated in her letter to Madame Erikson, her reading of the leading part was quite sure to be judged by the measure of all the greatest singers who had previously appeared in it. She had spared no labour in her endeavour to make it as perfect as possible. As is nearly always the case, when French *libretti* are translated into other languages, the text and music of the received version fitted together so imperfectly that without extensive revision it would have been impossible to do full justice to the composer's original intention. How this difficulty was surmounted when *Die Vestalin* was first produced in Berlin it does not fall within our province to consider Spontini was not an easy man to satisfy, even with regard to the minutest conceivable details of effect or expression ; but whether he was content or not with the German paraphrase provided for him, it is quite certain that it neither satisfied Mademoiselle Lind nor the only friend to whose assistance she could trust as a means of escape from the difficulty. We have before us, as we write, her own well-used copy of the little oblong edition, published by Meyer of Brunswick, in which page after page is filled, in her own handwriting, with pencilled corrections suggested by Madame Birch-Pfeiffer—

phrases substituted for those contained in the generally-received version, in order to rectify false emphasis, to provide better opportunities for taking breath, and to supply a smooth and more flowing translation of the entire part of Julia—the text allotted to the other performers remaining, of course, untouched. The amount of labour and anxiety expended upon the work may be conceived from the following letter to the talented authoress, written in December 1845—probably on the 18th of the month, though the exact day is not mentioned :—

"GOOD MOTHER! LITTLE MOTHER!*

" I cannot see you to-day. Why? Because the good King wishes to have some more music in Charlottenburg this evening.

" How are you to-day? I hope much better. Good mother, my refuge! What can I do with my *Vestalin?* the text is not yet in order. If you do not help me, things will go badly. Permit me, kind soul, to complain to you of my dire need, while I send you the part and the pianoforte score. Ah! if you have time, mother, help me, for Heaven's sake, for I cannot begin to study until the text is properly arranged. You will be quite weary of my large demands. Tell the servant how you are. Farewell, mother. May all good spirits float around your poor sick head! Greet all whom you will from

"Wednesday morning.   "Your

"JENNY."†

It is pleasant to know that the improvement effected in the text by this careful revision was worthily appreciated.

The impression the performance produced upon the German critics generally may be gathered from the notice which appeared in the *Berlinische Zeitung* three days after the first performance :—

* A paraphrase of the Swedish *Lilla Moder!*
† From Frau von Hillern's collection.

"A joy," says Herr Rellstab, "and more than a joy—a true elevation of the spirit has fallen to the share of the writer at the close of his year of critical activity, in that he is able to record an artistic achievement, among the most memorable that he himself has ever witnessed, and one which has deeply moved, not himself alone, but also a large and varied section of the public.

"Jenny Lind in the part of 'Julia.'

"Grand memories, rich in Art, revived themselves within us in connection with the work and with past interpreters of the *rôle* who have attained the sublimest heights.

"It placed a crown on the ravishing and lofty charm with which Nanette Schechner *—that star so brilliant, and so soon to vanish from the firmament of Art—enthralled her astonished hearers with an irresistible enchantment.

"Wilhelmina Schrœder-Devrient achieved, in the part of 'Julia,' one of her grandest Art-pictures, all glowing with the fire of genius.

"In short, the work marked, for many years, the culminating point of our noblest dramatic power at a time in which Nature still bestowed upon us her wondrous wealth of powerful and splendid voices.

"But let us now turn our eyes upon the present. It will give them plenty of material which cannot well be passed over. And this time we will occupy ourselves less with passing judgment than with giving a history of the impressions produced upon us by the performance.

"The first act was over. From first to last the singer had, through her womanly and noble bearing, excited the closest sympathy. The difficult entrance during the first chorus—a rock on which so many singers have been shipwrecked—naturally afforded our Artist the opportunity for a triumph, through the sweetness of her tones. † Her acting and singing were everywhere noble, but not with the victorious effect we expected from her. Sometimes in the latter she exhibited,

---

* See page 311.

† By a singular anomaly, "Julia," in *La Vestale*, is first introduced to the audience singing in unison with the chorus—but with different words adapted to the same notes. The intention no doubt is, that she may give utterance to her own sad thoughts, while singing the Hymn of the Vestals by compulsion. But it takes a very great singer and actress to make the audience understand this, and we can scarcely wonder that so many great singers have been shipwrecked on so dangerous a rock.

here and there, a trace of weariness and that veiling of the
organ which represents her only weakness.* After that all
expressed sweetest emotion. In holding forth the laurel-
crown to Licinius her acting displayed a magic charm, due
to the virgin purity with which the Artist glorified the
entire scene. But we cannot deny that her two great
predecessors, each in a different way, imparted to this very
scene a ravishing and altogether different effect. Nanette
Schechner had here painted the victory of the Roman
woman over the virgin, and her singing was a veritable
hymn of triumph. Wilhelmina Schrœder-Devrient, who
was not accustomed to enter into the lists with these
weapons, had exhibited here the whole creative power of her
mimic talent, and painted a changeful scene that moment
by moment rose higher and higher and held us in breathless thrall. In the face of this strife between the beautiful
expression of the present and the still greater recollections
of the past the first act closed. And it seemed to us—
perhaps too much preoccupied with the Roman spirit—as
if the Singer, whom we have always hitherto beheld as a
conqueror, had waged too rash a battle upon too unfavourable a field, and, goaded on by marvellous deeds of valour
and genius alike had lost!

"We found the audience under a similar impression,
and awaited the second act with an almost sorrowful depression of spirit.

"Sometimes, however—if we may still be permitted to
use the language of metaphor—a battle which, whether by
accident or design, may seem to have begun unfavourably,
recovers itself, to be crowned with the most glorious and
signal victory. And so it was in this case. From the very
beginning of the act certain passages breathed forth, as it
were, forecasts of the most fervid, the deepest, the grandest
feelings that could agitate a loving womanly breast. In the
grand air, ' *Götte, ach! hört mein Flehen!* '† lightning-
flashes of magic power gleamed forth as from some strange,

---

* This peculiar veiled tone of the middle register was always noticeable
in Mdlle. Lind's voice at the beginning of a new part, for the success of
which she was more than usually anxious, and the peculiarity remained
with her to the end of her career.

† ' *Impitoyables dieux!* ' in the original French. The German version
by Madame Birch-Pfeiffer is inserted, in pencil, in Mdlle. Lind's own
handwriting in her printed copy of the music.

unknown region; sounds, accents such as we had never
before heard. With an holy grandeur the artist sang the
words, ' *Was jetzo mich durchglüht, es ist die Liebe !* ' * The
acting before the appearance of Licinius, the greeting accorded
to him, the mimic recognition accompanying every tone of his
air, ' *Die Götter werden uns nicht gänzlich sinken lassen ;* ' †
all this formed a chain of the most ravishing beauties. It
was the picture of ecstatic love struggling by turns with the
shadow of the sombre presage of death. And emotion and
dread alternated, in like manner, in the breast of the hearer.
Words such as ' *Venus schütze mich, und die Liebe sei mein
Gott,* ' ‡ and ' *Er ist frei,* ' § rang out with the true blessed
inspiration of a love upborne by an inward power that
triumphed over every outward obstacle. And yet, with
these great effects, the artist mounted the first step only of
the heights to which she rose towards the close of the act.
At the words, ' *Schon fasst des Todes kaltes Grauen mich
an,* ' ‖ dim shadows began to creep in as from some doleful
world beyond. And it is worthy of remark that, through
an uninterrupted course of the most elevated and astonishing
appearances on the stage during the last twenty years,
nothing has so deeply moved us as the impression produced
by our Artist's acting from this moment onwards where
terror awakes her from her short dream of love. The strife
between greatness of soul and holiest faith in the might of
Love on the one side, and on the other the overpowering
recoil of Nature from the fear of death in a form so
terrible that it might well have crushed the shrinking
nerves of the boldest man; this strife, we say, is set
before us in such sort that the soul scarcely dares to
believe what the eye sees. It paints the last extremity of
horror, and yet the limit of the beautiful is never over-
passed even by a hair's-breadth.

"Yet we stand here on the threshold only of the realm

---

* ' *L'amour, le désespoir, usurpent dans mon cœur une entière puis-
sance.* '

† ' *Les dieux prendront pitié du sort qui vous accable.* ' Throughout
this air Licinius is addressing himself to Julia.

‡ ' *Eh bien ! fils de Vénus, à tes vœux je me rends !* '

§ ' *Il vivra !* '

‖ ' *Les horreurs du trépas sans espoir m'environne,* ' in the original
French. Here, again, Madame Birch-Pfeiffer's German differs widely
from the usual version.

of wonder over which our artist exercises her sway. It seemed to us impossible that such an achievement could have been surpassed. And yet!

"The third act, that hitherto has been for all other singers and actresses a mild and gentle echo only of the previous one, asserting its claim to nothing higher than the lyric expression of a weak emotion—this third act supplies to our Artist a point of union with still higher dramatic impressions; or, at least, with others so wholly different that they belong to an altogether foreign and unsuspected category that irresistibly proclaims her impersonation to be the most powerful of all.*

"Half hidden beneath the black veil, with difficulty supported by two veiled sisters, Julia glides, like a spirit, across the stage; advancing, with faltering step, in the funeral-procession of the Vestals, like a shadow from the depths below. It is but a memory of life that moves in the procession there; the horror of death holds her already in its freezing thrall. The sound of her voice trembles in ghostly whispers upon her lips. Over her pallid face flits, from time to time, a faint smile of love, like a dying sunbeam—a dream of the long-since-vanished past. How can one hope to paint, in words, a picture so incomprehensible? As we said above, the soul itself doubts the testimony of the living eye. And it could not be otherwise; for here Art works her miracles in the truest acceptation of the words. May we be forgiven if we defer all farther remarks to a future opportunity?"†

---

* The third act of *La Vestale* presents a difficulty which few, even of the greatest artists, can entirely overcome. The true catastrophe of the drama is represented by the ghastly procession to the living tomb, so powerfully described by Herr Rellstab in his next paragraph. The happy *dénouement* which follows forms an anti-climax quite out of harmony with the tragic complexion of the story, and Spontini leaves the heroine to create for herself the opportunity needed for the adequate expression of the joy she feels at her deliverance. When Herr Rellstab told his readers that the interest of Mdlle. Lind's ideal culminated in the third act he gave her the highest praise that it lay in his power to bestow. It *ought* to culminate there—but how consummate the power of the actress who can make it do so!

† *Kgl. priv. Berlinische Zeitung.* (Jan. 2, 1846.) See also, '*Gesammelte Schriften von Ludwig Rellstab.*' (Leipzig, 1861, tom. xx. pp. 397–402.)

We cannot but regard this eloquent panegyric as the most just as well as the most important expression of critical opinion that we have as yet had occasion to transcribe from the journals of this eventful epoch in Mdlle. Lind's artistic career. For Herr Rellstab was clearly writing under the influence of an almost irresistible predilection in favour of earlier interpretations of the *rôle* of "Julia," by German artists of the highest rank—one may almost say under the shadow of a foregone conclusion, against which nothing short of the conviction forced upon a thoroughly honest, though at the moment strongly prejudiced mind, by artistic power of the highest order, could ever have prevailed. That it did so prevail, in spite of such self-confessed resistance, adds infinite value to the final conquest, and the frankness with which Herr Rellstab proclaims his unqualified conversion does equal honour to his criticism and its subject.*

Those who were familiar with Mdlle. Lind's ideal conceptions of the great operatic *rôles* she interpreted, when at the zenith of her fame, will find no difficulty in understanding Herr Rellstab's disappointment at the effect she produced in the first act. It was her invariable custom to reserve her great effects, with true artistic self-abnegation, for certain points which the unerring instinct of her genius indicated as the fittest for the introduction of a logical climax, and to the power and perfection of such a climax she unhesitatingly sacrificed an indefinite number of those minor effects upon which too many artists gifted with less creative power are only too ready to seize for the purpose of securing a passing triumph at the expense of the logical whole. It is true that at some of her first appearances before an entirely new

---

* Mr. Chorley, who heard Mdlle. Lind, in *Die Vestalin* at Frankfort expressed his opinion of the performance in terms which entirely agree with Herr Rellstab's verdict.

audience she has been known to secure its sympathy by the
very first phrase she delivered; but it was the artistic
delivery alone that produced this magical effect.   Her
dramatic power she kept always in reserve, with a reticence
which none but the greatest artists are ever known to
exercise, for the predetermined situations in which she felt
that it could be successfully exhibited with logical consistency and deepest reverence for dramatic truth.   And
Herr Rellstab's conversion only proves how just was his
judgment on this point with regard to Spontini's masterpiece.

The particular performance of *Die Vestalin* criticised by
Herr Rellstab took place on the 30th of December.   The
Opera was given on two other occasions only during the
season, in consequence of the illness of several members of
the powerful cast.*

* For the dates of the performances, see p. 367.

CHAPTER XVIII.

AT WEIMAR.

WE have more than once had occasion to speak of Mdlle. Lind's intimacy with Hans Christian Andersen, whom, in accordance with the old-world Scandinavian usage, she was accustomed to address as her " brother."

Andersen spent the closing weeks of the year 1845 and the beginning of 1846 at Berlin; and, in his well-known autobiography, thus speaks of his Christmas festival :—

"Amidst all this festive excitement, this amiable and zealous interest in my behalf, one evening, and one only, was unoccupied, on which I suddenly felt the power of loneliness, in its most oppressive form—Christmas Eve, the exact evening on which I always feel most festive, feel so glad to stand beside a Christmas-tree, enjoy so much the happiness of the children, and love to see the elders become children again. I heard afterwards that, in each one of the family circles in which I had truly been received as a relative, it had been supposed that I was already engaged elsewhere: but, in reality, I sat quite alone in my room at the hotel and thought of home. I sat at the open window and looked up at the star-bespangled heavens. That was the Christmas-tree that had been lighted up for me. 'Father in heaven!' I prayed, as the children pray, 'what wilt Thou give me?'

"When my friends heard of my lonely Christmas feast, they lighted up many Christmas-trees for me on following evenings, and on the last evening in the year a little tree, with lights and pretty presents, was prepared for me alone— and that by Jenny Lind. The entire circle comprised herself her companion * and me. We three children of the North met together, on that Sylvester-evening, and I was the child for whom the Christmas-tree had been lighted up. With sisterly feeling, she rejoiced over my success in Berlin, and I felt almost vain of the sympathy of so pure, so womanly a being. Her praises were sounded everywhere, the praises, not of the artist only but of the woman. The two united awoke for her a true enthusiasm."†

And this homely little meeting, so touching in its child-like innocence—this pleasant and unrestrained intercourse between two pure honest-hearted souls, gifted, each in their measure, with the fire of genius—took place on the evening after Mdlle. Lind's splendid triumph on the first night of *Die Vestalin !*

The talented Dane tells another amusing little story connected with Mdlle. Lind's performances at the Opera at this period.

"One morning," he says, "as I looked out of my window, Unter den Linden, I saw, half hidden under the trees, a man, very poorly clad, who took a comb from his pocket, arranged his hair, smoothed his neck-tie, and dusted his coat with his hand. (I well know the shrinking poverty that feels oppressed by its shabby clothes.) A moment afterwards there was a knock at my door, and the man entered. It was the Nature-Poet, B * * * * *, who, though only a poor tailor, has the true poetical inspiration. Rellstab and others in Berlin have mentioned him with honour. There is something healthy in his poems, among which some breathe a true religious spirit. He had heard that I was in Berlin and had come to visit me. We sat side by side on the sofa, and his conversation betokened a contentedness so amiable, a spirit so pure and unsullied, that it truly grieved me that I was not rich enough to do something for him. I was ashamed to offer the little that lay in my power; but, in any case, I was anxious to put it in an acceptable form. I asked him, therefore, whether I might venture to invite him to hear Jenny

---

* Mdlle. Louise Johansson.

† '*Das Märchen meines Lebens,*' von *H. C. Andersen.* (Leipzig, 1880, pp. 206–207.)

Lind. 'I have already heard her,' he said, smiling. 'I could not afford to buy a ticket; so I went to the man who provides the "supers" and asked him if I could not go on as a "super" one evening in *Norma*. To this he agreed. So I was dressed up as a Roman soldier, with a long sword at my side, and in that guise appeared upon the stage; and I heard her better than any one else, for I stood close beside her. Ah! how she sang! and how she acted! I could not stand it: it made me weep. But they were furious at that. The manager forbade it, and would never permit me to set foot upon the stage again—for one must not weep upon the stage.'" *

Soon after this Andersen took leave of his friends in Berlin and proceeded to Weimar on a visit to the Hereditary Grand Duke, with whom he was on terms of the most affectionate intimacy. And here, again, he spent some happy days in the company of Mdlle. Lind, who had also been invited to Weimar, and sang there on five evenings, three of which were occupied by Court Concerts and two by performances of *Norma* and *La Sonnambula* at the Court Theatre.† Here, as in Berlin, her performances produced the most profound sensation. The Grand Duke and the various members of his Royal Highness's family received her with demonstrations of the warmest welcome. In company with Andersen and his friends, the Chancellor Müller, the Court Chamberlain Beaulieu, and the Court Secretary Schöll, she visited some of the most interesting places in the neighbourhood, and more especially those consecrated by memories of Goethe and Schiller.

On the 29th of January—two days after her last performance at Court—the Chancellor Müller escorted her, in company with Andersen, to the Fürstengruft—the burial-vault

* '*Das Märchen meines Lebens*,' von *H. C. Andersen*. (Leipzig, 1880, pp. 207, 208).

† The dates were: Jan. 23, Court Concert; Jan. 24, *Norma*, at the Court Theatre; Jan. 25, Court Matinée; Jan. 26, *La Sonnambula*, at the Court Theatre; Jan. 27, Court Concert, at the Theatre.

in the Neue Kirchof, beyond the Frauenthor, in which for many generations past, the remains of the departed Grand Dukes of Saxe-Weimar-Eisenach and their families have been laid to rest—and there showed to the little party of friends the coffins in which Goethe and Schiller now sleep their last long sleep.* The dimly lighted burial-place, and the solemn associations connected with it, made a deep impression upon the friends ; and amidst its ghostly shadows the Austrian poet, Hermann Rollet, who accidentally met the little party in the vault, wrote a poem, which Andersen has printed in his autobiography, and the original MS. of which was carefully preserved by Mdlle. Lind among her mementos of the past. We subjoin the verses in the original German, which would be seriously weakened by any attempt at translation :—

> Märchenrose, die Du oftmals
> Mich entzückt mit süssem Duft,
> Sah Dich ranken um die Särge
> In der Dichterfürstengruft.
>
> Und mit Dir an jedem Sarge
> In der todtenstillen Hall'
> Sah ich eine schmerzentzückte,
> Träumerische Nachtigall.
>
> Und ich freute mich im Stillen,
> War in tiefster Brust entzückt,
> Das die dunklen Dichtersärge
> Spät noch solcher Zauber schmückt.
>
> Und das Duften deiner Rose
> Wogte durch die Todtenhall'
> Mit der Wehmuth der in Trauer
> Stummgeworb'nen Nachtigall. †

* The late Grand-Duke, Carl Augustus, the father of Hans C. Andersen's friend, Carl Alexander, the heir-apparent, and the devoted admirer and intimate friend of the two great Poets, gave orders that their coffins should be placed on either side of his own ; but as this arrangement was found to be inconsistent with Court etiquette, they now stand, close together, in another part of the vault.

† '*Das Märchen meines Lebens ;*' von *Hans Christian Andersen.* (Leipzig, 1880, page 211.) See also, '*Hans Christian Andersens Briefwechsel ;*' *herausgegeben von Emil Jonas.* (Leipzig, 1887, page 29.)

The visit to the funeral-vault affected Mdlle. Lind very deeply; and she was evidently glad to relieve the sad impression by more cheerful thoughts. In a letter to Madame Birch-Pfeiffer, she wrote:—

Weimar, Jan. 27, 1846.

"I have just come out of the vault in which Goethe and Schiller lie entombed, and my whole heart is impressed and excited.

"On Friday afternoon I am going to Leipzig, where I have been most kindly invited to the Mendelssohns, for the evening, and on Saturday I return to Berlin." *

As her performances at the Opera at Berlin were *Gastrollen* only, and therefore subject to no iron rule with regard to specific dates, she enjoyed much greater freedom, in the matter of "leave of absence," than she could have hoped for had she formed one of the regular staff of the company. Thus privileged, she was able without difficulty to extend her little holiday some days beyond the time occupied by her engagements at Weimar, as we learn from the following letter, written in German, to Madame Wichmann:—

"Weimar, 27 January, 1846.

"ÄLSKADE † FRU!

"Yes! if I might only continue in my mother-tongue —then would my beloved Frau Professorin have the chance of receiving a fairly nice letter. But, in German! Ah! ‡

"Weimar is but a little place, but it is very interesting. However, I will not tell you all about that, but will work it out in Berlin.

"I remain here until Thursday § morning, when I go to Erfurt, to sing at a concert there. From thence I go on, on Friday, to Leipzig, where I stay for the night; and you can

---

* From Frau von Hillern's collection.

† 'Beloved.'

‡ It will be remembered, that Mdlle. Lind wrote the first of her long series of letters to Frau Wichmann in French.

§ January 29.

well understand, my gracious Professorin, from what source
my kind invitation comes : * can you not guess ? and on
Saturday we come, by the first train, to Berlin.

> " Your grateful and sincerely devoted,

> " JENNY LIND."†

The memory of this pleasant holiday—for it really was a
holiday, though not a time of idleness—was very dear to
her.   Soon after her return to Berlin she wrote thus to
her friend Hans C. Andersen :—

> "Berlin, February 19, 1846.

" MY DEAR GOOD BROTHER !

> " Thanks for our last meeting.   I did so enjoy it !   Do
you agree with me that we have scarcely ever before spent
a more charming pleasant time together ?

> " I thank you, ever so much, for your beautiful letter.   I
had a good cry over reading it.‡

> " Yes, yes ! Germany is a glorious country.   I certainly do
not long for any other except the very best—the last one.

> " Oh ! how I have wept over your story about the Grand
Duchess and her little sweep !   How lovely it is !

> " In the meantime I am perfectly enchanted with her—
and with the young Grand Duke and his wife also.
Dear Andersen, when you write to our high-born friend, tell
him—if you mention me §—that, as long as I live, I shall
remember those few days I spent in Weimar.   I can conscientiously say that I have nowhere else, as yet, found such
peace of mind and true joy ; and yet I have been treated
everywhere in the most friendly way.   I love these high-

---

* The invitation came from Dr. and Madame Mendelssohn.

† From the letters to Frau Wichmann.

‡ This letter does not appear to have been preserved.

§ Anderson had already mentioned Mdlle. Lind and described the visit
to the Fürstengruft in a letter to his friend, the young Grand Duke,
written from Leipzig, on the 14th of February—five days before the date
of Mdlle. Lind's letter to himself—and enclosing a copy of Rollet's Poem ;
and he afterwards sent the Duke a copy of that portion of her letter
which referred to her reception at the Court of Weimar, although it
was clearly intended for no other eye than his own.   See ' *H. C.
Andersen's Briefwechsel;*' *herausgegeben von Emil Jonas.*   (Leipzig, 1887,
pages 28–29.)

born personages; and, just as you say, Brother, not for the
stars and the diamonds they wear, but for their true and
loyal hearts. I get quite enthusiastic when I think of these
two people. May God preserve them and theirs!

"My friends, the Arnemanns, from Altona,* have been
here. They left yesterday. I wonder when we two shall
meet again?

"I have now quite decided upon going to Vienna. Are
you not going there, Andersen? I suppose you go on to
Italy direct?

"Do you know, Andersen, I appreciate your friend Beaulieu very highly indeed. I have really begun to feel a great
friendship for him. Give him my kindest regards when you
write.

"And now, *adieu!* I must start for the Theatre presently,
to sing in *Das Feldlager in Schlesien.*† God be with you!
Do not forget your sister. I shall remain here until the end
of March. After that letters will find me at Vienna, from
the middle of April until the middle of May. Write, either
Poste restante, or care of Herr Pokorny—the manager of the
Theatre.‡

"May the blessing of God go with you! then you will
have enough!

"I remain,

"Your true sister,

"JENNY."

She was by this time once more hard at work in
the dizzy whirl of the Berlin winter season. She had
reappeared, after her return from Weimar, on the 3rd of
February, in *Das Feldlager in Schlesien;* and, since then, had
been singing regularly twice a week, though on no fixed days,
in the above-mentioned Opera and in *Die Vestalin, Der Freischütz,* and *La Sonnambula.* But in the meantime her promised appearance in a new and very important part was
anxiously awaited by the art-loving public.

* See page 299.
† For the third time during this season.
‡ *I.e.* the Theater an der Wien, at which she was engaged to sing, in
Vienna.

CHAPTER XIX.

THE next—and last—new part in which Mdlle. Lind made
her appearance, at Berlin during the eventful winter of
1845–1846 was that of "Valentine," in Meyerbeer's Opera
Les Huguenots—or, as it was called in German, *Die Hugenotten.*

To the uninitiated, it may seem strange that, taking into
consideration Meyerbeer's all-powerful position and great
popularity in Berlin at this period, *Das Feldlager in Schlesien*
should have been the only one of his Operas put upon the
Stage, with a Singer for whose talent he entertained so
sincere an admiration in the principal part, until within a
few weeks of the close of the season. But the position will
not be thought at all strange by those who know how
severely punctilious Meyerbeer was, not only with regard to
the principal parts, but with all that concerned the perfection
of every minutest detail of his works. It was not enough
for him that the *prima donna* should be an artist of un-
approachable excellence. If all the other parts, great and
small, were not represented to his entire satisfaction he
would not allow the piece to be put upon the Stage at all.
Moreover, his independent position gave him advantages
which few other modern composers have enjoyed in an equal
degree; and the consequence was that, when he directed his
own Operas, they were brought out with a perfection of detail

comparable only with that insisted upon, some years earlier, by Spontini.

The demands upon the *personnel* of the opera-staff in *Les Huguenots* are very heavy. The part of "Queen Marguerite of Navarre" is not written for a *seconda donna*, but a second *prima donna*—a *Soprano leggiero*, as opposed to the *Soprano dramatico* of "Valentine." That of "Urbain," the page, needs a Mezzo-soprano of high capability. The Tenor— "Raoul de Nangis," and the two Baritoni—"Marcel," and "Saint Bris"—need representatives of the highest rank. And in face of these demands we can scarcely wonder that a man so hard to satisfy as Meyerbeer was not too ready to place his second great master-piece upon the Stage.

It must be supposed, however, that he was satisfied at last, for on the 26th of February *Die Hugenotten* was announced for representation, with Mdlle. Lind, as we have said, in the part of "Valentine"; and the performance was thus criticised in the journal from which we have so frequently and so freely quoted :—

"Our great Artist-visitor, Jenny Lind, has evolved from the character of 'Valentine,' in *Die Hugenotten*—a part as rich in dramatic and musical expression—a dramatic creation which, in noble individuality, occupies quite as high a position in the domain of Lyric Tragedy as the earlier *rôles* in which the artist enchained us with such irresistible power.

"We do not hesitate to say—as it is more than ever our duty to do, in the case of an artist of such acknowledged worth—that the first part of her performance, especially when she was in the presence of the Queen, did not produce an altogether agreeable impression upon us. However many various characters may be in sympathy with her individuality, she seemed unwilling to identify herself with that of the Court-lady. And, for us, this impression was heightened by the style of the dress she wore, though we admit that our reference to this savours of relapse into dilettantism.

"So far as the Actress was concerned, the *rôle* began with

the third act,[*] when she emerges from the natural forms of
life to plunge into the depths of the inner world with all its
profoundest impressions. Here she reached the highest and
most excellent point of all—the glorious virginal purity
which lighted up the tender romance of the character
throughout the whole of its development. At each fresh
entrance of the artist we debated within ourselves whether
the praise should be awarded to the Singer or to the Actress.
The two were often so completely melted into one that it
became impossible to separate them.

"Before the time of Jenny Lind, the grandest reading of
the part was decidedly that of Wilhelmina Schrœder-
Devrient. She threw more brilliant lights upon it and
invested certain passages with a more satisfactory colouring; as, for instance, at the well-known words, '*Ich bin ein
Mädchen das ihn liebt*,' &c. And yet the shrinking breath
with which our artist lightly veiled this expression cast a
more delicate fragrance over the deep inward glow, and
imparted to it a charm wholly its own.

"A similar idea—if we care to continue the parallel—
pervades the conception of the passage, '*Ich klammre mich
an Dich*,' in the fourth act. Jenny Lind undoubtedly
clothed this with a more spiritual expression. She scarcely
dared breathe it to her lover, whereas her great predecessor
gave way to a rush of passion and sensualised the glowing
confession with ravishing violence of gesture.

"But, as was only to be expected of an Artist so rich in
creative power, Jenny Lind also struck out for herself an
altogether original conception of the impersonation, impressed it in the most marked manner upon the character,

---

[*] Rellstab repeats this opinion, in a later critique on Madame Viardot's
appearance in the part of "Valentine," in 1847, and there finds the same
fault with Madame Viardot that he here finds with Mdlle. Lind, but
with the saving clause that, in both cases, the fault is inherent in the
part and must not be laid to the account of the performer (See the
'*Gesammelte Schriften von Ludwig Rellstab*;' Leipzig, 1861, tome xx.
p. 403.) The truth is, that it is not until the opening of the Third Act
that the part of "Valentine" becomes an important one. The scenes in
which she previously appears offer no opportunity for the introduction of
marked effects. We have already had occasion to direct our readers'
attention to the jealous reticence with which Mdlle. Lind was accustomed
to keep back her greatest effects until the proper moment arrived for
their introduction.

and filled us with astonishment at the rich variety of her
resources.   Her third act was a touching prayer to her
bitter fate; her fourth, a mighty battle waged against it;
her fifth, a splendid victory over it.   She sang the last
scene under truest inspiration of faith.

"If we would trace the course of these complications of the
character through single passages, the choice, amidst so
great a wealth of impressions, overwhelms us with difficulty.
Turning back to the duet with Marcel, we remember the
charm of its sadness; the trembling whisper with which it
opens; the ever-increasing warmth of its tones and passages,
as the certainty of love brings joy to her heart; and, last of
all, the fire of the vocalisation in the concluding divisions
raising the conception to its loftiest climax.

"In the fourth act, the silence of the Artist speaks almost
more strongly to us than the outpouring of her soul in sound.
Her acting, during the deliberation of the conspirators,
her struggling resistance, her listening, her comprehension,
her terror, her hope—her changes of position, which would
have afforded a painter opportunities for a hundred different
aspects of ever-varying expression—the living play of her
motions, corroborating and contradicting each other so
spiritually, with every scenic variation—this host of voiceless
expressions bore the artist to the loftiest heights which make
the history of her performance imperishable.[*]

"Towards the close of the act the strained action of the
eye is again exchanged for that of the ear, which the sweet
earnestness of the tones, here dwelt upon and enhanced by
the power of the composition, holds in sad and fettered
enchantment.

"But through this night of fatal destiny certain dramatic
gestures burst upon us like lightning-flashes of deepest
significance.   Such, for instance, as the inward terror manifested at the first boom of the *tocsin*, the ever-increasing
dread as the delineation of the scene of blood approaches its
climax, and at last the stunned fall upon the stage, with
eyes now closed, now open with staring gaze, as the last
power to resist this surfeit of horror and anxiety dies out!

"All these rich details, representing the sustained perseverance of the battle waged by the noblest and purest of
sentiments, against love and guilt and destiny, form a

---

[*] During a great portion of this powerful scene, "Valentine's" back is
turned to the audience.

dramatic whole, which, as we have already said, in no wise
fell short of the loftiest heights the artist has reached as yet
in her tragic greatness.

"If the fifth act, when compared with the fourth, betokens
some loss of power, in spite of the grand conception to one
phase of which we have already alluded, the fault certainly
does not lie with the performer, who here fulfils the whole
intention of the drama, but is probably due, in part at least,
to the fatigue of the hearer's overstrained attention.*

"So much, then, for the present.

"We have always found that the artist penetrates more
and more deeply into the heart of her task at every repetition,
and fulfils it with greater ease ; we may therefore in this, as
in other cases, look forward to even increased perfection.
Yet we may almost ask, 'What need of more?' in presence
of this noblest wealth of treasures." †

To sober-minded English readers the style of Herr
Rellstab's critiques—and of this one especially—may seem
high-flown and exaggerated. Moreover, as we have already
had occasion to remark, Herr Rellstab was not only
a critic, but a romancist and a poet on his own account ;
and he worked no less carefully at his critiques than
at his other writings, for which reason a great number of
his fugitive contributions to the *Berlinische Zeitung* are
included in the complete edition of his works. ‡   It
must be admitted that the style of these reviews differs
materially from that adopted in England at the present day ;
but they are of great value to us, as records of a form of
criticism now—in this country, at least—quite obsolete.
Moreover, in so far as our present purpose is concerned, they

---

* The last act of *Les Huguenots*, like that of *La Vestale*, undoubtedly
represents an unfortunate anti-climax, the weakness of which is increased
by the firing of musketry, and other stage-expedients of common-place
character.

† *Kgl. priv. Berlinische Zeitung.* (Feb. 28, 1846.)

‡ '*Gesammelte Schriften von Ludwig Rellstab*' (Leipzig, 1861); from
the twentieth volume of which we have reprinted, among others, the
critique on *Die Vestalin*, in Chapter XVII.

honestly reflect the feeling with which Mdlle. Lind's performances were listened to, at the time they were written, by the crowded audiences who flocked, night after night, to the Royal Opera-House to hear her. The performer concerning whom it was simply possible to write in a strain so exalted can have belonged to no common order in the Hierarchy of Art. And enough is known of the character of Herr Rellstab, and of his position in Berlin, to establish the certainty that he honestly meant every word he wrote.

CHAPTER XX.

AUF WIEDERSEHEN!

THE first performance of *Les Huguenots* took place on Thursday the 26th of February, the second on Sunday the 1st of March. A third, announced for Friday, March the 6th, was prevented by a most unfortunate accident; Mademoiselle Lind sprained her foot on the Thursday so seriously that for three weeks she was confined to the sofa.

The kindest sympathy was shown to the sufferer after this painful misadventure, and Mendelssohn, who had been informed of the accident, endeavoured, on the 18th of March, to cheer her loneliness with a long and delightful letter, half grave, half gay, in which the serious and the playful were intermingled with an easy grace in which few adepts in the art of letter-writing have ever been able to rival him.

We print this hitherto unpublished letter, in the belief that it cannot fail to prove generally interesting to the reader.

"Leipzig, March 18, 1846.

"MY DEAR FRÄULEIN,

"The account that Taubert brought of the state of your health was not so encouraging as I could have wished; * but as I used to like, on days such as these, to sit down to the piano, and play to you, so now—since, unhappily, I cannot come to you in person—I come, at least in writing, and fancy to myself that I ask, in the entrance hall, whether I can speak with you, and am told—'yes'; and Mademoiselle

* Herr Taubert had come to Leipzig, a few days before this, for the purpose of playing at one of the Gewandhaus Concerts.

Louise opens the door for me, and I see in your hand one of the ten thousand pictures and engravings with which you are now surrounded, and then I sit down beside you and begin like this:—

"Shall I tell you about Marie ? *

"She talks to me, all day long, about Fräulein Lind, and how she was so kind to her; and when I went to the children, yesterday, in the nursery, and found little fat Paul† practising his writing on a sheet of paper, I saw that he had written 'dear Fräulein Lind' over the whole page at least ten times. To-day he has finished a whole letter, and he made me promise that I would send it to you—I was absolutely obliged to promise it. Marie wanted to send her letter first, but I explained that one letter would be enough, and she was satisfied with signing it. Karl said he could not sign it as it was not his own letter.

"A funny thing happened to us this evening. Cécile ‡ said: 'It is a long time since we have had any Swedish bread; what a pity it is!' § I said, 'I will write to-day, and ask for some in your name.' Marie said, 'But Paul has already written to Fräulein Lind to-day.' I asked to see the letter—the beautiful scrawl I enclose—and as Paul came in at one door with his letter the servant brought in your present of Swedish bread at the other.

"The children think of you daily and hourly, and their parents also. We long very much indeed to hear soon that you are better, and once more free from all the weariness that such a long imprisonment brings with it.‖ May you soon send us, please God! an account of your complete cure.

"To-day we had a very pleasant rehearsal. Taubert conducted his symphony and made friends of the whole orchestra. To us, who are artists, must certainly be conceded one very delightful prerogative, in return for which we are willing to give up all other prerogatives whatever: viz. that in one short half-hour a host of strangers can be transformed into a host of good friends. That is a capital state of things, and many would like it, though it is given but to few. To my great joy, it was given very decidedly indeed to Taubert

* Mendelssohn's eldest daughter.
† Mendelssohn's second son.
‡ Madame Mendelssohn.
§ See foot-note, p. 122.
‖ I.e. the imprisonment caused by the sprained foot.

to-day; and when he adds to this his playing of the
Beethoven Concerto to-morrow he may build upon the Leipzig Musicians on both sides.*

"That which is called 'the Public' is exactly the same
here as elsewhere and everywhere; the simple 'Public,'
assembled together for an instant, so fluctuating, so full of
curiosity, so devoid of taste, so dependent upon the judgment
of the musician—the so-called connoisseur.   But against
this we must set the great 'Public,' assembling together year
after year, wiser and more just than connoisseur and musician,
and judging so truly! and feeling so delicately!

"A grand new vocal composition by Gade was also rehearsed, with full chorus, for performance next week.   I
hope it will turn out both poetical and beautiful.   The
text is from Ossian; and Fingal, with his warriors, and
harps, and horns, and spirits, plays an important part in it.
But Taubert will tell you all this much better by word of
mouth.†

"We also sang to-day, 'Come cow, come calf,' ‡ in such
sort that it was worthy to have been described as a noble
work of Art!   Taubert sings better than I; but I pronounce
Swedish better than he!

"You ask how things go with me.

"On the days when I was so quiet in my room, writing
music without interruption, and only going out from time to
time for a walk in the fresh air, they went very well indeed
with me—or, at least, I thought so.   But, since the day

---

* Herr W. Taubert's Symphony in F major was played at the Gewandhaus, under his own direction, on Thursday, March 19, 1846; and on
the same evening he played Beethoven's Pianoforte Concerto in E flat,
Op. 73.

† *Comala*, a Dramatic Cantata, by Herr Niels W. Gade—the composition alluded to in the text—was first produced at the Gewandhaus under
the direction of the Composer on the 23rd of March, 1846, at a Concert
given for the benefit of the poor, and repeated on the 26th of the same
month with great success.

‡ A national melody, afterwards known, in England as the 'Norwegian
Echo Song,' and in Germany as the '*Norwegisches Schäferlied*,' and
sung by Mdlle. Lind in both countries with immense success.   The
original title was, 'Kom kjyra! kom kjyra mi!'   It ended with a *coda*
added by herself, and sung in imitation of an echo with an effect quite
irresistible, and almost incredible, even to those who heard it.   (*See*
Appendix of Music.)

before yesterday, when I had more to do with the concert affairs and all sorts of correspondence connected with them, and things of that kind, to which I could only give half my attention because my own work lay so much nearer to my heart *—since then I have been a prey to such fatal excitement, and felt so miserably out of spirits, that, while every one says, 'How well you look,' *you* would rather say, 'What is the matter with you ?'

"Happily, however, this is the last week, for this year, during which I shall be concerned with these things ; and then I mean to work very hard, and after that I shall rejoice in the Rhine and the spring-time.

"Yes ; I rejoice in the thought of the Rhine and the Musical Festival,† and the real true spring—for, for many days past, I have been fearing that the winter would come back again, and that the spring would break off altogether, as in my old song in your book. ‡ And farther on, I, like yourself, rejoice very much indeed in thinking of the time when I shall be able to put aside the duty of conducting music and promoting Institutions, and quit this so-called 'sphere of activity,' and have no other 'sphere of activity' to think of than a quire of blank music-paper, and no need to conduct anything that I do not care for, and when I shall be altogether independent and free.   It will, indeed, be a few years before this can take place, but I hope *not more than that ;* and in this we are very much alike.   I believe, in good truth, that this is because we both have the love of Art so deeply implanted in our souls.

" But, I am fancying that I have been sitting by your side quite long enough, and must now take my leave ; or else that it is *Norma* to-night, and that it has already chimed half-past three §—in short, I must say good-bye.

" I hope I may soon hear that you are able to walk, run,

---

* Mendelssohn was then actively engaged on the composition of *Elijah*.

† The Lower Rhine Festival was to take place, on the 31st of May, 1846, and following days, at Aix-la-Chapelle; and it was arranged that Mdlle. Lind and Mendelssohn, who were both to take part in it, should meet at Frankfort in order that they might travel down the Rhine together.

‡ In allusion to a MS. Song-book, written by Mendelssohn for Mdlle. Lind, as a Christmas present, in 1845, and illustrated with pencil drawings by himself.

§ In those days the Opera began, at Berlin, at half-past six.

stand, jump, dance, play at billiards, sing at Ries's Concert,
and play the parts of 'Proserpina' and 'Valentine,' and
that you have become free of all farther inquiries.

" Your friend,

" FELIX MENDELSSOHN BARTHOLDY." *

Cheered by pleasant correspondence such as this, and still
more pleasant intercourse with the choice circle of sympathetic friends who enjoyed the privilege of *entrée* to the charmed
salon in the Hasenheger Strasse, the three long weeks of
dreary imprisonment passed more lightly than would otherwise have been expected.   And they were enlivened too, from
time to time, by another source of interest no less welcome
and agreeable.   Professor Wichmann seized upon this
excellent opportunity for securing the " sittings " necessary
for the modelling of a beautiful medallion-portrait of her
in profile, designed upon a circular plaque fourteen inches
in diameter, and eventually executed in white marble.
It is a charming work of Art, regarded, by all who have
seen it, as a valuable historical memorial.†

When modelling this beautiful profile the Professor did
not know that his guest was herself preparing a welcome
surprise for the family in anticipation of his idea.

Wishing to present her host and hostess with a grateful
memorial of the happy time she had spent beneath their roof,
she had commissioned Professor Magnus to paint her portrait,
on a large scale, in order that she might present it to them
before leaving Berlin.   Professor Magnus had accepted the
commission, and made some progress with the work, when the
" sittings " were interrupted by the accidental sprain, which

* Translated from the autograph letter in the possession of Mr. Goldschmidt.

† A representation of this medallion is impressed upon the binding of
these volumes.

for a time rendered the needful visits to his studio impossible.
As soon as these could be resumed, he proceeded with his
work, and in process of time produced a portrait not only
valuable as a striking likeness of the sitter but precious also
as a work of Art which may be fairly accepted as a
happy example of the best school of portrait-painting then
existing in Germany. That Professor Magnus himself
regarded it in that light is proved by the fact that, after it
had been presented to Madame Wichmann, and treasured for
fifteen years as a precious family possession, he consented, at
the request of Mr. Goldschmidt, to execute an exact *replica*,
forming so perfect a reproduction of the original picture,
that the Professor himself found it necessary to attach a
certain mark to it, in order that he might be able to dis-
tinguish the copy from the original. By his desire, and
that of the Prussian Government, this *replica* was exhibited,
in 1862, in the Prussian Court of the Universal Exhibition
at South Kensington, as the acknowledged representative
of this Artist's style at his best period—and it fulfilled this
intention perfectly and to the satisfaction of all concerned.

The original picture remained in the Wichmann family
until the year 1877, when the Professor's eldest son, Herr
Herrmann Wichmann, to whom it had passed by inheritance
after his mother's death in the previous year, consented to
its removal, at the price of twelve thousand thalers, to the
Berlin National Gallery, where, having now become national
property, it is treasured as a valuable artistic and historical
monument.* The sprain was healed, however, before the
picture was finished.

The public were perhaps more impatient at the duration
of the imprisonment than the prisoner herself. But it came
to an end at last; and, after a term of enforced captivity

---

* A copy of this forms the frontispiece to our present volume.

lasting for twenty-four days, Mademoiselle Lind reappeared on the 29th of March in *Norma*, before an audience who welcomed her return to the Stage with every demonstration of uncontrollable enthusiasm—an index of public opinion which might indeed, by this time, have been expected as a matter of course every time she appeared.

After this performance—the twenty-sixth in which she had taken part during the then current season—she appeared once more in *Das Feldlager in Schlesien* on the 31st of March; and on Thursday, the 2nd of April—her own 'benefit-night'—took leave of Berlin for the season.

The house, we need scarcely say, was crowded to the roof, and the performance in the highest degree satisfactory. Herr Rellstab thus feelingly describes the moment of the final parting :—

"The call before the curtain, which had already been anticipated at the end of the preceding Acts—the greetings represented by the wreaths thrown, in multitudes, by the hands of ladies—ladies too who well knew how to acknowledge worthily the noblest and the highest Art—all these demonstrations were renewed at the close of the performance, and with such increasing warmth as we have never before witnessed in our lives. The entire mass of the audience took part in the offering of applause : the profusion of flowers seemed inexhaustible. The curtain fell. But the summons before it was repeated, and the applause continued so long that the artist had no choice but to reappear ; yet no sooner had she again retired than she was yet again brought back by a newly repeated summons.

"A burning wish seemed to inspire the multitude—that for one farewell word. The Artist who, from a sense of shyness, combined with the unaccustomed tones of the language, had always hitherto expressed her thanks by dumb yet telling motions, yielded at last to this well-understood though unspoken wish (for how could it be spoken amidst such a storm of applause !), and uttered, with deepest inward emotion, the simple and almost inarticulate words, ' *Ich danke Ihnen—ich werde das in meinem ganzen Leben* *nicht vergessen!'* * And, like her Art, this expression of her thanks was a precious truth.

"And again the call was shouted by thousands of voices, and yet once again she had no choice but to respond to it; and then, at last, the audience was satisfied.

"And now let us cast a glance backwards from this brilliant, touching, overpowering moment, upon that which the Artist has given to us during the course of the last few months.

"In the first place; after her first wonderful appearance among us, last year, she has returned with all the purity, all the hallowing through and from her Art, that, to us, represents the highest attribute of her personality. In all her triumphs she has lost nothing of the noblest quality that adorns her, and therein lies her priceless reward. But she has also gained much in another sense. She has returned to us developed in many ways. She draws forth her creations from a deeper source. Much that was a charming bud has blossomed into a still more charming flower. There is not one of her impersonations, already known to us, that has not spread forth its branches to form a richer crown. To the old creations she has added new ones—the sweet wild-flower fragrance of her 'Agathe'; the wonderful picture of her 'Vestal,' beautiful, even amidst the terrors of the grave; the unapproachably rich painting of her grief and love in the tragic part of 'Valentine.' Who shall say which of her Art-creations is the highest? To scarcely any other Artist has it happened in the same degree as it has to her that the judgment of the public has differed so widely. Each one has chosen a *rôle* on his own account. The wavering extends from the gayest to those who listen only to grief and horror. We believe the secret lies in this, that she everywhere fulfils her task with the highest perfection of which it is susceptible. One sentiment, however, pervades all her Art-pictures—the spirit of holiness; the transfiguration resulting from the purest reverence for Art, absolute freedom from all secondary objects and endeavours. And therein lies all, all that lends to her artistic representations that moral consecration, which we once heard very beautifully described by a lady in the words—simple enough, yet full of *esprit*— 'One becomes better through having seen her.'

"And therefore it is that the Artist is everywhere spoken

---

* "I thank you—never, in my whole life, shall I forget this!"

of with wonder as well as with the feeling of gratitude; therefore it is that she is accompanied by thousands and thousands
of wishes that the most beautiful blessings of life may be added
to the noblest gifts of Art that she possesses. Vacillating
rumours whisper that she will soon vanish from the Stage
and from us for ever! May they prove false! We can only
express the hope, in which all will certainly join with us,
that she may belong to Art so long as Art belongs to her, and
that her desire to bring it back again to us may be measured
by the certainty of her welcome." *

And thus was the second winter season at Berlin brought
to an end, with mutual regret and warmest good wishes on
either side.†

* *Kgl. priv. Berlinische Zeitung*, April 4, 1846.

† Our account of the Art-work of these two eventful seasons would be
incomplete without a detailed list of the performances in which Mdlle.
Lind took part; but, in order to avoid interrupting the course of our
narrative, we have thought it best to supply this in the form of a note.

FIRST WINTER SEASON (1844–5).

1844.

Dec. 15 (Sun.)   *Norma.*
„ 20 (Fri.)   *Norma.*
„ 26 (Thur.) *Norma.*

1845.

Jan. 5 (Sun.)   *Das Feldlager in
                Schlesien.*
„ 10 (Fri.)   *Das Feldlager in
                Schlesien.*
„ 14 (Tue.)   *Das Feldlager in
                Schlesien.*
„ 19 (Sun.)   *Das Feldlager in
                Schlesien.*
„ 21 (Tue.)   *Norma.*
„ 23 (Thur.) *Norma.*
„ 28 (Tue.)   *Norma.*
„ 31 (Fri.)   *Norma.*
Feb. 4 (Tue.)   *Das Feldlager in
                Schlesien.*
„ 7 (Fri.)   *Euryanthe.*
„ 9 (Sun.)   *Norma.*

Feb. 11 (Tue.)   *Euryanthe.*
„ 14 (Fri.)   *Euryanthe.*
„ 18 (Tue.)   *Die Nachtwand-
                lerin.*
„ 21 (Fri.)   *Die Nachtwand-
                lerin.*
„ 23 (Sun.)   *Euryanthe.*
Mar. 2 (Sun.)   *Die Nachtwand-
                lerin.*
„ 4 (Tue.)   *Das Feldlager in
                Schlesien.*
„ 7 (Fri.)   *Die Nachtwand-
                lerin.*
„ 9 (Sun.)   *Die Nachtwand-
                lerin.*
„ 11 (Tue.)   *Norma* (for Mdlle.
                Lind's benefit).

[In all, twenty-four performances.]

CONCERTS.

1844.

Nov.   Soirée at the Prin-
                cess of Prussia's.
Dec. 18 (Wed.) Court concert.

1845.

Jan. 2 (Thur.) Court concert.
Feb. 2 (Sun.) Court concert.
 „ 13 (Thur.) Concert of the Brothers Ganz.
Mar. 10 (Mon.) Concert of Herr Nehrlich.
 „ 13 (Thur.) Concert for Blind Soldiers at the Sing-Akademie.

SECOND WINTER SEASON 1845-6.

1845.

Nov. 9 (Sun.) *Norma.*
 „ 13 (Thu.) *Norma.*
 „ 19 (Wed.) *Don Juan.*
 „ 21 (Fri.) *Don Juan.*
 „ 25 (Tue.) *Don Juan.*
 „ 30 (Sun.) *Der Freischütz.*
Dec. 2 (Tue.) *Der Freischütz.*
 [The visit to Leipzig.]
 „ 9 (Tue.) *Don Juan.*
 „ 12 (Fri.) *Norma.*
 „ 16 (Tue.) *Der Freischütz.*
 „ 19 (Fri.) *Die Nachtwandlerin.*
 „ 23 (Tue.) *Die Nachtwandlerin.*
 „ 30 (Tue.) *Die Vestalin.*

1846.

Jan. 2 (Fri.) *Die Vestalin.*
 „ 6 (Tue.) *Die Nachtwandlerin.*
 „ 11 (Sun.) *Norma.*
 „ 15 (Thu.) *Don Juan.*

Jan. 18 (Sun.) *Das Feldlager in Schlesien.*
[*Norma* and *Die Nachtwandlerin* at Weimar.]
Feb. 3 (Tue.) *Das Feldlager in Schlesien.*
 „ 5 (Thu.) *Die Vestalin.*
 „ 10 (Tue.) *Der Freischütz.*
 „ 19 (Thu.) *Das Feldlager in Schlesien.*
 „ 24 (Tue.) *Die Nachtwandlerin.*
 „ 26 (Thu.) *Die Hugenotten.*
Mar. 1 (Sun.) *Die Hugenotten.*
 (The Sprained ankle.)
 „ 29 (Sun.) *Norma.*
 „ 31 (Tue.) *Das Feldlager in Schlesien.*
Apr. 2 (Thu.) *Die Nachtwandlerin.*
(For Mademoiselle Lind's Benefit.)
[In all, twenty-eight performances.]

CONCERTS.

1845-6.

Six Court Concerts.

1845.

Dec. 13. (Sat.) Concert (Swedish) of Herr Musik-direktor Ahlström.

1846.

Mar. 2 (Mon.) Concert given by Mdlle. Lind for some poor families.
 „ 28 (Sat.) A grand concert.

BOOK V.

PROGRESS.

CHAPTER I.

THE engagement at Vienna, vaguely alluded to in the letter
to Madame Erikson, and more decidedly, in that to Herr
Josephson, was now finally arranged, and on the eve of fulfilment. The terms of this contract—five hundred gulden *
each, for five performances, with an extra benefit night—
had been carefully discussed, and gladly accepted, by Herr
Franz Pokorny, the then manager of the Theater an der
Wien, during the latter part of Mdlle. Lind's stay at Berlin ;
and, as soon as she could conveniently do so, after the
exciting scene at the Royal Opera-House on the evening
of her benefit, she took leave of her kind host and hostess,
and started, with her companion, Mdlle. Louise Johansson,
for Vienna, *viâ* Leipzig, in which last-named town she had
been invited to spend a few days, as the guest of Herr
Heinrich Brockhaus, and had also decided upon giving a
concert, at the Gewandhaus, on her own account.

On the 8th of April, 1846, Herr Brockhaus wrote in his
diary :—

"At home, I found all well, and in high good humour with
an amiable visitor—Fräulein Lind—who, early this morning,
fulfilled a long-standing promise to stay with us.

- " I was heartily pleased to see, once more, the amiable and

* Equal to about fifty pounds, in English money. The terms for the
"benefit" were to be, half the receipts, after payment of the evening's
expenses.

2 B 2

unaffected girl, whose natural simplicity is so beautifully
united to the greatness of the Artist. She was sociable and
cheerful throughout the evening, which was still farther
enlivened by the presence of Mendelssohn."

In a farther entry, on the 9th of April, Herr Brockhaus
continues :—

"Unhappily, Fräulein Lind can stay no longer with us, as
she has met with her friend from Hamburg, with whom she
had made an appointment.

"We lunched with her, at Mendelssohn's, where I also met
Dr. Emanuel Geibel, whom I had previously seen in Berlin.
One must like the girl from the very bottom of one's heart.
She has such a noble and beautiful nature. And yet, she
does not feel happy. I am convinced that she would gladly
exchange all her triumphs, for simple homely happiness. She
sees that, in Mendelssohn's house, where the wife and
children make his happiness complete." *

The "friend from Hamburg," by whose arrival Herr
Brockhaus's arrangements were thus unfortunately interrupted, was Madame Arnemann. Mdlle. Lind had stayed in
this lady's house at Nienstädten, near Altona, in the autumn
of 1845; and had promised to travel with her as far as
Carlsbad, on her way to Vienna. She had now come to
Leipzig, for the purpose of putting her long-cherished
design into execution ; and the visit to the Brockhaus
family was necessarily shortened, in conformity with the
earlier arrangement.

But this change of plan did not prevent the welcome visitor
from thoroughly enjoying her brief stay in Leipzig, or from
happy intercourse with her most valued friends there.
Among other incidents connected with this memorable visit,
the domestic happiness of Mendelssohn, whose devotion to
his wife and family were no less remarkable than his artistic

* '*Aus den Tagebüchern von Heinrich Brockhaus,*' Band ii. s. 100.
(Leipzig, 1884.) See p. 326, *et seq.*

talent, made a deep impression upon her. She had been equally impressed, at Berlin, by the charming pictures of home life daily presented to her in the family circle at Professor Wichmann's. Of such a life her own early experience had taught her nothing. As a child, at home, she had never been truly understood; and, in consequence of this, had suffered cruelly from want of sympathy and domestic happiness. Who can wonder, then, at the emotion she felt, when witnessing, in other families, the peaceful effect of social relations to which her own childhood had been an utter stranger? She alludes to this, in touching terms, in a letter, written about this time, to Madame Wichmann:—

Leipzig, April (8?*), 1846.

"DEARLY BELOVED AMALIA,—

"God bless you all, and give you, some day, tenfold the good that you have given me! For, Amalia, I have felt, for the first time in my life, as if I had tasted the blessedness of home.

"What can I say more? All the rest, you can imagine for yourself. This only will I confide to you, that, if I had not before me the prospect of soon seeing you again, it would go very sadly indeed with me; for my heart now clings to you so that nothing else can satisfy me.

"I am staying with the Brockhauses, and they are all so kind and friendly.

"Yours,

"JENNY."†

In the meanwhile, the necessary arrangements for the forthcoming concert had been satisfactorily completed, under the superintendence of Mendelssohn himself. The performance was fixed for Sunday, the 12th of April; and, as there was to be no orchestra, Mendelssohn had undertaken to

---

* The day of the month is not given; but, the letter must have been written on the 8th or 9th of April, since Mdlle. Lind left Herr Brockhaus's house on the morning of the last-named day.

† From the Wichmann collection.

"preside at the pianoforte," as well as to play at least one
solo. His friend, Herr Ferdinand David, had also promised
to contribute a solo on the violin ; and, when these details
had been finally decided upon, the following programme was
issued to the public :—

Sonntag, den 12 April, 1846,

im Saale des Gewandhauses.

Concert

von Fräulein

JENNY LIND.

___

ERSTER THEIL.

Sonate von L. v. Beethoven, G dur, vorgetragen von den Herren G. M. D.
   Felix Mendelssohn Bartholdy und C. M. David.
Arie aus *Niobe*, von Pacini, gesungen von Fräulein Lind.
Solo, für die Violine, componirt und vorgetragen von Herrn C. M. David.
*Arie** aus *Don Juan*, von Mozart, gesungen von Fräulein Lind.

ZWEITER THEIL.

Sonate in Cis moll,† von Beethoven, vorgetragen von Herrn Dr.
   Mendelssohn.
Cavatine aus *Euryanthe* (Glöcklein im Thale), und *Cavatine* aus dem
   Freischütz ('Und ob die Wolke sie verhülle') von C. M. von Weber,
   gesungen von Fräulein Lind.
Lied ohne Worte, componirt und vorgetragen von Herrn Dr. Mendelssohn.
Lieder, gesungen von Fräulein Lind.

No sooner did this announcement make its appearance
in the *Leipziger Tageblatt*, than the usual rush for tickets
began, with a vigorous onslaught which exhausted the
supply in the course of a few hours. The most ardent
music-lovers in the town lost not a moment in their endeavours to secure the best places. It soon became evident
that, had the room been even much larger than it really
was, it could easily have been filled, over and over again.

* 'Ueber alles bleibst du theuer.' ('Non mi dir.')
† Now popularly known as "The Moonlight Sonata"—a name which
Beethoven never applied to it, and never heard.

And it cannot be said that the excitement was extravagant,
or unnatural; for it would be difficult to recall to memory
a concert, within the experience of the oldest musical
critic now living, in which three such artists * united their
forces for the production of so attractive a programme—
an entertainment in which there was not one single
weak point, one single piece falling short of the highest
level that Art, in the department of "chamber music," could
reach.

Madame Clara Schumann (*née* Wieck), who was then
residing in Dresden, came to Leipzig in the course of the
afternoon, with the intention of taking a seat among the
audience.   On arriving at the railway-station, after her four
hours' journey, she drove at once to Mendelssohn's house,
for the purpose of paying him a visit.   She found him a
little anxious about his share in the duties of the evening,
which was exceedingly onerous, since, beside his own solos,
he had accepted the responsibility of accompanying every
piece in the programme.   Thus circumstanced, he begged
Madame Schumann to add to the interest of the performance
by taking part in it herself.   She was tired with her journey;
quite unprepared to play, and not even provided with a
suitable toilette for the evening; but she unhesitatingly
consented; and Mendelssohn well knew that she would
prove more than equal to the occasion, when the moment
for the fulfilment of her promise arrived.

Long before the appointed time, the room was crowded,
to its remotest corner.   The *beneficiaire* sang—as she always
did, when supported by Mendelssohn's matchless accompaniment—her very best.   Mendelssohn played Beethoven's

---

* Though almost unheard in England, Herr Ferdinand David (for whom
Mendelssohn had, not long before, composed his Violin Concerto in E)
enjoyed, on the Continent, a reputation scarcely inferior to that of Spohr,
and Ernst, in Germany, or Baillot, in Paris.

' Sonata in C♯ minor,' as no one but he could play it ; and, when the point in the programme was reached, at which he was expected to play his own ' *Lieder ohne Worte*,' he came down to the place in which Madame Schumann was seated among the audience, and led her, in her travelling dress, to the piano. She was received with an ovation ; and played two of the ' *Leider* '—Nos. I. and IV.* in the Sixth Book—and a 'scherzo' of her own, with an effect which could scarcely have been surpassed. The performance concluded, in accordance with the previous announcement, with a selection of songs, by Mdlle. Lind, accompanied by Mendelssohn, in his own inimitable manner ; and the audience departed in raptures.

Could those present have looked forward less than two short years into the future, how different would have been their feelings! Who could have believed that, even then, over the world-famous concert-room, which had witnessed so many of the most striking artistic triumphs of the period, the Angel of Death was hovering—that his dusky wing was, at that very moment, overshadowing the greatest musical genius of the age—that, in less than one year and seven months after that delightful evening, Felix Mendelssohn Bartholdy himself was destined to be the recipient of his fatal message.

Yet, so it was.

We little thought that the concert which had given us such unclouded pleasure was fated to be the last but one at which Mendelssohn would play, in public, at the Gewandhaus ; or that the concluding symphony of Mdlle. Lind's last song would represent (with one exception) his last touch upon the

---

* No. IV. is now commonly called, the *Spinnlied*; and, more vulgarly known by the ridiculous title of "The Bee's Wedding"—another instance of the application of sentimental names, unsanctioned by, and unknown to, the composer.

pianoforte, in the concert-room which, through his influence, had become so justly celebrated.*

But, we must not anticipate the day of sadness. No one foresaw it, then ; and, though the audience at the Gewandhaus was so soon to bid its last farewell to the beloved composer who had so long represented its heart and soul, Mdlle. Lind enjoyed the privilege of his friendship for a full year and a half after this eventful evening.†

* Mendelssohn's *last* performance in the Gewandhaus took place on the 19th of July, 1846, when he played the pianoforte part of Beethoven's "Kreutzer Sonata" (Op. 47) with Ferdinand David.

† Mendelssohn died on the 4th of November, 1847. The circumstances above related, and still remembered by many, are corroborated by entries made in the writer's diary, at the time.

CHAPTER II.

THE DÉBUT AT VIENNA.

In accordance with the arrangement previously made with Madame Arnemann, Mdlle. Lind left Leipzig, on the 13th of April—the day after the concert—and proceeded, first, to Carlsbad, where she remained until the 16th. She then took leave of her friend, and, accompanied by Mdlle. Louise Johansson, continued her journey to Prague; remained there for one night, and started, the next morning, for Vienna, where she arrived on Saturday, April the 18th.

In the meantime, accommodation had been prepared for her, at the house of Dr. Vivanot, a physician of some repute, who occupied a conveniently-situated residence in one of the principal streets of Vienna—Am Graben.

The place was a convenient one, in every respect; and here she remained *en pension*, until the termination of her engagement for the season, perfectly satisfied with the arrangements made for her personal comfort, though, in its social aspect, her position in Vienna was far more trying than that which had awaited her on her first visit to Berlin in the autumn of 1844. For, the influence of Meyerbeer was all-powerful in the Prussian capital; and the introductions with which he was able to furnish her had undoubtedly done much towards ensuring her a favourable reception, both at Court, and in the best circles of Berlin society, before she had had time to secure it for herself, either by her talent, or by the charm of her personal character—while, in Vienna, she knew no one,

and, except for the *prestige* of her artistic reputation, had no
claim whatever upon the good-will of the people among
whom she had come to reside.   Her friends in the North of
Germany felt this strongly; and did their best to overcome
the difficulty.   Madame Birch-Pfeiffer wrote a letter to a
friend in Vienna, which gives so true a delineation of her
young friend's character that we need no apology for introducing it *in extenso*:—

"On Sunday," she says, "our Angel fled from us; and
to-day only have I brought myself to introduce her to you by
this letter.

"Jenny Lind, indeed, needs no introduction to a lady so
truly artistic as yourself; and I only venture to give you a
few slight indications of her northern proclivities, which your
own fine tact would easily have discovered without them.

"She is reserved, and self-contained; pure, through and
through, and sensitive to the last degree; so strangely tender,
that she is easily wounded, and thereupon becomes silent,
and serious, when no reason for it is apparent—and I have
long studied this marvellous character, and penetrated its profoundest depths.

"A word will often quickly shut her up in herself; and I
tell you this, in order that you may see how you stand with
her.   When she suddenly becomes dumb to you, you may be
certain that something has wounded her delicate sensibility.
She is a true *Mimosa*, that closes itself at the lightest touch.
Do not think, from this, that she is intolerable.   She is, by
nature, a truly lovable creature.   True, in everything that she
does.   Do not suffer yourself to be misled, by her persistent
silence, into thinking that she is *sans esprit*.   She speaks
little, and thinks deeply.   She is full of perception, and the
finest tact—a mixture of devotion, and energy, such as you
have probably never before met with.

"Free, herself, from the slightest trace of coquetry, she
regards all coquetry with horror.   In short, she stands alone,
of her kind, from head to foot.

"I adjure you, tell all your *coterie* that Jenny must be
brilliantly received; otherwise, she will never forgive me for
having persuaded her to perform in so large a theatre, for she
fears that her voice will not fill it.   She stands alone in
modesty, as in everything else.

"If you invite her to your house, and she does not sing,
when first you ask her, let it pass. Do not suffer any one to
press her; otherwise, it is possible that she may not come
again. This has often happened with her, here. She is
passionately fond of dancing; and cares but very little for
the table. Nothing is more hateful to her than sitting long
at dinner.

"Here you have a little confidential description of her
person. It is well that you should be forewarned; for, every
genius has her own peculiarities.

"If you wish to make her really happy, invite her companion, Louise Johansson, to accompany her to your parties.
She is an excellent girl, and Jenny looks upon her as a
sister.

"Since she has left me, I have felt as if in my grave. I
can listen to no singing now. You will soon understand
why."

No one who really knew Mdlle. Lind will fail to recognise
the fidelity of this charming portrait; so delicately drawn;
so truthfully delineated; so conscientiously describing, in
every well-weighed word, the minutest traits of a character
which needed so liberal a share of philosophical discernment
for its successful analysis, and so deep an insight into the
poetry of the human heart for its full and loving appreciation.
Such a portrait could only have been drawn by one who had
deeply and worthily studied the moving spirit by which a
character so lovely had been dominated, through life; and the
truth of the picture is proved by the ready assent accorded to
it by all who had the privilege of knowing the original.
That it helped to prepare the way for the cordial reception
that awaited Mdlle. Lind in Vienna we cannot doubt; and, in
order that nothing might be left undone which could conduce
to that most desirable end, Mendelssohn, on his part, fore-
seeing that she might possibly need the assistance of an
experienced adviser, should any unfortunate misunderstand-
ing occur in her dealings with the strangers by whom she was
surrounded, endeavoured to meet the difficulty, by providing

her, when she left Leipzig, with the following letter to his friend, Herr Franz Hauser : *—

"Leipzig, April 12, 1846.

DEAR FRIEND,

"These lines will reach you, through my friend, Jenny Lind; and I beg you, as soon as you receive them, to call upon her, and to be as friendly and as useful to her as you possibly can during the time of her residence in Vienna. For, I take it for granted that it will be with you, as with me; and that you will never be able to look upon her as a stranger, but as one of ourselves—a member of that invisible Church,† concerning which you write to me sometimes. She pulls at the same rope with all of us who are really in earnest about that; thinks about it; strives for it; and, if all goes well with her in the world, it is as pleasant to me as if it went well with me : for it helps me, and all of us, so well on our road. And to you, as a singer, it must be especially delightful to meet, at last, with the union of such splendid talents, with such profound study, and such heartfelt enthusiasm. But I will say no more. I only ask you to be friendly, and helpful to her, whenever, and wherever you can ; and to let her depend upon you ; and, when she sings for the first time, write to me, on the same day, and tell me how it all went off.

"You are angry with me, I know, about the barbarous letter that I sent to you with the *Antigone;* but you must not be cross, for it was not so bad as you thought. And, send me these lines that I ask of you ; for it is from you that I particularly wish to hear about it.

"For ever and ever yours,

"FELIX MENDELSSOHN BARTHOLDY."‡

---

* Franz Hauser was born on the 12th of January, 1794; and was first known in Germany as a bass singer of exceptional talent. After having taught singing, in Vienna, for many years, with great success, he was appointed Director of the Conservatorium in Munich, and held this important post from the year 1846 to 1864.

† It must be remembered that Mendelssohn looked upon the worship of Art as a veritable religion ; and endeavoured to impress that view upon all who were in familiar intercourse with him.

‡ Translated from the original autograph, forming part of the valuable collection of letters in the possession of Herr Joseph Hauser, by whose kind permission we are enabled to present our readers with numerous extracts which, in future, will be acknowledged as "From the Hauser letters."

By a strange fatality Herr Hauser's kind offices were needed, before Mdlle. Lind had even made her first appearance on the stage.

The Theater an der Wien, at which she was engaged to sing for Herr Franz Pokorny, stood very nearly on the site of an older theatre, rich in historical memorials of a very brilliant period. Towards the close of the last century the original building was licensed, by Prince Starhemberg, to a restless manager and hot-headed Freemason, named Emmanuel Schickaneder, who, finding himself in difficulties, thought to repair his fortunes by producing an Opera, based upon a masonic *libretto*, and enriched with music by Mozart, who himself was a Freemason also. Mozart, who was generosity incarnate, yielded to the entreaties of his unhappy 'brother mason,' and produced for him, as an act of pure charity, his last great dramatic inspiration, *Die Zauberflöte*, imposing, as Schickaneder could not pay for it, the condition that the score should not be allowed to pass out of his hands. Schickaneder accepted the gift; but broke the conditions, by supplying, to every provincial manager who was able to pay him for it, a copy of the score. Mozart died, shortly afterwards, in cruel poverty. He never received anything for his latest masterpiece; while the success of *Die Zauberflöte* so enriched Schickaneder that, out of his ill-gained profits, he was able to build the present "Theater an der Wien," which, at the time of which we are now treating,* was the largest and handsomest theatre in Vienna.

So large did it seem to the timid *débutante*—still timid, and distrustful as ever of her own powers, in spite of her triumphs at Berlin—that, when she entered it for the first time, in order to take her part in the rehearsal of *Norma*, she was appalled at the sight of its vast circumference; felt con-

---

* That is to say, before the splendid new Opera-House was built.

vinced that her voice would prove insufficient to fill it ; and, under the influence of an utterly causeless terror, refused even to make the attempt.

Herr Pokorny was in despair. He could not understand the lady's fears ; nor could she comprehend his remonstrances. Fortunately, he remembered having seen her in company with Herr Hauser, to whom he sent a hurried message, entreating him to come to the rescue, without the loss of a moment. By great good fortune, the messenger found Herr Hauser at home. He instantly responded to the appeal ; and reached the theatre while Mdlle. Lind was still standing on the stage, in an agony of nervousness and indecision. As it was impossible to discuss the question, in presence of the assembled artists, he led her to the "green-room," where he set the case so clearly before her, made her so plainly see that her fears would be misunderstood, and her position as an artist ruined, that the Viennese would treat the matter as a joke, and hold Herr Pokorny responsible for having befooled them, spoke, in short, so sensibly and so earnestly, that, with a great effort, she overcame her terror, returned to the stage, where Herr Pokorny was anxiously awaiting her decision, and at once took her part in the rehearsal, with every prospect of a successful *début* on the following evening.

How right Herr Hauser was in his judgment she never forgot ; nor did Herr Pokorny ever forget the kindness of his intervention. During the whole remaining portion of the season, he reserved a box for Herr Hauser, at every performance, even when the prices were at their highest, and applicants were sent away, in crowds, for want of room. And this was no small thing ; for never, within the memory of the Viennese, had such crowds assembled at the theatre, or such prices been demanded for admission.

The paralysing fear with regard to the size of the house proved, we need scarcely say, entirely illusory. Mdlle.

Lind's voice was sonorous enough to have filled the largest
theatre in Europe ; and the " Theater an der Wien," spacious
as it was, was far from being that.　The scene, on the
evening of the *début*—Wednesday, the 22nd of April, 1846—
was simply a *replica* of that which had taken place, in Berlin,
on the 9th of November, in the previous year.　The same
Opera—*Norma*—was wisely chosen as the work best calculated to produce a favourable effect upon the general public ;
and the result proved all that could possibly be desired, notwithstanding the patent fact that a very unfair share of
responsibility was thrown upon the *débutante*.　For, except
by Herr Staudigl, the representative of Oroveso, who was a
host in himself, and Demoiselle Henriette Treffz,* who sang
the part of Adalgisa very charmingly, she was by no
means worthily supported.　Concerning the tenor, who took
the part of Pollio—called " Sever," in the German version—
the *Wiener Musik-Zeitung* could find nothing better to
say, than that " he sang no worse than usual."　The chorus
sang, not only without expression, but incorrectly ; and the
orchestra fulfilled its functions very inefficiently indeed.　At
any other time such faults as these would have been very
heavily visited indeed upon the management of an Opera-
House of such high repute as the Theater an der Wien ; but,
in presence of Mdlle. Lind, all collateral shortcomings were
not only forgiven, but forgotten—if even noticed at all ; and
the success of the performance could scarcely have been
exceeded.

After having entered so largely into detail, in our description of the performances at Berlin, it is unnecessary that we
should supplement Herr Rellstab's exhaustive critiques, by
quoting, at length, those that appeared in the Vienna newspapers ; we shall, therefore, content ourselves with saying that

---

* This lady, not long afterwards, became well known, in London as a
concert-singer, under the name of Jetty Treffz.

Herr August Schmidt, the editor of the *Wiener Allgemeine Musik-Zeitung*—a journal by no means enthusiastically devoted to Mdlle. Lind's interests—after saying, in one part of his paper—

" For the initiated in music—those who listen, not with the ear only, but with the soul, and the spirit—the appearance of Jenny Lind is an event altogether exceptional ; such as has never before been witnessed, and will probably never be repeated," *

sums up his critique of *Norma*, with the words :—

" The appearance of Fräulein Lind is of the deepest interest, in all its aspects ; and her achievements in Art deserve, in the highest degree, the universal acknowledgment that they have received. She is the perfect picture of noblest womanhood ; and has, through her artistic aims, and the high perfection of her artistic cultivation, united to her great and many-sided talents, already won the sympathy of the entire public, on her first appearance, in a way in which few other singers have won it before her. I count the moments that passed at her *début*, among the most enjoyable artistic pleasures that I have ever yet experienced ; and eagerly look forward to her forthcoming performances." †

* *Wiener Allgemeine Musik-Zeitung*, April 19, 1846, p. 179.
† *Ibid.* April 25, 1846, p. 198.

CHAPTER III.

CORRESPONDENCE WITH MENDELSSOHN.

FOR her second appearance, on Friday, the 24th of April, Mdlle. Lind again selected *Norma*, the reception of which was, if possible, still more enthusiastic than that with which it had been greeted on the evening of the *début*. The Viennese were delighted with the new reading of the part, so full of passion and true womanly feeling, and so power-fully dramatic in all its varied shades of expression. Even the recollections of former triumphs—such as those of Mesdames Pasta, and Fodor, and Malibran—were cited by old and experienced critics as telling rather in her favour than otherwise.

It is true, there was a strong party against her. Three rival *prime donne*—Mesdames Stoeckel-Heinefetter and Has-selt-Barth and Fräulein Anna Zerr—though bitterly jealous of each other's triumphs at the "Kärntnerthor Theater," * united their forces, in opposition to the rising star, and formed what a certain section of the press called a Kärntner clique for the purpose of preventing her from singing in Vienna.

In allusion to this opposition, the well-known poet Grillparzer, wrote the following clever epigram :—

Der Hund bellt an den Mond ;
Der leuchtet wie gewohnt,
Giebt sich durch Strahlen kund,
Uhr bleibt—der holde Mond,
Sowie der Hund—ein Hund.

* A famous Opera-House, known also as the "Hofoperntheater."

But Mdlle. Lind triumphed over everything: over present rivalry; over inefficient support, in the general *ensemble* of the works in which she appeared; and—a harder task still—over the shades of the great *virtuose* who had preceded her. In spite of these adverse influences, she created a profound impression, on Wednesday, the 29th of April, in Bellini's *La Sonnambula*, by her inimitable union of the purest vocal method, with acting so touching, that the coldest heart could not witness it unmoved. It was this combined effect of legitimate vocalization and dramatic sensitiveness that alone could explain the secret charm to which none who heard her in the part of Amina ever failed to yield. The Viennese understood it at once; and sympathised with it, as unreservedly as they had sympathised with, and thoroughly comprehended, the new reading of *Norma.* No sooner had they heard and seen, than they rose, one and all, to a pitch of enthusiasm, in no degree inferior to that which had been manifested, night after night, at the Royal Opera-House in Berlin. She herself was more than satisfied with the reception she met with; and, on the day after her first appearance in *Norma,* wrote the following account of it to Madame Birch-Pfeiffer:—

"Wien, 23 April, 1846.

" DEAR FRIEND,

"It is over, at last—THANK GOD! and I hasten, good Mother, to describe it to you, though I know that the kind-hearted Director, Pokorny, has written all about it to you to-day.

"Well, then! Yesterday was the all-important day on which I appeared here in *Norma;* and the good God did not desert me, though I deserved it, for my unreasonable nervousness.

"Do not be angry with me, I beg you! I can do nothing with regard to that, and I myself suffer enough for it. The three days beforehand were dreadful. The idea of turning back was ever in my mind; and I should have done it, if it would not have given offence to so many people.

" But, now, we shall be jolly here, for a little while, and sing nine times; and then we can go on still farther!

" But, this Public! At the close, I was called back sixteen times, and twelve or fourteen before that. Just count that up! And this reception! I was quite astounded!

" The *salle* is considerably smaller than that in Berlin—Ah! but I shall always love my Berlin theatre, and my Berliners, immensely; they have grown into my heart! Neither the Viennese, nor any others, can weaken this impression

" How are you all? A raging headache prevents me from writing more. I have not yet been calmed down since yesterday.

" Your truly loving

" JENNY." *

It is evident that this description of the excitement of the Viennese, and the countless calls before the curtain, is not written in sportive exaggeration; for, on the same day, Mdlle. Lind wrote a similar account of the circumstances to Mendelssohn, from whom, a few days later, she received the following reply :—

" Leipzig, May 7, 1846.

" MY DEAR FRÄULEIN,

" You are indeed a good, and excellent, and very kind Fräulein Lind. That is what I wanted to say to you (and I have said it often enough, in thought), after receiving your first letter from Vienna, written so soon after your opening performance.

" That you wrote to me on the very next day; that you knew there was no one to whom it would give greater pleasure than to myself; and, that you found time for it, and let nothing hinder you, or hold you back—all this was too good and kind of you!

" Your description of the first evening, and of the twenty-five times you were called before the curtain, &c., &c., re-minded me of an old letter written to me by my sister, when I was in London, a long time ago: and I looked for the old letter until I found it.

" It was the first time that I had left the shelter of the parental roof, or had produced anything in public; and it

---

* From Frau von Hillern's collection.

had gone well, and a stone had been lifted from my heart; and I had written an account of it all to her. And, there-upon, she answered me thus:—

"There was nothing new to her, she said, in all that, for she had known it all, quite certainly, beforehand; she could not, therefore, very clearly explain to herself why, in spite of this, it had been so very pleasant to her to hear it all con-firmed—but it was very pleasant, nevertheless.*

"It was precisely so with me, when I received your letter. And then, you write so well! In fact, when I get a letter like that from you, it is just exactly as if I saw you, or heard you speak. I can see the expression of your face, at every word that stands written before me; and I understand all that took place on the first *Norma* evening at Vienna, almost as well as if I had been there.

"There came also a very pretty description from Hauser; a happier letter than I ever before received from him. And in this way you give me so much, and such great pleasure, even in a secondary form, through the soul of my friends.

"But, tell me, now; how comes it that half the Berlin Opera is so suddenly in Vienna, the Kapellmeister included? Hauser wrote to tell me that your Viennese associates in *Norma* were by no means excellent;† so, Bötticher‡ and the others could, after all, give the Viennese something worth hearing—if only Taubert beat time to it!

"I really feel, however, more pleasure in the enthusiasm of the Viennese, and the twenty-five calls before the curtain, than these few lines will perhaps express to you. It is great fun for me, too—not because of what people call triumph, or success, or anything of that kind, but, because of the succes-sion of pleasant days and evenings that it expresses, and the numbers of delighted and friendly faces with which you are surrounded. You must tell me all about this, very particu-larly; or rather, I must worm it out of you.

---

* The letter here spoken of is not included in the collection printed, by Herr S. Hensel, in 'Die Familie Mendelssohn;' which, however, contains one, of as nearly as possible, the same period, addressed, by Mendelssohn's sister, Fanny, to Herr Klingemann, and dated, "Berlin, June 4, 1829," in which she writes exactly in the strain here indicated, declaring that, with reference to his successes, she has "an almost silly belief in pre-destination." (See 'Die Familie Mendelssohn,' Berlin, 1879.)

† See page 384.

‡ The principal bass at Berlin.

" You are, undoubtedly, quite right in what you say about
Vienna, in your second letter. Where, then, is there more
than a little nucleus that feels anything sincerely, or honestly
rejoices about *anything at all ?*

" How pleased I am that you like Hauser! He is one who
has crept very much into my heart; and for whom I could,
at no time, or for any reason, feel diminished affection. And,
how much good has he not done to me !

"And now, let me send you a thousand thanks for what
you have written to me about *Antigone.* Yes ; I should like
to do that over again. But, out of this, I must weave the
material for a new letter, and a consultation with Madame
Birch-Pfeiffer—not, indeed, about *Antigone* itself, but about
something else of the same kind.

" But, my paper has come to an end. We are all well,
here, and think of you every day. I shall write once more,
before long, to Vienna ; and then, please God, we shall see
each other again, on the Rhine, and make a little music together, and talk to each other a little, and I think I shall
enjoy myself a little over it ! *Au revoir.**

> " Your friend,
>
> " FELIX MENDELSSOHN BARTHOLDY." †

The allusion to Madame Birch-Pfeiffer, in the above letter,
is connected with an episode of some importance in Mendelssohn's Art-life, concerning the details of which the public has
never been very fully informed.

It will be remembered that it was under the superintendence of this lady that Mdlle. Lind resumed those studies in
the German language which had been interrupted, at Dresden,
by her recall to Stockholm, for the coronation of King Oscar I. ‡

---

* These remarks refer to the " Lower Rhine Festival " which was to be
held on the 31st of May, and two following days, at Aix-la-Chapelle.
Mdlle. Lind had been engaged as the principal soprano ; and Mendelssohn,
who had accepted the office of conductor, had promised to act as her
escort, during her journey down the Rhine.

† This and other letters inserted in this work, addressed by Mendelssohn to Mdlle. Lind, are translated from the originals in the possession of
Mr. Goldschmidt, and now published for the first time.

‡ *Vide* pp. 220–221.

While prosecuting this course of study, she had met with frequent opportunities of observing, and appreciating at their true value, Madame Birch-Pfeiffer's literary talent and thorough acquaintance with what is known, in dramatic circles, as "the business of the stage." And this experience led to negotiations, which, though they afterwards broke down completely, seemed, at the time, to promise very important results indeed.

During their conversations, Mdlle. Lind and Mendelssohn had frequently discussed the possibility of a union of forces, which, had it not been interrupted by his early death, would probably have exerted a marked effect upon the future of the musical drama. The scheme was, the production of a serious Opera, for which he should compose the music, with special reference to the character and scope of her vocal and dramatic talent. The one great difficulty with which the project was threatened, was that of procuring a really good *libretto* suitable for the purpose. On this point, Mendelssohn was well-known to be severely *exigeant*. But both he and Mdlle. Lind thought that they had found, in Madame Birch-Pfeiffer, a colleague on whom they could thoroughly depend; and, as we shall see, from the following letter—written a week later than that just quoted—Mendelssohn was already in active correspondence with the lady upon this engrossing topic; and, while his friend was gathering new laurels in Vienna, was endeavouring to open a still wider field for the exercise of her talents in the future.

"Leipzig, May 15, 1846.

" MY DEAR FRAULEIN,

"If I am not mistaken, my last letter to you must have seemed very stupid—with absolutely nothing in it.* Moreover, I fear it will not be very different with the present one; and that the two together will mean no more than just a hearty greeting.

* See Mendelssohn's letter to Herr Hauser, p. 403.

"You must have been suffering severely from home-sickness! I can see that, plainly enough, from your last letter; and Hauser also wrote something to me about it. But, I hope this has long since passed away; and, that you are again fresh and cheerful, and make music, and gladden the hearts of the people by means of the many noble gifts with which God has endowed you, and which you yourself have now made your own.

"Will you not, then, sing 'Donna Anna' at Vienna? I have long been looking for news of it; but it has never come.

"How happy you have again made my dear good Hauser! Such a delightful letter came from him, after you had been to his house for the second time. And, about this, I am always thinking—what if, of all the true joy that you shed around you, the brightest rays could fall back upon yourself, and could as thoroughly warm and quicken you as you warm and quicken others! But this is not to be. And, when we meet again, I will show you a passage from Goethe, in which it stands written why it is not to be. Yet, how I wish it could be!

"You must know, my dear Fräulein, that I have now again good hope of coming to a satisfactory arrangement with Madame Birch-Pfeiffer. We have lately exchanged several letters; and, as it seems to me, she has had a very lucky find, and, out of it, will work up a subject that speaks to me strongly, and unites in itself a great deal of that which you like so much in *Antigone*. And yet it is not antique. However, I will not write to you about it, but describe it, *vivâ voce*, when we meet again. We have quite given up the subject of the *Peasant War*; and I have no other wish than, (1) that the whole idea may please you; (2) that Madame Birch-Pfeiffer may put it together dramatically, and truthfully; and, (3) that I may write really good music for it. Apart from these little matters, all is in order.

"I write these stupid letters, because, for the last fortnight I have been kept at home by a very bad cold; and, still more, because I have been working very hard, and without intermission. To-morrow, or the day after to-morrow, the first part of my Oratorio * will be quite finished; and many pieces out of the second part are already finished also. This has given me immense pleasure during these last weeks. Some-

* *Elijah.*

times, in my room, I have jumped up to the ceiling, when it
seemed to promise so very well. (Indeed, I shall be but too
glad if it turns out only half as good as it now appears to me.)
But I am getting a little confused, through writing down,
during the last few weeks, the immense number of notes that
I previously had in my head, and working them backwards
and forwards upon the paper into a piece, though not quite in
the proper order, one after another. Would that the Opera
were already as far advanced as this! I would then play some
of it to you. But, what if it should not please you at all!—
Sometimes it seems to me as if it were an imperative duty to
compose an Opera for you, and to try how much I could accomplish in it—and it is, in fact, a duty. However, it does
not altogether depend upon me, and it will certainly not be
my fault, if only the thing be possible. If it were but possible! *Au revoir.*

> "Ever your friend,
>
> "FELIX MENDELSSOHN BARTHOLDY."

It is evident, from passages in this letter, that the difficulties
in the way of obtaining a satisfactory *libretto* for the projected Opera were very grave indeed. In fact, it is impossible
to read Madame Birch-Pfeiffer's letters to Mendelssohn *—
written in a hand sometimes almost illegible — without
arriving at the conclusion that, so far at least as co-operation with that lady was concerned, the cause was hopeless,
however sanguine Mendelssohn himself may have felt about
it. Madame Birch-Pfeiffer wrote, sometimes, while suffering
from painful headaches. Her letters contain allusions to
an endless variety of historical and other subjects, which
she passes in review, one after another, only to condemn them
as unsuitable. The *Bauernkrieg*—or "Peasant War"—and
Der Truchsess von Waldburg; Tieck's *Genofeva,* and another

---

* It is well known, through the medium of his biographers, that Dr. Felix
Mendelssohn's correspondence was systematically preserved by him, in a
series of volumes bound in green, which are now carefully preserved by
his children, through whose kindness we are enabled to present copious
extracts from them to our readers. In future cases, these extracts will be
acknowledged as taken " From the Green volumes."

Genofeva, by Hebbel; De la Motte Fouquet's *Kronenwächter;* and other like subjects, including a sentimental hint at *Consuelo,* are all treated in turn, and in turn dismissed. She was much disheartened, too, by a remark of Meyerbeer's to the effect that she had talent for the elaboration of a plot, but, that her verses were not suitable for musical treatment. But we shall have so much to say on this subject, in a future chapter, that it is needless to discuss its minute details here.

All this worried Mdlle. Lind, no less than Mendelssohn; though the letters she received from him, and from other friends at a distance, gave her great comfort, in her loneliness —for, lonely indeed she was, in the midst of her constantly-recurring triumphs. It was evident, that she was far less happy, in Vienna, than she had been in Berlin. Yet, though suffering from the home-sickness alluded to by Mendelssohn, and—through the painful mistrust of her own merits, concerning which we have so frequently had occasion to speak— oppressed, rather than elated, by the enthusiastic adoration which everywhere awaited her, she could not close her eyes to the fact that her visit to the Austrian capital had been successful beyond the wildest expectations of her most sanguine admirers. More than once, she described her new and brilliant triumphs to Madame Wichmann, in the unfamiliar German in which she still found it difficult to express her thoughts with clearness. The following letter, written nine days after her arrival in Vienna, gives a graphic picture of her then frame of mind:—

                                          " Vienna, 27 April, 1846.

" MEIN ÄLSKADE ! *

        " I have again been suffering from home-sickness; and, though I may well say that I am at home everywhere, I really feel quite homeless. Do you understand me, Amalia ? That is the way it is with me: it is so. Only, during the time that I lived with you, I had no such longings.

                    * " Beloved."

" Hitherto, all has gone here splendidly. I have appeared twice in *Norma;* and was called so many times before the curtain that I was quite exhausted. Bah! I do not like it. Everything should be done in moderation; otherwise it is not pleasing.

" How glad I should be, if Taubert were really to come here. I dare not build too much upon it; but it would be very pleasant.

" Thine,

" JENNY." *

And, again, nine days later :—

" Vienna, May 6, 1846.

" ÄLSKADE,

" I think of you, daily, and hourly; and it goes badly with me, since I parted from you, my beloved friends.

" I have been so home-sick, that I scarcely knew whether I should live or die; and so frightfully melancholy, and sad, that it is a long long time since I have felt anything like it. Do you understand me ? I never felt this anguish while I was with you.

" But, I am better, now; and the day before yesterday, Taubert came. Ah! This joyful suprise !—this reminiscence of the past existence!—all now comes so brightly before me!

" And, now, I must tell you a little about the Theatre, and things of that sort.

" Dearest, dearest lady !

" Do you know, I have been placed in the very worst, and the most unfavourable circumstances ; and yet, I have never had a greater triumph ! Just think of this !

" To begin with ; Herr Pokorny actually had the rashness to demand such frightful prices, that a single reserved seat cost eight gulden, and a box forty ! † So that, since the time of Catalani, such a thing has never been heard of; and the public were furious about it.

" Secondly ; with these high prices, Pokorny engaged, for the first ten performances, a tenor, at whom everyone

---

* From the Wichmann collection.

† Eight gulden = about sixteen shillings, in English money, and forty gulden, about four pounds. The usual prices were, thirty-six or forty-eight kreuzers, for a single seat; and five gulden for a box on the grand tier : that is to say, about one shilling and twopence ; one shilling and eight pence; and ten shillings.

laughed. Everything depended upon me; so I was made the sacrifice. And all this, I had to bear, and do penance for.

" In the third place; the whole Italian faction was opposed to me; * and was determined to hiss if there was the slightest thing that could be found fault with. Nevertheless, everything has gone well; and my success is only so much the greater.

" Taubert is sitting with me, now, and playing to me; and I persuade myself that I am with you, and live in quietness and peace, and am assured that you all know with what deep and true love I cling to you, and how impossible it would be for me ever to love you less."†

The last leaf of this letter, together with the signature, is missing; but enough has been preserved, to show the state of the writer's feeling, both with regard to the attitude of the public, and her own inner life.

Though it contains no allusion to the circumstance, this account is proved, by its date, to have been written exactly a week after the first performance of *La Sonnambula*. This was followed, on the 8th of May, by *Der Freischütz*; and, on the 15th, by *Die Ghibellinen in Pisa*. The first of these proved, as in Berlin, an immense success; the second was less warmly received—and, not without good reason. Few English readers, we think, will be prepared to hear that *Die Ghibellinen in Pisa* was neither more nor less than a German version of Meyerbeer's *Les Huguenots*, the music of which had been tortured into association—or the reverse — with another historical event, more closely in sympathy with religious and social conditions in Vienna at the time. Under the title of *Die Welfen und Ghibellinen*, this version had been brought out, with the same *libretto*, at the " Hoftheater," in 1844; and on this, its first introduction at Vienna, it had proved by no means a brilliant success. On the present

* See page 386.
† From the Wichmann collection.

occasion, moreover, neither the chorus, nor the orchestra, proved equal to the demand made upon them for the general effect, and neither Mdlle. Lind, Herr Tichatschek, nor Herr Staudigl, felt at home, in *rôles* dissevered from their logical connection with the story they were originally designed to illustrate. It was, really, very much to the credit of those three great artists, that they found it impossible to lend themselves to so barbarous a travestie, the comparative failure of which was a real gain to the cause of true Art. Mdlle. Lind never sang in it again, and the blame of its cold reception was certainly not visited upon her; for, on the 20th of May—the night fixed for her benefit—she received an ovation, accompanied by circumstances, which, even among the brilliant triumphs to which she was now so well accustomed, can only be described as altogether exceptional.

Of *Der Freischütz*, she writes, on the 18th of May, to Madame Birch-Pfeiffer's sister—whom she familiarly called "Tante":—

"Yesterday, *Der Freischütz* was given. Tichatschek sings beautifully in it; and it is the only Opera that has gone fairly well; for Taubert was good enough to conduct it himself, and the public was beside itself." *

For Mdlle. Lind's "benefit" *La Sonnambula* was again announced, as the Opera most likely to please the public, who had been delighted with it, on its first presentation, and flocked, in crowds, to hear it a second time. Every available seat in the house was filled with the *élite* of the Austrian capital. The noblest representatives of Art and Literature, the highest of the nobility, and the various members of the Imperial family, assembled, *en masse*, to do honour to the occasion. Each act of the Opera, each scene in which the *bénéficiaire* took part, was received with acclamation; and

* From Frau von Hillern's collection.

when the curtain fell, after the last *Finale,* and she was recalled before it, to receive the grateful acknowledgments of
the audience for the pleasure she had given them, while
flowers were falling in showers upon the stage, the Empress-
Mother dropped a wreath, with her own hand, at Mdlle.
Lind's feet.

Such a favour, involving so bold a departure from the
severity of Court etiquette, had never before been granted,
by a member of the Imperial family, to any artist of any
rank whatever, though Vienna had not been slow to acknowledge the claims of true genius, or to crown it with well-
earned laurels.

As at Berlin, the audience seemed bent upon obtaining a
spoken word of farewell; and, when silence had been
obtained, Mdlle. Lind came forward, to the foot-lights, and
said, in German: "You have well understood me. I thank
you, from my heart." * These few heartfelt words were
received with a shout of sympathetic recognition; and it
was only when that had subsided, that the audience,
quite overcome with excitement, consented at last to
disperse.

And, this was not all.

When, after the performance was over, the heroine of the
evening prepared to return to her temporary home, *Am
Graben,* the street, in front of the stage-door, was found to be
so crowded with worthy citizens, anxious to catch a glimpse
of her, that it was thought imprudent to make the attempt.
Hour after hour, she waited, in the hope that the watchers
would disperse. But, the crowd was as patient as she was.
The honest burghers, who had brought their wives and
daughters to see the singer, at least, if they could not hear
her, were determined not to be cheated of their hardly-

* "Sie haben mich recht verstanden. Ich danke Ihnen aus meinem
Herzen."

earned pleasure. They waited on, in perfect order, until the
day began to dawn; and then only did she think it safe
to step into the carriage, with Mdlle. Louise Johansson
by her side, and her man-servant in attendance, on the
"dicky," behind. Up to this time, there was no attempt at
disorder, though the greatest excitement prevailed; but,
before the carriage had had time to traverse the "Drei-
hufeisengasse," a band of enthusiastic young men unharnessed
the horses, and would have dragged the vehicle, with its
occupants, through the crowded streets to the door of Dr.
Vivanot's house, had they not been prevented from doing
so by a detachment of cavalry. Fortunately, the military
force arrived in time to prevent a serious disturbance;
but, even with this protection, the carriage was escorted
to the Graben by a crowd of excited spectators, who
insisted upon walking by its side; and, when Mdlle. Lind
reached her hand out of the lowered window, those who
were near enough rushed up, in the hope of respectfully
kissing it.

Unhappily, the excitement produced a very serious accident. The man-servant, Görgel, who, as we have said, was
seated behind the carriage, either fell, or was dragged from
his place, while the enthusiasm was at its highest, and so
severely crushed, that, even with the best medical assistance
that could be procured, he was unfit to travel for some considerable time, in consequence of which, the departure
from Vienna was seriously delayed, at a time when the
hindrance proved of the greatest possible inconvenience to
her.

She mentions the circumstance, though without entering
into the details—which she probably thought too closely
connected with her unbounded popularity to admit of nar-
ration by herself without appearance of conceit—in a letter
addressed to Madame Birch-Pfeiffer :—

"Wien, 23 May, 1846.

"DEAR GOOD FRIEND,

"I really do not know whether I am dead, or alive—so you must just ask the Director, Pokorny, who will, no doubt, tell you all about it.

"It gives me unspeakable regret, to think that you will perhaps come here to-day, just as I am going away!

"It is four o'clock on Saturday morning. Two hours ago, I came from Herr Pokorny; and, think of my horror! my poor Görgel has been almost crushed to death!* He was brought home in a frightful condition; and it does not look at all well with him. I have already postponed my journey four hours later. God grant that it may not turn out to be anything dangerous.

"Except for this, I have spent delightful days here. I have never met with such kind people as the Viennese in general. I can find no words in which to describe my stay in Vienna. Enough! Thank Heaven for helping me so much!

"I had much to fight against, here; and some day, I will tell you all about it. For the present, good bye, dear Mother. I am as I have ever been, and shall never change. May all good attend you. May the good God shield you, on your way, from all that is called grief, and sorrow! I shall always think of you with heart-felt love.

"From,

"JENNY." †

The style of this letter sufficiently shows the haste and excitement amidst which it was despatched; but no surrounding circumstances, however trying, could make the writer forget her affection for those whom she loved.

---

* *Zerquetscht!*
† From Frau von Hillern's collection.

CHAPTER IV.

CORRESPONDENCE WITH MENDELSSOHN (*suite*).

HERR HAUSER had not forgotten Mendelssohn's wish to be kept *au courant* with regard to the events which took place at the *Theater an der Wien.* He had written more than one account of the various occurrences we have described ; * and, on the morning after the "benefit," he wrote again, giving his friend a brief general description of the events of the evening, but leaving the details to be "wormed out" by Mendelssohn himself during the projected voyage down the Rhine.

To the first and second of these letters Mendelssohn sent the following reply, containing much that will interest the reader, even in certain passages which are not very closely connected with our present subject :—

"Leipzig, 11th May, 1846.

" MY DEAR FRIEND,

" I well knew how pleased you would be with Jenny Lind—I never for a moment doubted it ; and I was pleased indeed to find, from your letter, that I had not been mistaken, and that you had been so truly refreshed and encouraged by an artistic nature so splendid and so thoroughly genuine.

"Tell her that no day passes on which I do not rejoice anew that we are both living at the same epoch, and have learned to know each other, and are friends, and that her voice sounds so joyous, and that she is exactly what she is, and, with that, give her my heartiest greetings.

* See pp. 382–383, 388–389, &c.

"And accept my best thanks for your two good letters.
It says something when you—miserable correspondent that
you are!—awake out of your sleep, or when I—miserable
correspondent that I am!—awake out of mine. I should,
indeed, have thanked you long ago for your first letter, had
not my time been so wholly absorbed by music that writing
was impossible, for I sit, over both my ears, in my *Elijah*,
and if it only turns out half as good as I often think it will,
I shall be glad indeed! The first part will be quite finished
within the next few days, and a goodly portion of the second
part also. I like nothing more than to spend the whole day
in writing the notes down, and I often come so late to dine
that the children come to my room to fetch me, and drag me
out by main force; and people seem to have agreed together
just at this particular time to worry me with all sorts of
business letters and questions, and such like odious things,
so that, sometimes, I feel inclined to rush out of the house—
for, at such moments, one can neither converse to any
purpose by word of mouth, nor by letter. So now you know
what I mean, and how I am, and I only wish we could soon
see each other again.

"But, really, I must come some day to Vienna. I hear
so much said about it, right and left, and you all say such
kind things about my music, and give me such extraordinary
accounts of your performances, that you make my mouth
water. Perhaps I may bring my *Elijah*, while it is quite
new, about the winter-time—for, naturally, it cannot be
given at Aix-la-Chapelle, since it is barely half-finished; or,
perhaps I may wait until I have found a subject for my
Opera, and composed the music—if Jenny Lind is still there
—and this last would be the best. But, in some way or
other, I hope to see our imperial city; and I shall not then
make my first visit to the tower of St. Stephen's, or to the
Sperl, but to the Bärenmühle.* But perhaps you no longer
live there, in which case I shall come wherever you do live.

"As soon as our copyist is free again he shall transcribe
the score of the *Œdipus* for you, since you wish to have it,
sub rosâ, and I shall rejoice if it gives you any pleasure. In

---

* Literally, the "Bear's Mill." This was the name of the house in
which Herr Hauser had formerly lived; though Mendelssohn was right
in thinking that he had now removed to another part of the city. The
tower of St. Stephen's Cathedral, and the Sperl, have always been two of
the great attractions of Vienna.

any case, find a place for it in your library, and perhaps that, or the other piece, may prove suitable for your society. Is it still going on happily? Are you very much worried with stupidity? Have you not yet got over that? I have sworn, a thousand times, that I would never allow myself to be vexed about it again, and, a thousand times, I have broken my oath. But I have lately discovered, from some passages in Goethe's later works, that, to the end of his life, he never attained to that, and, since then, I have preferred not to swear any more, for it does not help one in the least. Sometimes I fancy that the Devil—the real Evil One—is nothing else than stupidity, though, truly, there are other degrees that one does not love.

"But it is getting late, and I must leave off. Do you know whether Jenny Lind is going to sing the part of Donna Anna in Vienna? I should like you to hear it. If she does not sing it, ask her to sing the last or the first *aria* to you in your room; and, when you greet her, from me, tell her that I will write to her this week, but she must forgive me if my letter is stupid, for, just now, I cannot do anything better.

"Let me soon hear from you again. What happened at the second performance of *Antigone?* And how are your sons, and your wife? Greet them all many times, and continue kind to

"Thine,
"FELIX." *

Herr Hauser's letter of May 21—the day after the benefit —was, in some sort, an answer to this. He renews the invitation to Vienna, though complaining that he is not living so comfortably as in his former house in the Bären-mühle. He says that he duly reported to Mdlle. Lind Mendelssohn's thankfulness that they were both born in the same epoch, and himself hopes that they will all long continue to give thanks to God for so artistic a nature—and not without grave reason, for there are some still living who thank God heartily that they were, to a certain extent, contemporary with Mendelssohn. And he speaks of the

* From the Hauser letters.

Antigone as having been sung to an audience in fullest sympathy with it "body and soul." It was not quite fair to call him a "miserable correspondent." He was scarcely a less voluminous letter-writer than his accuser, who certainly repeats the playful charge against himself; but the most interesting part of his correspondence is almost exclusively addressed to his friend, Herr Moritz Hauptmann—the then Cantor of the Thomas-Schule at Leipzig, and one of the most distinguished successors of the great John Sebastian Bach in that responsible office. A few days after hearing Mdlle. Lind for the first time, he thus described his impression in a letter addressed to the learned Cantor:—

"Vienna, 4 May, 1846.

"DEAREST FRIEND,

"Jenny Lind is singing here, and I will say no more than that I have caught the 'fever,' and that in its most violent form. I tell you she is a dear one to devour, and a dear, genial, honest, intellectual, lovely, &c., &c., &c., &c., &c., child she is! Such a voice I have never heard in all my life, nor have I ever met with so genial, so womanly, so musical a nature. Yet I can quite understand that she might easily be so put out in the concert-room that she might almost fail to be recognised as an extraordinary singer. On the stage she is the loveliest, purest, most charming creature that one can possibly see or hear. There is a charm in her voice that I have never known before, surpassing all that other singers have attained to, however powerful their acting on the stage. The Lind soars above all; but not through any single quality. It is the mastery wielded by this *anima candida* that works the magic."

And—let it be clearly understood!—this high eulogium is addressed to one of the most conscientious and least impressionable musicians then living, and proceeds from the pen of a critic noted for the deliberate caution with which he was accustomed to hedge round his published opinions on matters connected with Art. A vestige of this deliberation is discernible in the saving clause referring to possible weakness in the concert-room.

Mdlle. Lind had sung, with her usual success, at Herr Taubert's *matinée* in Streicher's Konzert-Salon on the 10th of May, contributing to the programme two of Taubert's songs, and a northern melody; and, on the 21st, she sang, for the last time that season, at a grand orchestral concert, given for an institution for the support of little children at the *Theater au der Wien* under the patronage of His Imperial Highness the Archduke Franz Carl.

On this last-named occasion—a *matinée*, beginning at half-past twelve in the afternoon—she sang the *aria* from *Il Don Giovanni* which Mendelssohn so much wished Herr Hauser to hear; a *Wiegenlied*, by Taubert, and the *Norwegisches Schäferlied*, and *Tanzlied aus Dalekarlien*, which had already produced so marked a sensation in Berlin and Leipzig, but had not previously been heard in Vienna.

"Jenny Lind's rendering of the *Lied*," said the *Wiener Musik Zeitung*, in criticising this performance, "is so tender and full of feeling, so simple and expressive, that the hearer is irresistibly impressed by it, and even the exotic element in these Swedish songs, which, performed by any other singer, would certainly sound strange to us, rejoices the very soul through her interpretation. She yielded to the wish of the enraptured audience in repeating the *Schäferlied*, and afterwards sang a little German song, which concluded the performance." *

And thus ended the first short season in Vienna. It had been, for all concerned, a tentative one, for no one could predicate, until trial had been made, the temper in which the Viennese might feel inclined to accept it. But the experiment had proved eminently successful, and there could be no possible doubt on the mind of any one as to the result

---

* *Wiener Allgemeine Musik-Zeitung*, May 26, 1846, p. 251.

of a similar enterprise undertaken during the ensuing winter. If the Viennese critics had seemed somewhat more cautious in their expressions than those of Berlin, the public had certainly been very much less so in their actions.

We can hardly give a clearer idea of the profound impression produced upon the literary world, in Vienna, than by closing our present chapter with the charming verses,* addressed to Mdlle. Lind, on the 2nd of May, by the poet, Grillparzer :—

> Sie nennen dich die Nachtigall
> Mit dürst'gem Bilderraube;
> So süß auch deiner Lieder Schall,
> Doch nenn' ich dich die Taube.
>
> Und bist du Rose, wie du's bist,
> Sey's denn die Alpenrose,
> Die, wo sich Schnee und Leben küßt,
> Ausglüht aus dunklem Moose.
>
> Du bist nicht Farbe, bist nicht Licht;
> Das Farbe erst verkündet,
> Das, wenn sein Weiß an Fremden bricht,
> Die bunte Pracht entzündet.
>
> Und freuten Sie des Beifalls Lohn
> Den Wundern deiner Kehle,
> Hier ist nicht Körper, ist nicht Ton,
> Ich höre deine Seele.

---

* The poem is here given on the authority of Grillparzer's autograph, found among Madame Goldschmidt's papers, after her death.　It was also printed, at Vienna, in a volume entitled, ‘ *Austria ; oder Oesterreichischer Universal Kalender für das gemeine Jahr* 1847.’　In this version, however, the last line but one differs from the MS., and reads thus :

> Hier ist nicht Körper, kaum auch Ton.

CHAPTER V.

As early as the month of January, 1846, the committee of the "Lower Rhine Musical Festival" * entered into negotiations with Mdlle. Lind in the hopes of obtaining her assistance at the twenty-eighth meeting of the Association, which was appointed to take place that year on the 31st of May and the 1st and 2nd of June, at Aix-la-Chapelle.

The Association was, and still is, one of the most important in Europe, and one of the oldest also. First suggested in 1811, and regularly organised in 1818, it had since that year given an annual festival at Whitsuntide, either at Cologne, Düsseldorf, or Aix-la-Chapelle, each town taking upon itself the responsibility of arrangement, in its regular turn. Up to the year 1833 two concerts had been given annually, on Whitsunday and Whitmonday; but Mendelssohn, who that year had been for the first time appointed conductor, proposed an additional concert on the Tuesday morning; and, as the programme was on that day miscellaneous, it was called "The Artists' Concert," under which title it has ever since been annually repeated. The festival was held that year at Düsseldorf. Mendelssohn again conducted, in 1835, at Cologne; and in 1836 he produced his *Saint Paul*, at the eighteenth festival at Düsseldorf. Since then he had conducted three times; and now he was engaged again for 1846.

* Das Niederrheinische Musikfest.

Many hindrances had arisen, and many changes been made with regard to the arrangements, chiefly in consequence of the difficulty of engaging an efficient company of artists to support Mdlle. Lind; for, unlike Herr Pokorny, the committee had determined that she should not be asked to sing with vocalists of inferior merit. But all was satisfactorily arranged before she left Berlin in April, and the programmes for the two first days decided upon in the following order :—

WHITSUNDAY, MAY 31, 1846.

1. Symphony in D major (No. 5) . . . . . *Mozart.*
2. Oratorio, *The Creation* . . . . *Haydn.*

> (Mdlle. Lind singing the music of Gabriel, in Parts I. and II.; and that of Eve, in Part III.)

WHITMONDAY, JUNE 1, 1846.

PART I.

1. Symphony in C minor (No. 5) . . *Beethoven.*
2. Motett, with Chorus, *Iste dies* . . *Cherubini.*

PART II.

Overture, *Oberon* . . . . . *C. M. von Weber.*
Oratorio, *Alexander's Feast* . . *Handel.*

TUESDAY, JUNE 2, 1846.

("The Artists' Concert.")

Miscellaneous Programme.

The first grand rehearsal was fixed for Wednesday, the 27th of May, and it had been arranged that Mdlle. Lind should leave Vienna on the 23rd, meet Mendelssohn at Frankfort on the evening of the 26th, and proceed with him down the Rhine to Aix-la-Chapelle on the 27th. But when the hour fixed for the departure from Vienna arrived it was found that the injured man-servant was quite unfit to travel.

Always thinking of others before caring for herself, Mdlle. Lind consulted with the doctors, and found that they demanded twelve hours longer in order that the sufferer might be comfortably bandaged and prepared, in so far as was possible under such circumstances, for the fatigues of the journey. To this delay she consented, in preference to leaving him friendless in Vienna. It was a great risk, and involved a terrible increase of fatigue for her at a time when she needed all her physical powers, as well as those of the mind, in preparation for the responsibilities devolving upon her at the festival. But she did not hesitate; though in consequence of the lateness of the hour at which she was obliged to start, it was nearly midnight on Tuesday, the 26th of May, before she arrived at Frankfort, where Mendelssohn had been awaiting her all the afternoon at the well-known hotel *Der Weisse Schwan*, in an agony of anxiety and suspense.

It was, indeed, a desperate venture; if, through any accidental hindrance, either of them had failed to appear at the rehearsal on Thursday the 28th, the success of the entire festival would have been endangered. But all fear of that was now at an end; and, leaving Görgel the wounded man-servant under careful medical attendance in Frankfort, the two friends, accompanied by Mdlle. Louise Johansson, started down the Rhine, on Wednesday the 27th, by the steamboat, and in due time reached Aix-la-Chapelle, where Mdlle. Lind, in accordance with the previous arrangement, became the guest of the Marquis and Marquise de Sassenay, and Mendelssohn occupied an apartment provided for him by the committee at the principal hotel—the *Grand Monarque*.

The festival was declared by all present to have been the best that had taken place within the memory of the public. The two principal songs in Haydn's oratorio, *On mighty pens* and *With Verdure Clad*, and the solo and chorus, *The marvellous Work*, were calculated to display Mdlle. Lind's powers, whether of voice, method, or poetical conception, to the greatest possible advantage—indeed, they became great favourites everywhere in later years. And yet it was undoubtedly in the third part of the Oratorio that her ideal conception of the work reached its culminating point. Would it have been a true conception, a natural, a logical one, if it had been otherwise? There can be no doubt that her version of it coincided with Haydn's, in every particular. Both saw that the whole interest of the work must of necessity concentrate itself upon the point at which the whole purpose of the Almighty Creator is consummated—the creation of man. Neither she, nor Haydn, had studied in the school of philosophy which teaches us than man's place in the great scheme of nature is that of a mere accidental atom. They believed that the material world was designed as a fitting residence for the being who had been created in the image of God. Penetrated with this idea, Haydn clothed the part of Gabriel with florid beauty perfectly in keeping with the most perfect ideal he was able to form of the angelic nature; and that of Eve, with the tender grace which he supposed to express the noblest conception of ideal woman. And it was in closest sympathy with this conception—whether true or false—that his careful interpreter sang the music assigned by the composer to " the mother of us all." Can we believe that either he, or she, was mistaken? That their joint ideal was a false one? that the "Third Part" of *The Creation* forms an anti-climax, which may be dispensed with, at will, without injury to the logical development of the whole? It is clearly possible to arrive at this extravagant conclusion; for, since the Lower Rhine Festival of 1846, this portion of the Oratorio has been omitted, over and over again, both in Germany, and in England, at performances conducted upon a very

grand and liberal scale.   But it is equally clear that this
opinion was irreconcilable with Mdlle. Lind's, for she
threw the whole poetry of her womanly nature into this
part of Eve, and emphasised its importance in a way which
attracted the attention of every deep thinker among the
audience.

Her part too in *Alexander's Feast* was a very important one, demanding the combined powers of *virtuosa* and
poetess.   But her greatest success, perhaps, was achieved
on the Tuesday morning, at the "Artists' Concert," in
Mendelssohn's *Auf Flügeln des Gesanges* and *Frühlingslied*,
in which, say the critics of the period, "she produced
an effect wholly unparalleled," insomuch that the meeting
of 1846 was afterwards known as the "*Jenny-Lind-
Fest.*"

Many dear friends, both of the conductor, and the singer,
assembled that year at Aix-la-Chapelle to do honour to the
occasion; and it was altogether a very happy time, as some
letters, fortunately preserved, sufficiently prove.

It will interest the reader to glance at three descriptions
of the same pleasant Whitsuntide holiday, drawn from three
different points of view—like P. de Champaigne's threefold
portrait of the great Cardinal de Richelieu in the National
Gallery—less gorgeously toned, indeed, and by no means
so grandly modelled; but certainly not less true to nature,
though only in playful miniature.

Among the sympathetic friends who flocked to Aix-la-
Chapelle, and certainly not among the least welcome of these,
were Professor Geijer of Upsala and his wife, who had not
breathed a word to any one of their intention to come.   Their
presence in the town was a surprise indeed; and Madame
Geijer thus describes the meeting, in a letter forwarded to us
by her son-in-law Count Hamilton, the Lord-Lieutenant of
the province of Upland.

"Aachen, Whitsunday, 1846.

"Geijer was informed that 'Fräulein' Lind and Dr. Mendelssohn were at home, so he went to Madame la Marquise de Sassenay's, where Jenny was staying during her visit to Aachen.

"Jenny, however, was at rehearsal, so he went to the theatre and enquired for her there.

"Soon afterwards Jenny came out, and could hardly believe her eyes. She did not know whether she was dreaming, whether she was in Germany or in Sweden!

"She put her hands to her forehead, and was ready to cry. Later on, she followed Geijer to the hotel at which we were staying. She was joyous, excited, and exceedingly interesting and animated. She asked with warmth and emotion after friends and acquaintances at home, and more particularly after the Lindblads. Geijer told her that Lindblad was engaged on an Opera. 'Well,' she cried, 'and who is to sing it?' Geijer answered, 'You had better say who.' 'Yes,' she said, 'I may help him to bring out an Opera, both at home, and here in Germany; there is no doubt about that.'

"She spoke of the great success she had had in Vienna, and told him how, after her last appearance, an attempt had been made to draw her carriage, in consequence of which her man-servant had been severely injured, so much so that she had been obliged to leave him behind.*

"Jenny promised to get tickets for us for the concert, adding, 'I shall tell them that I will not sing, if they do not give me tickets for you.' She also promised that she would arrange for Mendelssohn to play to us, and, since the world now turns round according to her wishes and commands, one may feel quite safe when she has pronounced her *fiat* in one's favour.

"In the evening we were present at the rehearsal of the *Creation*, and we then heard the good news that Mendelssohn had declared his willingness to play to us, and that he would have a piano sent to our rooms for that purpose.

"So, in the evening, Jenny and Mendelssohn came to us. Jenny sang some *Lieder*, and I need neither describe nor praise them. Geijer was quite beside himself with delight and pleasure.

---

* *I.e.* at Frankfort, as already related.

"Mendelssohn thought Agnes * and Jenny so like each other that they might be taken for sisters." †

Five days after his departure from Aix-la-Chapelle, Mendelssohn, who was then in Düsseldorf, sent the following account of the Festival to his friend Franz Hauser, at Vienna :—

"Düsseldorf, June 8, 1848.

"You wish me to tell you about the musical festival at Aachen. Well, it was very good, very splendid, towering above all the others, and chiefly owing to Jenny Lind; for, as to the orchestra, I have heard it perhaps better on some other occasions, and the chorus, though splendid, has been equally so at previous festivals. But they were all so uplifted, so animated, so artistically moved by Lind's singing and manner, that the whole thing became a delight, a general success, and worked together as it never did before.

"I had the clearest evidence of this at the last rehearsal, when I had begged of her, for once, not to be the first and most punctual in attendance, but to take some rest and come in towards the end of the rehearsal. To this she agreed, and it was quite a misery to notice how feebly things went— so devoid of swing that even I became listless, like all the others, until, thank God! Jenny Lind appeared, when the needful interest and good humour came back to us, and things moved on again.

"There were, of course, wreaths and poems, and fanfares, again and again, and the audience was seized with that excitement which manifests itself wherever she goes. The manner of its manifestation is of no consequence.

"After the Festival, we went together a little way on the Rhine ; spent a very pleasant day at Cologne, Bonn, up the Drachenfels, at Königswinter, and back (to Cologne), and on the following day she left for Hanover, and I for this place, where I took part yesterday in a concert which also would have been a fine one if Jenny Lind had been there.

"To-morrow I leave for Liège, in order to hear the *Lauda*

---

* Professor Geijer's daughter ; the late Gräfin Hamilton.

† Translated from an extract from the original letter, kindly furnished by Count Hamilton.

Sion, which I have composed for the Festival of *Corpus Christi* there." *

The rest of the story is told in Mendelssohn's letter to his sister, Madame Fanny Hensel:—

"Leipzig, June 27, 1846.

"You ask what I did on the Rhine, but, unfortunately, Cécile's letter to Paul (giving, at my request, all the particulars of my journey) crossed your letter to me, so that I cannot possibly tell what you do or do not know.

"The best way will be for me to write only what I know Cécile cannot have told you, for there is much choice of material.

"The principal feature of my stay in Aix-la-Chapelle was that both the Marquis de Sassenay and Bürgermeister Nellesen made incredible exertions to feast me upon rice-milk, Mdlle. Lind having told them of my weakness for it. But they did not succeed, for their French cooks always produced something quite different—much grander, but not rice-milk.

"A Frenchman—a real Parisian—asked me, on Sunday, ' *Qu'est-ce qu'elle chante ce soir, Mdlle. Lind?* ' I replied, ' *La Création,*' whereupon he turned upon me and said, ' *Comment peut elle chanter La Création? La dernière fois que j'ai entendu La Création en France, c'était un basse-taille qui la chantait!* '

"The choruses were splendidly sung, and if Paul could have heard Jenny Lind sing the two first airs in *Alexander's Feast,* he would have applauded as he did that time at the concert.

"On the Saturday before Whit Sunday, Simrock spent an hour with me over *Elijah.* At 8 (A.M.) the rehearsal began, and lasted till two, when there was a grand dinner, at which I was obliged to be present, and which was not over until half-past four. At five, the general rehearsal of *The Creation* began, and lasted till about nine. At nine I went to see the Swedish Professor Geijer—you remember him at Lindblad's—when we had some music, and I played the *Sonata in C♯ Minor* and some *Lieder ohne Worte,* &c., &c.

"Immediately after Aix-la-Chapelle came Düsseldorf, where they serenaded me twice, for the two local *Lieder-*

* From the collection of Herr Joseph Hauser.

tafeln hate each other so thoroughly that they could not be persuaded to unite." *

Finally, Mdlle. Lind recorded her own impressions of this Whitsuntide holiday—for earnest work in the cause of Art is really a holiday to earnest artists, however hard it may be—in the following letter to Herr Rudolph Wichmann, the Professor's second son :—

"Aachen, June 2, 1846.

" My dear Rudolph,

"My pleasure in Aachen will soon come to an end, for all will be over to-day, and early to-morrow we leave. But I believe Mendelssohn means to accompany us a little way, and we hope to see the view from the Drachenfels, which will be very nice.

"How well everything went with me in Vienna! only my man-servant was very nearly crushed to death, owing to the enthusiasm, so that I had to leave him behind in Frankfort, and he has only just now rejoined me.

"Farewell, my dear boy. Greetings from

"Thy Sister." †

Mdlle. Lind was evidently sorry to leave the gloomy old city of Charlemagne, but she was not allowed to do so without an ovation. On the day of her departure she was presented with a poem, beautifully printed in black and gold, on a sheet of white satin, twelve inches in height by ten broad. The feeling displayed in the verses is so good, and the occasion—entirely unconnected with the dramatic successes we have recorded—was so important in its bearing upon a concert performance, that we think no apology necessary for the introduction of a portion of the poem, of which we subjoin the first stanza :—

> " Wie aus des Chaos dunklem Schoos entsprungen
> Die junge Welt in bräutlich holder Pracht,
> Der erste Lenz zu Gottes Lob erwacht,
> Hast mit des Engels Stimme DU gesungen," &c.

---

* Translated from the ' Familie Mendelssohn,' by Mr. Sebastian Hensel.
† Translated from the original letter, by the kind permission of Herr Rudolph Wichmann.

It had been a happy time for all; but for Mendelssohn, with *Elijah* not yet finished, though on the eve of production, and some hard days' work still waiting for accomplishment in Düsseldorf, Cologne, and Liège, the fatigue was dangerously heavy, and the amount of excitement with which it was accompanied more disproportioned still to the then condition of his mental and physical powers, which sorely needed the rest he was nevermore able to accord to them.

But when did Prudence ever come to the front, to calm the suicidal eagerness of Genius?

CHAPTER VI.

THE view from the Drachenfels answered all the bright expectations that had been formed of it; and, after supplementing it with an afternoon at Königswinter, and a pleasant day at Cologne, Mdlle. Lind proceeded to Hanover, where she was engaged for four performances at the Court Theatre, and a concert.

The Operas selected were *Norma* (June 6), *La Sonnambula* (June 8), *Der Freischütz* (June 9), and *Lucia di Lammermoor* (June 11). The concert took place on the 13th of June. The success, on each occasion, was that to which all concerned had so long been accustomed, that it was now looked for as a matter of course. But, of far greater importance than any amount of local enthusiasm was the fact, that, during this visit to Hanover, Mdlle. Lind was brought into immediate relations with the then Crown Prince and Princess—afterwards King George V., and Queen Marie—who, amidst the heavy trials destined afterwards to fall upon them, never forgot the friendship with which they then learned to regard her; a friendship which remained undiminished until the day of her death, and which, even since then, has been most touchingly alluded to by Her Majesty, Queen Marie.

After fulfilling her engagement at Hanover, and singing once at a concert at Bremen, Mdlle. Lind proceeded to Hamburg, where she was engaged for a series of twelve

" Guest-performances " at the Stadt Theatre, supplemented
by a benefit in aid of the " Theatrical Orchestra Pension
Fund"; another for herself, and a Concert for the poor.

During this visit, she did not reside in Hamburg itself,
having accepted an invitation to the house of her friend,
Consul Arnemann, at Nienstädten, near the neighbouring
township of Altona.   Here she spent many pleasant weeks
with her host and hostess and their family, who had invited
another friend—Mdlle. Mina Fundin—to keep her company,
and had also sent a pressing invitation to Mendelssohn, in
the hope that he would be able to take Nienstädten on his
way to England, whither he was bound, in August, for the
purpose of producing his *Elijah* at the Birmingham Festival.
This project, however, failed entirely.   Though Mendelssohn
would have been pleased indeed to have availed himself of
so pleasant an opportunity for refreshing himself with a
brief rest, before his heavy work began, it was quite impossible for him to do so.   He was working beyond his
strength, as he himself well knew; and let the consequences
be what they might, there was no help for it.

Mdlle. Lind arrived at Nienstädten, on the 19th of June;
and began her second season at Hamburg, on the 22nd, with
her favourite Opera, *Norma*, followed, in turn, by *La Sonnambula, Don Juan, Lucia di Lammermoor*, and, for the first
time in Germany, *La Figlia del Reggimento*,* concerning
which she wrote from Nienstädten to Madame Birch-Pfeiffer,

---

* The dates were:—June 22, *Norma;* June 25, *La Sonnambula;*
June 27, *Norma;* July 1, *La Sonnambula;* July 3, *Don Juan;* July 8,
Lucia di Lammermoor; July 11, *Don Juan;* July 14, *La Figlia del
Reggimento;* July 18, *La Figlia del Reggimento;* July 21 (for the benefit
of the " Orchestra Pension Fund" at the Stadt-Theater), *Norma;* July 24,
Lucia di Lammermoor; July 26, *La Figlia del Reggimento;* July 28,
La Sonnambula ; July 30 (benefit), *La Sonnambula* (act iii.), *La Figlia
del Reggimento* (act ii.), with *Swedish Songs* introduced, in the scene at
the piano.   August 1, Concert, at the Stadt-Theater, for the poor.

on the 26th of June :—" Cornet * plagues me about *Die Tochter des Regiments;* and, although I do not know how that can be managed without your help, dear mother, I must try " —a sentence which proves how deeply she was indebted to this lady for the help afforded to her in the German translations of works which she had already sung, in her own language, at Stockholm.

The terms of the engagement were one hundred *Louis d'or* for each performance—about eighty pounds in English money.   During her first season at Hamburg, she had received forty *Louis d'or* only—about thirty-two pounds sterling.   But she did not forget to devote a large share of her earnings to charitable purposes.   The performance in aid of the " Orchestra Pension Fund " realised twelve hundred and forty-one marks—more than sixty pounds sterling; and the concert for the poor, about five pounds less.   The performances were received with even greater enthusiasm than those of the previous year; and no less hearty were the demonstrations of personal respect, and grateful recognition of benefits afforded, for charitable purposes, to the old Hanse Town.

If a local journal of the period may be trusted, Mdlle. Lind's horses were again unharnessed, after the Concert on the 1st of August, and her carriage drawn home by the crowd.   And she was also serenaded with a Farewell-Ode, composed for the occasion by Herr Krebs, the conductor at the Theatre.

Yet, during the course of this visit to Hamburg, she was made, for the first time in her Art-life, the subject of a long series of virulent attacks, prompted by the spirit of petty jealousy with which inept mediocrity never fails to resent the respect paid to true genius.

* A well-known tenor singer, and, at that time, the manager of the Stadt-Theater at Hamburg.

In 1845, an anonymous author published a little biographical sketch, entitled, 'Jenny Lind, the Swedish Nightingale,'* giving a short and fairly correct account of Mdlle. Lind's early career, prettily written, and accompanied by a pleasing, if not very accurate lithographic portrait.

This little *brochure*, pleasant enough to read, met with a very extensive sale, and its success tempted certain pamphleteers of low degree to venture into the field, on their own account, either with weak imitations of the original, or with attempts to turn it into ridicule.

In the same year appeared, ' Jenny Lind in Hamburg. An Apotheosis,'† and 'Jenny Lind and the Hamburgers; or half an hour in the Jungfernstieg.' ‡

But it was not until the following year that the annoyance reached its climax. In 1846, the booksellers' shops were deluged with *feuilletons*, in which vulgar *calembours* and senseless epigrams were made to do duty for wit and humour. A disappointed genius lamented, in coarsest satire, the fate of the ill-used poet, who received less, for the work that had cost him months of labour, than the singer could gain in three hours in a single evening. At the ' Theater im Vorstadt S. Pauli,' a singer appeared under the pseudonym of ' Jenny Bind,' and nightly attracted large audiences of the lower orders, and the name of Lindwurm—a word used in old German romances as a synonym for Dragon—was passed, from mouth to mouth, among the envious and disappointed, as an excellent joke.

But the loyalty of the public itself never wavered for a moment. Hamburg was as true to its allegiance as Berlin,

* ' Jenny Lind, die schwedische Nachtigall.' (Hamburg, 1845.)

† ' Jenny Lind in Hamburg. Apotheose.' (Hamburg, 1845.)

‡ ' Jenny Lind und die Hamburger: ein Stündchen im Jungfernstieg.' Hamburg, 1845. The Jungfernstieg is the principal street around the Alsterbassin; in it stood Mdlle. Lind's hotel, the Alte Stadt London.

or Vienna. As at the Royal Opera House, and the Theater an der Wien, the prices for admission to the Stadt-Theater were raised, whenever a "guest-performance" took place; the local journals were loud, and unanimous, in their praise; and the demonstrations in the Theatre were of the warmest and most enthusiastic character.

Mdlle. Lind prolonged her visit at Nienstädten—with interruptions—for some considerable time, after the termination of her engagement at the Theatre. Like Mendelssohn, she had, for some time past, been working far beyond her strength, and the fatigue was now beginning to tell upon her with serious effect. She herself saw this very plainly. Madame Wichmann, with two of her sons, had spent four days with her in Hanover, and tried to persuade her to accompany the family on a journey to Switzerland, towards the close of the summer; and had written to Mendelssohn, telling him of her hope that the plan was finally and successfully arranged. But, on the day after the first performance of *Don Juan*, at Hamburg, Mdlle. Lind wrote to her friend, deploring her long neglect of rest, and explaining that the journey was impossible :—

"Nienstädten, July 4, 1846.

" DEAR AMALIA !

"Beloved Amalia! I feel very much pulled down. After all, these fatigues leave their trace, and convince me that I am not strong enough to undertake such a journey, without injury to my health. I must sing here a few times more—but that cannot be helped. I have consulted a physician; for, these nervous contractions from which I am suffering rendered it indispensable. He says it is imperatively necessary that I should go to some bathing place. My nerves, he says, are seriously attacked; and I ought to have done it, long before this. I know that the doctors in Sweden recommended this, four years ago; but I could not possibly do it, then.

"I have quite made up my mind, that, next summer, or next autumn at the latest, I will leave the stage. I will, therefore, make the best use I can of the time; and, as I have already arranged for the coming season, it will be only reasonable, now, to provide the necessary strength for next winter.

"Greet my beloved there, from thine ever loving

"JENNY." *

The project for retiring from the stage was, as we are already aware, no new one; but it was forced into greater prominence, just at this time, by the inroads that excessive fatigue was making upon Mdlle. Lind's health and strength. Indeed, one can only look on in wonder at the amount of work she was able to accomplish, without actually breaking down. The constant performance of familiar parts, with new associates, needing, every time, laborious rehearsal; the exposure to draughts on the stage, and to changing weather on the long journeys between; the excitement of the calls before the curtain; the nocturnal serenades; the social claims; the constant appeals for pecuniary help, afterwards so strongly animadverted against by Mendelssohn; all these might well have worn out a constitution of steel. The work of older and more firmly established *prime donne*, such as Madame Persiani, or Madame Grisi, with regular seasons in London, during the summer, and in Paris in the winter, was light indeed compared with it. But it had to be done, for the present at least, whatever the sacrifice might be.

In the meantime, the correspondence with Mendelssohn was not allowed to languish. Towards the end of July, he wrote thus:—

"Leipzig, July 23, 1846.

"MY DEAR FRÄULEIN,

"As usual, I come to you, to-day, asking a favour. I mean, that I am anxious to know how matters stand, with regard to your travelling arrangements, both now, and in the future—and I hope you will explain them to me. In your last letter, you told me that you were going to Switzerland,

* From the Wichmann collection.

with the Wichmanns, on the first of August. Does this plan still hold good? And, is it true, or not, that you will be at Frankfort in September? Also, are you going straight from Hamburg to Berlin, to fetch the Wichmanns? All this I want to know. And it is because I want to know this, that I ask you to tell me of your plans, both before and after your journey to Switzerland and Vienna; and whether you still adhere both to the one and the other intention. The reason is, that, since my return from the Rhine, I have lived the life of a marmot. I was rather frightened, when, on coming back, I saw the amount of work that lay unfinished,* and compared it with the time that remained to me. Then, I made up my mind not to write to you until my Oratorio was quite complete; but, for the last few days I have not been well (you will find it out, sooner or later), so now I shall not be ready till August, and I dare not delay my letter so long as that, or it will be brought to you while on the back of some mule or other, to some cow-herd's hut.

"Madame Arnemann has written me a very friendly letter, and invited me to Nienstädten. As yet, I have not been able even to thank her for it; and yet, how gladly would I have accepted the invitation! But, I cannot get away from here before the middle of August; and, even then, I must make haste, in order to reach England in time. To-day, however, I really will write to Madame Arnemann, or she will be vexed—and with good cause.

"Is it true that you have been singing the '*Regimentstoch-ter*' in German? If so, I should have liked to have been one of the audience. And, do you know that the Geijers have lately been here? and, that they invited me to go to Sweden, to feast on a roasted reindeer? (I can get rice-milk at your house!) And, that Fräulein Geijer sang '*Vorwärts so heisst des Schicksals Gebot*' to me again? and the song, by Lindblad, in C major.

"But, I will leave off, for to-day. My letter is tiresome, and stupid, and will continue so to the end. Only, grant my requests. And tell me all about yourself, and how you are getting on, and whether you are having much music, and whether you are in good spirits, and in first-rate voice?

"We are all well, at home, and often remember you.

"Your friend,

"Felix Mendelssohn Bartholdy."

* For *Elijah*, which was to be produced, at the Birmingham Festival, in August.

The idea of the journey to Switzerland was never revived, after the doctor had recommended a course of baths; and the changed plans for the autumn were thus detailed, in a letter to Madame Wichmann:—

"Nienstädten, August 1, 1846.

"DEARLY BELOVED AMALIA!

"To-day, I sing for the poor; and positively for the last time.

"On Thursday, the fourth of August, I go to Cuxhaven, with the Brunton family. (Do you remember the long letters that the daughter * used to write to me?) They have always been very kind to me. But there, I shall be quite at rest; and take the sea baths for four weeks.

"In the meantime, Louise stays here, to take care of her health; for she is ordered to drink the mineral waters. When I have done with Cuxhaven, I shall come here again; for I am very happy here, and I can only compare this family with yours.

"I shall rest until about the 20th of September. Then I go, first, to Frankfort; and, from thence, to Munich, as you know; and, from Munich, to Stuttgard—but this will be later on. From Stuttgard, I go to Vienna.

"When shall I see you again? If we could only go to Paris together, next summer, somewhere about the month of June! I should so much like to see Garcia again, before I leave Germany for ever.

"God keep you! Farewell! Write to me soon again; and I will duly answer you. Ah, Amalia! Next spring, I shall be free! I am afraid so great a happiness will never fall to my lot.

"Your ever truly loving

"JENNY."

"P.S.—Many thanks for the portrait of Mendelssohn.† Remember me to Magnus, and thank him for it." ‡

---

* Fräulein von Seminoff.

† This was a *replica* of the portrait painted by Magnus, and by him presented to Mdlle. Lind, who subsequently bequeathed it to Mendelssohn's daughter, Mrs. Victor Benecke.

‡ From the Wichmann collection.

The events which took place between this period, and the beginning of September need no detailed record. It was a time of rest, much needed, and hardly earned. We shall, therefore, resume our history, with the return to a more active Art-life, in the autumn.

CHAPTER VII.

CONTRACT WITH MR. LUMLEY.

AFTER leaving Cuxhaven, Mdlle. Lind wrote again to Madame Wichmann :—

> "Nienstädten, 3 Sept. 1846.

" BELOVED AMALIA,

"I am thinking whether I can, by any possible means, manage to visit you for a few days. For I long for you all with my whole soul, and you would not believe, Amalia, what an impression my stay in your house has left upon my inner life.

"You will write to me soon, and tell me you are well. I shall stay here a fortnight or three weeks longer. My good Louise has been ill, and is not yet so well that I can put a strain upon her. So I am not going to begin my 'guest-performances' just yet.

"The baths seem to have done me a great deal of good. I am at Nienstädten again, and shall continue to rest myself here.

"All good angels be with you! Farewell, dear friend. Forget not your for ever and ever loving and grateful

> "JENNY." *

Mdlle. Johansson's illness was not a serious one, and soon after the middle of September she was able to accompany Mdlle. Lind to Frankfort, where the business of the autumn season began.

Mdlle. Lind had by this time acquired a thoroughly methodical and business-like way of keeping records, and one of her first acts, on arriving at Frankfort, was the pur-

---

* From the Wichmann letters.

chase of a thick and sturdy memorandum-book, a square bulky volume, of quarto size, labelled, "Annotation-Book * of Jenny Lind," and filled with ruled "sermon-paper," in which she entered every one of her engagements, from that time forward, up to the moment of her marriage, in America, in the year 1852.

The value of this document to her biographers may be imagined. Henceforward we shall no more have to send to Berlin, or to Vienna, for official lists of the various performances with which we are concerned. It is true that, up to this date, such lists have been furnished to us through the intervention of Mr. Goldschmidt, with never-failing courtesy, by the officers in whose charge the archives of the different theatres are placed. The information for which we have asked, whether at Berlin, Vienna, Stockholm, Copenhagen, Hamburg, or elsewhere, has never once been refused to us, and as much care has been bestowed upon the verification of a date as if the welfare of the theatre itself had depended upon its correctness. For this we tender our best and most sincere thanks; but henceforth every date, in whatever country, will be given on the authority of Mdlle. Lind's own hand-writing, and the advantage of this is manifest.

The first entries in the book are :—

```
" Frankfort a/M.                              1846.
    Sonnambula .        .  .  .       .  .  .  . Sept. 25
    Norma  .  .        .  .  .       .  .  .  .    „   28
    Figlia  .          .  .  .       .  .  .  .    „   30
    Figlia  .  .       .  .  .       .  .  .  . Oct.  2
    Sonnambula .  .  .  .  .  .  .  .  .  .  .     „    5
    Vestale (50 Louis d'or for the members of the
                      chorus) x  .  .  .  .  .  .  .  „    7
    Figlia (benefit for the orchestra pension-fund) x   „   10
```

We subjoin a fac-simile of the first page. The little cross means that the performance was given, wholly or in part, for

---

* ' Annotations-Bok.'

charitable or benevolent purposes, and the number of such
crosses in a single page is sometimes very remarkable. In
the present case fifty *Louis d'or* of the proceeds, on the 7th
of October, were given to the chorus, and on the 10th the
whole was devoted to the "Orchestra Pension Fund" of the
Frankfort Stadt Theatre.

The performances were crowned with the usual success,
and followed by the usual demonstrations of enthusiastic
admiration; but this visit to Frankfort was memorable for
reasons quite unconnected with its individual triumphs, for
it was here that the idea of an engagement at Her Majesty's
Theatre, in London, first took a definite and palpable form.

When, in her letter of October 18, 1845, Mdlle. Lind
assured Mr. Bunn that she "did not count upon taking any
other engagement in England," she wrote in perfect good
faith. She had made no engagement with any other English
manager, and did not contemplate making one.

On the other hand, when Mr. Bunn, in his letter of
October 30, accused her of trying to get rid of her liability
at his theatre, in order that she might make an engagement
at the Italian Opera, he probably believed that he was telling
the truth, though he based his conclusions upon reports which
might or might not have reached the ears of his correspondent.

Long before that, some of her friends in London—
including Mrs. Grote, who herself mentions the fact in the
MS. "Memoir" from which we have so frequently quoted—
had "urged Mr. Lumley to make efforts in this direction," [*]
and he had, in fact, "made more than one tentative to obtain
the services of the celebrated songstress for Her Majesty's
Theatre." [†] Hearing of this—as no doubt he did—Mr. Bunn,
looking at the circumstance from his own point of view, put
the worst possible construction upon it, and took it for

[*] MS. 'Memoir,' by Mrs. Grote.
[†] *Ibid.*

Jenny Lind

Representationen 1846

Frankfurt a/M.	Sömmgängerskan	Sept	25.
Oct —	Norma	—	28
— —	Regementets Dotter	—	30
— —	Regementets Dotter	Oct	2.
— —	Sömmgängerskan	—	5
— —	Westalen /50 Louisd'or à Chor. Personalen/	✱	7.
— —	Regementets Dotter /Benefice för orchester personalen/	/✱	10.
Darmstadt.	Sömmgängerskan	—	13.
—	Norma	—	16
—	Regementets Dotter	/	18.
	Consert hos Vieweg's gesse /Kll./ ✱		19.
München	Sömmgängerskan	—	23.
	Norma	—	25
	Friskytten	—	26.
	Consert för barnen ✱	Nov.	1
	Regementets Dotter		3.
	Sömmgängerskan		5.
	Regementets Dotter		8.
Stuttgard	Sömmgängerskan	—	11.
	Norma	—	13.
	Consert hos Kungen af Würtemberg	—	14.

FACSIMILE PAGE OF ENGAGEMENT BOOK. [To face p. 428.

granted that his correspondent was cognizant of all that took place—which was not true. She did not know of it, until the period affected by Mr. Bunn's contract had long been over-passed. It was not until long after that date that Mr. Lumley made her a definite and tangible offer for Her Majesty's Theatre : and, when the offer came, she refused even to think of it. She was so terrified at the penalties, the law-suits, and the disgrace with which Mr. Bunn had threatened her, that her dearest and most trusted friends could not persuade her to entertain the idea of appearing at an English theatre, under any circumstances, or upon any terms whatever.

And yet her destiny seemed to be weaving a net round about her, from which no way of escape was visible. She was brought, apart from her own will entirely, under the steadily increasing influence of English friends. Mrs. Grote was most anxious that she should come to London. Her brother, Mr. Edward Lewin—of whom more will be said in a future chapter—saw no insurmountable difficulties in the way of an engagement at Her Majesty's Theatre. Mr. Lumley was un-ceasing in his endeavours to induce her to rescind her decision ; and, while she was still in Frankfort, the musical correspon-dent of one of the most influential art journals in England turned aside from his travels, in the hope of hearing her sing, and begged an introduction to her, from a quarter whence he well knew that it would be favourably received.

The following letter from Mendelssohn, which arrived in Frankfort almost simultaneously with Mdlle. Lind herself, will explain the situation exactly :—

" Leipzig, September 23, 1846.

" MY DEAR FRÄULEIN,

"If you will do me a real favour, and if you are not too much occupied and worried during your stay in Frank-fort, let me beg of you to receive the bearer of these lines,

Mr. Chorley (an acquaintance of mine of long standing, and a great lover of music), with your usual kindness, and to sing him one of my songs.*

"He is an excellent listener, and you will make him very happy if you grant my wish. I believe he is going to Frankfort solely on this account, so that I have really no choice but to come to you with this new request.

"Many thanks for your last letter, which I only received after I had left London, and at the moment of starting for Ostend. †

"I have so much to say about England, and your journey thither, that I really do not know how I am to write it.‡ In any case, everything depends upon the way in which one establishes oneself there; or, rather, upon the way in which *you* establish *yourself*, for you have the whole thing entirely in your own hands, and English lovers of music are expecting you, in a frame of mind, and speaking of you, in terms, which please me very much indeed—a thing which very seldom happens—when I hear you spoken of. So you can manage it exactly *as you will;* though, for that very reason, you alone are in a position to decide upon it.

"Till we meet again, merry, happy, unchanged,

"FELIX MENDELSSOHN BARTHOLDY."

Thus prepared for Mr. Chorley's visit, Mdlle. Lind received him when he called, a few days later, with the friendly courtesy which she felt it no less a pleasure than a duty to extend to the friends of those with whom she was herself on terms of intimacy. He repeated his visit more than once, heard her sing in *La Figlia del Reggimento*, and afterwards in *La Sonnambula* and *Die Vestalin*, and wrote, on the 4th of October, to Mrs. Grote, describing, in the most enthusiastic terms, the pleasure he had felt in hearing her sing. "And now let me tell you," he says, "how thoroughly, with my

---

* Mr. Chorley was the musical critic, attached to the *Athenæum.*

† That is, on his return home, after the first performance of *Elijah,* at the Birmingham Festival.

‡ Mendelssohn evidently supposed the negotiations with Mr. Lumley to have advanced farther than they really had at this moment.

whole heart, I like her as a singer, more, by twenty times,
than I had expected. The only fault I can find, or fancy, is,
that she is too fond of using all her powers, the end of which
is a feeling of heaviness—the one tinge of Germanism which
remains about her style. . . . . I was really delighted to find
that I am not past the old thrill, or the old beating of the
heart, and that I could not go to bed till I had written a note
(in horrible French) to say ' Thank you.' " *

On the same day (October 4th) he also wrote to Mendelssohn, to thank him for " the very very intense pleasure " that
had made him " laugh and cry like a child again," after " a
fear of disappointment " which he " hardly liked to describe,"
ending his letter with the words, " She says *she will not* come
to London," †—from which it is evident, that, if he did not
endeavour to persuade her to come, he had, at least, discussed
the subject with her.

She would have liked to come, very much indeed, if only
to please Mendelssohn, who was most anxious that she
should do so, and whose wish was shared by many other
friends in whose judgment she placed great confidence ; but,
believing, as she did, that Mr. Bunn's threats were no mere
idle words, but menaces which he possessed full power to
carry out, and certainly had the will to carry out, if she
ventured to set foot upon English soil, she did not dare to
listen, either to the whispers of her own feelings on the subject, or the wishes of her friends. Her fears overcame every
other consideration ; and, against these fears, Mr. Lumley
found himself absolutely powerless to contend.

The next engagement was at Darmstadt, where she sang
three times at the Court Theatre, in *La Sonnambula*,
on the 13th of October, and in *Norma* and *La Figlia
del Reggimento*, on the 16th and 19th. The memory of the

---

* From Mrs. Grote's MS. ' Memoir.'
† From the original letter, preserved in the ' Green Volumes.'

previous performances in September 1845 were still green and
flourishing, and the success of the second visit was greater than
that of the first. The account of *La Sonnambula*, given in the
local journal, on the day after the performance, was written
in a strain as exalted as that of Herr Rellstab himself; and
described a wealth of wreaths and flowers rivalling those of
Berlin and Vienna. The prices were raised, after the usual
manner, for these three performances; and, when these were
over, Mdlle. Lind gave a concert, for the young son of a
musician named Panny, who stood in need of help for the
development of his talent, and thus supplemented her
engagement, as she had so often done before, by an act of
benevolence.

In the meantime, Mr. Lumley had not been idle. He had
now abundant hope—having gained the all-powerful support
of Mendelssohn—and the engagement of Mdlle. Lind was
a matter of such vital importance to him that he could
not afford to let the subject drop. Since the close of the
previous season, the affairs of Her Majesty's Theatre had
been in the utmost possible disorder. The company, with
Mesdames Grisi and Persiani at their head, had revolted, and
there was no one to take their place. Mr. Lumley's friends
in England—among them, Mrs. Grote, who took the keenest
interest in his negotiations, and in whose judgment and
discretion he placed great faith—and a host of amateur
musicians who had the interests of the musical drama really
at heart, saw, in the proposed engagement, his only chance
of escape from absolute ruin, and urged him to leave no
stone unturned that might help to bring the matter to a
successful issue. By their advice, he followed Mdlle. Lind
from Frankfort to Darmstadt, and there again presented
himself to her, armed, this time, with a letter from Mendelssohn, whom he had seen in Leipzig, and to whom he had
taken a letter from herself.

Feeling sure that the missive with the delivery of which
he was entrusted was a very valuable one, and not at all
likely to be written in opposition to his own interests, Mr.
Lumley lost no time in presenting it in person ; and thus it
ran :—

" Leipzig, October 12, 1846.

" My dear Fräulein,

          " I intended to write to you on the day on which
your first letter arrived ; but a few hours afterwards came
your second letter, and Mr. Lumley, who brought it. All
that he said to me, and all that passed through my mind in
connection with it, and the different thoughts that crossed
each other hither and thither, made it impossible for me to
write to you until to-day ; and I told Mr. Lumley that, if he
should be coming here again after his journey to Berlin, I
would meanwhile think it all carefully over, and would then
tell him whether I could advise you to go to London
or not.

" Upon that—*i.e.*, upon my advice—he seems to set great
store, and I have already told you in my former letter that
the whole success of his undertaking depends upon your
coming.

" In short, I can only repeat what I then wrote—I should
like you, as far as is humanly possible, to arrange, *as
completely as one could wish*, for your own comfort, and,
when that has all been settled, I should like you to go
there.

" I should have strongly urged Mr. Lumley—at least, on
his return here—to speak clearly and exactly about money
matters ; because that is a very serious point, in England ; and
because you could, and ought, to make such terms as no one
else could at this moment, since you are the *only* one upon
whom alone the whole thing depends. But—do not be
angry with me !—I had not the courage to do this : not even
for you, though I know that you understand that kind of
thing even less than I do—in other words, not at all. But
it is such a very sore point with me, and I rejoice so much
when I have nothing to hear or say about it, that I could
not bring the words to my lips. And, at last, I thought, ' It
is not my province,' and so, after all, I let it pass.

" Therefore I can only repeat, it must all be as is just and
right to you.

"Nevertheless, you will certainly meet with such a reception there, that you will be able to think of it with pleasure throughout the whole of your future life. When the English once entertain a personal liking for anyone, I believe that no people are more friendly, more cordial, or more constant; and such a feeling you will find there. For, as I told you before, I have noticed that they entertain this true feeling there, not only about your singing, but about your personality, and your whole being, and upon this last they even set more store than upon the singing itself. And this is as it should be.

"In my opinion, therefore, it cannot for a moment be doubted that you will be received there as you deserve—more warmly, enthusiastically, and heartily, perhaps, than in all your former experience: and you have experienced a great deal in that way. You will therefore give your friends great pleasure if you go there; and I, for my part, should be very glad indeed if you were to go.

"Insist upon all possible conditions that can in the least degree make things agreeable to you, and insist upon them very firmly, and strictly, and clearly. Do not forget anything that may be pleasant for you, and have nothing to say to anything that may be unpleasant. Going to London, and singing there, can, in itself, be nothing but pleasant—of that I am firmly persuaded. Everything else depends only upon the manner in which this is done, and all that you have in your own hands.

"I am selfish, too, in my advice: for I hope that we shall there meet in the world again. While still in England, I had half promised to return there next April; had I only known that you would be there at that time, or would be going there, you may imagine how much more willingly I should have settled it. Mr. Lumley, also, in the kindest manner, proposed that I should compose an Opera for him next May, and I could only answer, that, on the self-same day on which I succeeded in getting a good *libretto*, on a good subject, I would begin to write the music; and that, in doing so, I should be fulfilling my greatest wish. He hopes soon to be able to procure such a *libretto*, and has already taken some decided steps with regard to it. God grant that some good results may follow. From Madame Birch-Pfeiffer, I have not heard a single word, for a long time. In the meantime, I have music-paper and finely-nibbed pens lying on the table—and wait.

" But, apart from this, I hope, as I have told you, to visit London again next spring, and what a pleasure it will be to me to witness there the most brilliant and hearty reception that can possibly fall to an artist's lot! For I know full well that that is what your reception will be, and it will be great fun for me that you yourself will be the fêted artist.

" For myself, I am doing well; but, during the three weeks that have elapsed since I returned here, I have done scarcely anything but rest, so tired was I—and still am, sometimes—with the work that preceded the journey to England, and the journey itself. The performance of my *Elijah* was the best first performance that I have ever heard of any one of my compositions. There was so much go, and swing, in the way in which the people played, and sang, and listened. I wish you had been there. But I have now fallen back into the concert trouble, and can neither get true rest, nor quietness here. So I have built myself a grand castle in the air; namely, to travel, next summer, with my whole family, in my favourite country—which, as you know, is Switzerland—and then to study uninterruptedly for two months on one of the lakes, living in the open air. If God gives us health, we will carry out this plan; and when I think of such a quiet time in the country after all the hurry and bustle, and all the brightness of a London season, and remember how dear both of them are to me, and how well they please me, I almost wish that the spring were already here, and that I was taking my seat in the travelling carriage.

" And now, to-day, I have still a request to make. Write to me, *at once*, when you have come to a decision concerning England; and tell me everything, with all the details : for you know how much it all interests me. Before all things, then, write to me, from time to time; and think kindly of me, sometimes.

" As for myself, you know that I am, and remain,

" Your friend,

" FELIX MENDELSSOHN BARTHOLDY."

The result of Mendelssohn's advice will be most clearly manifested, by a letter which Mr. Lumley wrote to him after his interview with Mdlle. Lind—a letter which is all the more interesting, inasmuch as it treats, also, of the long hoped-for *libretto* in such sort as to show that the manager had already begun to look upon it as "a matter of business."

"Darmstadt, October 17.

"DEAR MR. MENDELSSOHN,

"I am delighted to tell you that your letter has had its effect; and that the lady has signed an engagement. *

"Your letter charmed her so much. It was a most pleasing picture—her countenance, when reading it. No sun could have infused more joy into a beautiful landscape, than your letter did on her.

"To give her peace of mind, I added clauses to the engagement, which, if known by persons not intimately acquainted with her charming character and feeling of honour, would perhaps incur for me the charge of folly. But, I know I can depend on her honour; and I am perfectly happy and contented on that head. I have prepared the engagement wholly in her favour: but I proposed to her to add anything else that you might think advisable, and I added a clause to that effect.

"She would not enter into the question of money; but I am quite sure you will be satisfied that I have done everything right in that way.

"I need not tell you how truly grateful I am to you. The English, as a nation, will owe you a debt of gratitude; for I look upon the engagement of Lind as a new era in the progress of Art in England. Her success will be transcendent. Independently of her great genius, she has that purity and chastity of manner which none but a really good person can possess, and which, in England, will gain her partisans on all sides. I say 'on all sides,' because, even with the vile, there is that in real goodness and virtue which *commands* admiration.

"Pray remember me most kindly to Madame Mendelssohn, and to her mother,† and permit me to send my love to your children, not forgetting the baby, and that beautiful boy Carl, who, though suggestive of the pictures of Raphael, and Correggio, reminds us that there is an artist far above

---

* The document was formally signed, on the 17th of October, 1846.

† Madame Jeanrenaud.

the greatest of human artists, and that the real is frequently more beautiful than the ideal.

"My joy on the completion of the affair is not unsullied. I am fearful that she may, for a time, at least, tease herself with fears, which, though entirely groundless, may equally torment her.   I will venture to entreat you to assure her of the absolute certainty of her great success to give her encouragement.

"I shall lose no time in occupying myself, immediately, with the *libretto* for our grand affair ; and I do not despair of providing you with a *libretto* which shall give you pleasure and ensure your valuable aid.

"It is of importance that this affair of Lind should be kept private for the present.   I shall lose no time in occupying myself about the '*affaire Bunn.*'

"I need not say that it will give me great pleasure to hear from you.

" Yours most truly,

" B. LUMLEY." *

Without wearying our readers with a literal transcript of the " Lumley Contract," with its endless circumlocutions and technical legal phraseology, we may briefly say that it provided :—

(1.) An *honorarium* of 120,000 francs (£4800) for the season, reckoned from the 14th of April to the 20th of August, 1847.

(2.) A furnished house, a carriage, and a pair of horses, free of charge, for the season.

(3.) A farther sum of £800 if Mdlle. Lind wished to spend a month in Italy before her *début*, for the purpose of studying the language, or for rest.

(4.) Liberty to cancel the engagement, if, after her first appearance, she felt dissatisfied at the measure of its success, and wished to discontinue her performances.

(5.) Mdlle. Lind was not to sing at concerts, public or private, for her own emolument.

---

* Transcribed from the original letter, preserved in the 'Green Volumes.'

So, the question of appearing at Her Majesty's Theatre was decided at last; and, when Mdlle. Lind left Darmstadt, for Munich, she had bound herself to the most important dramatic engagement, and prepared the way for the most solid artistic triumph that ever had been, or was ever destined to be, associated with her name.

END OF VOLUME I.

www.ingramcontent.com/pod-product-compliance
Lightning Source LLC
Chambersburg PA
CBHW022013110726
47901CB00006B/1508